The Books of FAERIE
AUBERON'S TALE

BRONWYN CARLTON ~ JOHN NEY RIEBER
writers

PETER GROSS ~ MARK BUCKINGHAM
RYAN KELLY ~ HERMANN MEJIA
pencillers

VINCE LOCKE ~ MARK BUCKINGHAM
DICK GIORDANO ~ RYAN KELLY
HERMANN MEJIA
inkers

GLORIA VASQUEZ ~ JAMES SINCLAIR
DANNY VOZZO ~ ALEX SINCLAIR
colorists

RICHARD STARKINGS & COMICRAFT
letterer

Auberon created by Neil Gaiman and Charles Vess

Timothy Hunter and The Books of Magic created by

Neil Gaiman and John Bolton

Jenette Kahn ~ *President & Editor-in-Chief* Paul Levitz ~ *Executive Vice President & Publisher* Karen Berger ~ *Executive Editor*
Stuart Moore ~ Julie Rottenberg ~ *Editors-original series* Dale Crain ~ *Editor-collected edition* Cliff Chiang ~ *Assistant Editor-original series*
Michael Wright ~ *Assistant Editor-collected edition* Georg Brewer ~ *Design Director* Robbin Brosterman ~ *Art Director*
Richard Bruning ~ *VP-Creative Director* Patrick Caldon ~ *VP-Finance & Operations* Dorothy Crouch ~ *VP-Licensed Publishing*
Terri Cunningham ~ *VP-Managing Editor* Joel Ehrlich ~ *Senior VP-Advertising & Promotions* Alison Gill ~ *Exec. Director-Manufacturing*
Lillian Laserson ~ *VP & General Counsel* Jim Lee ~ *Editorial Director-WildStorm* John Nee ~ *VP & General Manager-WildStorm*
Bob Wayne ~ *VP-Direct Sales*

THE BOOKS OF FAERIE: AUBERON'S TALE

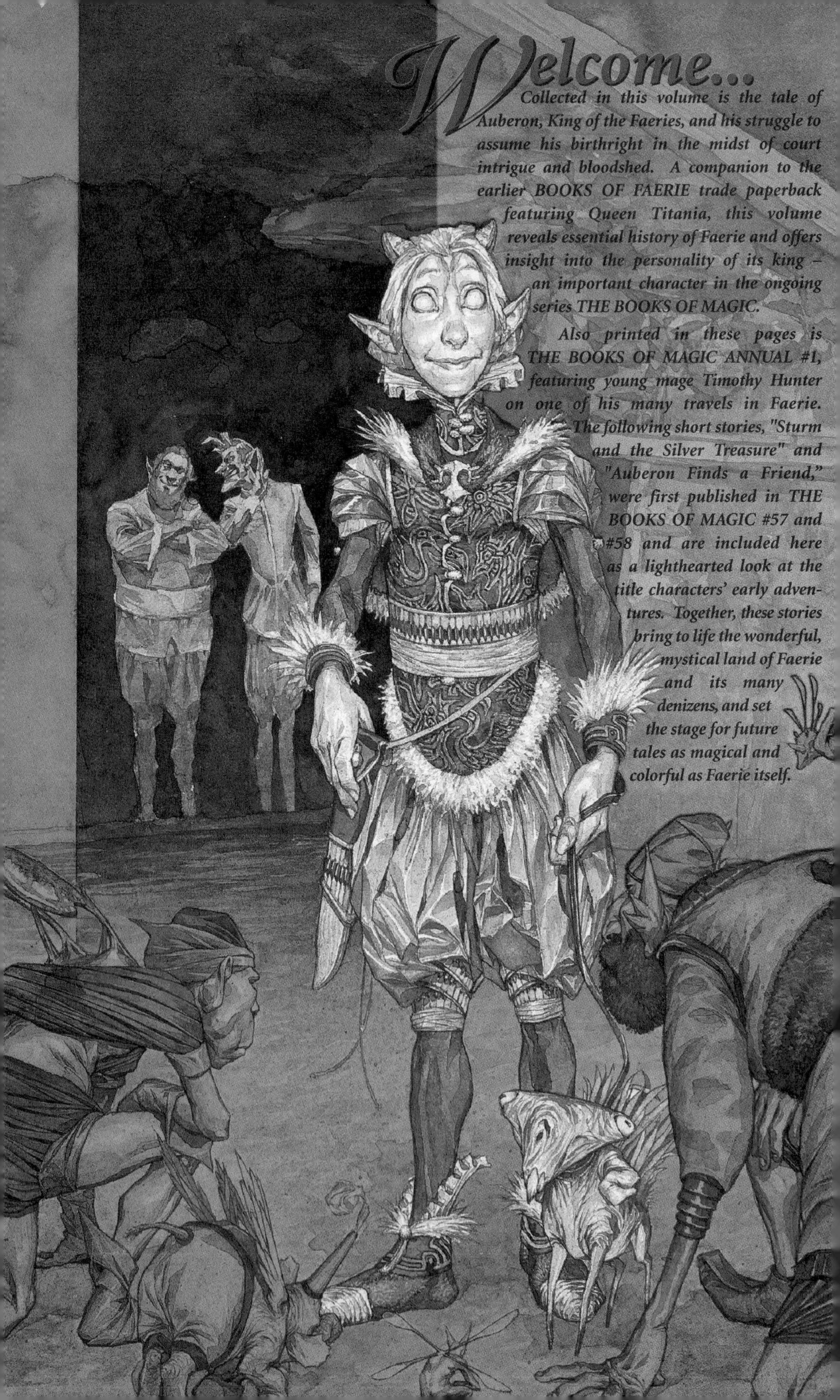

Welcome...

Collected in this volume is the tale of Auberon, King of the Faeries, and his struggle to assume his birthright in the midst of court intrigue and bloodshed. A companion to the earlier BOOKS OF FAERIE trade paperback featuring Queen Titania, this volume reveals essential history of Faerie and offers insight into the personality of its king – an important character in the ongoing series THE BOOKS OF MAGIC.

Also printed in these pages is THE BOOKS OF MAGIC ANNUAL #1, featuring young mage Timothy Hunter on one of his many travels in Faerie. The following short stories, "Sturm and the Silver Treasure" and "Auberon Finds a Friend," were first published in THE BOOKS OF MAGIC #57 and #58 and are included here as a lighthearted look at the title characters' early adventures. Together, these stories bring to life the wonderful, mystical land of Faerie and its many denizens, and set the stage for future tales as magical and colorful as Faerie itself.

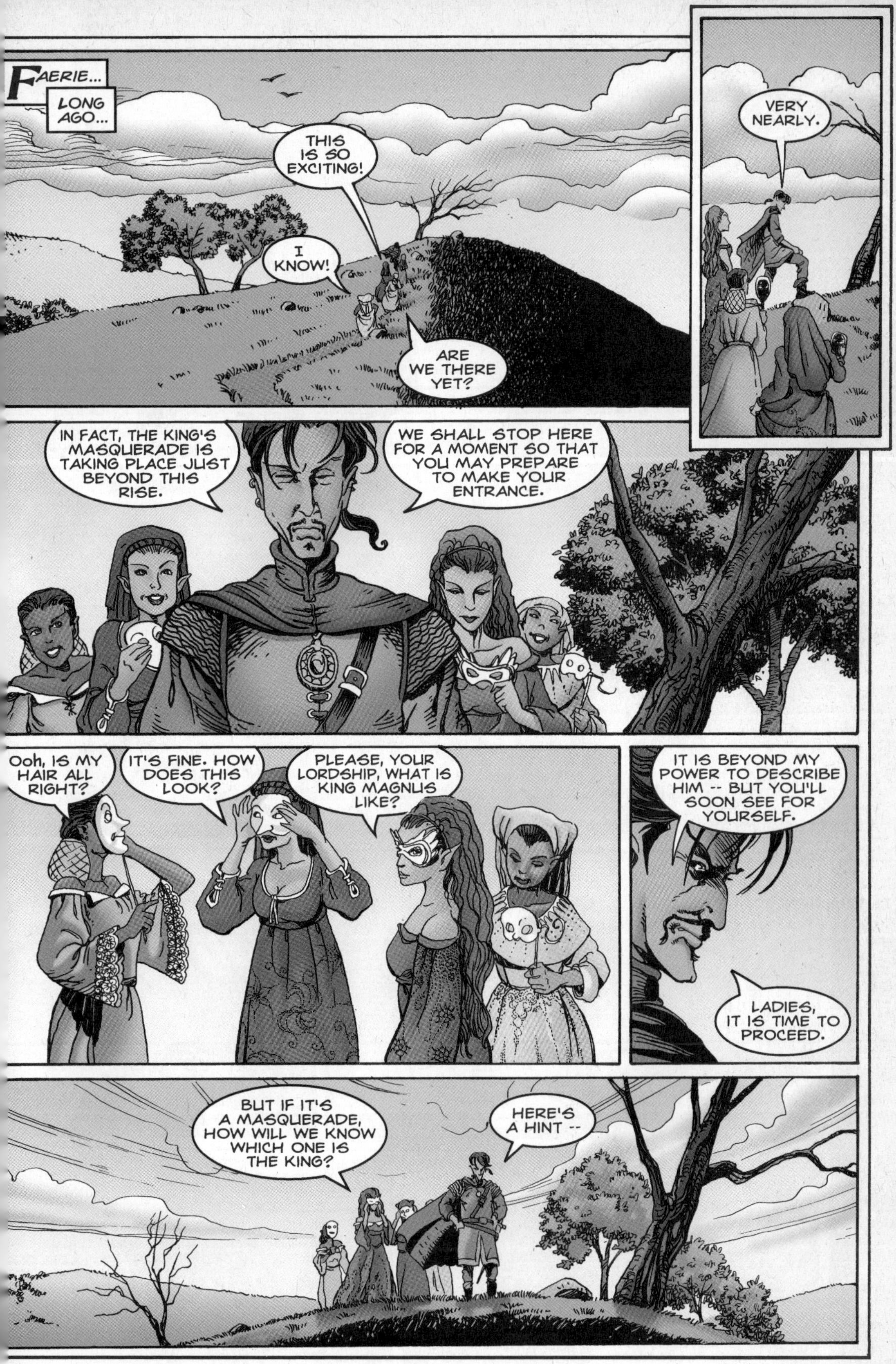
FAERIE...
LONG AGO...
THIS IS SO EXCITING!
I KNOW!
ARE WE THERE YET?
VERY NEARLY.
IN FACT, THE KING'S MASQUERADE IS TAKING PLACE JUST BEYOND THIS RISE.
WE SHALL STOP HERE FOR A MOMENT SO THAT YOU MAY PREPARE TO MAKE YOUR ENTRANCE.
Ooh, IS MY HAIR ALL RIGHT?
IT'S FINE. HOW DOES THIS LOOK?
PLEASE, YOUR LORDSHIP, WHAT IS KING MAGNUS LIKE?
IT IS BEYOND MY POWER TO DESCRIBE HIM -- BUT YOU'LL SOON SEE FOR YOURSELF.
LADIES, IT IS TIME TO PROCEED.
BUT IF IT'S A MASQUERADE, HOW WILL WE KNOW WHICH ONE IS THE KING?
HERE'S A HINT --

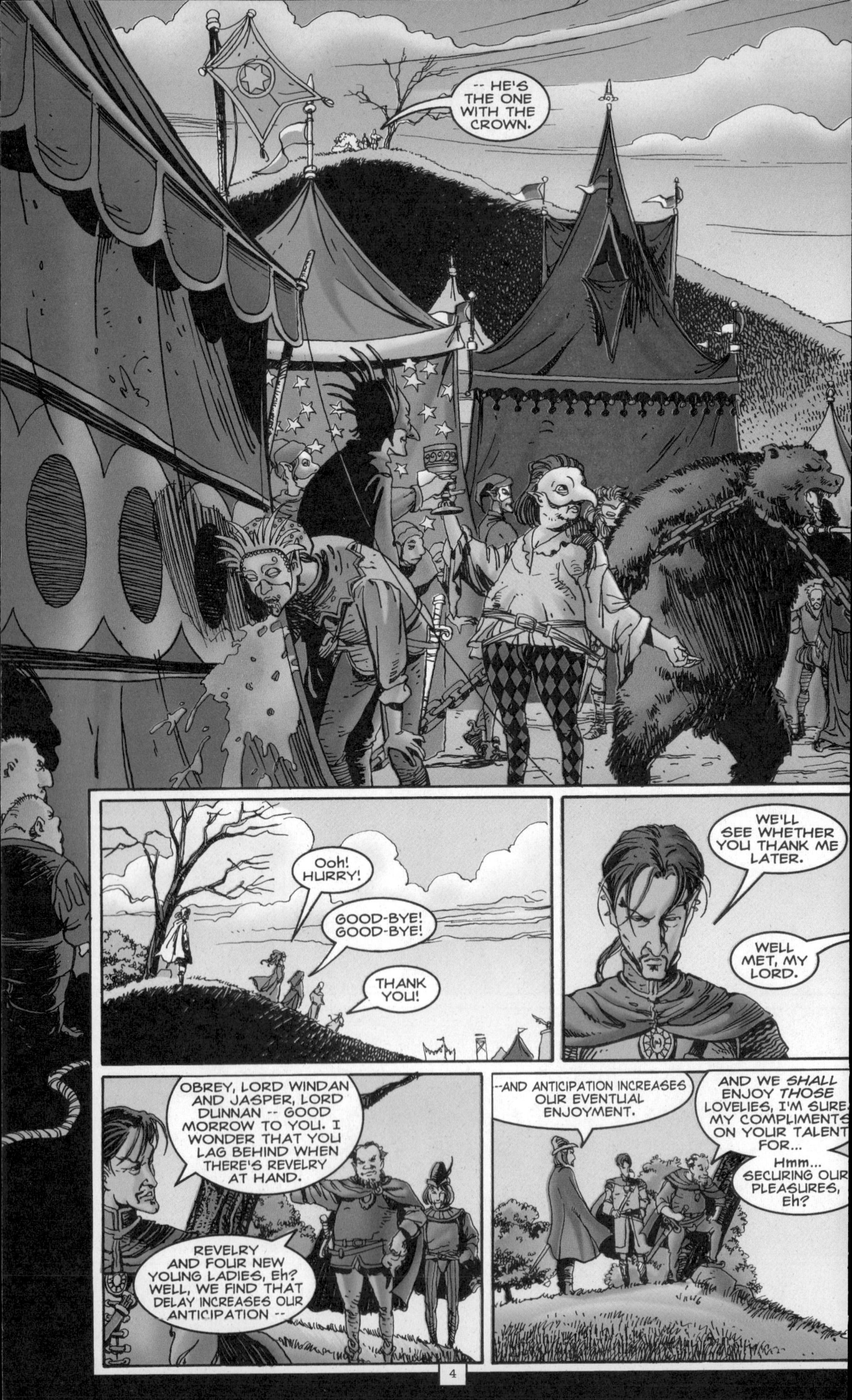

-- HE'S THE ONE WITH THE CROWN.
Ooh! HURRY!
GOOD-BYE! GOOD-BYE!
THANK YOU!
WE'LL SEE WHETHER YOU THANK ME LATER.
WELL MET, MY LORD.
OBREY, LORD WINDAN AND JASPER, LORD DUNNAN -- GOOD MORROW TO YOU. I WONDER THAT YOU LAG BEHIND WHEN THERE'S REVELRY AT HAND.
REVELRY AND FOUR NEW YOUNG LADIES, Eh? WELL, WE FIND THAT DELAY INCREASES OUR ANTICIPATION --
--AND ANTICIPATION INCREASES OUR EVENTUAL ENJOYMENT.
AND WE SHALL ENJOY THOSE LOVELIES, I'M SURE. MY COMPLIMENTS ON YOUR TALENT FOR...
Hmm... SECURING OUR PLEASURES, Eh?

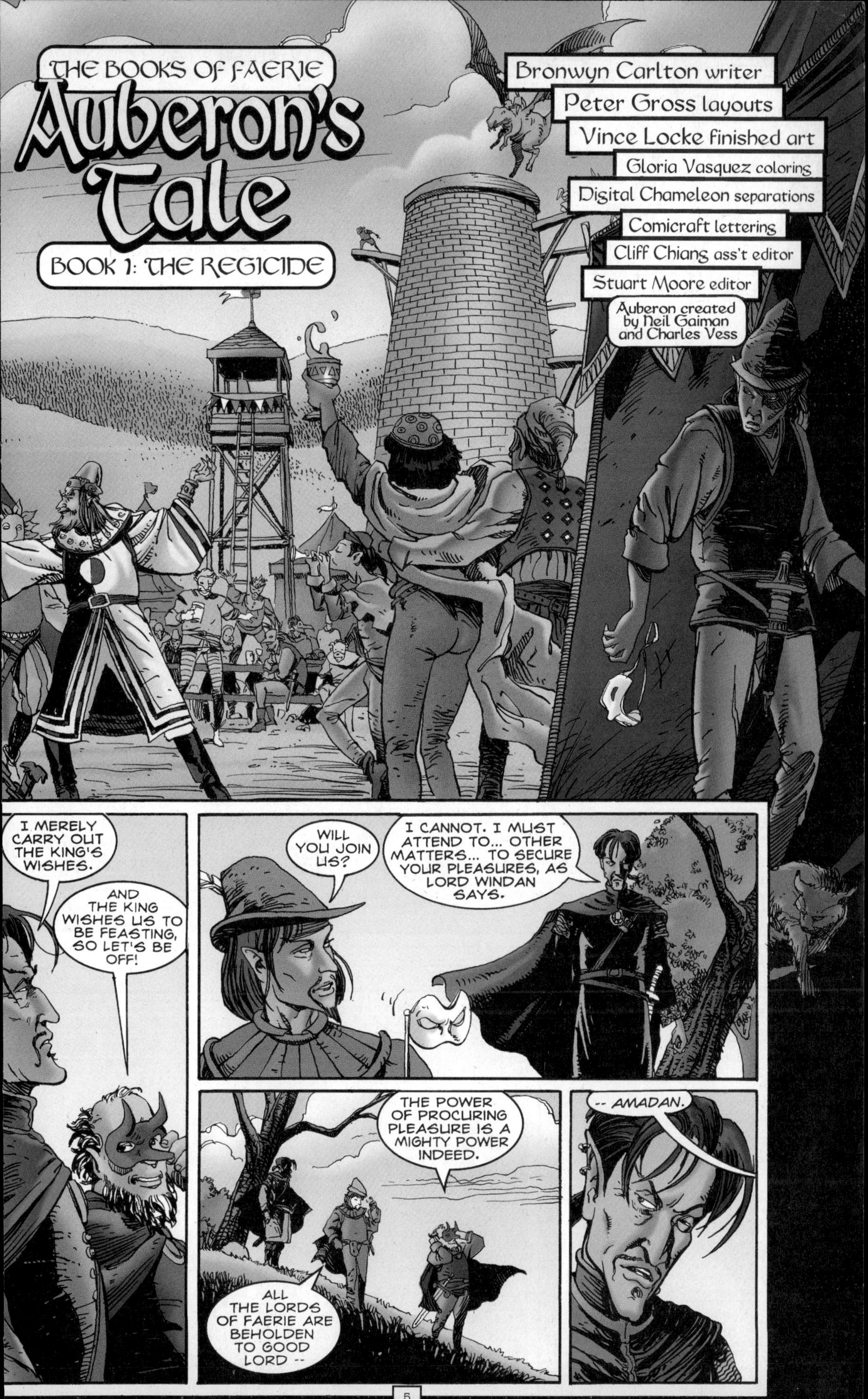

THE BOOKS OF FAERIE
Auberon's Tale
BOOK 1: THE REGICIDE
Bronwyn Carlton writer
Peter Gross layouts
Vince Locke finished art
Gloria Vasquez coloring
Digital Chameleon separations
Comicraft lettering
Cliff Chiang ass't editor
Stuart Moore editor
Auberon created by Neil Gaiman and Charles Vess
I MERELY CARRY OUT THE KING'S WISHES.
AND THE KING WISHES US TO BE FEASTING, SO LET'S BE OFF!
WILL YOU JOIN US?
I CANNOT. I MUST ATTEND TO... OTHER MATTERS... TO SECURE YOUR PLEASURES, AS LORD WINDAN SAYS.
THE POWER OF PROCURING PLEASURE IS A MIGHTY POWER INDEED.
ALL THE LORDS OF FAERIE ARE BEHOLDEN TO GOOD LORD --
-- AMADAN.

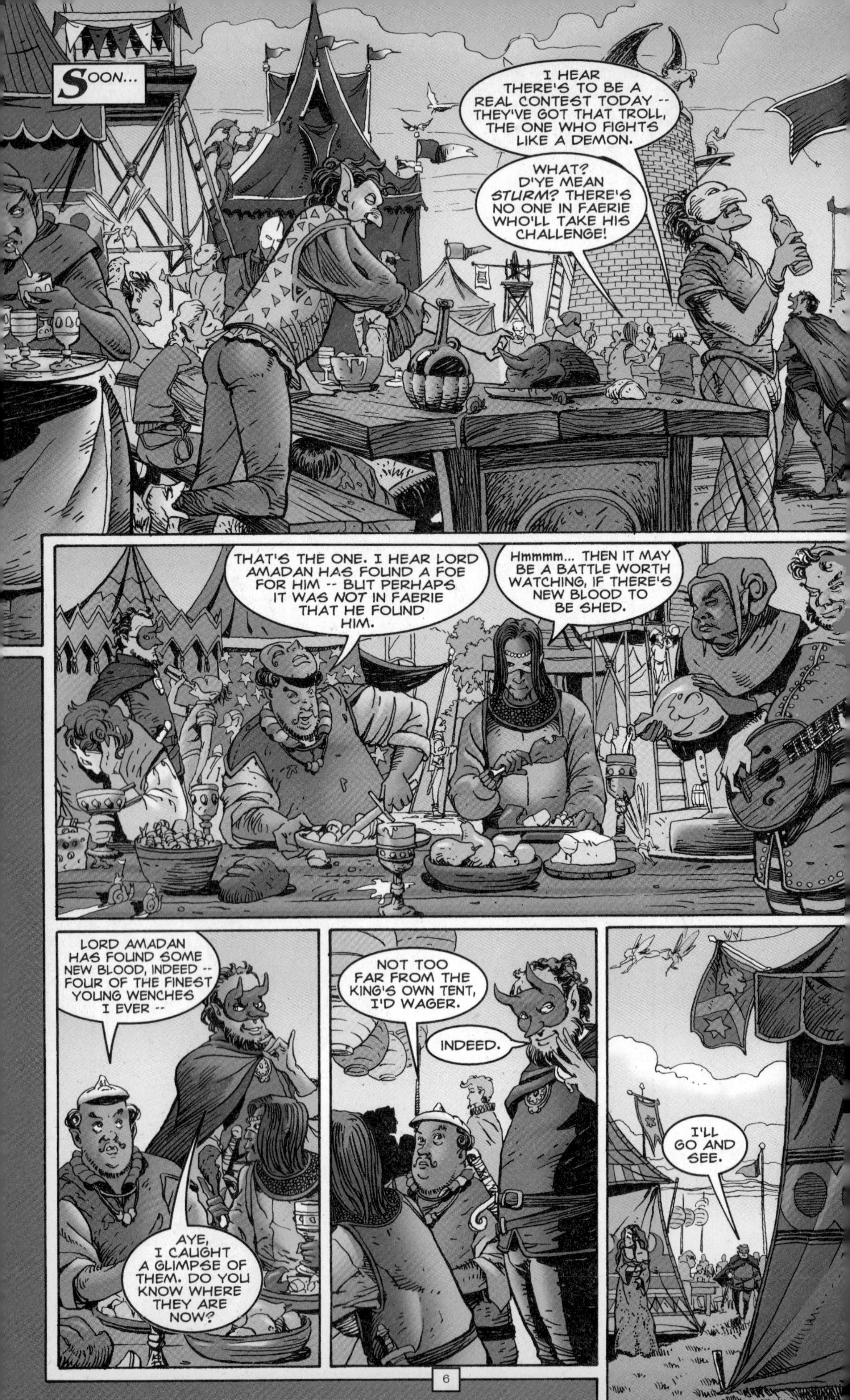
SOON...
I HEAR THERE'S TO BE A REAL CONTEST TODAY -- THEY'VE GOT THAT TROLL, THE ONE WHO FIGHTS LIKE A DEMON.
WHAT? D'YE MEAN STURM? THERE'S NO ONE IN FAERIE WHO'LL TAKE HIS CHALLENGE!
THAT'S THE ONE. I HEAR LORD AMADAN HAS FOUND A FOE FOR HIM -- BUT PERHAPS IT WAS NOT IN FAERIE THAT HE FOUND HIM.
Hmmmm... THEN IT MAY BE A BATTLE WORTH WATCHING, IF THERE'S NEW BLOOD TO BE SHED.
LORD AMADAN HAS FOUND SOME NEW BLOOD, INDEED -- FOUR OF THE FINEST YOUNG WENCHES I EVER --
AYE, I CAUGHT A GLIMPSE OF THEM. DO YOU KNOW WHERE THEY ARE NOW?
NOT TOO FAR FROM THE KING'S OWN TENT, I'D WAGER.
INDEED.
I'LL GO AND SEE.

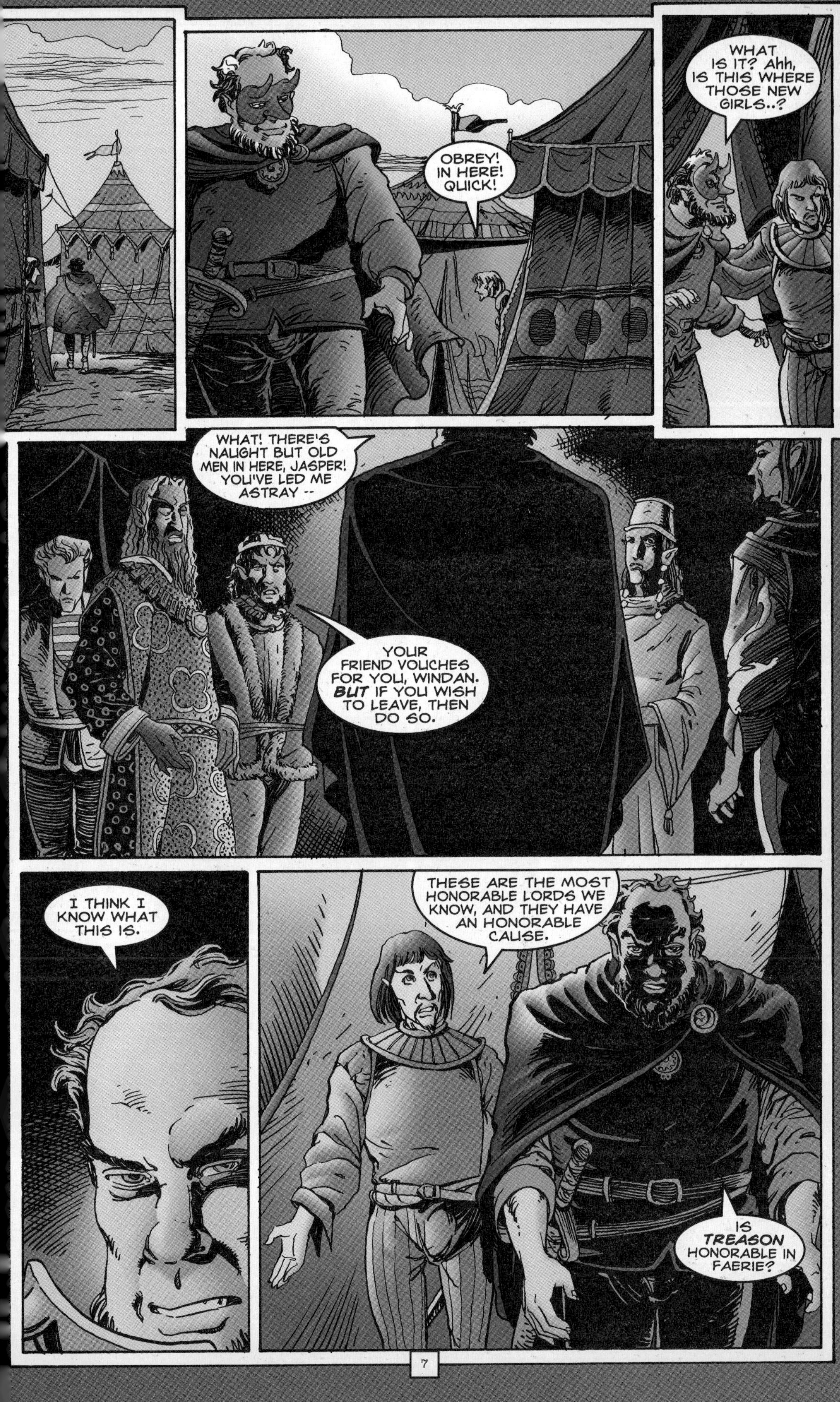
OBREY! IN HERE! QUICK!
WHAT IS IT? Ahh, IS THIS WHERE THOSE NEW GIRLS..?
WHAT! THERE'S NAUGHT BUT OLD MEN IN HERE, JASPER! YOU'VE LED ME ASTRAY --
YOUR FRIEND VOUCHES FOR YOU, WINDAN. BUT IF YOU WISH TO LEAVE, THEN DO SO.
I THINK I KNOW WHAT THIS IS.
THESE ARE THE MOST HONORABLE LORDS WE KNOW, AND THEY HAVE AN HONORABLE CAUSE.
IS TREASON HONORABLE IN FAERIE?

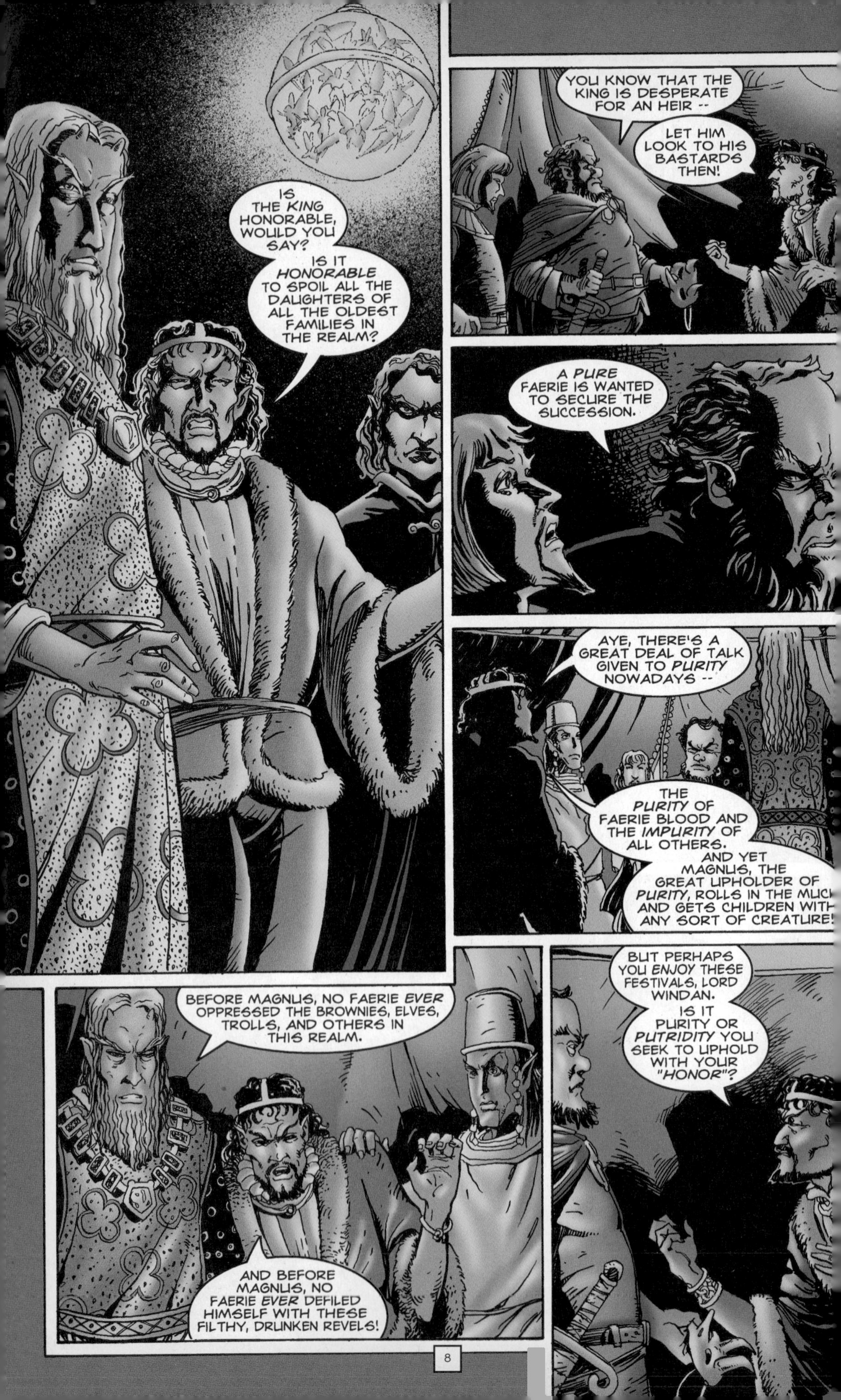

IS THE *KING* HONORABLE, WOULD YOU SAY?
IS IT *HONORABLE* TO SPOIL ALL THE DAUGHTERS OF ALL THE OLDEST FAMILIES IN THE REALM?
YOU KNOW THAT THE KING IS DESPERATE FOR AN HEIR --
LET HIM LOOK TO HIS BASTARDS THEN!
A *PURE* FAERIE IS WANTED TO SECURE THE SUCCESSION.
AYE, THERE'S A GREAT DEAL OF TALK GIVEN TO *PURITY* NOWADAYS --
THE *PURITY* OF FAERIE BLOOD AND THE *IMPURITY* OF ALL OTHERS.
AND YET MAGNUS, THE GREAT UPHOLDER OF *PURITY*, ROLLS IN THE MUCK AND GETS CHILDREN WITH ANY SORT OF CREATURE!
BEFORE MAGNUS, NO FAERIE *EVER* OPPRESSED THE BROWNIES, ELVES, TROLLS, AND OTHERS IN THIS REALM.
AND BEFORE MAGNUS, NO FAERIE *EVER* DEFILED HIMSELF WITH THESE FILTHY, DRUNKEN REVELS!
BUT PERHAPS YOU *ENJOY* THESE FESTIVALS, LORD WINDAN.
IS IT PURITY OR *PUTRIDITY* YOU SEEK TO UPHOLD WITH YOUR "*HONOR*"?

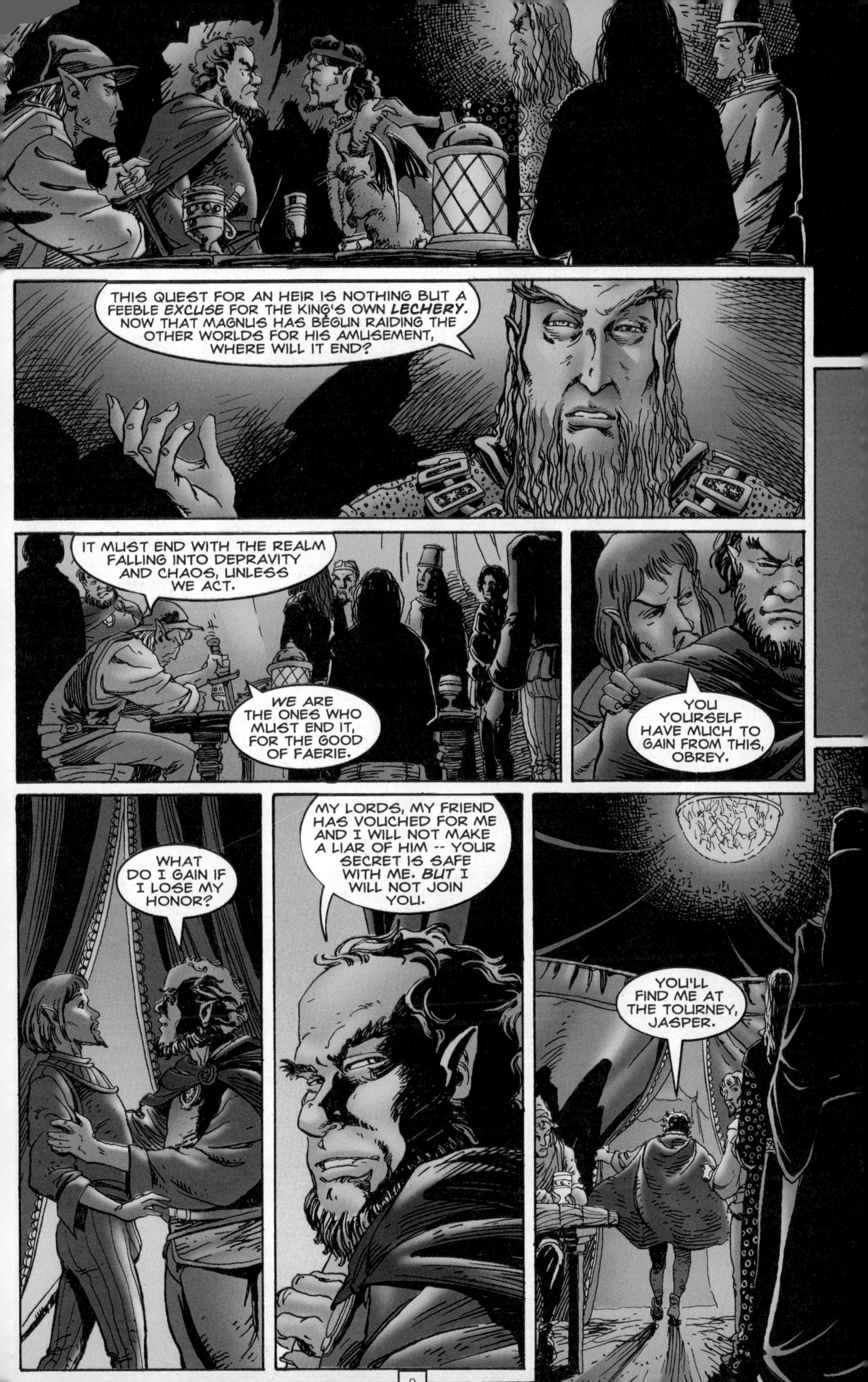
THIS QUEST FOR AN HEIR IS NOTHING BUT A FEEBLE EXCUSE FOR THE KING'S OWN LECHERY. NOW THAT MAGNUS HAS BEGUN RAIDING THE OTHER WORLDS FOR HIS AMUSEMENT, WHERE WILL IT END?
IT MUST END WITH THE REALM FALLING INTO DEPRAVITY AND CHAOS, UNLESS WE ACT.
WE ARE THE ONES WHO MUST END IT, FOR THE GOOD OF FAERIE.
YOU YOURSELF HAVE MUCH TO GAIN FROM THIS, OBREY.
WHAT DO I GAIN IF I LOSE MY HONOR?
MY LORDS, MY FRIEND HAS VOUCHED FOR ME AND I WILL NOT MAKE A LIAR OF HIM -- YOUR SECRET IS SAFE WITH ME. BUT I WILL NOT JOIN YOU.
YOU'LL FIND ME AT THE TOURNEY, JASPER.

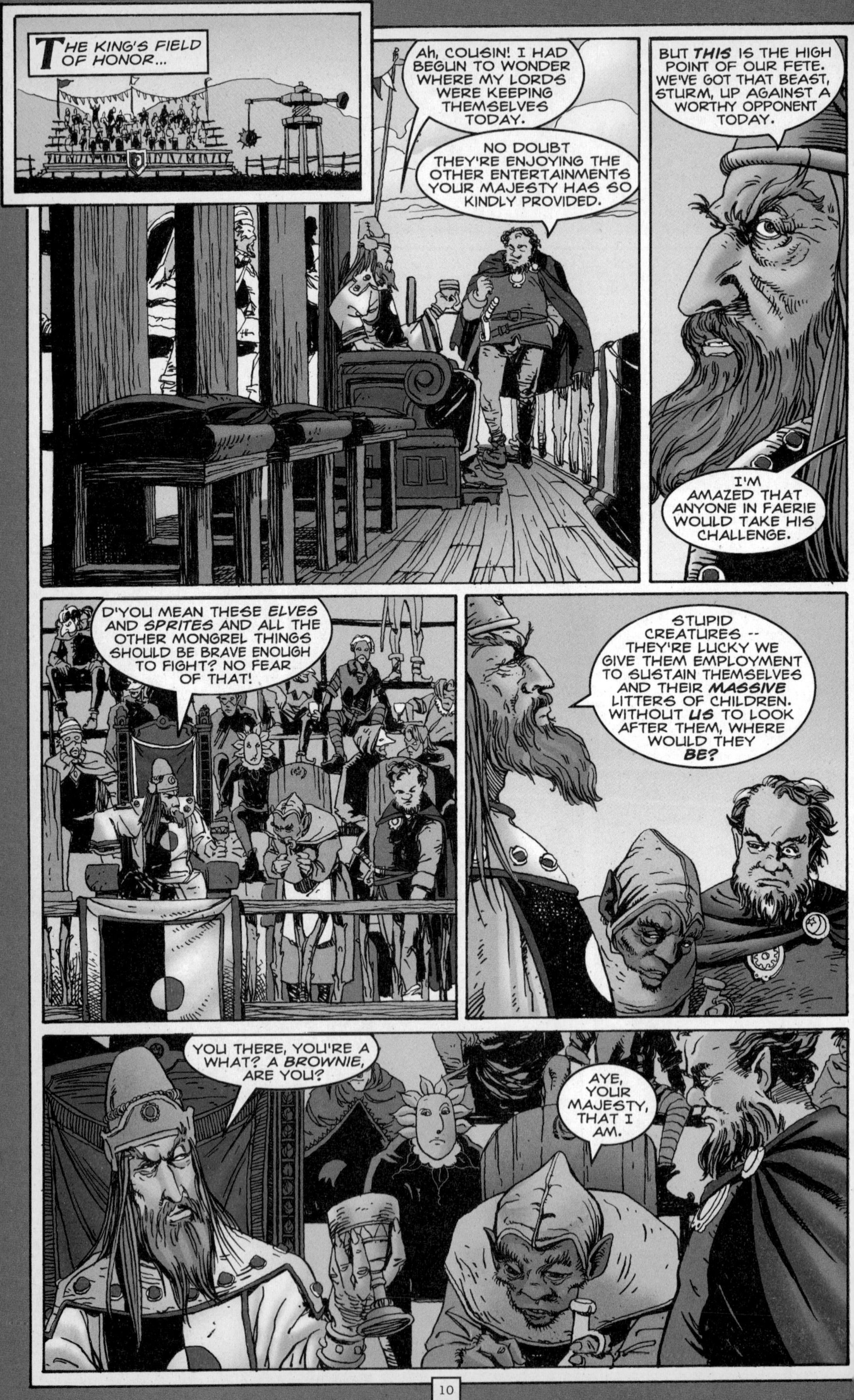
THE KING'S FIELD OF HONOR...
Ah, COUSIN! I HAD BEGUN TO WONDER WHERE MY LORDS WERE KEEPING THEMSELVES TODAY.
NO DOUBT THEY'RE ENJOYING THE OTHER ENTERTAINMENTS YOUR MAJESTY HAS SO KINDLY PROVIDED.
BUT *THIS* IS THE HIGH POINT OF OUR FETE. WE'VE GOT THAT BEAST, STURM, UP AGAINST A WORTHY OPPONENT TODAY.
I'M AMAZED THAT ANYONE IN FAERIE WOULD TAKE HIS CHALLENGE.
D'YOU MEAN THESE *ELVES* AND *SPRITES* AND ALL THE OTHER MONGREL THINGS SHOULD BE BRAVE ENOUGH TO FIGHT? NO FEAR OF THAT!
STUPID CREATURES -- THEY'RE LUCKY WE GIVE THEM EMPLOYMENT TO SUSTAIN THEMSELVES AND THEIR *MASSIVE* LITTERS OF CHILDREN. WITHOUT *US* TO LOOK AFTER THEM, WHERE WOULD THEY *BE?*
YOU THERE, YOU'RE A WHAT? A *BROWNIE*, ARE YOU?
AYE, YOUR MAJESTY, THAT I AM.

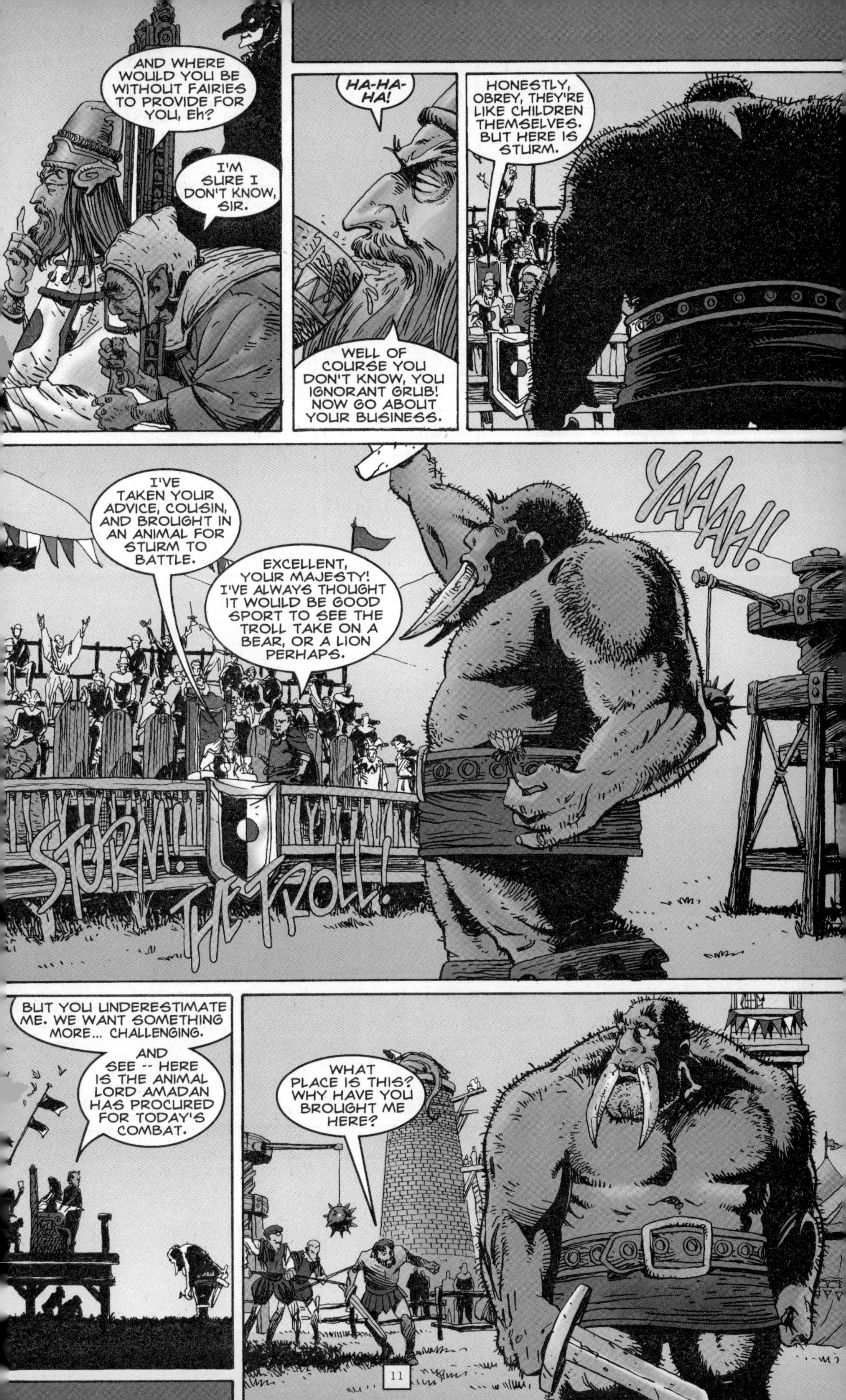
AND WHERE WOULD YOU BE WITHOUT FAIRIES TO PROVIDE FOR YOU, EH?
I'M SURE I DON'T KNOW, SIR.
HA-HA-HA!
WELL OF COURSE YOU DON'T KNOW, YOU IGNORANT GRUB! NOW GO ABOUT YOUR BUSINESS.
HONESTLY, OBREY, THEY'RE LIKE CHILDREN THEMSELVES. BUT HERE IS STURM.
I'VE TAKEN YOUR ADVICE, COUSIN, AND BROUGHT IN AN ANIMAL FOR STURM TO BATTLE.
EXCELLENT, YOUR MAJESTY! I'VE ALWAYS THOUGHT IT WOULD BE GOOD SPORT TO SEE THE TROLL TAKE ON A BEAR, OR A LION PERHAPS.
YAAAAH!
STURM! THE TROLL!
BUT YOU UNDERESTIMATE ME. WE WANT SOMETHING MORE... CHALLENGING.
AND SEE -- HERE IS THE ANIMAL LORD AMADAN HAS PROCURED FOR TODAY'S COMBAT.
WHAT PLACE IS THIS? WHY HAVE YOU BROUGHT ME HERE?

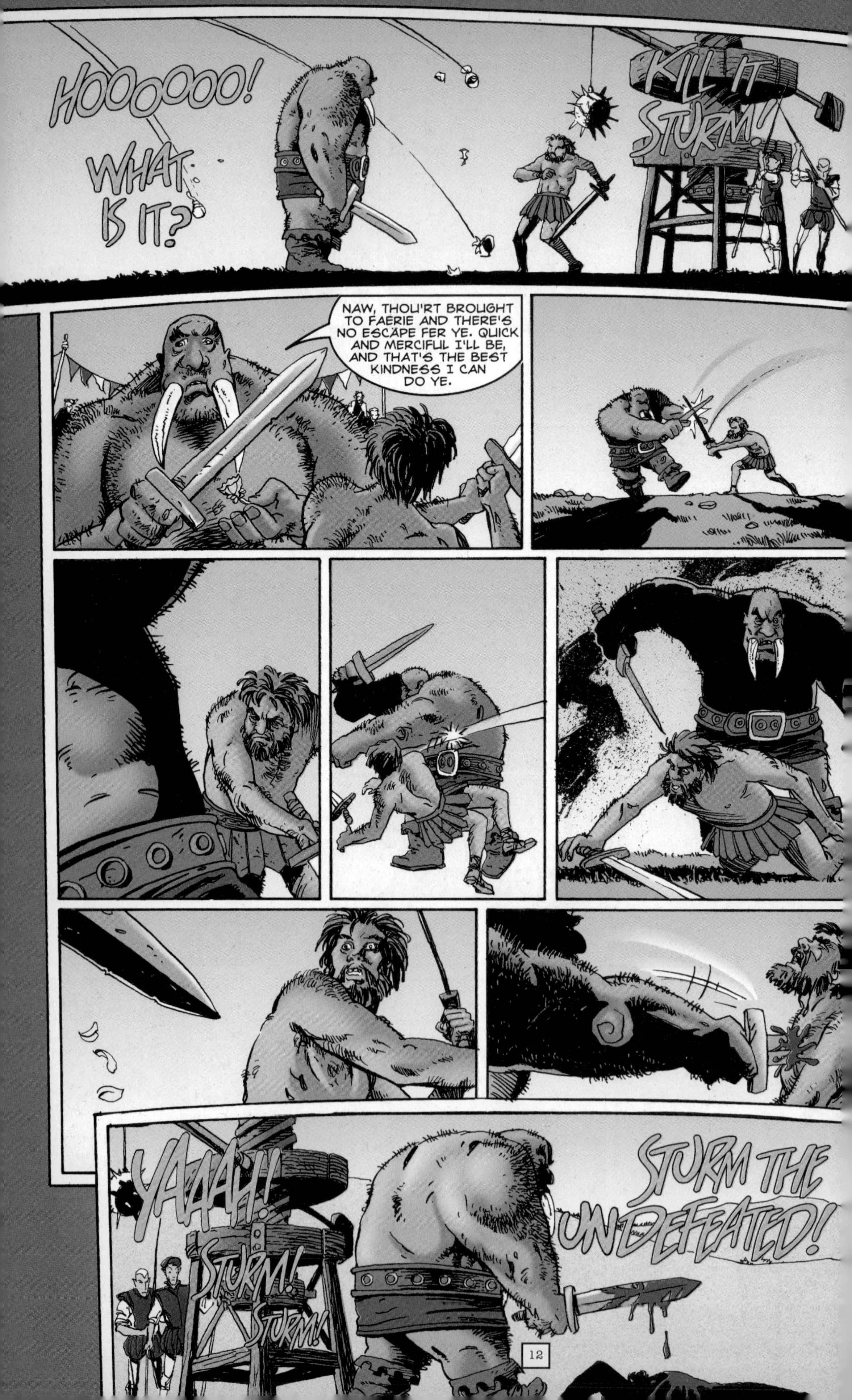
HOOOOOOO!
WHAT IS IT?
KILL IT STURM!
NAW, THOU'RT BROUGHT TO FAERIE AND THERE'S NO ESCAPE FER YE. QUICK AND MERCIFUL I'LL BE, AND THAT'S THE BEST KINDNESS I CAN DO YE.
YAAAH!
STURM!
STURM!
STURM THE UNDEFEATED!

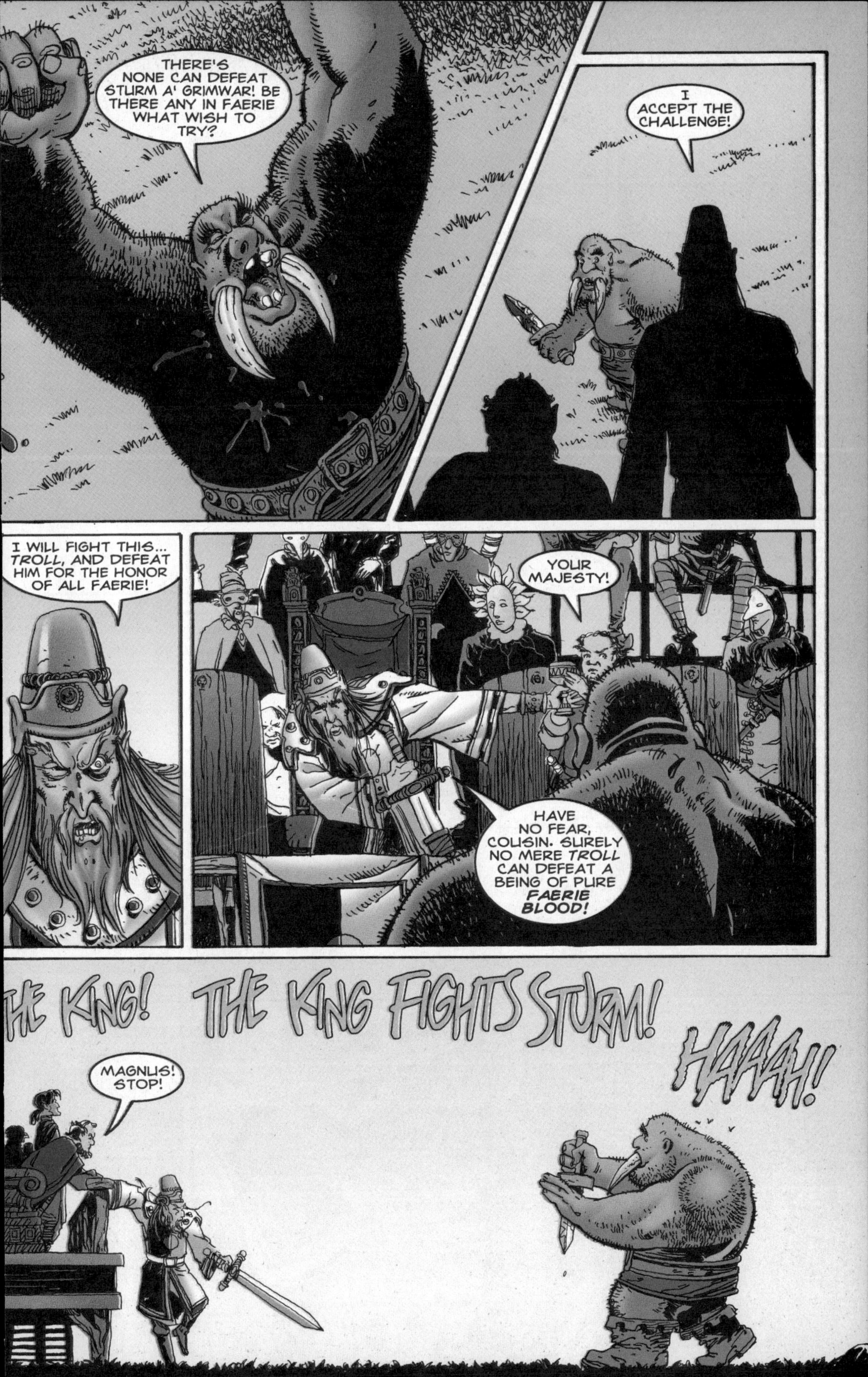
THERE'S NONE CAN DEFEAT STURM A' GRIMWAR! BE THERE ANY IN FAERIE WHAT WISH TO TRY?
I ACCEPT THE CHALLENGE!
I WILL FIGHT THIS... TROLL, AND DEFEAT HIM FOR THE HONOR OF ALL FAERIE!
YOUR MAJESTY!
HAVE NO FEAR, COUSIN. SURELY NO MERE TROLL CAN DEFEAT A BEING OF PURE FAERIE BLOOD!
HE KING!
THE KING FIGHTS STURM!
HAAAH!
MAGNUS! STOP!

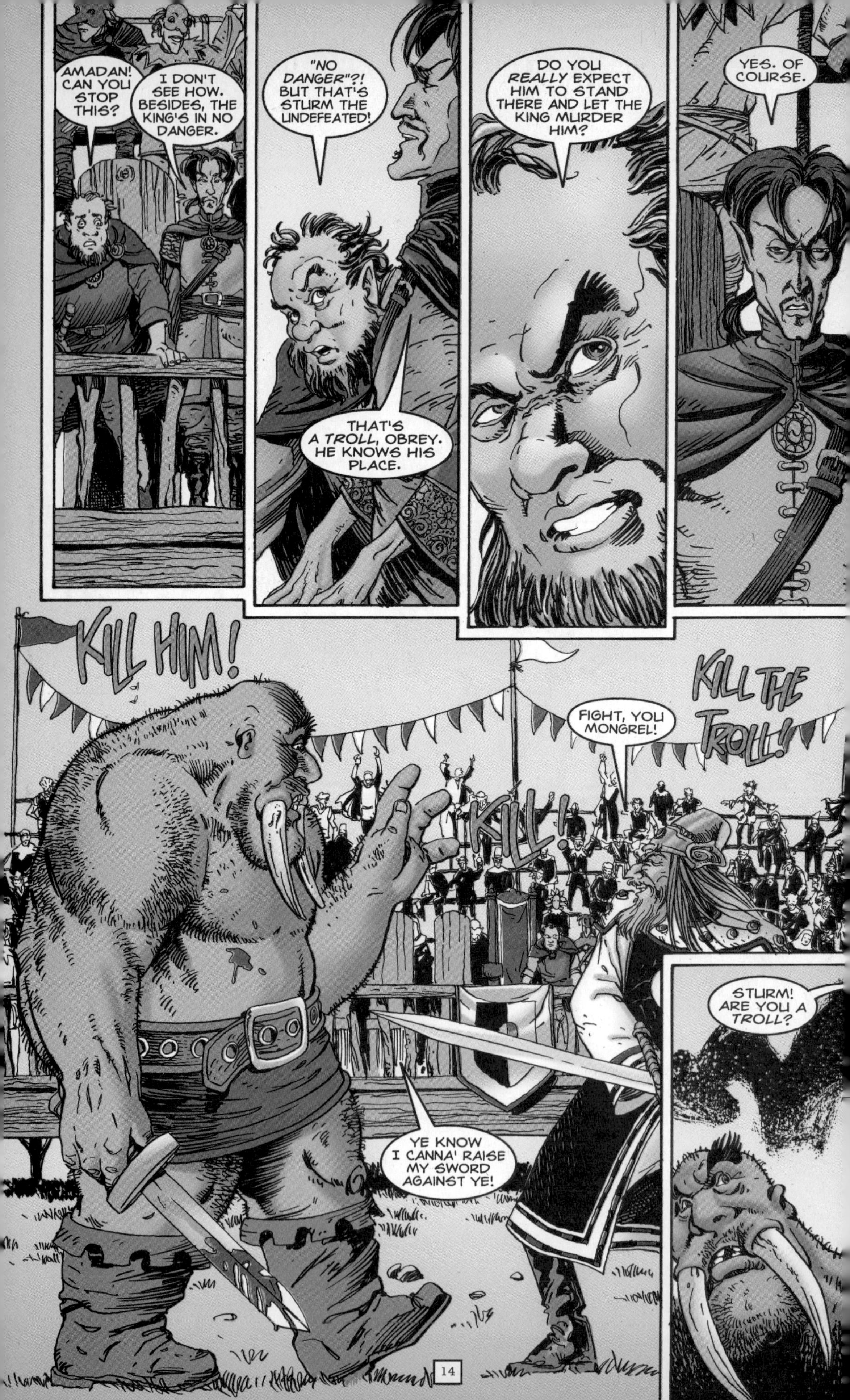

AMADAN! CAN YOU STOP THIS?
I DON'T SEE HOW. BESIDES, THE KING'S IN NO DANGER.
"NO *DANGER*"?! BUT THAT'S STURM THE UNDEFEATED!
THAT'S A *TROLL*, OBREY. HE KNOWS HIS PLACE.
DO YOU *REALLY* EXPECT HIM TO STAND THERE AND LET THE KING MURDER HIM?
YES. OF COURSE.
KILL HIM!
FIGHT, YOU MONGREL!
KILL THE TROLL!
KILL!
YE KNOW I CANNA' RAISE MY SWORD AGAINST YE!
STURM! ARE YOU A *TROLL*?

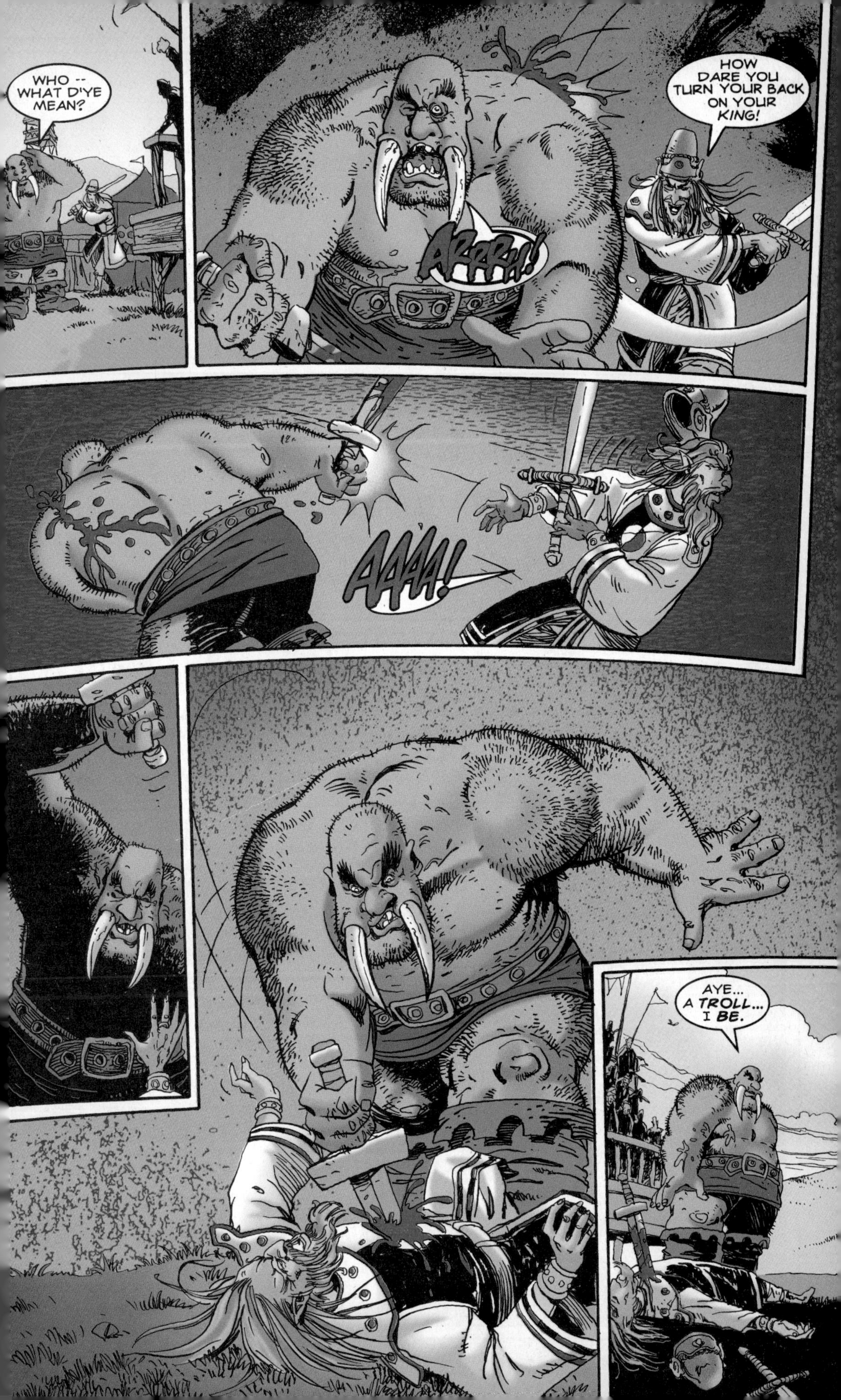
WHO -- WHAT D'YE MEAN?
HOW DARE YOU TURN YOUR BACK ON YOUR KING!
ARRRH!
AAAA!
AYE... A TROLL... I BE.

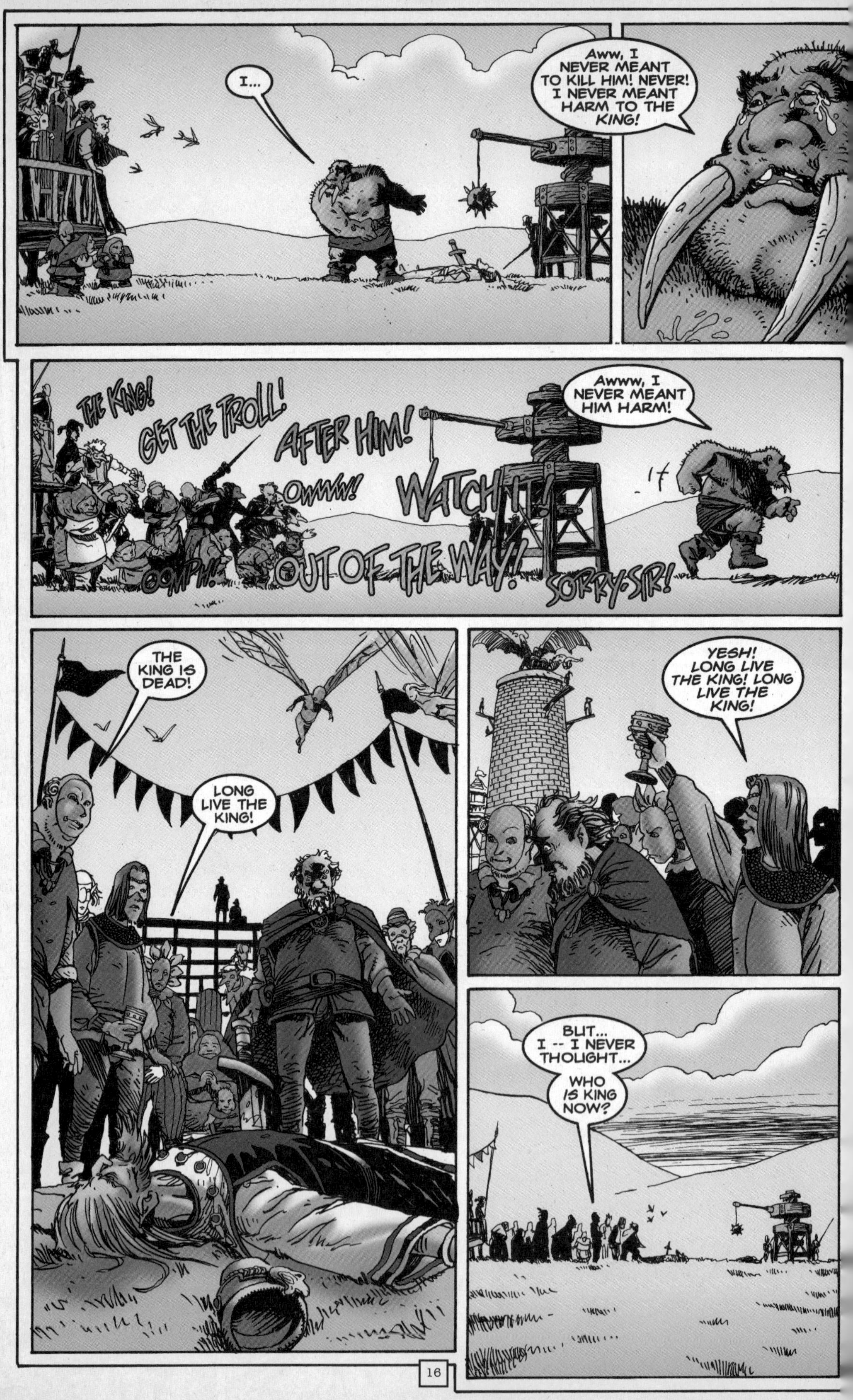
I...
Aww, I NEVER MEANT TO KILL HIM! NEVER! I NEVER MEANT HARM TO THE KING!
THE KING!
GET THE TROLL!
AFTER HIM!
OWWW!
WATCH IT!
OOMPH!
OUT OF THE WAY!
SORRY SIR!
Awww, I NEVER MEANT HIM HARM!
THE KING IS DEAD!
LONG LIVE THE KING!
YESH! LONG LIVE THE KING! LONG LIVE THE KING!
BUT... I -- I NEVER THOUGHT...
WHO IS KING NOW?

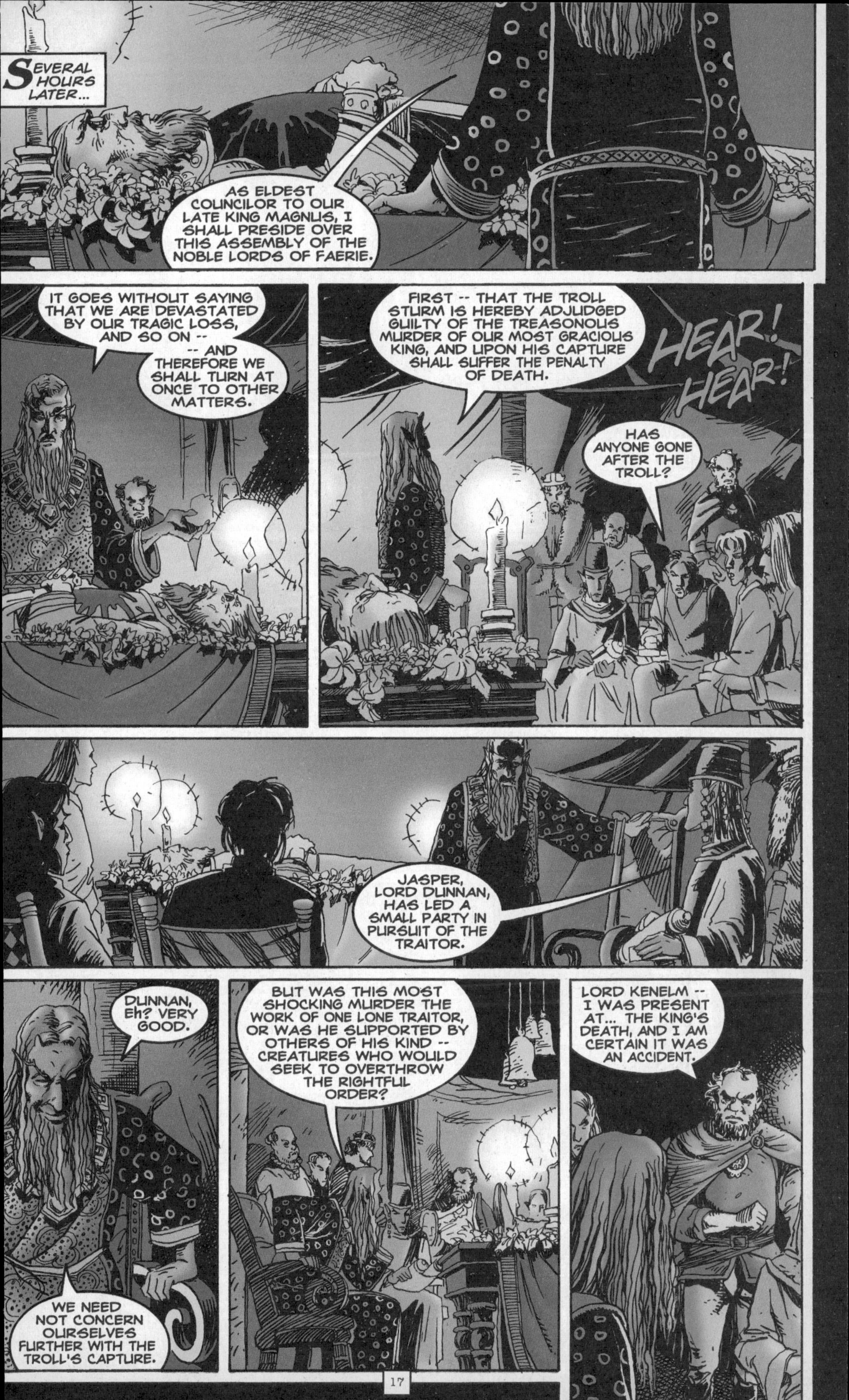
SEVERAL HOURS LATER...
AS ELDEST COUNCILOR TO OUR LATE KING MAGNUS, I SHALL PRESIDE OVER THIS ASSEMBLY OF THE NOBLE LORDS OF FAERIE.
IT GOES WITHOUT SAYING THAT WE ARE DEVASTATED BY OUR TRAGIC LOSS, AND SO ON --
-- AND THEREFORE WE SHALL TURN AT ONCE TO OTHER MATTERS.
FIRST -- THAT THE TROLL STURM IS HEREBY ADJUDGED GUILTY OF THE TREASONOUS MURDER OF OUR MOST GRACIOUS KING, AND UPON HIS CAPTURE SHALL SUFFER THE PENALTY OF DEATH.
HEAR! HEAR!
HAS ANYONE GONE AFTER THE TROLL?
JASPER, LORD DUNNAN, HAS LED A SMALL PARTY IN PURSUIT OF THE TRAITOR.
DUNNAN, EH? VERY GOOD.
WE NEED NOT CONCERN OURSELVES FURTHER WITH THE TROLL'S CAPTURE.
BUT WAS THIS MOST SHOCKING MURDER THE WORK OF ONE LONE TRAITOR, OR WAS HE SUPPORTED BY OTHERS OF HIS KIND -- CREATURES WHO WOULD SEEK TO OVERTHROW THE RIGHTFUL ORDER?
LORD KENELM -- I WAS PRESENT AT... THE KING'S DEATH, AND I AM CERTAIN IT WAS AN ACCIDENT.

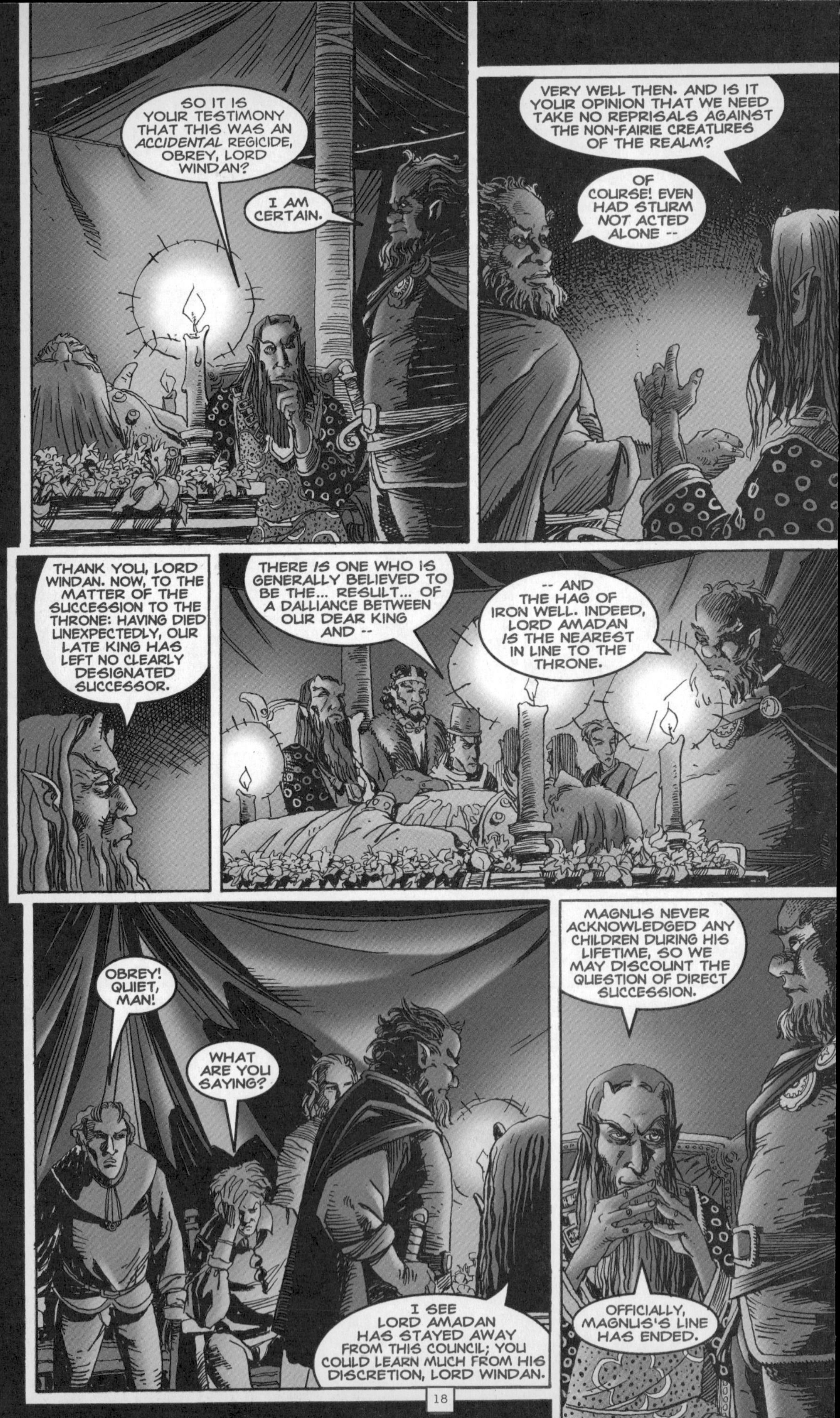
SO IT IS YOUR TESTIMONY THAT THIS WAS AN *ACCIDENTAL* REGICIDE, OBREY, LORD WINDAN?
I AM CERTAIN.
VERY WELL THEN. AND IS IT YOUR OPINION THAT WE NEED TAKE NO REPRISALS AGAINST THE NON-FAIRIE CREATURES OF THE REALM?
OF COURSE! EVEN HAD STURM *NOT* ACTED ALONE --
THANK YOU, LORD WINDAN. NOW, TO THE MATTER OF THE SUCCESSION TO THE THRONE: HAVING DIED UNEXPECTEDLY, OUR LATE KING HAS LEFT NO CLEARLY DESIGNATED SUCCESSOR.
THERE *IS* ONE WHO IS GENERALLY BELIEVED TO BE THE... RESULT... OF A DALLIANCE BETWEEN OUR DEAR KING AND --
-- AND THE HAG OF IRON WELL. INDEED, LORD AMADAN *IS* THE NEAREST IN LINE TO THE THRONE.
OBREY! QUIET, MAN!
WHAT ARE YOU SAYING?
I SEE LORD AMADAN HAS STAYED AWAY FROM THIS COUNCIL; YOU COULD LEARN MUCH FROM HIS DISCRETION, LORD WINDAN.
MAGNUS NEVER ACKNOWLEDGED ANY CHILDREN DURING HIS LIFETIME, SO WE MAY DISCOUNT THE QUESTION OF DIRECT SUCCESSION.
OFFICIALLY, MAGNUS'S LINE HAS ENDED.

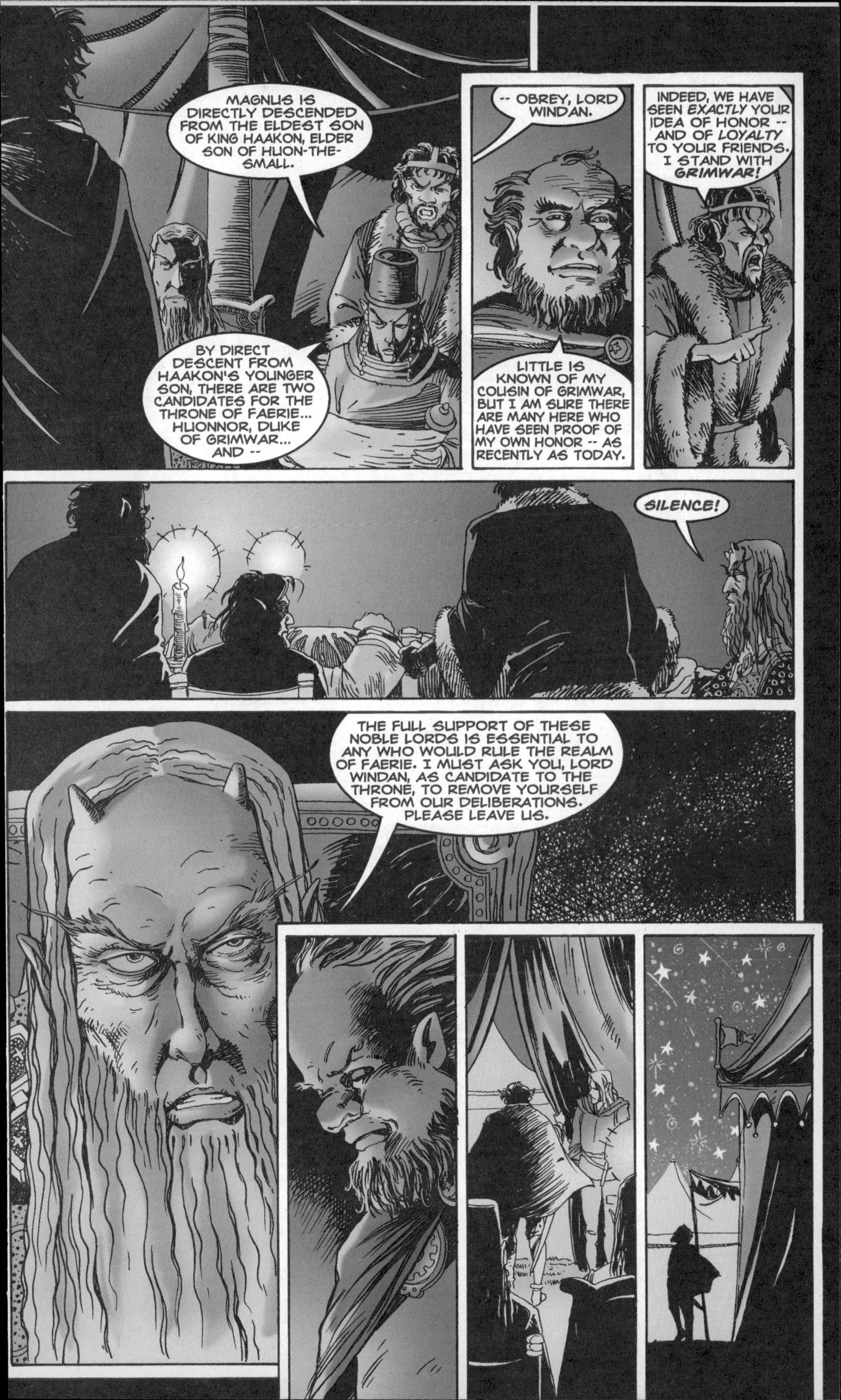
MAGNUS IS DIRECTLY DESCENDED FROM THE ELDEST SON OF KING HAAKON, ELDER SON OF HUON-THE-SMALL.
BY DIRECT DESCENT FROM HAAKON'S YOUNGER SON, THERE ARE TWO CANDIDATES FOR THE THRONE OF FAERIE... HUONNOR, DUKE OF GRIMWAR... AND --
-- OBREY, LORD WINDAN.
LITTLE IS KNOWN OF MY COUSIN OF GRIMWAR, BUT I AM SURE THERE ARE MANY HERE WHO HAVE SEEN PROOF OF MY OWN HONOR -- AS RECENTLY AS TODAY.
INDEED, WE HAVE SEEN EXACTLY YOUR IDEA OF HONOR -- AND OF LOYALTY TO YOUR FRIENDS. I STAND WITH GRIMWAR!
SILENCE!
THE FULL SUPPORT OF THESE NOBLE LORDS IS ESSENTIAL TO ANY WHO WOULD RULE THE REALM OF FAERIE. I MUST ASK YOU, LORD WINDAN, AS CANDIDATE TO THE THRONE, TO REMOVE YOURSELF FROM OUR DELIBERATIONS. PLEASE LEAVE US.

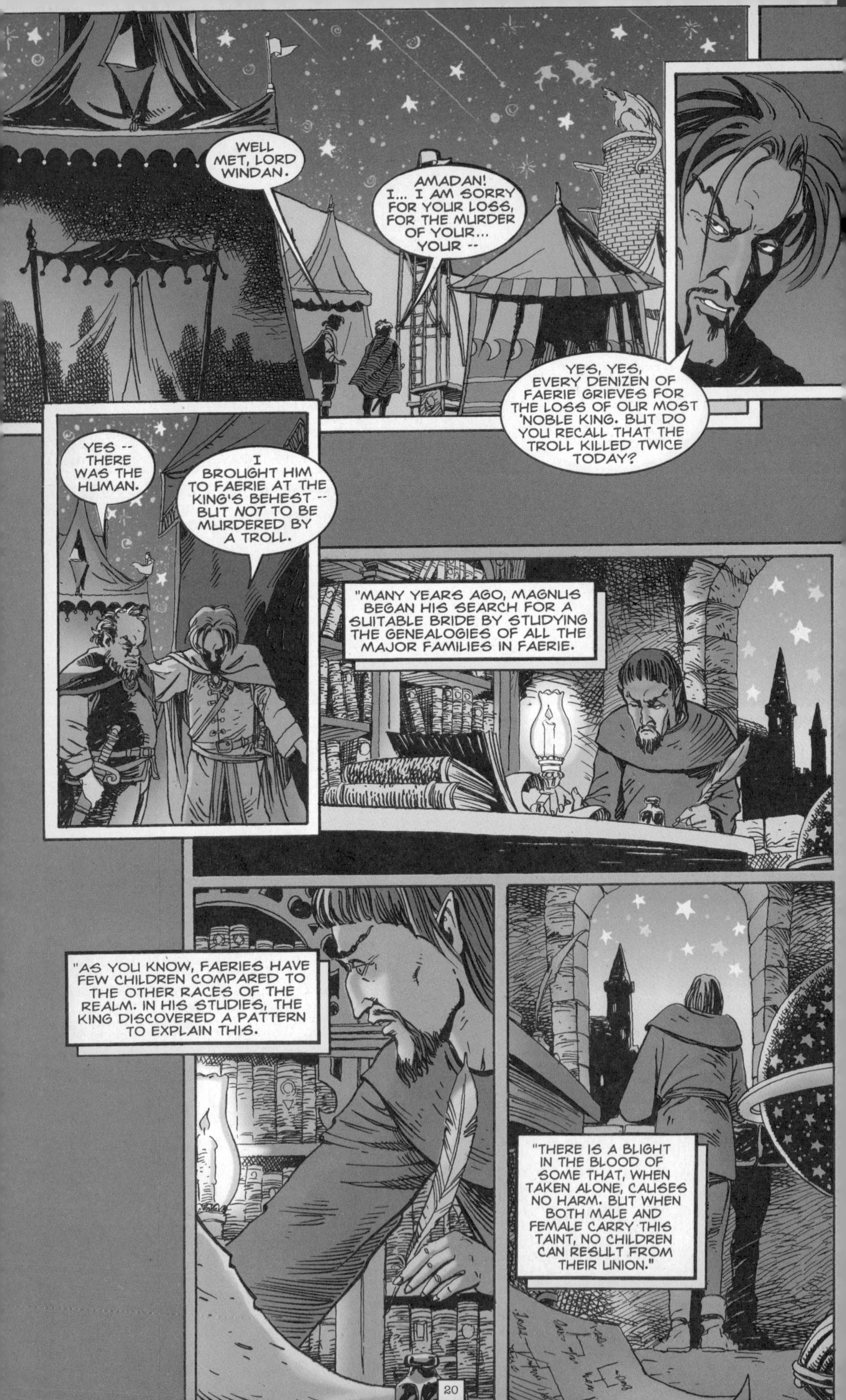
WELL MET, LORD WINDAN.
AMADAN! I... I AM SORRY FOR YOUR LOSS, FOR THE MURDER OF YOUR... YOUR --
YES, YES, EVERY DENIZEN OF FAERIE GRIEVES FOR THE LOSS OF OUR MOST 'NOBLE KING. BUT DO YOU RECALL THAT THE TROLL KILLED TWICE TODAY?
YES -- THERE WAS THE HUMAN.
I BROUGHT HIM TO FAERIE AT THE KING'S BEHEST -- BUT NOT TO BE MURDERED BY A TROLL.
"MANY YEARS AGO, MAGNUS BEGAN HIS SEARCH FOR A SUITABLE BRIDE BY STUDYING THE GENEALOGIES OF ALL THE MAJOR FAMILIES IN FAERIE.
"AS YOU KNOW, FAERIES HAVE FEW CHILDREN COMPARED TO THE OTHER RACES OF THE REALM. IN HIS STUDIES, THE KING DISCOVERED A PATTERN TO EXPLAIN THIS.
"THERE IS A BLIGHT IN THE BLOOD OF SOME THAT, WHEN TAKEN ALONE, CAUSES NO HARM. BUT WHEN BOTH MALE AND FEMALE CARRY THIS TAINT, NO CHILDREN CAN RESULT FROM THEIR UNION."

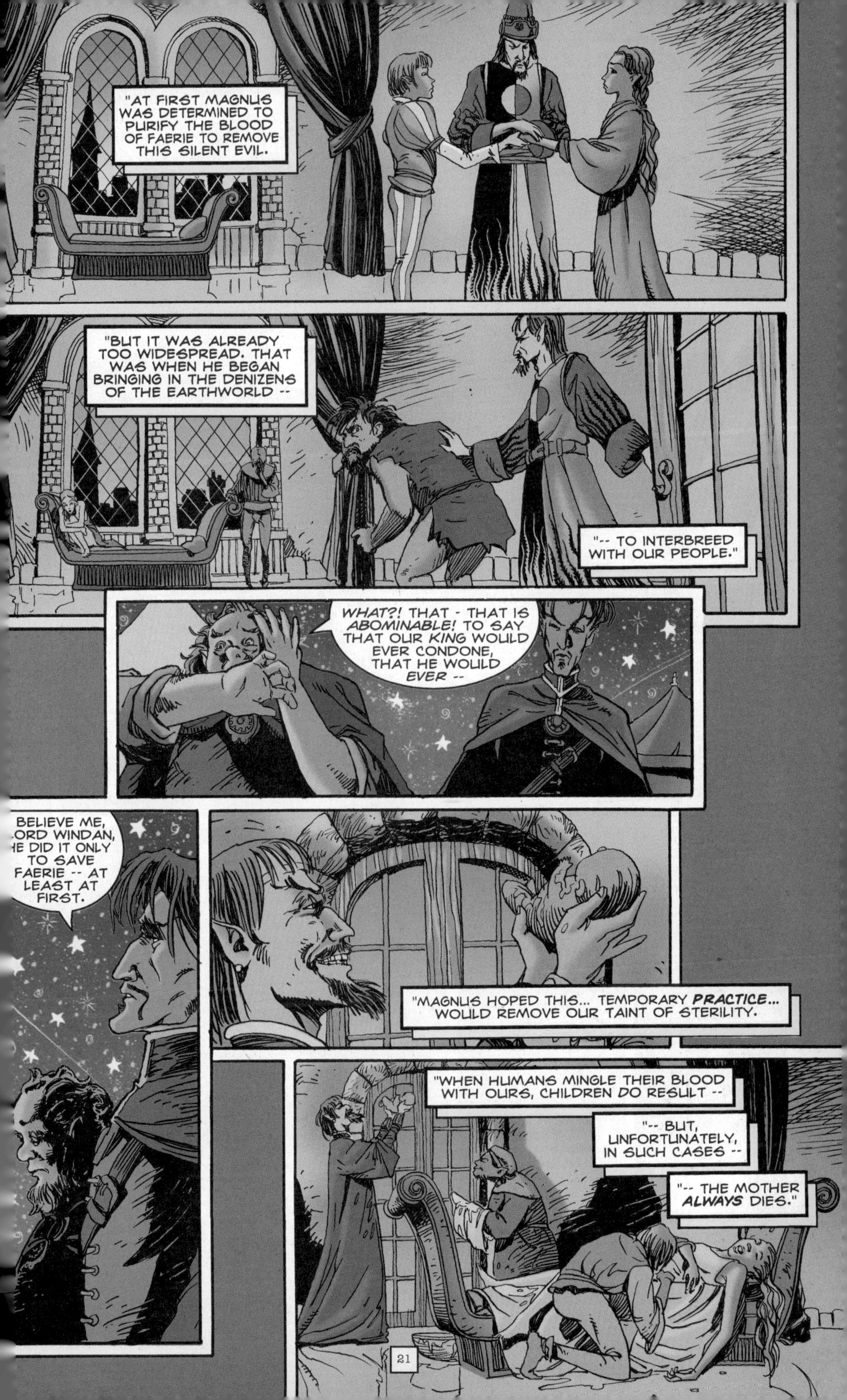
"AT FIRST MAGNUS WAS DETERMINED TO PURIFY THE BLOOD OF FAERIE TO REMOVE THIS SILENT EVIL.
"BUT IT WAS ALREADY TOO WIDESPREAD. THAT WAS WHEN HE BEGAN BRINGING IN THE DENIZENS OF THE EARTHWORLD --
"-- TO INTERBREED WITH OUR PEOPLE."
WHAT?! THAT - THAT IS *ABOMINABLE!* TO SAY THAT OUR *KING* WOULD EVER CONDONE, THAT HE WOULD *EVER* --
BELIEVE ME, LORD WINDAN, HE DID IT ONLY TO SAVE FAERIE -- AT LEAST AT FIRST.
"MAGNUS HOPED THIS... TEMPORARY ***PRACTICE...*** WOULD REMOVE OUR TAINT OF STERILITY.
"WHEN HUMANS MINGLE THEIR BLOOD WITH OURS, CHILDREN *DO* RESULT --
"-- BUT, UNFORTUNATELY, IN SUCH CASES --
"-- THE MOTHER ***ALWAYS*** DIES."

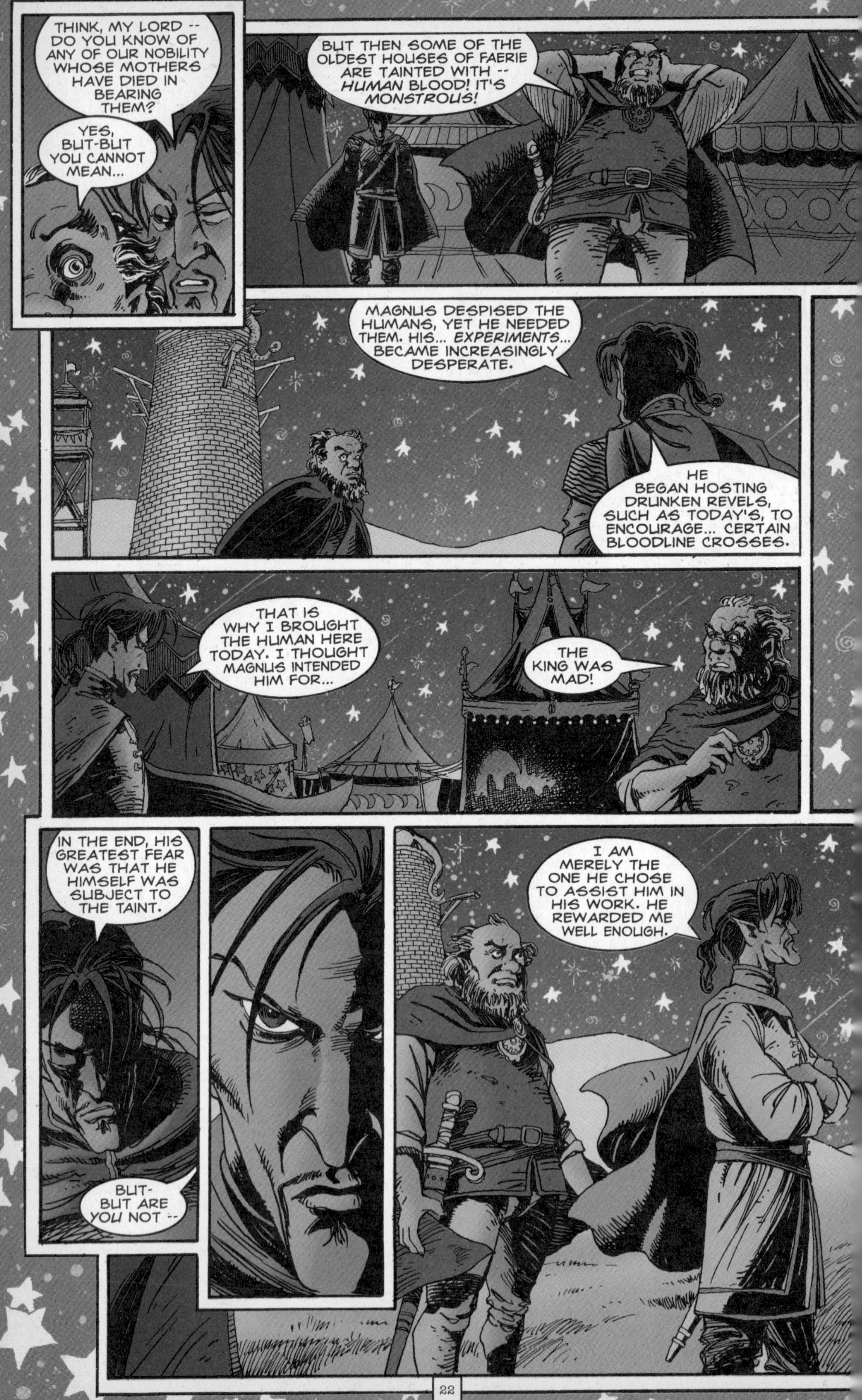
THINK, MY LORD -- DO YOU KNOW OF ANY OF OUR NOBILITY WHOSE MOTHERS HAVE DIED IN BEARING THEM?
YES, BUT-BUT YOU CANNOT MEAN...
BUT THEN SOME OF THE OLDEST HOUSES OF FAERIE ARE TAINTED WITH -- *HUMAN* BLOOD! IT'S *MONSTROUS!*
MAGNUS DESPISED THE HUMANS, YET HE NEEDED THEM. HIS... *EXPERIMENTS*... BECAME INCREASINGLY DESPERATE.
HE BEGAN HOSTING DRUNKEN REVELS, SUCH AS TODAY'S, TO ENCOURAGE... CERTAIN BLOODLINE CROSSES.
THAT IS WHY I BROUGHT THE HUMAN HERE TODAY. I THOUGHT MAGNUS INTENDED HIM FOR...
THE KING WAS MAD!
IN THE END, HIS GREATEST FEAR WAS THAT HE HIMSELF WAS SUBJECT TO THE TAINT.
BUT-BUT ARE *YOU* NOT --
I AM MERELY THE ONE HE CHOSE TO ASSIST HIM IN HIS WORK. HE REWARDED ME WELL ENOUGH.

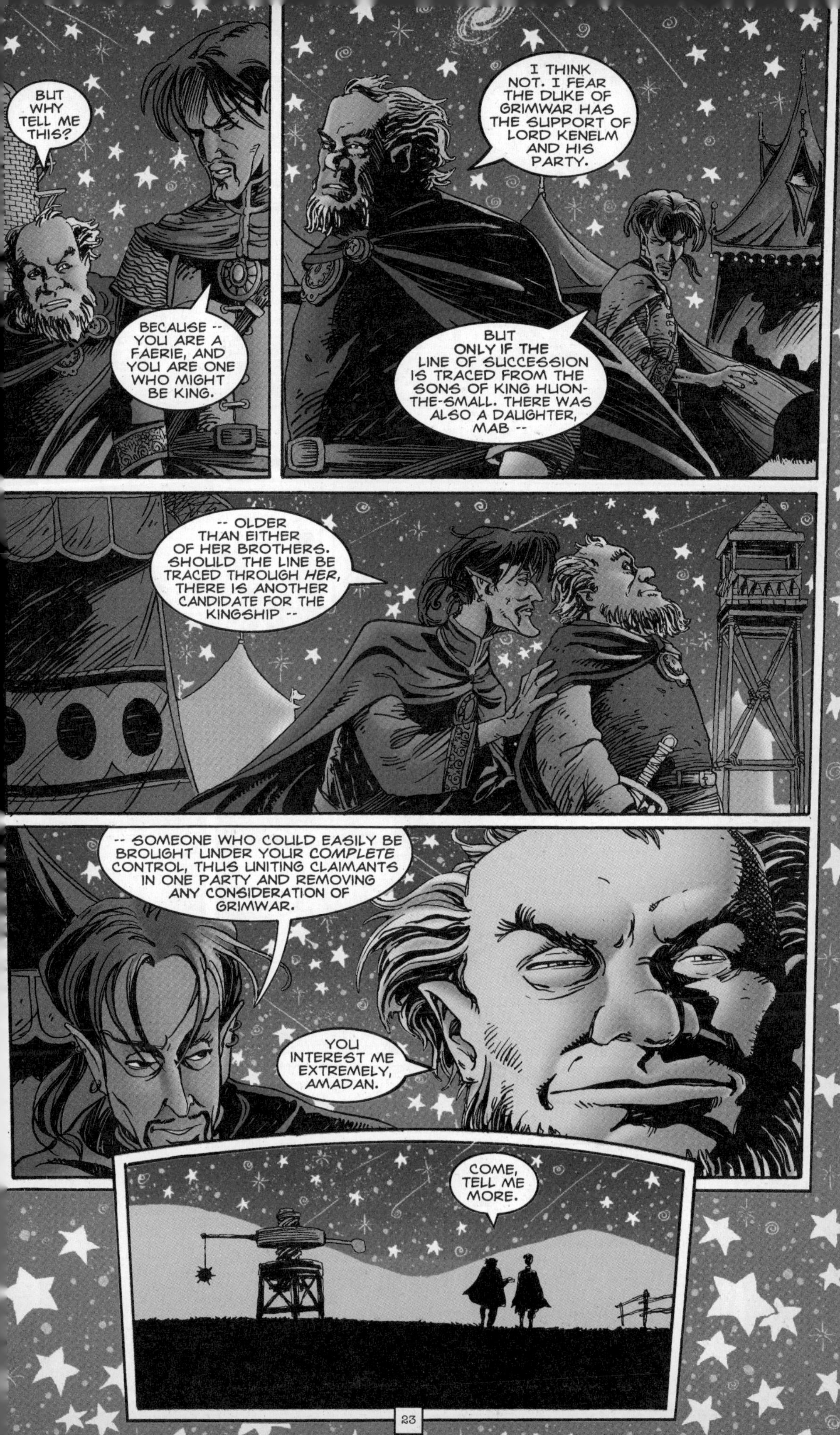
BUT WHY TELL ME THIS?
BECAUSE -- YOU ARE A FAERIE, AND YOU ARE ONE WHO MIGHT BE KING.
I THINK NOT. I FEAR THE DUKE OF GRIMWAR HAS THE SUPPORT OF LORD KENELM AND HIS PARTY.
BUT ONLY IF THE LINE OF SUCCESSION IS TRACED FROM THE SONS OF KING HUON-THE-SMALL. THERE WAS ALSO A DAUGHTER, MAB --
-- OLDER THAN EITHER OF HER BROTHERS. SHOULD THE LINE BE TRACED THROUGH *HER*, THERE IS ANOTHER CANDIDATE FOR THE KINGSHIP --
-- SOMEONE WHO COULD EASILY BE BROUGHT UNDER YOUR *COMPLETE* CONTROL, THUS UNITING CLAIMANTS IN ONE PARTY AND REMOVING ANY CONSIDERATION OF GRIMWAR.
YOU INTEREST ME EXTREMELY, AMADAN.
COME, TELL ME MORE.

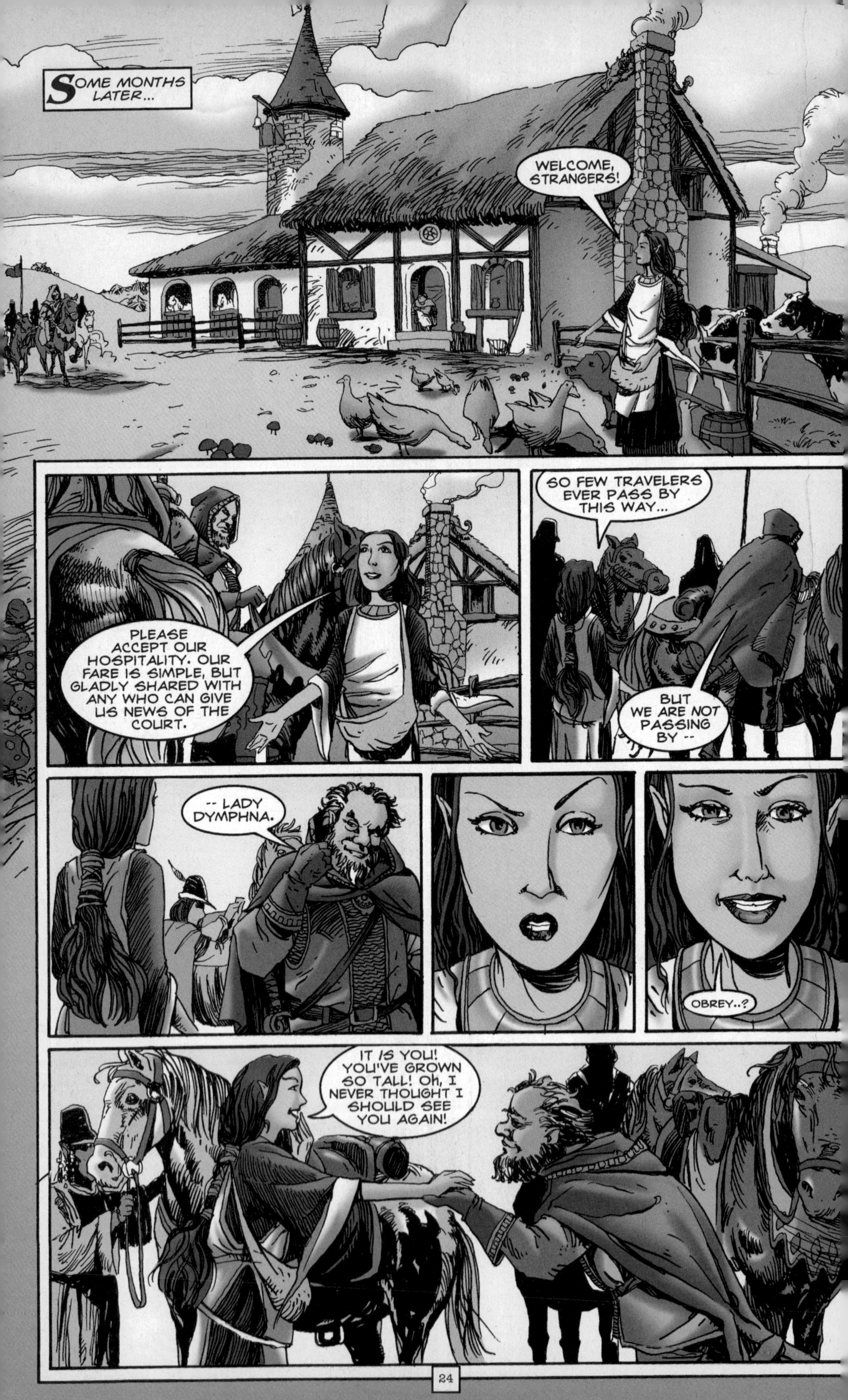
SOME MONTHS LATER...
WELCOME, STRANGERS!
PLEASE ACCEPT OUR HOSPITALITY. OUR FARE IS SIMPLE, BUT GLADLY SHARED WITH ANY WHO CAN GIVE US NEWS OF THE COURT.
SO FEW TRAVELERS EVER PASS BY THIS WAY...
BUT WE ARE NOT PASSING BY --
-- LADY DYMPHNA.
OBREY..?
IT IS YOU! YOU'VE GROWN SO TALL! Oh, I NEVER THOUGHT I SHOULD SEE YOU AGAIN!

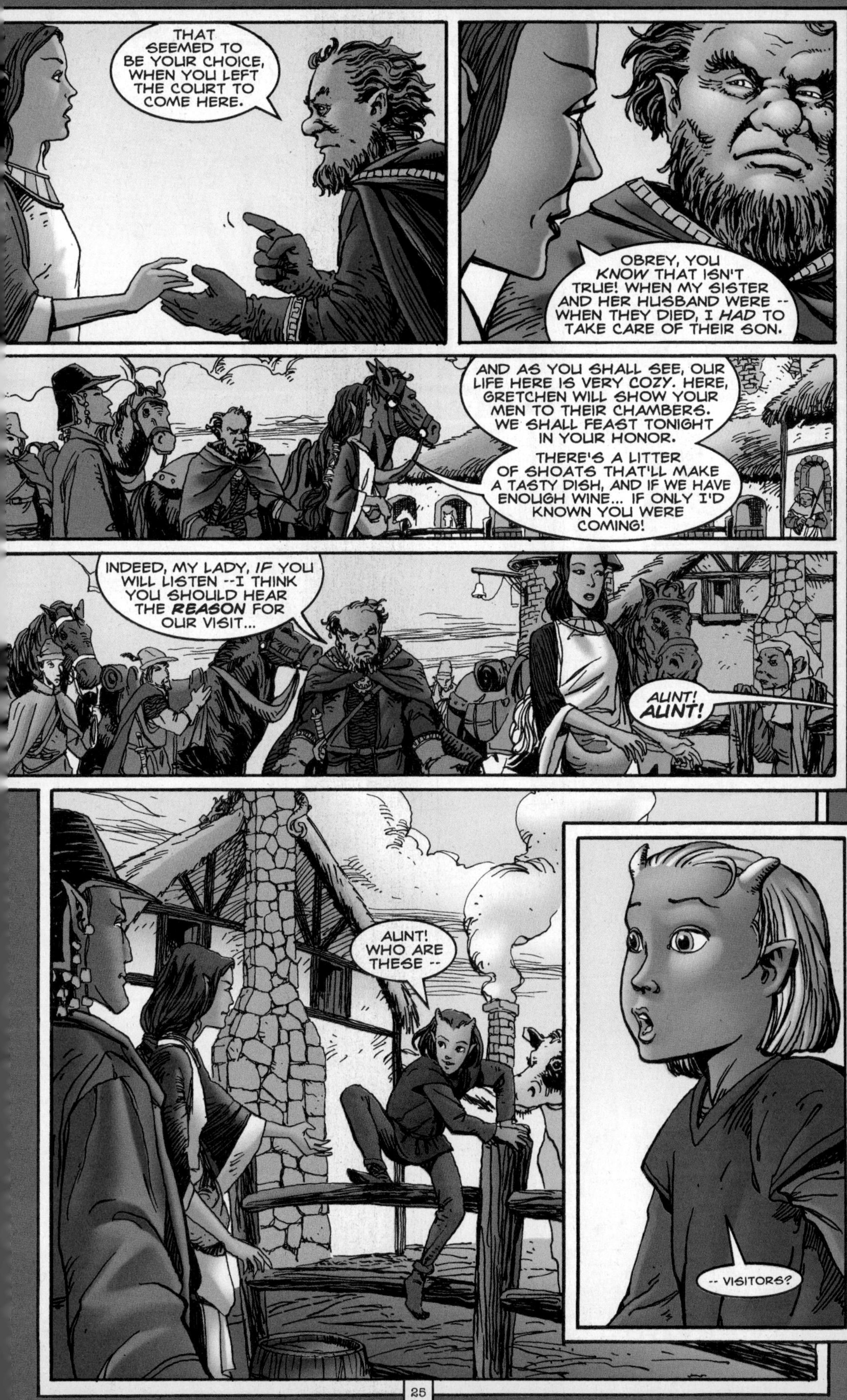

THAT SEEMED TO BE YOUR CHOICE, WHEN YOU LEFT THE COURT TO COME HERE.
OBREY, YOU *KNOW* THAT ISN'T TRUE! WHEN MY SISTER AND HER HUSBAND WERE -- WHEN THEY DIED, I *HAD* TO TAKE CARE OF THEIR SON.
AND AS YOU SHALL SEE, OUR LIFE HERE IS VERY COZY. HERE, GRETCHEN WILL SHOW YOUR MEN TO THEIR CHAMBERS. WE SHALL FEAST TONIGHT IN YOUR HONOR.
THERE'S A LITTER OF SHOATS THAT'LL MAKE A TASTY DISH, AND IF WE HAVE ENOUGH WINE... IF ONLY I'D KNOWN YOU WERE COMING!
INDEED, MY LADY, *IF* YOU WILL LISTEN --I THINK YOU SHOULD HEAR THE ***REASON*** FOR OUR VISIT...
AUNT! ***AUNT!***
AUNT! WHO ARE THESE --
-- VISITORS?

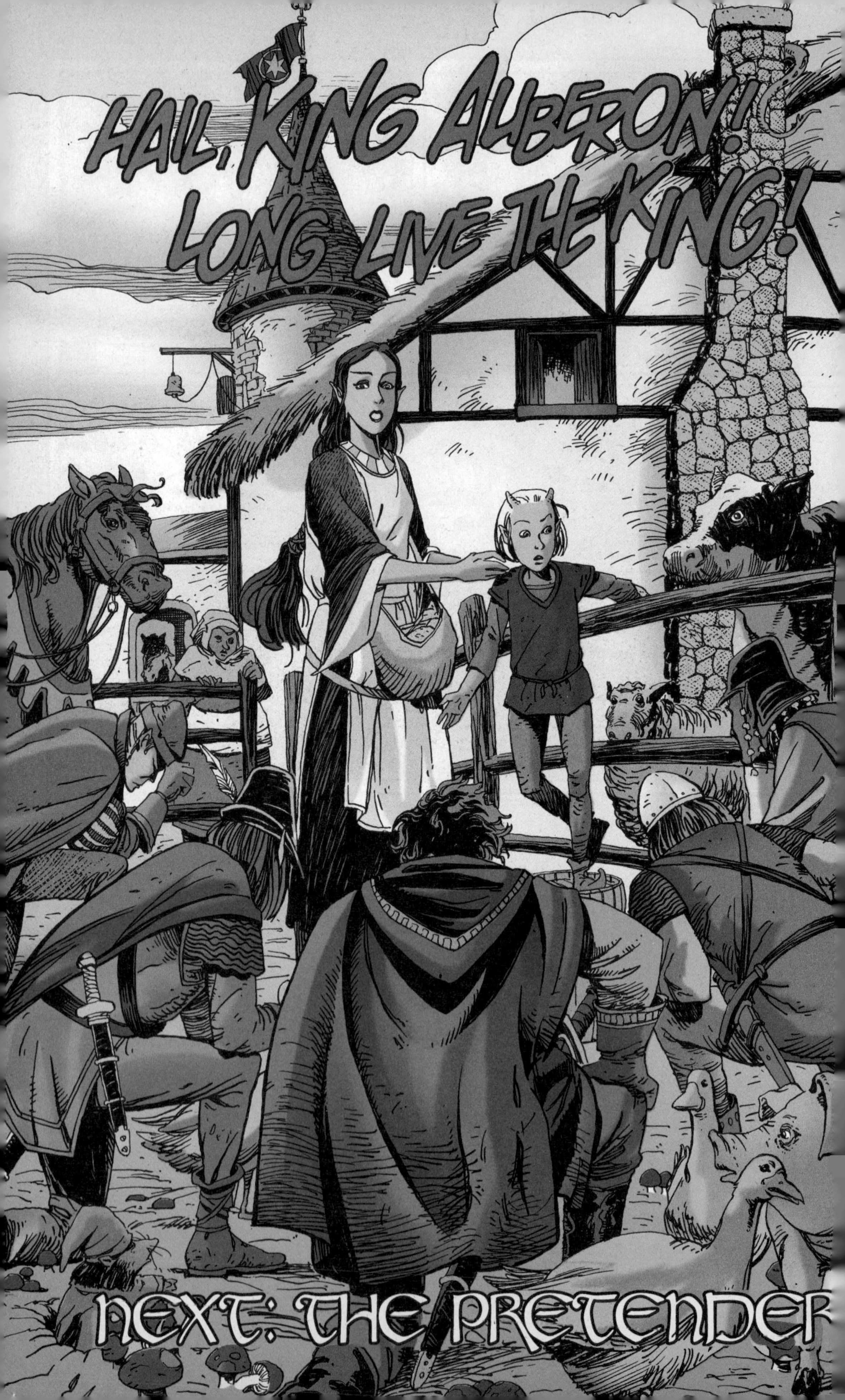
HAIL, KING AUBERON! LONG LIVE THE KING!
NEXT: THE PRETENDER

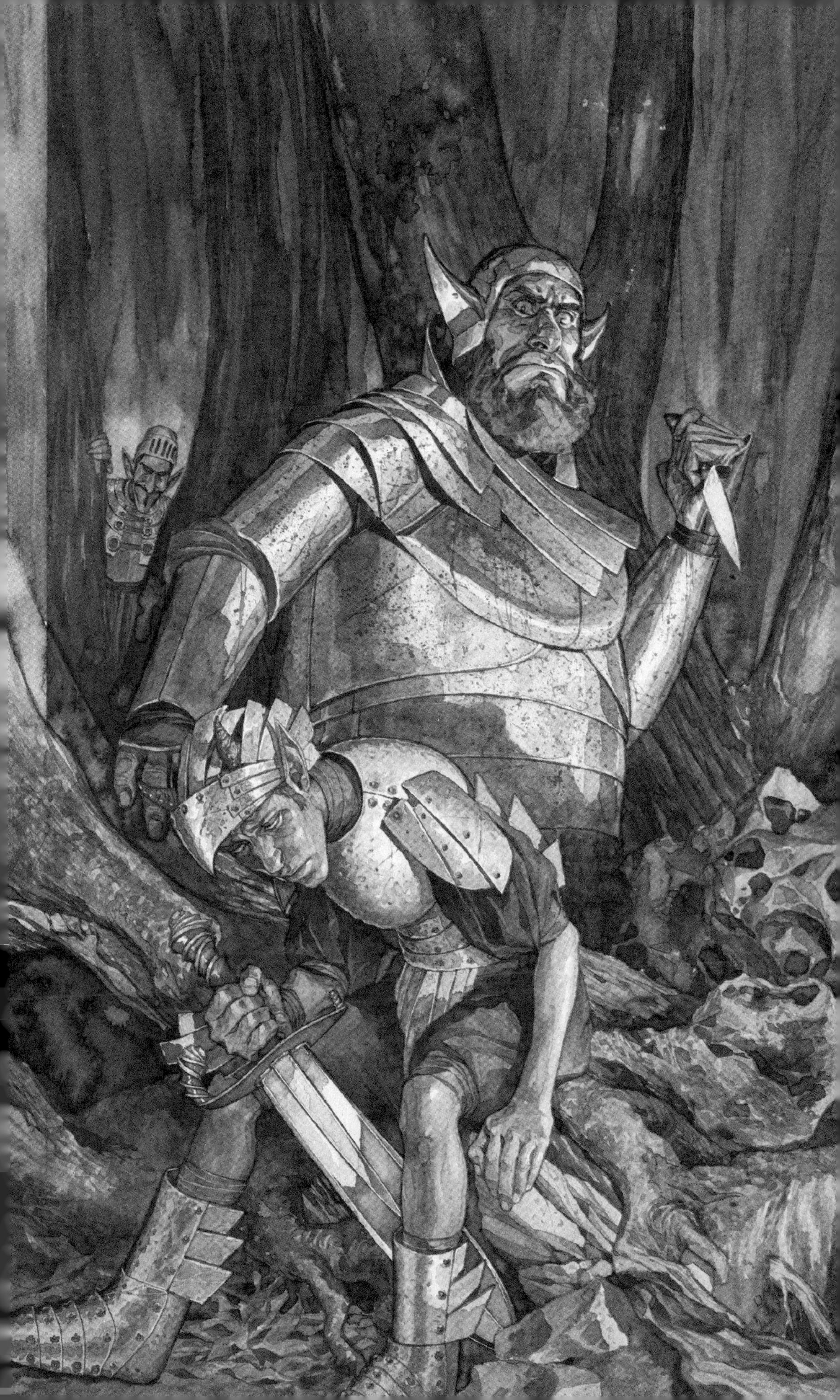

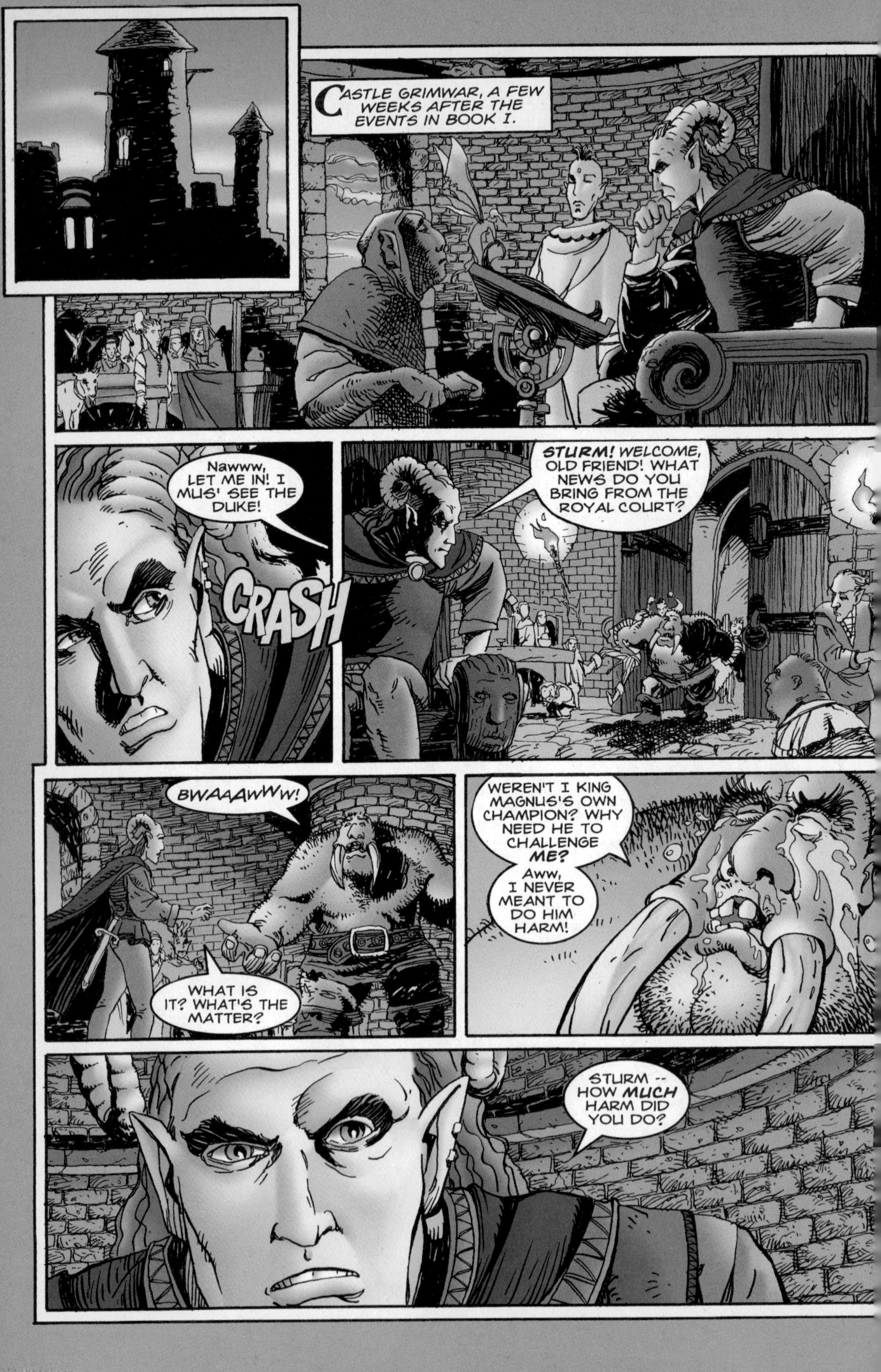
CASTLE GRIMWAR, A FEW WEEKS AFTER THE EVENTS IN BOOK I.
Nawww, LET ME IN! I MUS' SEE THE DUKE!
CRASH
STURM! WELCOME, OLD FRIEND! WHAT NEWS DO YOU BRING FROM THE ROYAL COURT?
BWAAAAWWW!
WHAT IS IT? WHAT'S THE MATTER?
WEREN'T I KING MAGNUS'S OWN CHAMPION? WHY NEED HE TO CHALLENGE ME?
Aww, I NEVER MEANT TO DO HIM HARM!
STURM -- HOW MUCH HARM DID YOU DO?

Awww, I *KILLED* HIM, BUT I NEVER *MEANT* TO DO IT! AN' NOW THEY'VE NAMED ME *TRAITOR* IN THEIR COUNCIL!

PLEASE, YOUR HIGHNESS, I NEVER MEANT HIM HARM!

KNG!

BUT, STURM... AH... THIS IS VERY GRAVE.

WHAT IS IT YOU'D HAVE ME DO?

CAN YE NOT PARDON ME, DUKE HUONNOR, YOUR HIGHNESS, NOW THAT YE ARE KING?

BY HUON'S BONES, SO I *AM*... THOUGH THERE'S MY COUSIN OF WINDAN -- BUT THE COUNCIL WILL *NEVER* BACK OBREY. STILL, HE'S THERE, AND I AM NOT...

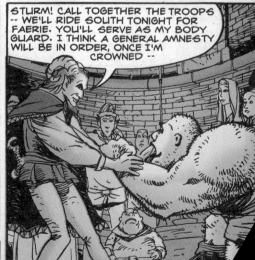

STURM! CALL TOGETHER THE TROOPS -- WE'LL RIDE SOUTH TONIGHT FOR FAERIE. YOU'LL SERVE AS MY BODY GUARD. I THINK A GENERAL AMNESTY WILL BE IN ORDER, ONCE I'M CROWNED --

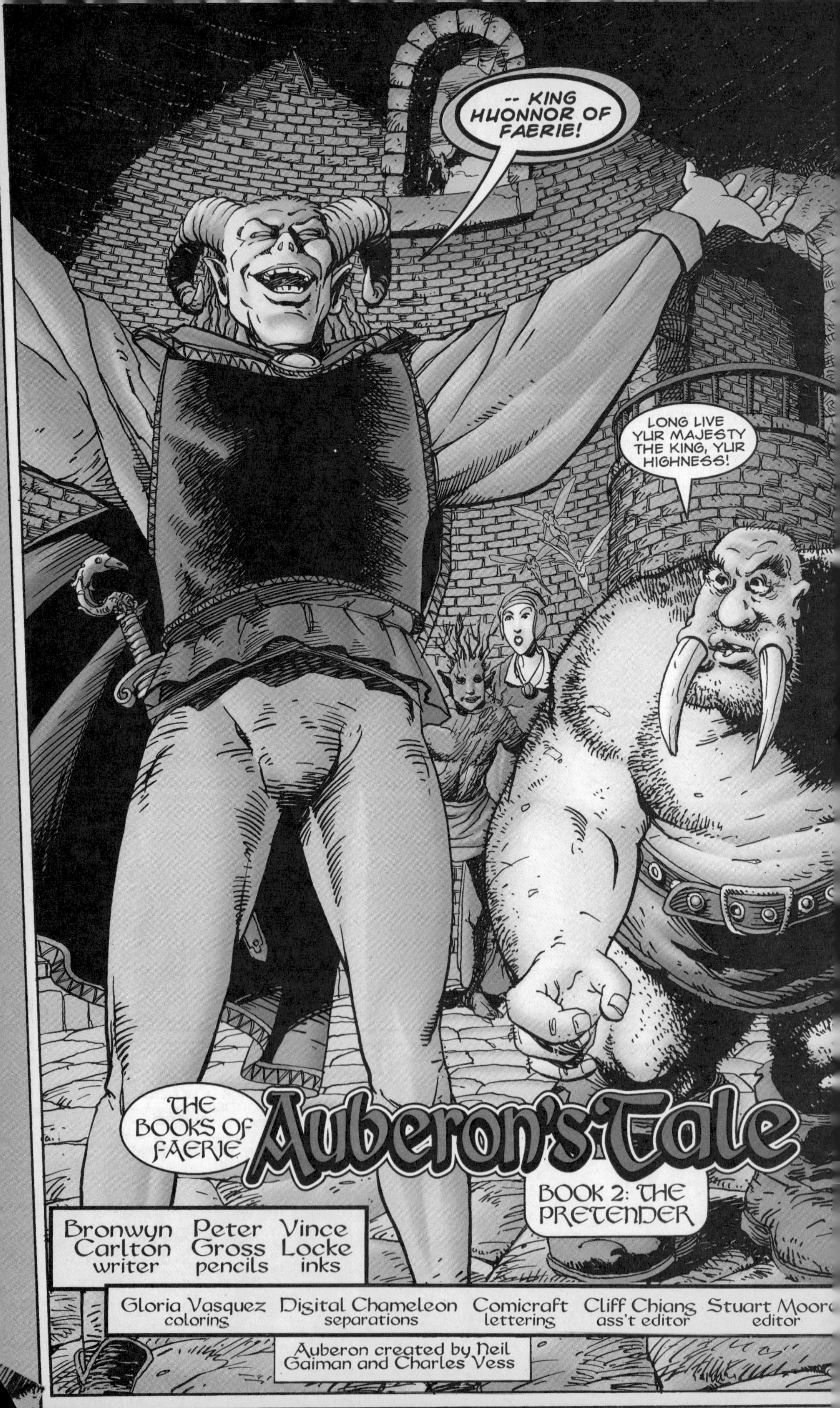
-- KING HUONNOR OF FAERIE!
LONG LIVE YUR MAJESTY THE KING, YUR HIGHNESS!
THE BOOKS OF FAERIE
Auberon's Tale
BOOK 2: THE PRETENDER
Bronwyn Carlton writer
Peter Gross pencils
Vince Locke inks
Gloria Vasquez coloring
Digital Chameleon separations
Comicraft lettering
Cliff Chiang ass't editor
Stuart Moore editor
Auberon created by Neil Gaiman and Charles Vess

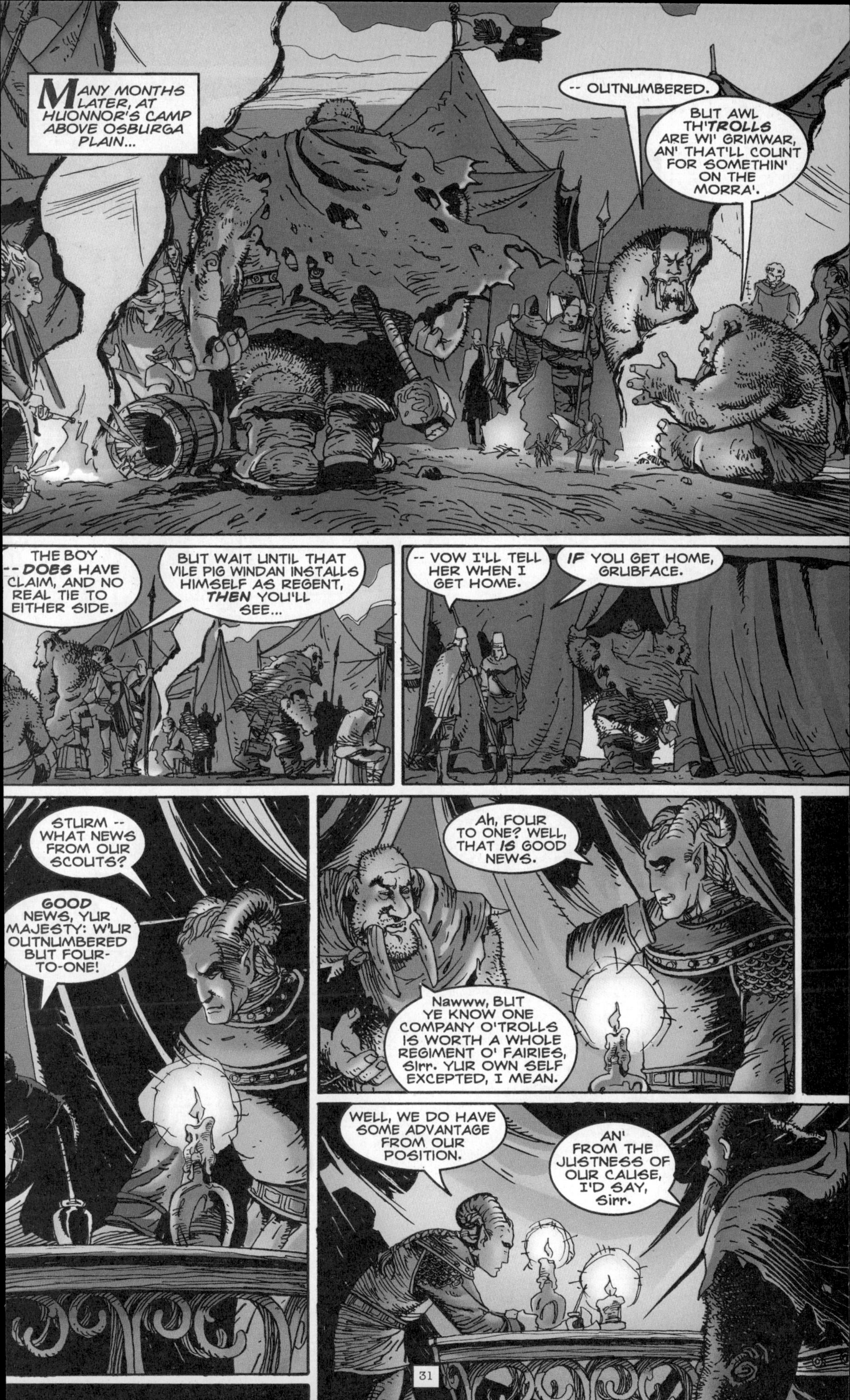
MANY MONTHS LATER, AT HUONNOR'S CAMP ABOVE OSBURGA PLAIN...
-- OUTNUMBERED.
BUT AWL TH'TROLLS ARE WI' GRIMWAR, AN' THAT'LL COUNT FOR SOMETHIN' ON THE MORRA'.
THE BOY --DOES HAVE CLAIM, AND NO REAL TIE TO EITHER SIDE.
BUT WAIT UNTIL THAT VILE PIG WINDAN INSTALLS HIMSELF AS REGENT, THEN YOU'LL SEE...
-- VOW I'LL TELL HER WHEN I GET HOME.
IF YOU GET HOME, GRUBFACE.
STURM -- WHAT NEWS FROM OUR SCOUTS?
GOOD NEWS, YUR MAJESTY: W'UR OUTNUMBERED BUT FOUR-TO-ONE!
Ah, FOUR TO ONE? WELL, THAT IS GOOD NEWS.
Nawww, BUT YE KNOW ONE COMPANY O'TROLLS IS WORTH A WHOLE REGIMENT O' FAIRIES, Sirr. YUR OWN SELF EXCEPTED, I MEAN.
WELL, WE DO HAVE SOME ADVANTAGE FROM OUR POSITION.
AN' FROM THE JUSTNESS OF OUR CAUSE, I'D SAY, Sirr.

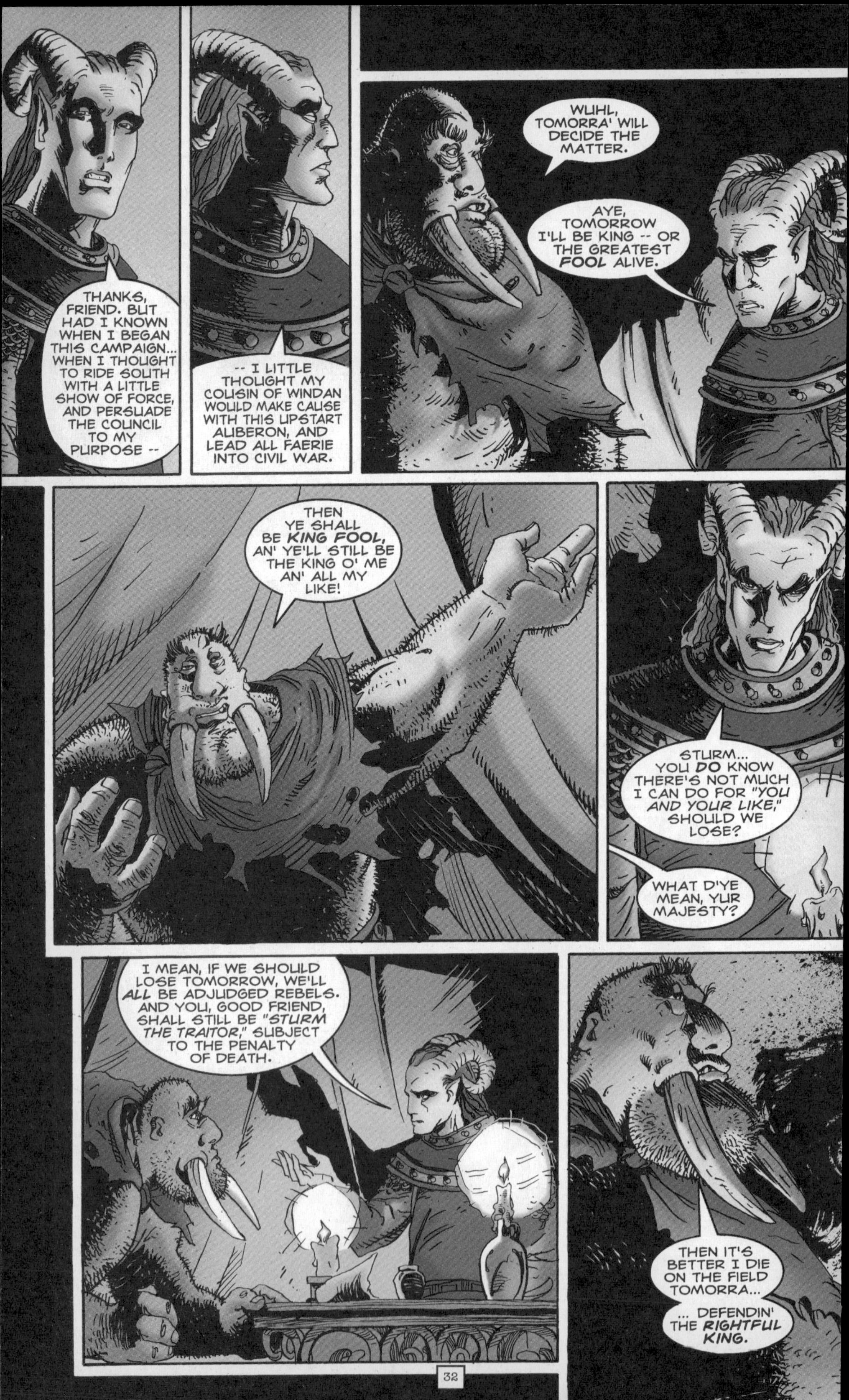
THANKS, FRIEND. BUT HAD I KNOWN WHEN I BEGAN THIS CAMPAIGN... WHEN I THOUGHT TO RIDE SOUTH WITH A LITTLE SHOW OF FORCE, AND PERSUADE THE COUNCIL TO MY PURPOSE --
-- I LITTLE THOUGHT MY COUSIN OF WINDAN WOULD MAKE CAUSE WITH THIS UPSTART AUBERON, AND LEAD ALL FAERIE INTO CIVIL WAR.
WUHL, TOMORRA' WILL DECIDE THE MATTER.
AYE, TOMORROW I'LL BE KING -- OR THE GREATEST **FOOL** ALIVE.
THEN YE SHALL BE **KING FOOL,** AN' YE'LL STILL BE THE KING O' ME AN' ALL MY LIKE!
STURM... YOU **DO** KNOW THERE'S NOT MUCH I CAN DO FOR *"YOU AND YOUR LIKE,"* SHOULD WE LOSE?
WHAT D'YE MEAN, YUR MAJESTY?
I MEAN, IF WE SHOULD LOSE TOMORROW, WE'LL ***ALL*** BE ADJUDGED REBELS. AND YOU, GOOD FRIEND, SHALL STILL BE *"STURM THE TRAITOR,"* SUBJECT TO THE PENALTY OF DEATH.
THEN IT'S BETTER I DIE ON THE FIELD TOMORRA...
... DEFENDIN' THE ***RIGHTFUL KING.***

I SAW A MESSENGER COME FROM THE NORTH TODAY -- WERE IT NEWS FROM GRIMWAR?

INDEED -- THOUGH NOT AS GOOD AS YOUR NEWS OF OUR ENEMIES' FOUR-TO-ONE ADVANTAGE.

MY LADY IS WITH CHILD.

Awwww, THAT'S FINE, FINE NEWS INDEED, THE HAPPIEST NEWS THAT EVER WAS HEARD IN FAERIE!

HOW SO?

SURELY YE REMEMBER THE *PROPHECY*... Aww, I DISRECOLLECT THE WORDS OF IT, BUT ITS MEANIN' WERE THAT THE CHILDREN OF GRIMWAR SHALL RULE FAERIE UNTIL FAERIE CEASES TO BE!

YES, I'VE HEARD OF IT.

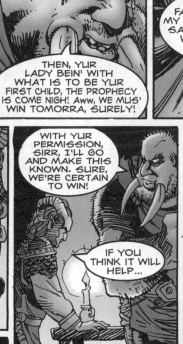

THEN, YUR LADY BEIN' WITH WHAT IS TO BE YUR FIRST CHILD, THE PROPHECY IS COME NIGH! Aww, WE MUS' WIN TOMORRA, SURELY!

WITH YUR PERMISSION, SIRR, I'LL GO AND MAKE THIS KNOWN. SURE, WE'RE CERTAIN TO WIN!

IF YOU THINK IT WILL HELP...

BUT BEWARE OF FAERIE PROPHECIES, MY FRIEND -- THEY MAY SAY WHAT THEY MEAN WITHOUT MEANING WHAT THEY SAY.

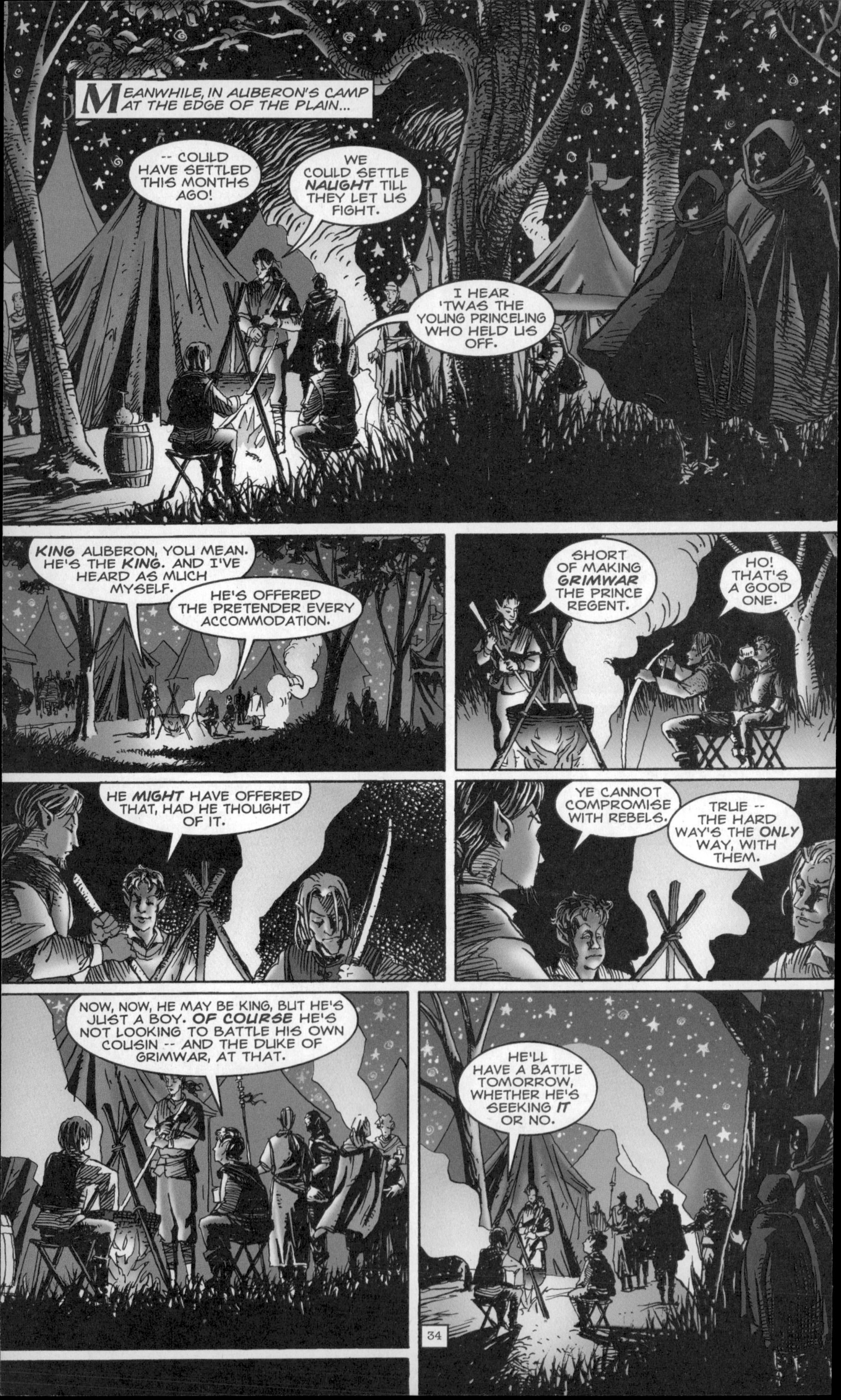
MEANWHILE, IN AUBERON'S CAMP AT THE EDGE OF THE PLAIN...
-- COULD HAVE SETTLED THIS MONTHS AGO!
WE COULD SETTLE NAUGHT TILL THEY LET US FIGHT.
I HEAR 'TWAS THE YOUNG PRINCELING WHO HELD US OFF.
KING AUBERON, YOU MEAN. HE'S THE KING. AND I'VE HEARD AS MUCH MYSELF.
HE'S OFFERED THE PRETENDER EVERY ACCOMMODATION.
SHORT OF MAKING GRIMWAR THE PRINCE REGENT.
HO! THAT'S A GOOD ONE.
HE MIGHT HAVE OFFERED THAT, HAD HE THOUGHT OF IT.
YE CANNOT COMPROMISE WITH REBELS.
TRUE -- THE HARD WAY'S THE ONLY WAY, WITH THEM.
NOW, NOW, HE MAY BE KING, BUT HE'S JUST A BOY. OF COURSE HE'S NOT LOOKING TO BATTLE HIS OWN COUSIN -- AND THE DUKE OF GRIMWAR, AT THAT.
HE'LL HAVE A BATTLE TOMORROW, WHETHER HE'S SEEKING IT OR NO.

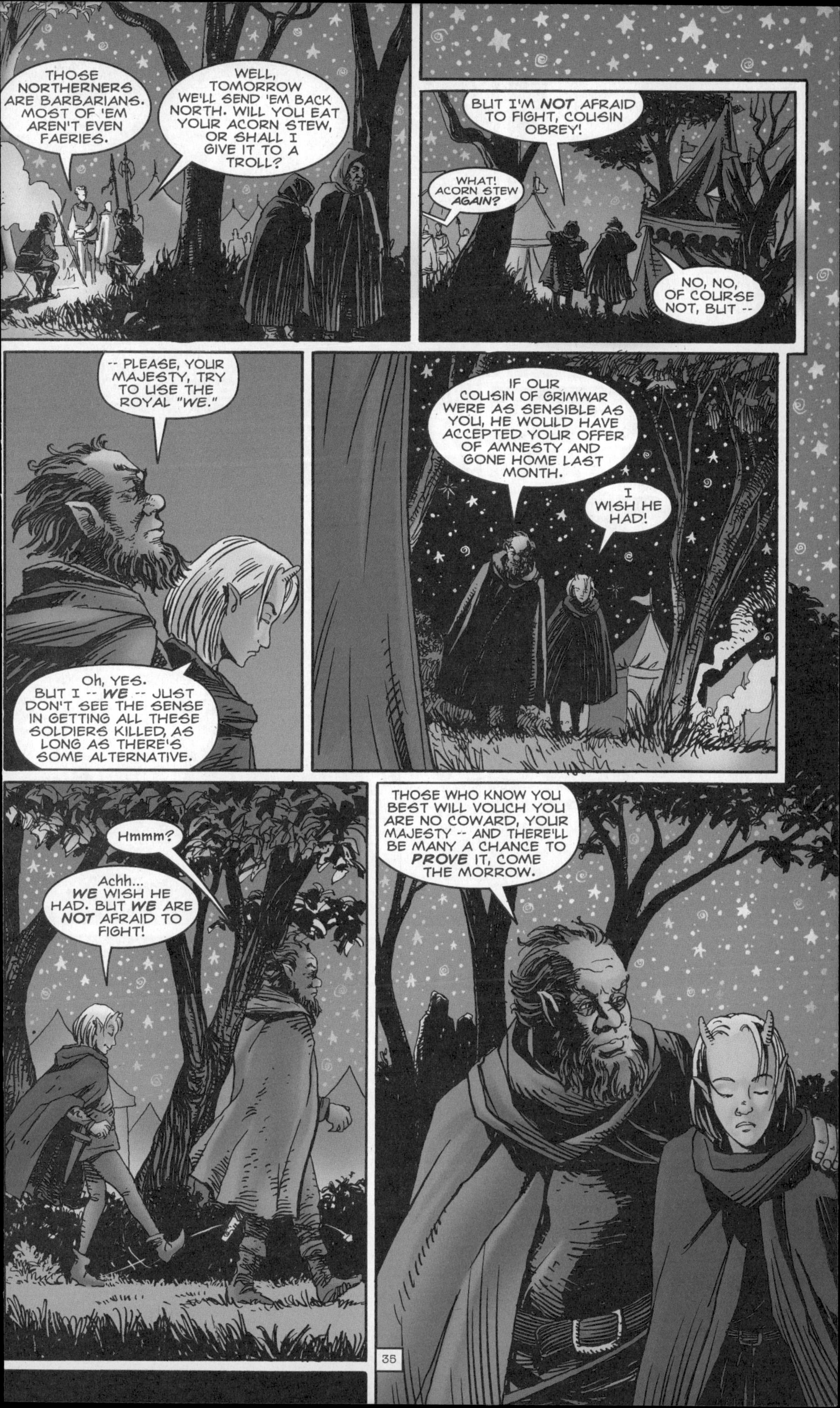
THOSE NORTHERNERS ARE BARBARIANS. MOST OF 'EM AREN'T EVEN FAERIES.
WELL, TOMORROW WE'LL SEND 'EM BACK NORTH. WILL YOU EAT YOUR ACORN STEW, OR SHALL I GIVE IT TO A TROLL?
BUT I'M NOT AFRAID TO FIGHT, COUSIN OBREY!
WHAT! ACORN STEW AGAIN?
NO, NO, OF COURSE NOT, BUT --
-- PLEASE, YOUR MAJESTY, TRY TO USE THE ROYAL "WE."
Oh, YES. BUT I -- WE -- JUST DON'T SEE THE SENSE IN GETTING ALL THESE SOLDIERS KILLED, AS LONG AS THERE'S SOME ALTERNATIVE.
IF OUR COUSIN OF GRIMWAR WERE AS SENSIBLE AS YOU, HE WOULD HAVE ACCEPTED YOUR OFFER OF AMNESTY AND GONE HOME LAST MONTH.
I WISH HE HAD!
Hmmm?
Achh... WE WISH HE HAD. BUT WE ARE NOT AFRAID TO FIGHT!
THOSE WHO KNOW YOU BEST WILL VOUCH YOU ARE NO COWARD, YOUR MAJESTY -- AND THERE'LL BE MANY A CHANCE TO PROVE IT, COME THE MORROW.

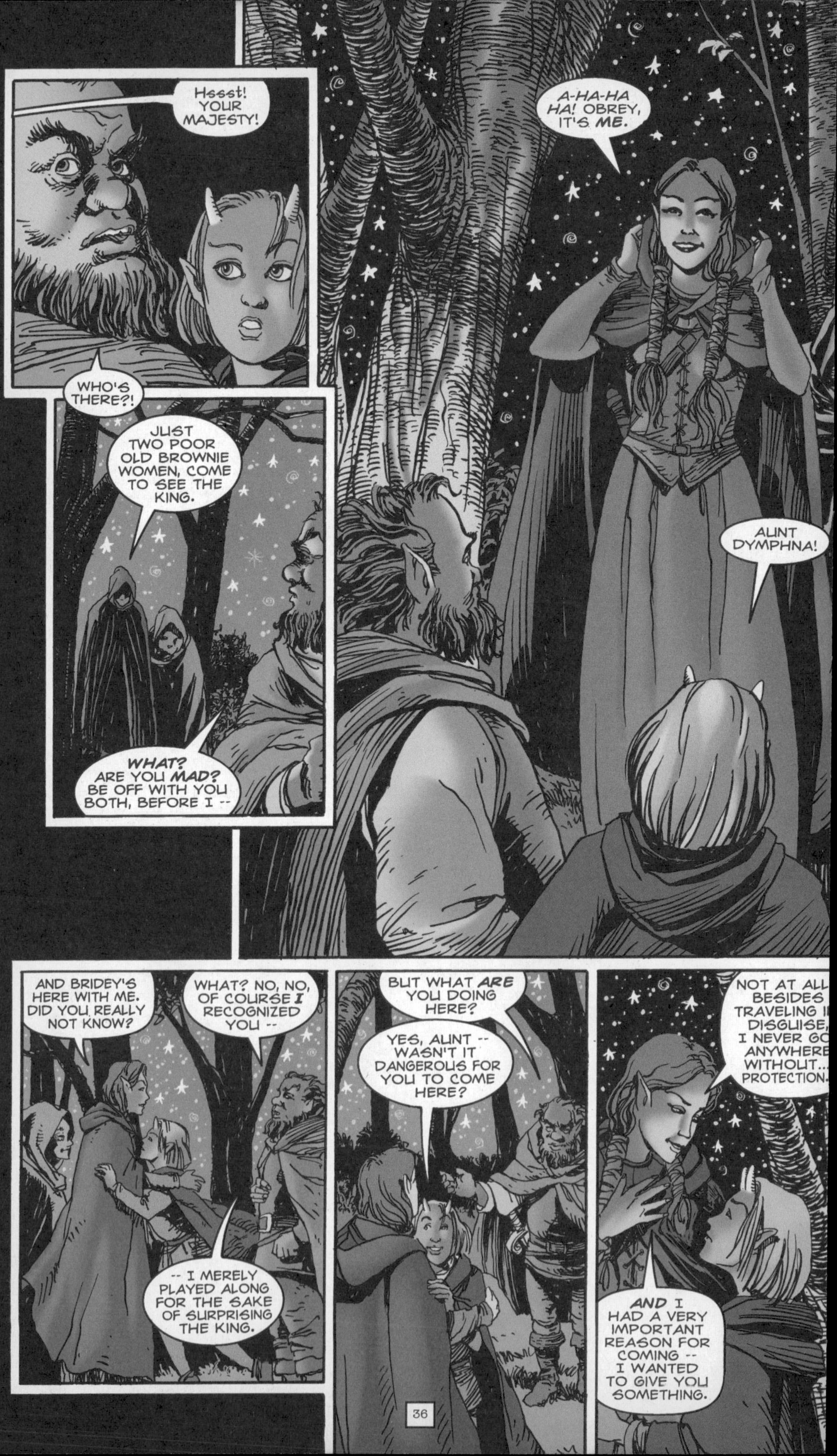
Hssst! YOUR MAJESTY!
WHO'S THERE?!
JUST TWO POOR OLD BROWNIE WOMEN, COME TO SEE THE KING.
WHAT? ARE YOU MAD? BE OFF WITH YOU BOTH, BEFORE I --
A-HA-HA HA! OBREY, IT'S ME.
AUNT DYMPHNA!
AND BRIDEY'S HERE WITH ME. DID YOU REALLY NOT KNOW?
WHAT? NO, NO, OF COURSE I RECOGNIZED YOU --
-- I MERELY PLAYED ALONG FOR THE SAKE OF SURPRISING THE KING.
BUT WHAT ARE YOU DOING HERE?
YES, AUNT -- WASN'T IT DANGEROUS FOR YOU TO COME HERE?
NOT AT ALL BESIDES TRAVELING I DISGUISE, I NEVER GO ANYWHERE WITHOUT... PROTECTION.
AND I HAD A VERY IMPORTANT REASON FOR COMING -- I WANTED TO GIVE YOU SOMETHING.

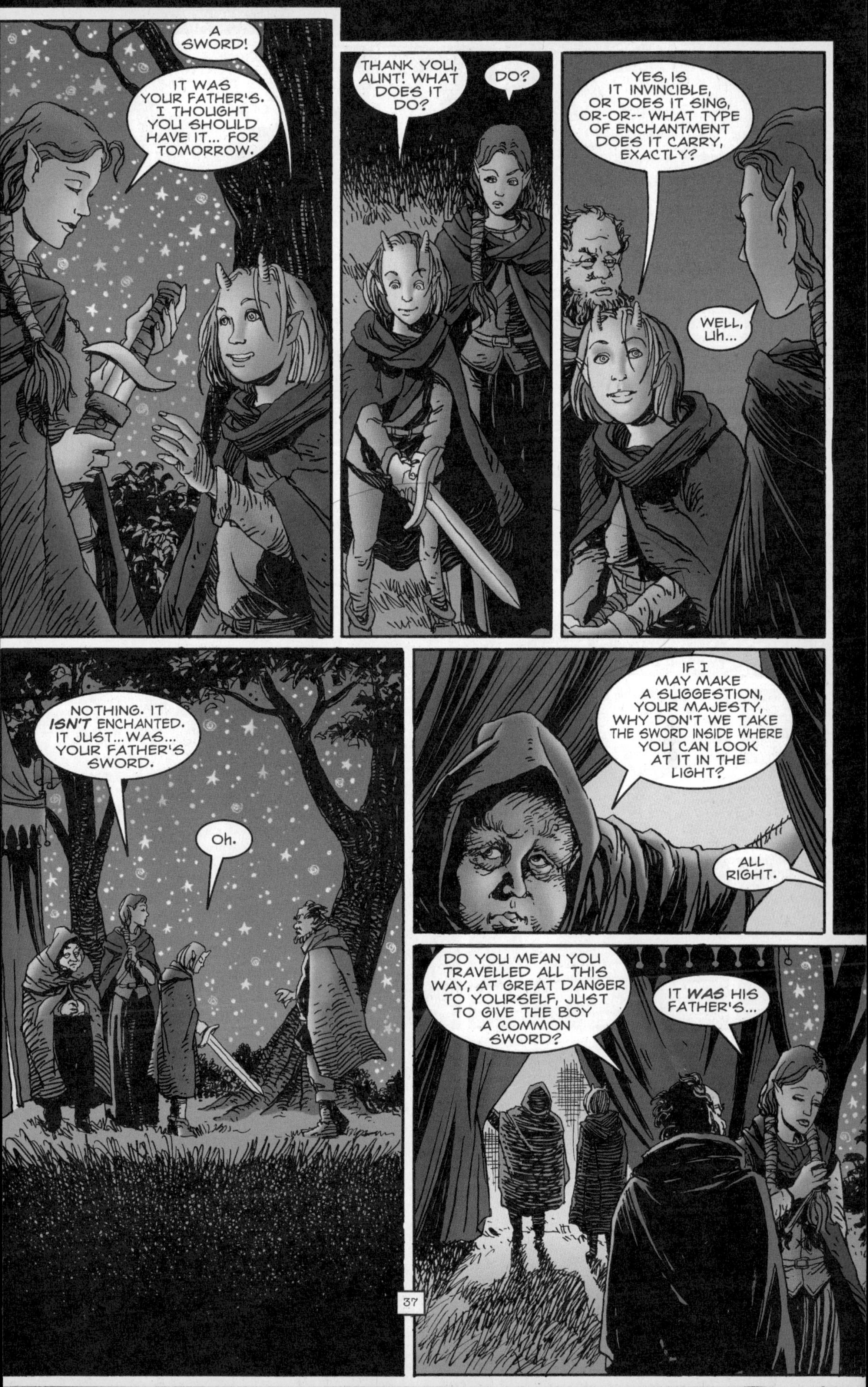
A SWORD!
IT WAS YOUR FATHER'S. I THOUGHT YOU SHOULD HAVE IT... FOR TOMORROW.
THANK YOU, AUNT! WHAT DOES IT DO?
DO?
YES, IS IT INVINCIBLE, OR DOES IT SING, OR-OR-- WHAT TYPE OF ENCHANTMENT DOES IT CARRY, EXACTLY?
WELL, Uh...
NOTHING. IT *ISN'T* ENCHANTED. IT JUST...WAS... YOUR FATHER'S SWORD.
Oh.
IF I MAY MAKE A SUGGESTION, YOUR MAJESTY, WHY DON'T WE TAKE THE SWORD INSIDE WHERE YOU CAN LOOK AT IT IN THE LIGHT?
ALL RIGHT.
DO YOU MEAN YOU TRAVELLED ALL THIS WAY, AT GREAT DANGER TO YOURSELF, JUST TO GIVE THE BOY A COMMON SWORD?
IT *WAS* HIS FATHER'S...

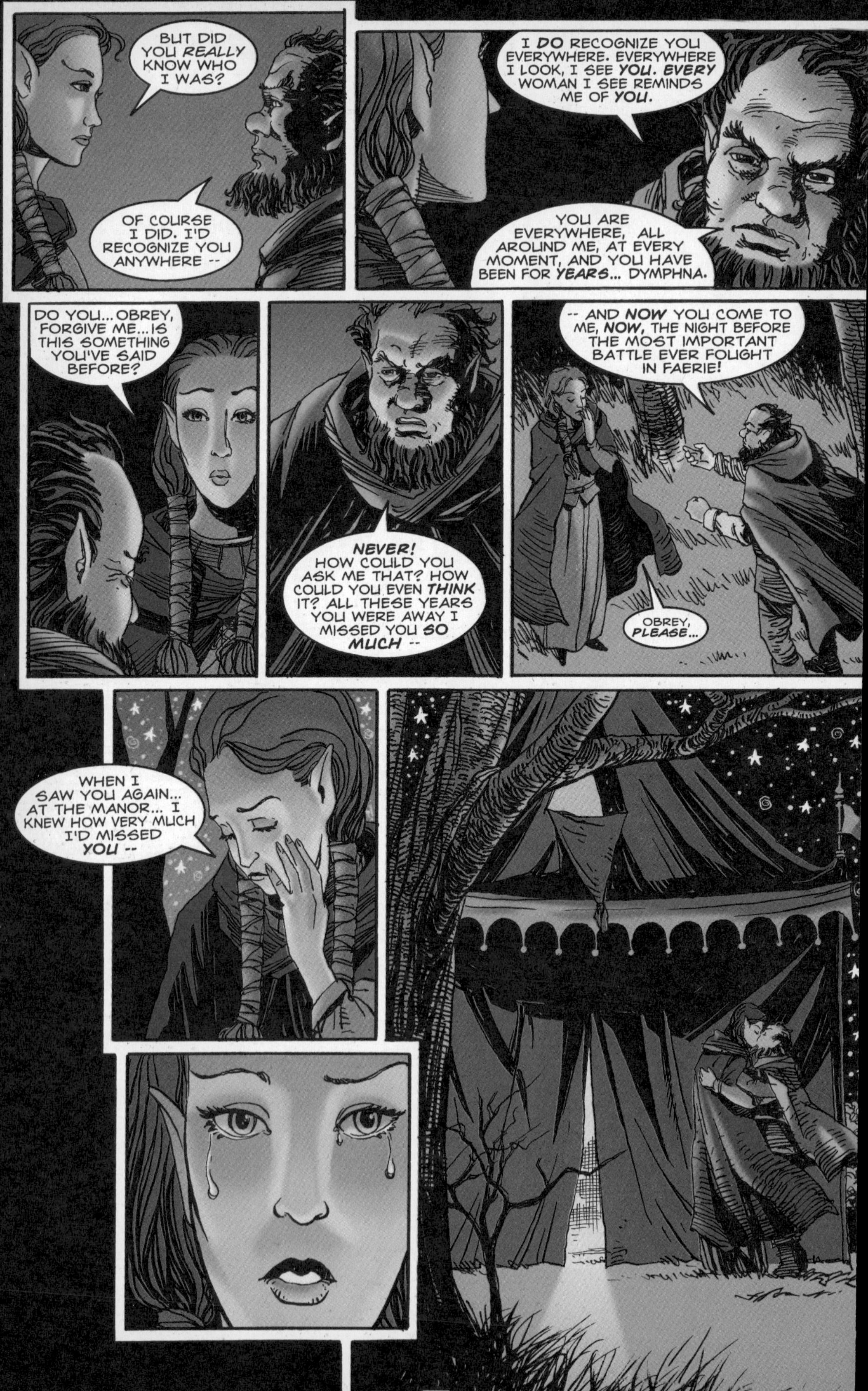
BUT DID YOU REALLY KNOW WHO I WAS?
OF COURSE I DID. I'D RECOGNIZE YOU ANYWHERE --
I DO RECOGNIZE YOU EVERYWHERE. EVERYWHERE I LOOK, I SEE YOU. EVERY WOMAN I SEE REMINDS ME OF YOU.
YOU ARE EVERYWHERE, ALL AROUND ME, AT EVERY MOMENT, AND YOU HAVE BEEN FOR YEARS... DYMPHNA.
DO YOU... OBREY, FORGIVE ME... IS THIS SOMETHING YOU'VE SAID BEFORE?
NEVER! HOW COULD YOU ASK ME THAT? HOW COULD YOU EVEN THINK IT? ALL THESE YEARS YOU WERE AWAY I MISSED YOU SO MUCH --
-- AND NOW YOU COME TO ME, NOW, THE NIGHT BEFORE THE MOST IMPORTANT BATTLE EVER FOUGHT IN FAERIE!
OBREY, PLEASE...
WHEN I SAW YOU AGAIN... AT THE MANOR... I KNEW HOW VERY MUCH I'D MISSED YOU --

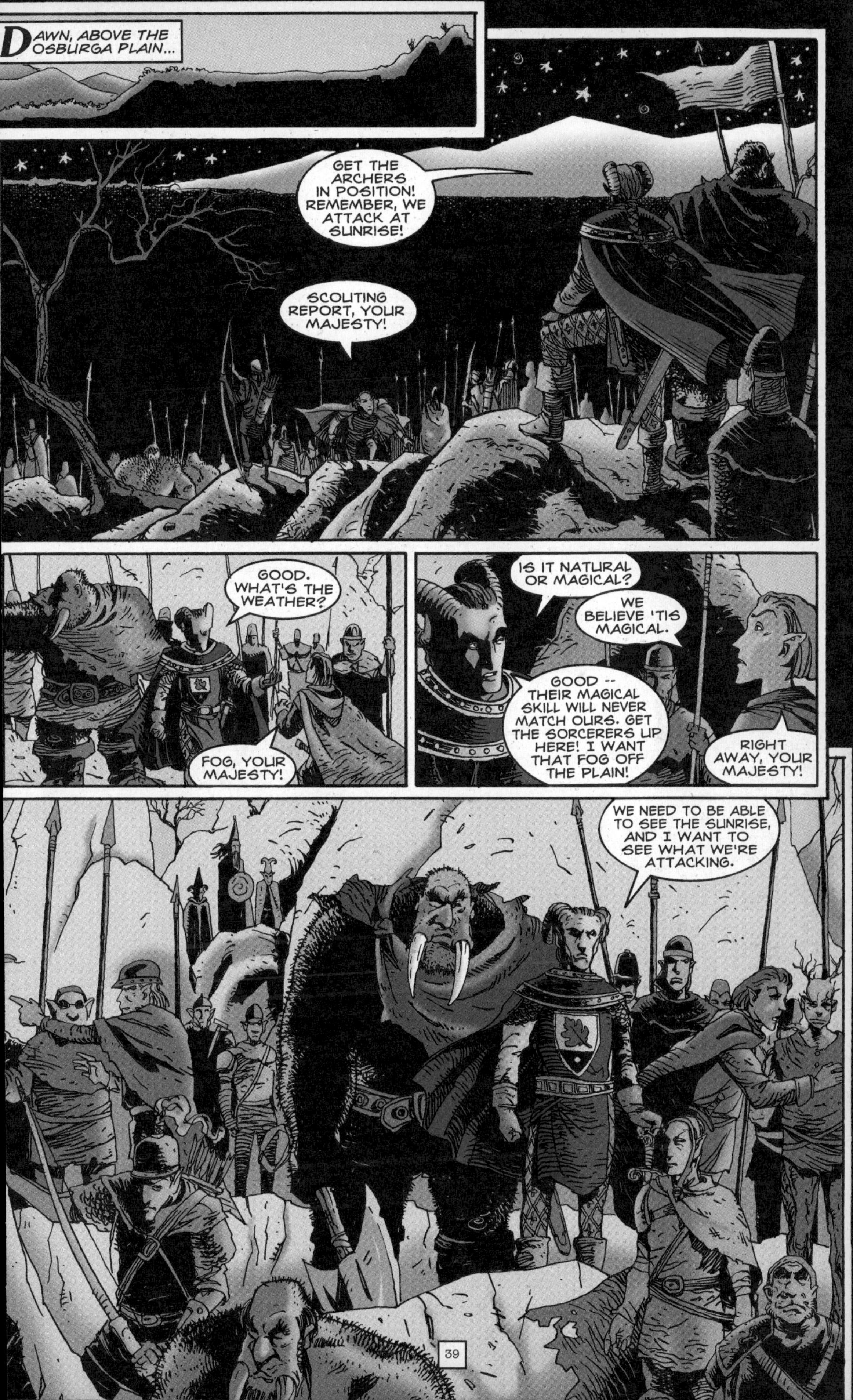
DAWN, ABOVE THE DOSBURGA PLAIN...
GET THE ARCHERS IN POSITION! REMEMBER, WE ATTACK AT SUNRISE!
SCOUTING REPORT, YOUR MAJESTY!
GOOD. WHAT'S THE WEATHER?
FOG, YOUR MAJESTY!
IS IT NATURAL OR MAGICAL?
WE BELIEVE 'TIS MAGICAL.
GOOD -- THEIR MAGICAL SKILL WILL NEVER MATCH OURS. GET THE SORCERERS UP HERE! I WANT THAT FOG OFF THE PLAIN!
RIGHT AWAY, YOUR MAJESTY!
WE NEED TO BE ABLE TO SEE THE SUNRISE, AND I WANT TO SEE WHAT WE'RE ATTACKING.

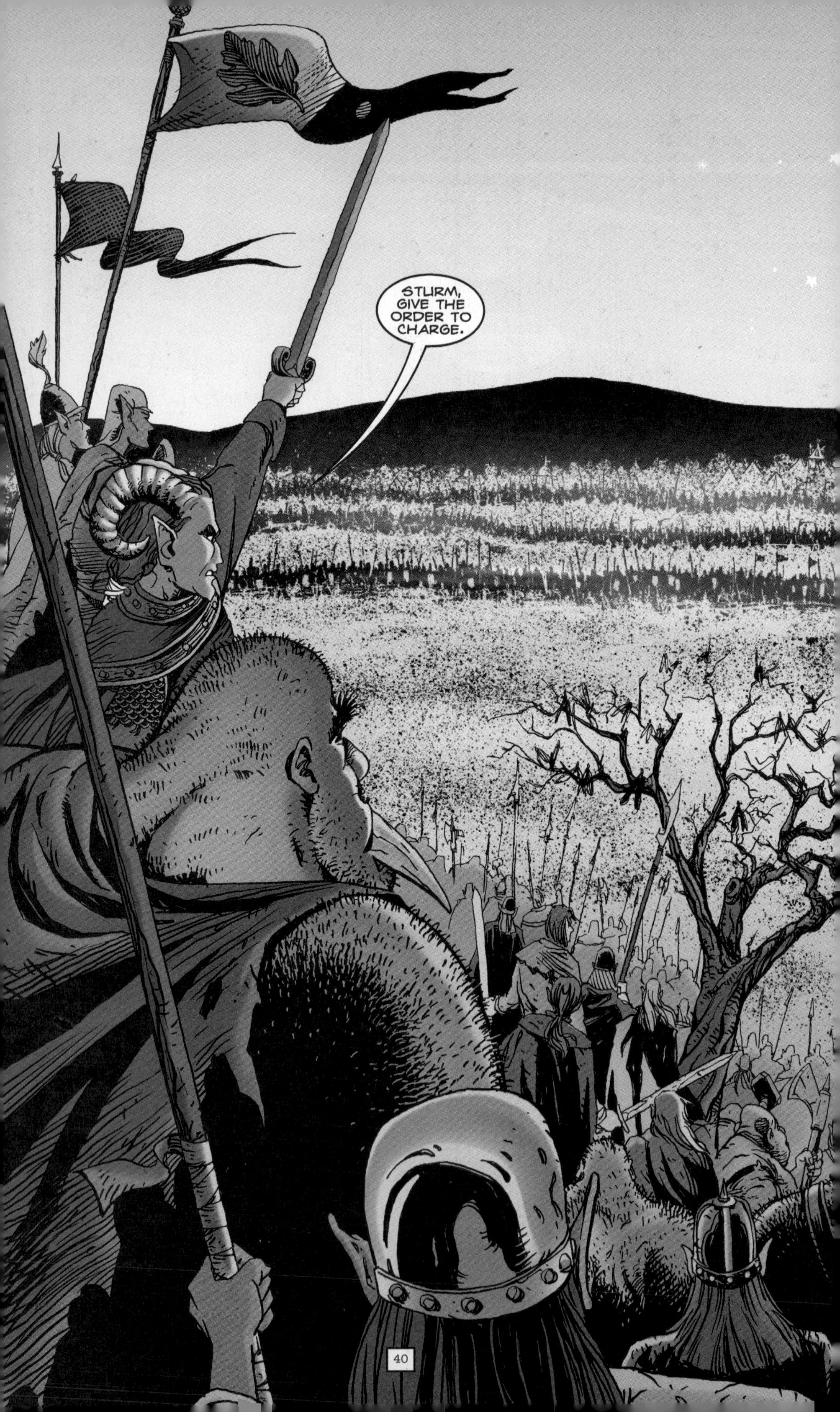
STURM, GIVE THE ORDER TO CHARGE.

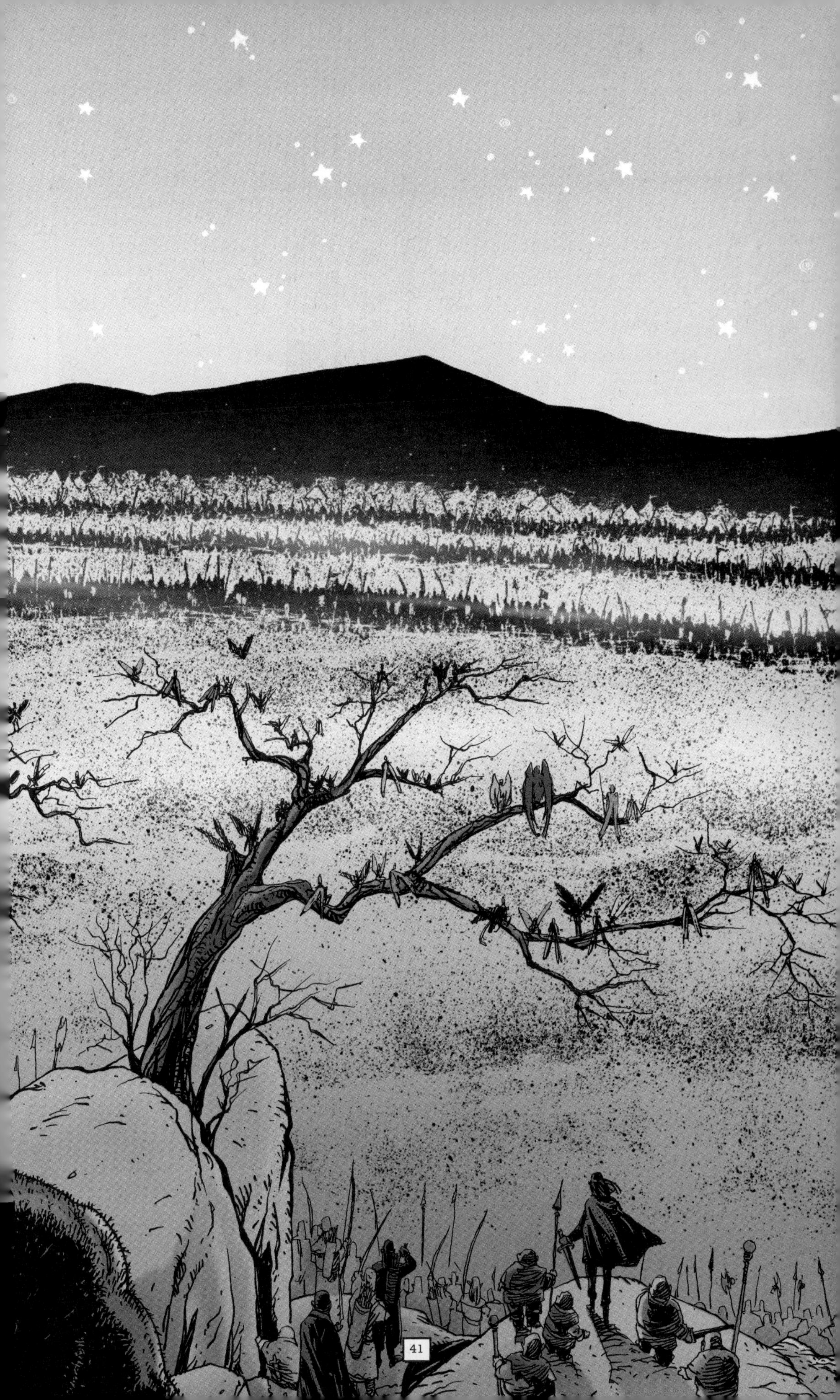

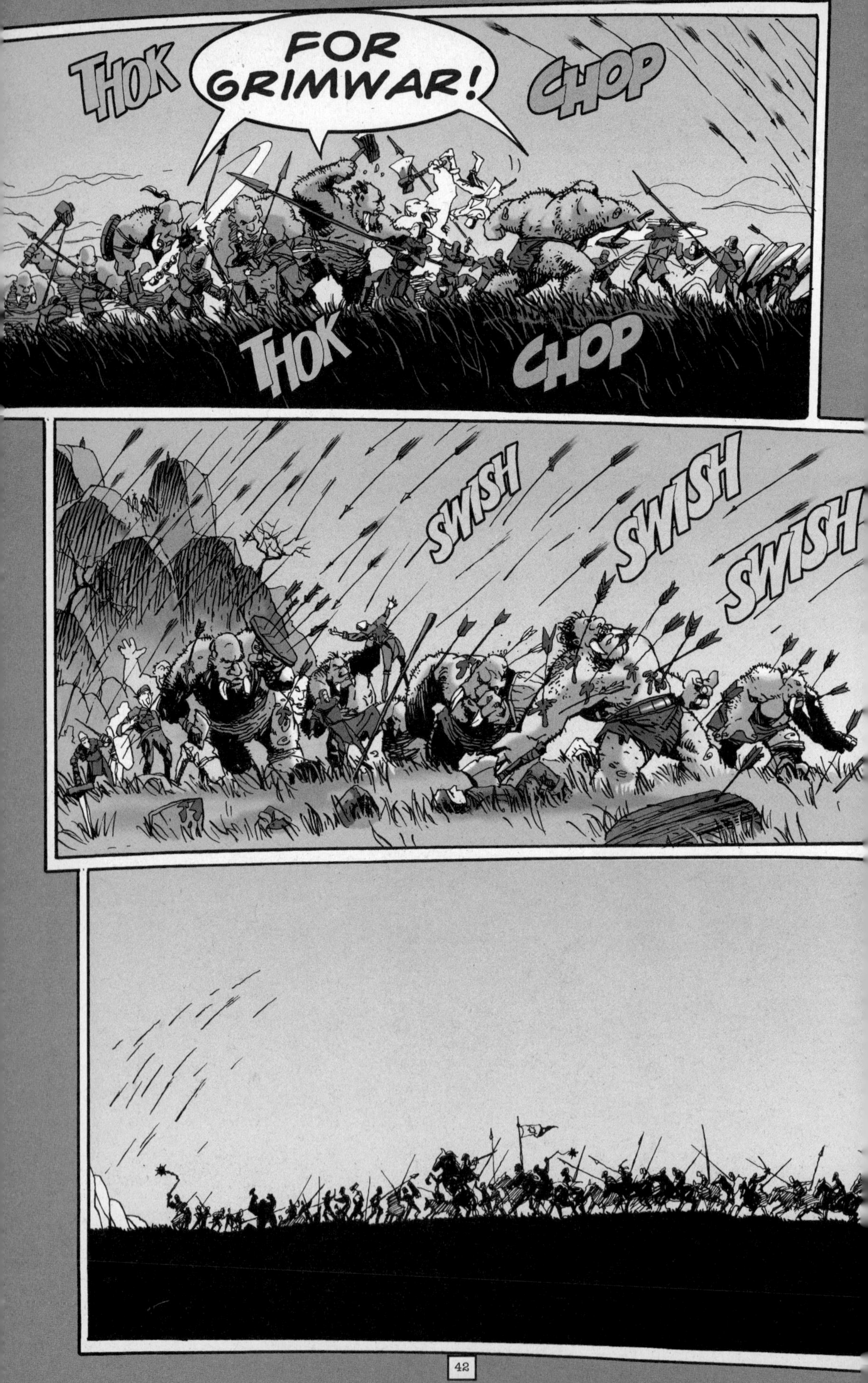
THOK
FOR GRIMWAR!
CHOP
THOK
CHOP
SWISH
SWISH
SWISH

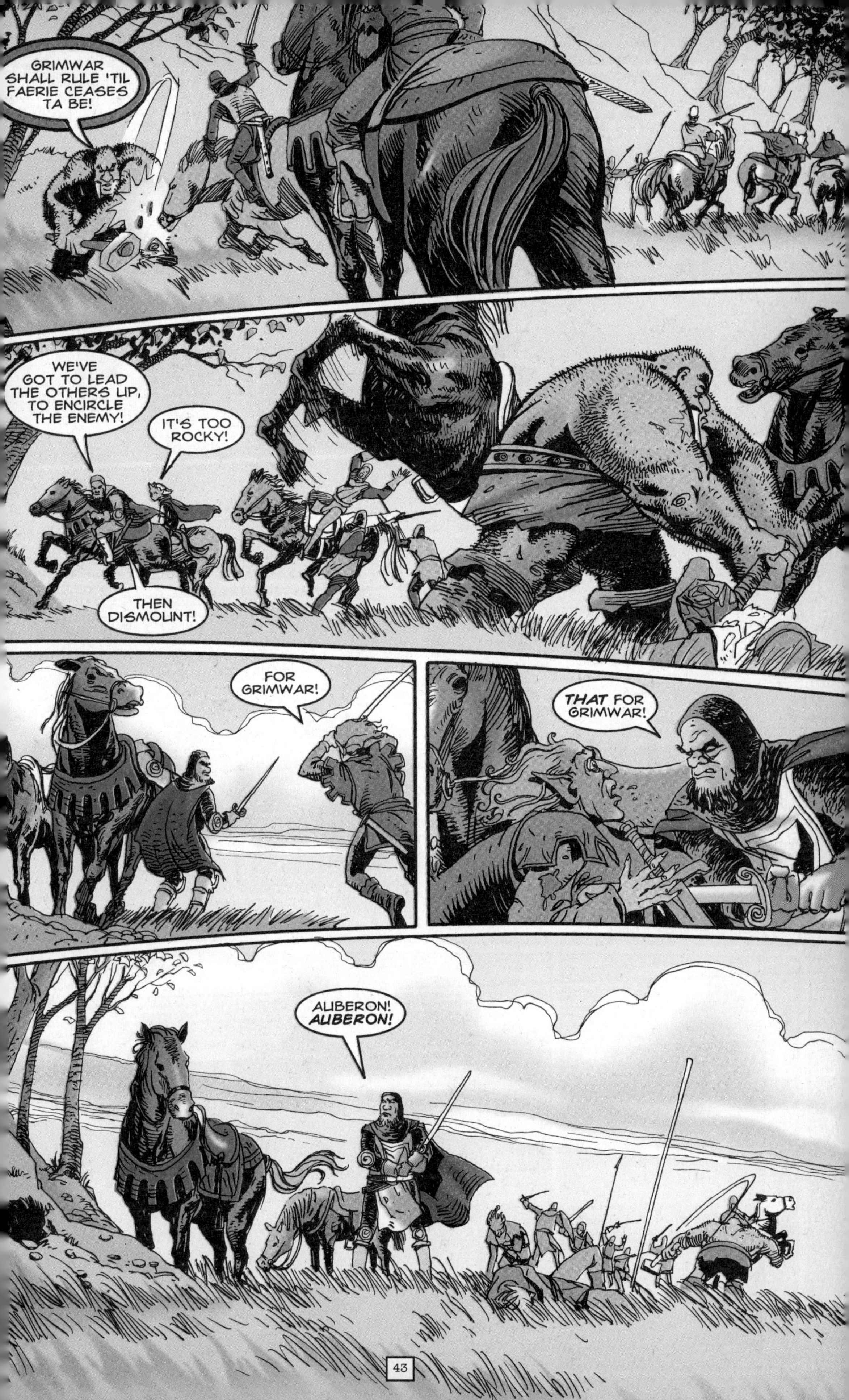
GRIMWAR SHALL RULE 'TIL FAERIE CEASES TA BE!
WE'VE GOT TO LEAD THE OTHERS UP, TO ENCIRCLE THE ENEMY!
IT'S TOO ROCKY!
THEN DISMOUNT!
FOR GRIMWAR!
THAT FOR GRIMWAR!
AUBERON! ***AUBERON!***

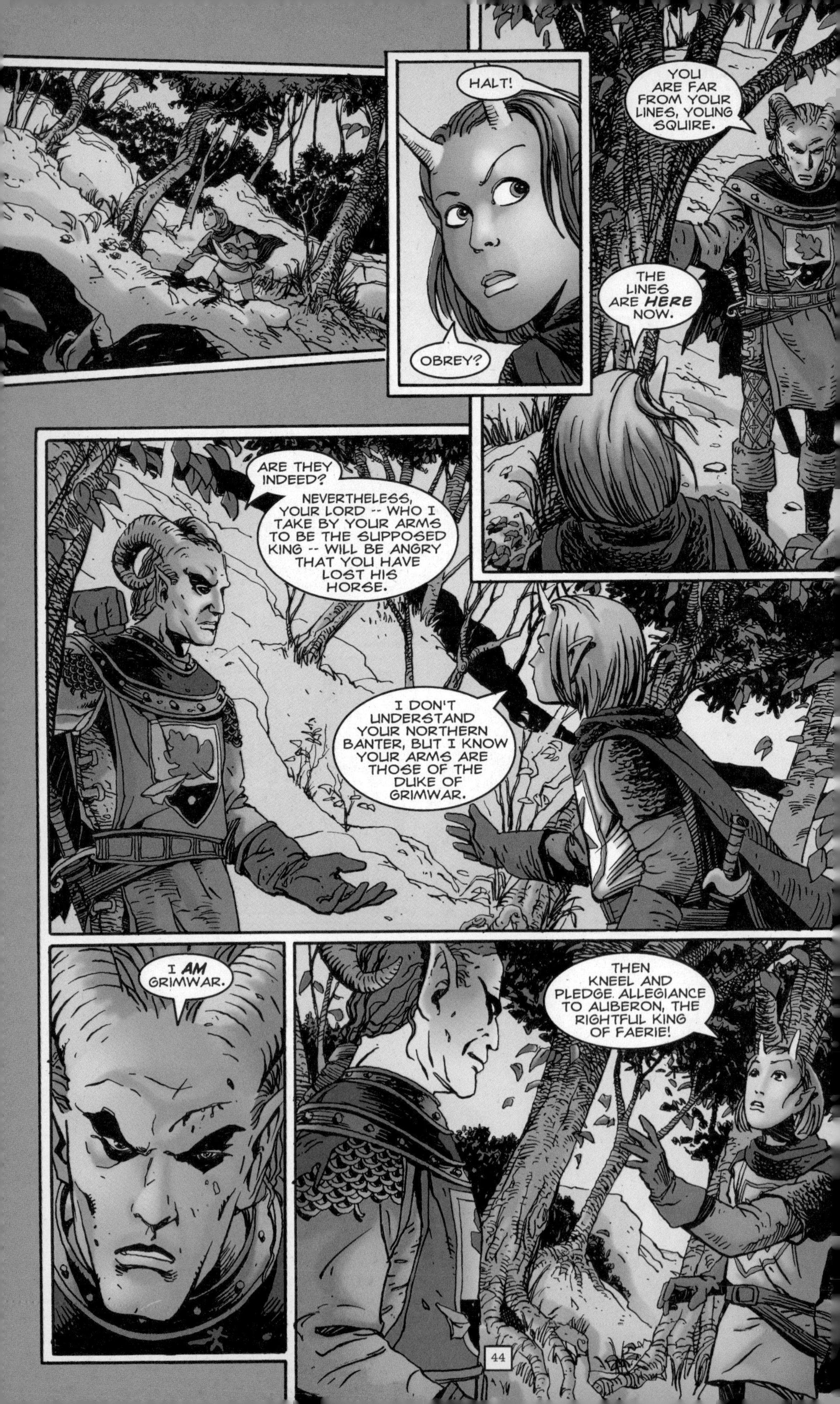
HALT!
OBREY?
YOU ARE FAR FROM YOUR LINES, YOUNG SQUIRE.
THE LINES ARE *HERE* NOW.
ARE THEY INDEED?
NEVERTHELESS, YOUR LORD -- WHO I TAKE BY YOUR ARMS TO BE THE SUPPOSED KING -- WILL BE ANGRY THAT YOU HAVE LOST HIS HORSE.
I DON'T UNDERSTAND YOUR NORTHERN BANTER, BUT I KNOW YOUR ARMS ARE THOSE OF THE DUKE OF GRIMWAR.
I *AM* GRIMWAR.
THEN KNEEL AND PLEDGE ALLEGIANCE TO AUBERON, THE RIGHTFUL KING OF FAERIE!

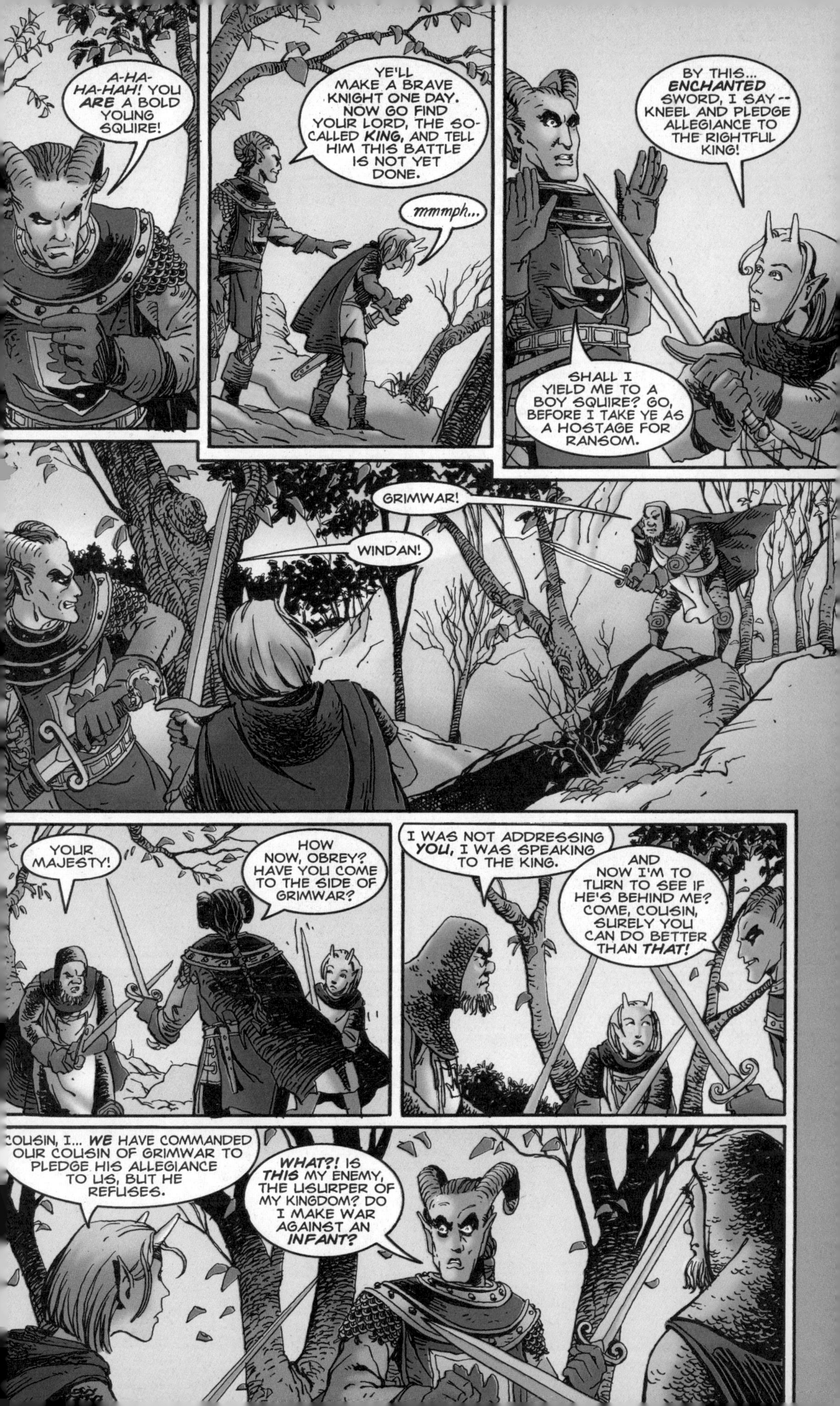
A-HA-HA-HAH! YOU ARE A BOLD YOUNG SQUIRE!
YE'LL MAKE A BRAVE KNIGHT ONE DAY. NOW GO FIND YOUR LORD, THE SO-CALLED KING, AND TELL HIM THIS BATTLE IS NOT YET DONE.
mmmph...
BY THIS... ENCHANTED SWORD, I SAY -- KNEEL AND PLEDGE ALLEGIANCE TO THE RIGHTFUL KING!
SHALL I YIELD ME TO A BOY SQUIRE? GO, BEFORE I TAKE YE AS A HOSTAGE FOR RANSOM.
GRIMWAR!
WINDAN!
YOUR MAJESTY!
HOW NOW, OBREY? HAVE YOU COME TO THE SIDE OF GRIMWAR?
I WAS NOT ADDRESSING YOU, I WAS SPEAKING TO THE KING.
AND NOW I'M TO TURN TO SEE IF HE'S BEHIND ME? COME, COUSIN, SURELY YOU CAN DO BETTER THAN THAT!
COUSIN, I... WE HAVE COMMANDED OUR COUSIN OF GRIMWAR TO PLEDGE HIS ALLEGIANCE TO US, BUT HE REFUSES.
WHAT?! IS THIS MY ENEMY, THE USURPER OF MY KINGDOM? DO I MAKE WAR AGAINST AN INFANT?

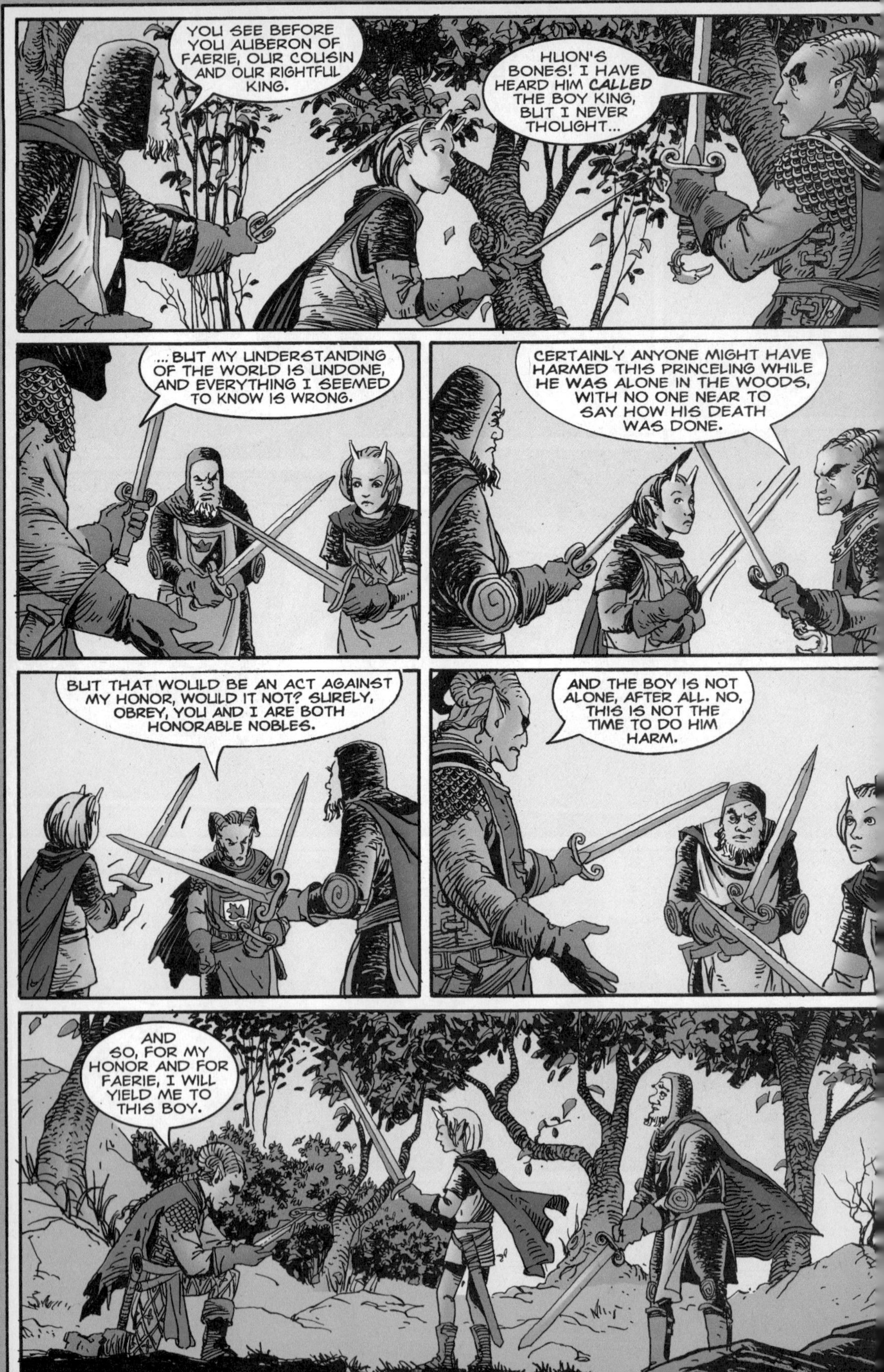
YOU SEE BEFORE YOU AUBERON OF FAERIE, OUR COUSIN AND OUR RIGHTFUL KING.
HUON'S BONES! I HAVE HEARD HIM CALLED THE BOY KING, BUT I NEVER THOUGHT...
...BUT MY UNDERSTANDING OF THE WORLD IS UNDONE, AND EVERYTHING I SEEMED TO KNOW IS WRONG.
CERTAINLY ANYONE MIGHT HAVE HARMED THIS PRINCELING WHILE HE WAS ALONE IN THE WOODS, WITH NO ONE NEAR TO SAY HOW HIS DEATH WAS DONE.
BUT THAT WOULD BE AN ACT AGAINST MY HONOR, WOULD IT NOT? SURELY, OBREY, YOU AND I ARE BOTH HONORABLE NOBLES.
AND THE BOY IS NOT ALONE, AFTER ALL. NO, THIS IS NOT THE TIME TO DO HIM HARM.
AND SO, FOR MY HONOR AND FOR FAERIE, I WILL YIELD ME TO THIS BOY.

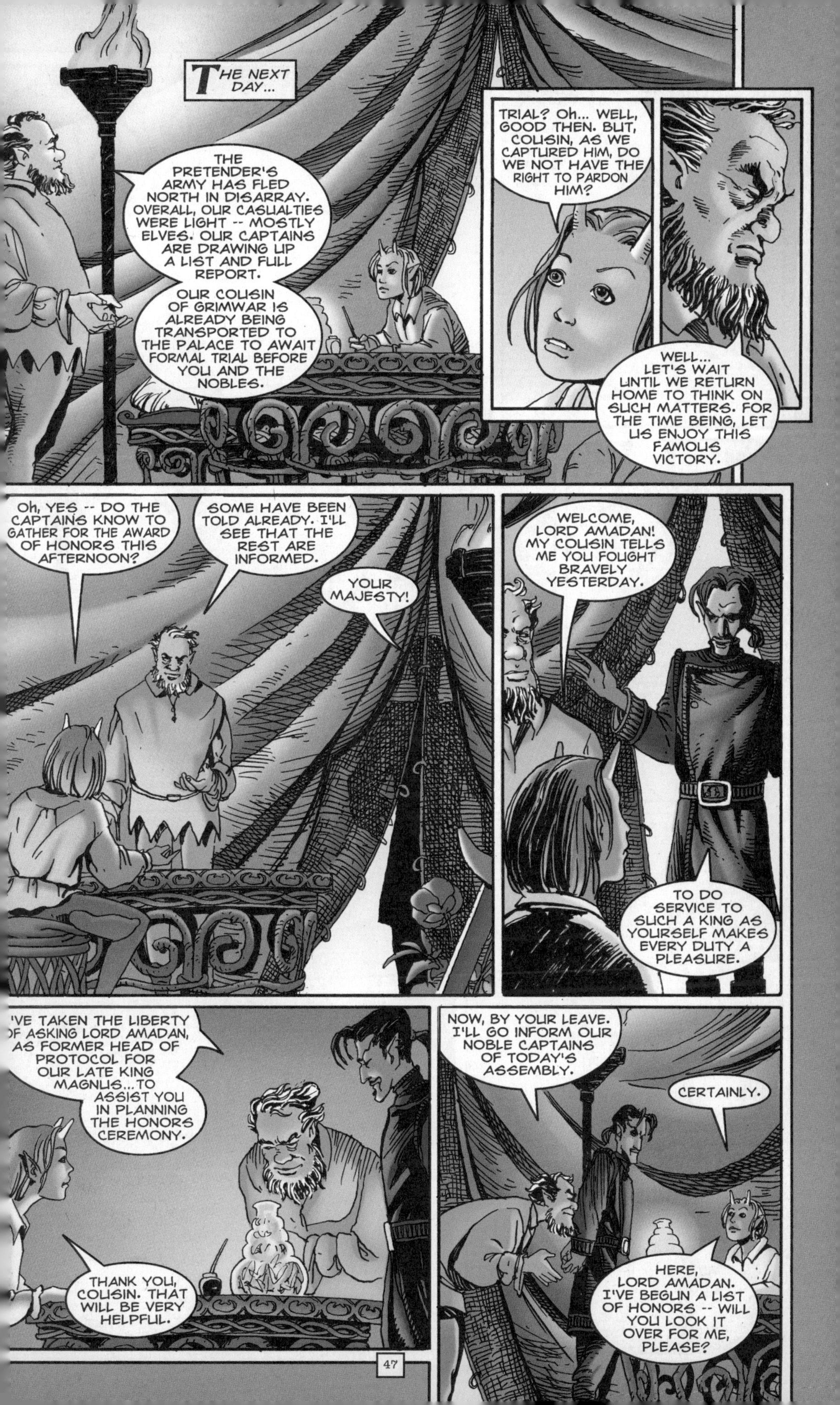
THE NEXT DAY...
THE PRETENDER'S ARMY HAS FLED NORTH IN DISARRAY. OVERALL, OUR CASUALTIES WERE LIGHT -- MOSTLY ELVES. OUR CAPTAINS ARE DRAWING UP A LIST AND FULL REPORT.
OUR COUSIN OF GRIMWAR IS ALREADY BEING TRANSPORTED TO THE PALACE TO AWAIT FORMAL TRIAL BEFORE YOU AND THE NOBLES.
TRIAL? Oh... WELL, GOOD THEN. BUT, COUSIN, AS WE CAPTURED HIM, DO WE NOT HAVE THE RIGHT TO PARDON HIM?
WELL... LET'S WAIT UNTIL WE RETURN HOME TO THINK ON SUCH MATTERS. FOR THE TIME BEING, LET US ENJOY THIS FAMOUS VICTORY.
Oh, YES -- DO THE CAPTAINS KNOW TO GATHER FOR THE AWARD OF HONORS THIS AFTERNOON?
SOME HAVE BEEN TOLD ALREADY. I'LL SEE THAT THE REST ARE INFORMED.
YOUR MAJESTY!
WELCOME, LORD AMADAN! MY COUSIN TELLS ME YOU FOUGHT BRAVELY YESTERDAY.
TO DO SERVICE TO SUCH A KING AS YOURSELF MAKES EVERY DUTY A PLEASURE.
I'VE TAKEN THE LIBERTY OF ASKING LORD AMADAN, AS FORMER HEAD OF PROTOCOL FOR OUR LATE KING MAGNUS...TO ASSIST YOU IN PLANNING THE HONORS CEREMONY.
THANK YOU, COUSIN. THAT WILL BE VERY HELPFUL.
NOW, BY YOUR LEAVE. I'LL GO INFORM OUR NOBLE CAPTAINS OF TODAY'S ASSEMBLY.
CERTAINLY.
HERE, LORD AMADAN. I'VE BEGUN A LIST OF HONORS -- WILL YOU LOOK IT OVER FOR ME, PLEASE?

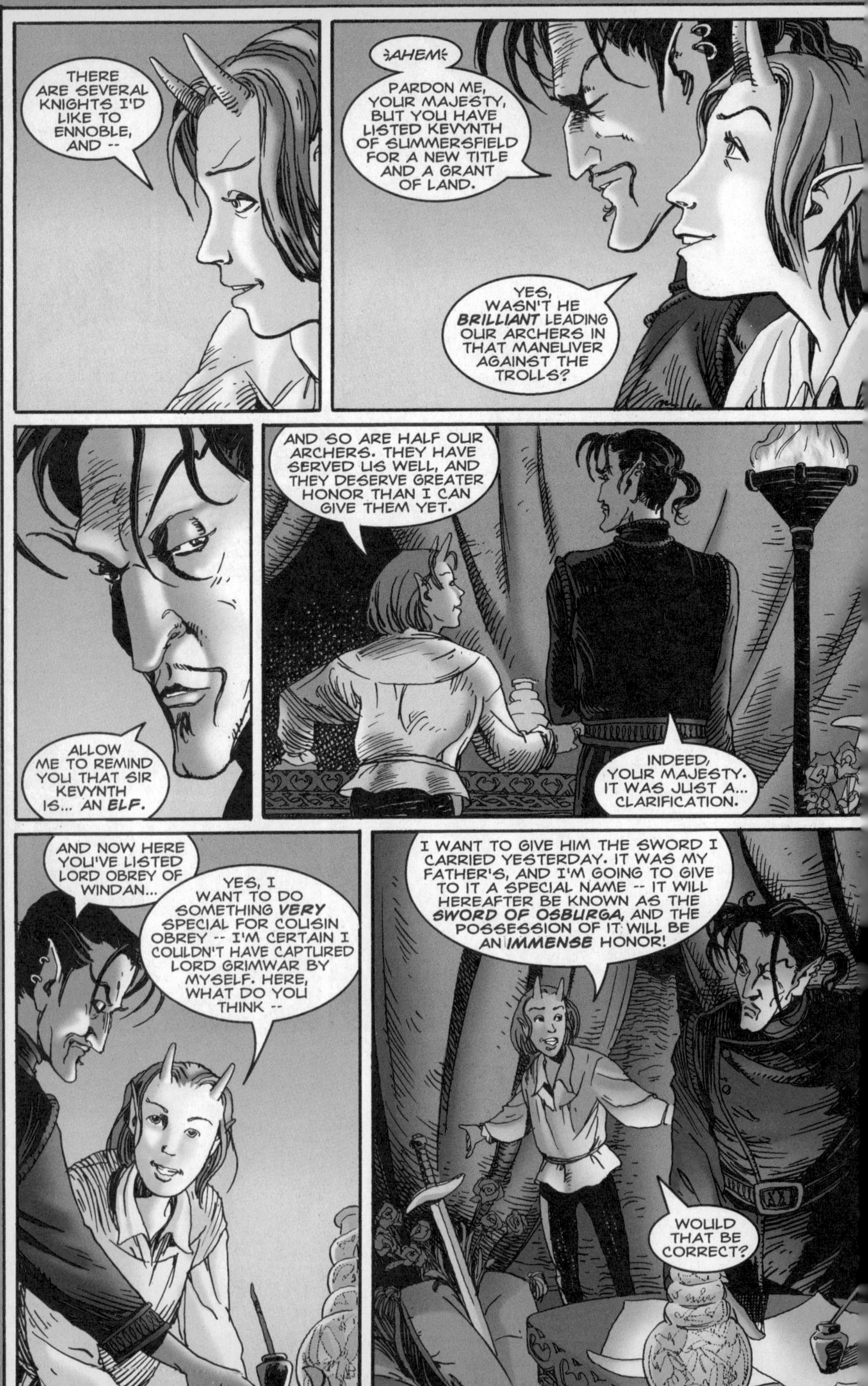
THERE ARE SEVERAL KNIGHTS I'D LIKE TO ENNOBLE, AND --
AHEM
PARDON ME, YOUR MAJESTY, BUT YOU HAVE LISTED KEVYNTH OF SUMMERSFIELD FOR A NEW TITLE AND A GRANT OF LAND.
YES, WASN'T HE BRILLIANT LEADING OUR ARCHERS IN THAT MANEUVER AGAINST THE TROLLS?
ALLOW ME TO REMIND YOU THAT SIR KEVYNTH IS... AN ELF.
AND SO ARE HALF OUR ARCHERS. THEY HAVE SERVED US WELL, AND THEY DESERVE GREATER HONOR THAN I CAN GIVE THEM YET.
INDEED, YOUR MAJESTY. IT WAS JUST A... CLARIFICATION.
AND NOW HERE YOU'VE LISTED LORD OBREY OF WINDAN...
YES, I WANT TO DO SOMETHING VERY SPECIAL FOR COUSIN OBREY -- I'M CERTAIN I COULDN'T HAVE CAPTURED LORD GRIMWAR BY MYSELF. HERE, WHAT DO YOU THINK --
I WANT TO GIVE HIM THE SWORD I CARRIED YESTERDAY. IT WAS MY FATHER'S, AND I'M GOING TO GIVE TO IT A SPECIAL NAME -- IT WILL HEREAFTER BE KNOWN AS THE SWORD OF OSBURGA, AND THE POSSESSION OF IT WILL BE AN IMMENSE HONOR!
WOULD THAT BE CORRECT?

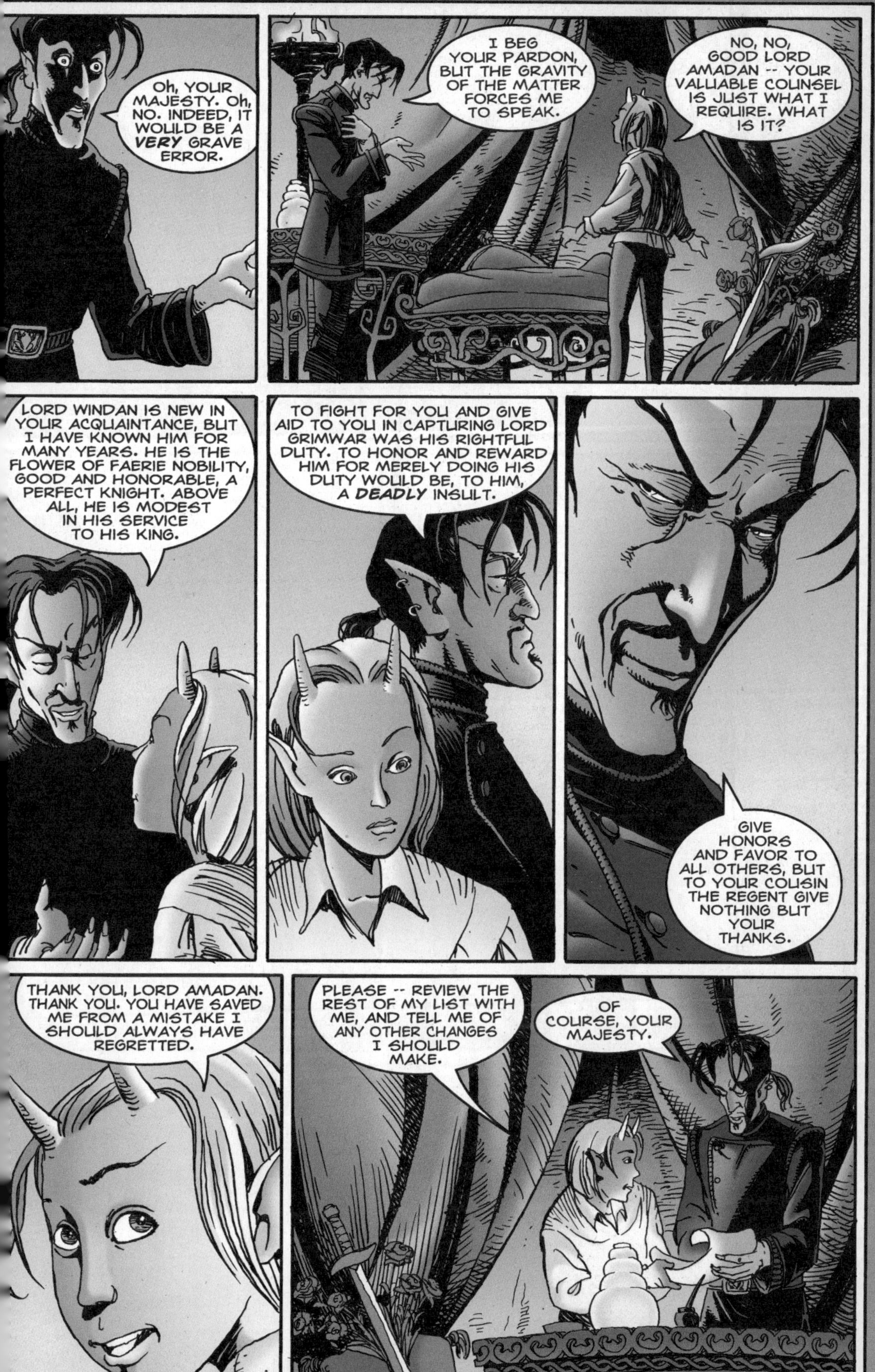
Oh, YOUR MAJESTY. Oh, NO. INDEED, IT WOULD BE A VERY GRAVE ERROR.
I BEG YOUR PARDON, BUT THE GRAVITY OF THE MATTER FORCES ME TO SPEAK.
NO, NO, GOOD LORD AMADAN -- YOUR VALUABLE COUNSEL IS JUST WHAT I REQUIRE. WHAT IS IT?
LORD WINDAN IS NEW IN YOUR ACQUAINTANCE, BUT I HAVE KNOWN HIM FOR MANY YEARS. HE IS THE FLOWER OF FAERIE NOBILITY, GOOD AND HONORABLE, A PERFECT KNIGHT. ABOVE ALL, HE IS MODEST IN HIS SERVICE TO HIS KING.
TO FIGHT FOR YOU AND GIVE AID TO YOU IN CAPTURING LORD GRIMWAR WAS HIS RIGHTFUL DUTY. TO HONOR AND REWARD HIM FOR MERELY DOING HIS DUTY WOULD BE, TO HIM, A DEADLY INSULT.
GIVE HONORS AND FAVOR TO ALL OTHERS, BUT TO YOUR COUSIN THE REGENT GIVE NOTHING BUT YOUR THANKS.
THANK YOU, LORD AMADAN. THANK YOU. YOU HAVE SAVED ME FROM A MISTAKE I SHOULD ALWAYS HAVE REGRETTED.
PLEASE -- REVIEW THE REST OF MY LIST WITH ME, AND TELL ME OF ANY OTHER CHANGES I SHOULD MAKE.
OF COURSE, YOUR MAJESTY.

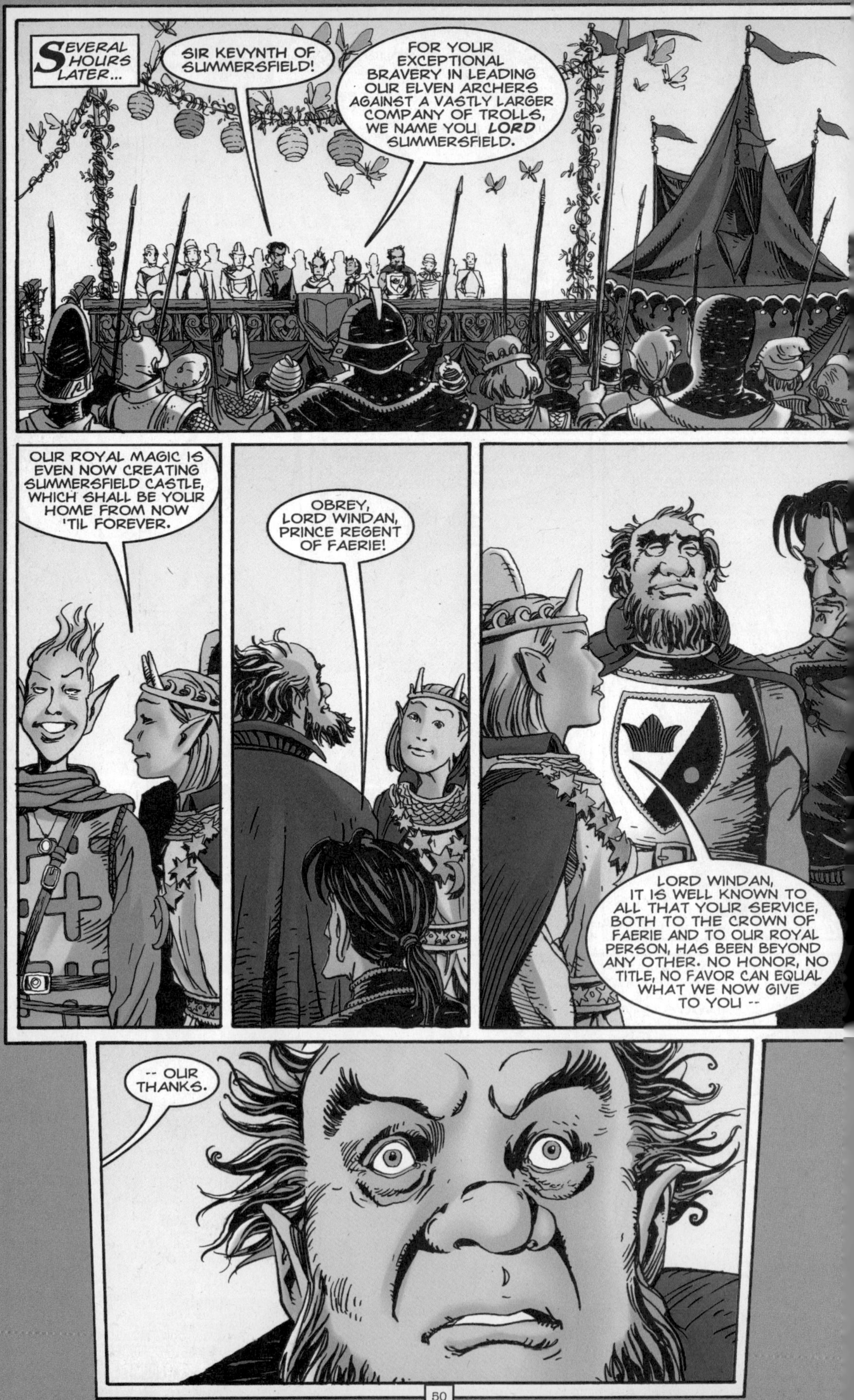
SEVERAL HOURS LATER...
SIR KEVYNTH OF SUMMERSFIELD!
FOR YOUR EXCEPTIONAL BRAVERY IN LEADING OUR ELVEN ARCHERS AGAINST A VASTLY LARGER COMPANY OF TROLLS, WE NAME YOU **LORD** SUMMERSFIELD.
OUR ROYAL MAGIC IS EVEN NOW CREATING SUMMERSFIELD CASTLE, WHICH SHALL BE YOUR HOME FROM NOW 'TIL FOREVER.
OBREY, LORD WINDAN, PRINCE REGENT OF FAERIE!
LORD WINDAN, IT IS WELL KNOWN TO ALL THAT YOUR SERVICE, BOTH TO THE CROWN OF FAERIE AND TO OUR ROYAL PERSON, HAS BEEN BEYOND ANY OTHER. NO HONOR, NO TITLE, NO FAVOR CAN EQUAL WHAT WE NOW GIVE TO YOU --
-- OUR THANKS.

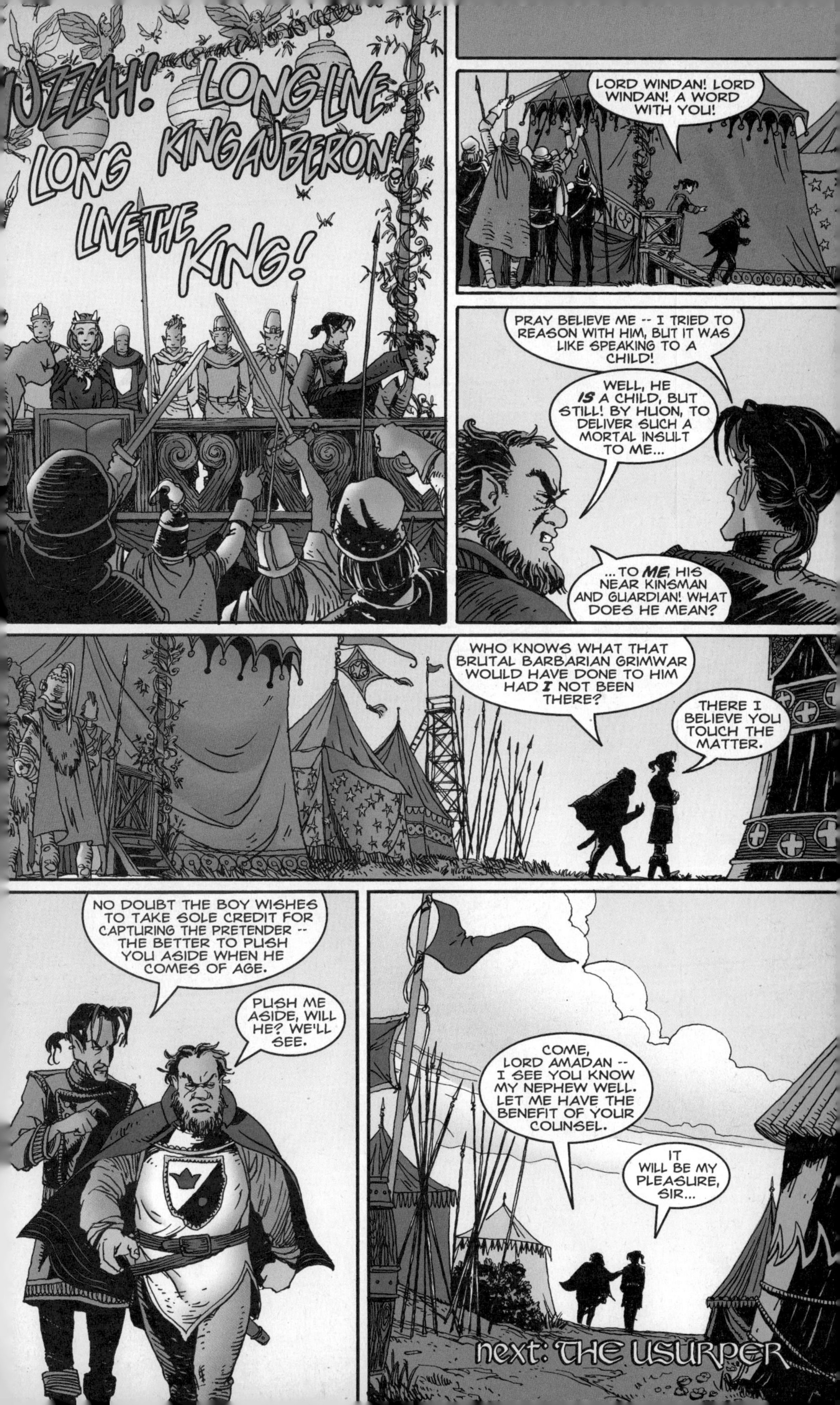

HUZZAH! LONG LIVE LONG KING AUBERON! LIVE THE KING!
LORD WINDAN! LORD WINDAN! A WORD WITH YOU!
PRAY BELIEVE ME -- I TRIED TO REASON WITH HIM, BUT IT WAS LIKE SPEAKING TO A CHILD!
WELL, HE IS A CHILD, BUT STILL! BY HUON, TO DELIVER SUCH A MORTAL INSULT TO ME...
...TO ME, HIS NEAR KINSMAN AND GUARDIAN! WHAT DOES HE MEAN?
WHO KNOWS WHAT THAT BRUTAL BARBARIAN GRIMWAR WOULD HAVE DONE TO HIM HAD I NOT BEEN THERE?
THERE I BELIEVE YOU TOUCH THE MATTER.
NO DOUBT THE BOY WISHES TO TAKE SOLE CREDIT FOR CAPTURING THE PRETENDER -- THE BETTER TO PUSH YOU ASIDE WHEN HE COMES OF AGE.
PUSH ME ASIDE, WILL HE? WE'LL SEE.
COME, LORD AMADAN -- I SEE YOU KNOW MY NEPHEW WELL. LET ME HAVE THE BENEFIT OF YOUR COUNSEL.
IT WILL BE MY PLEASURE, SIR...
next: THE USURPER

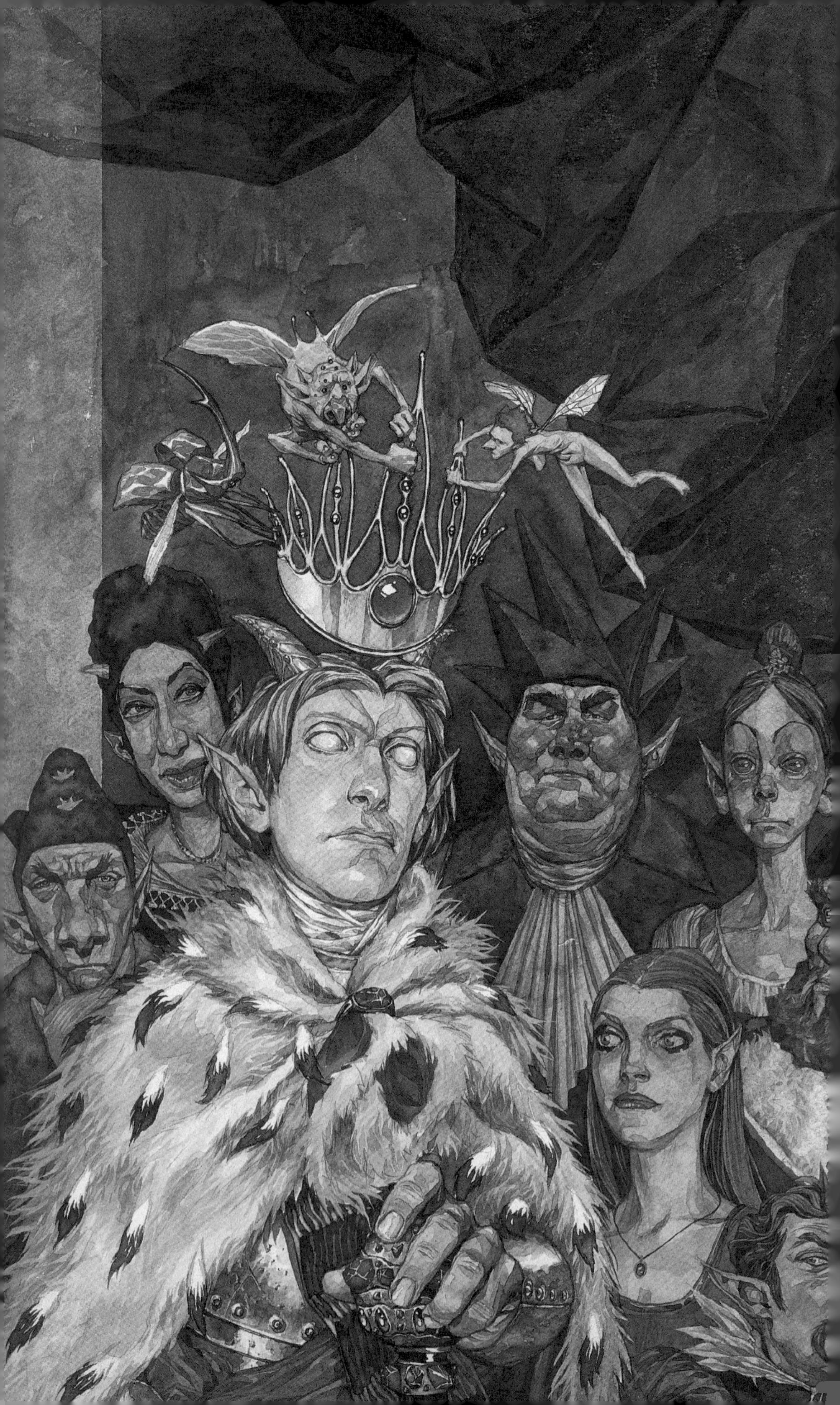

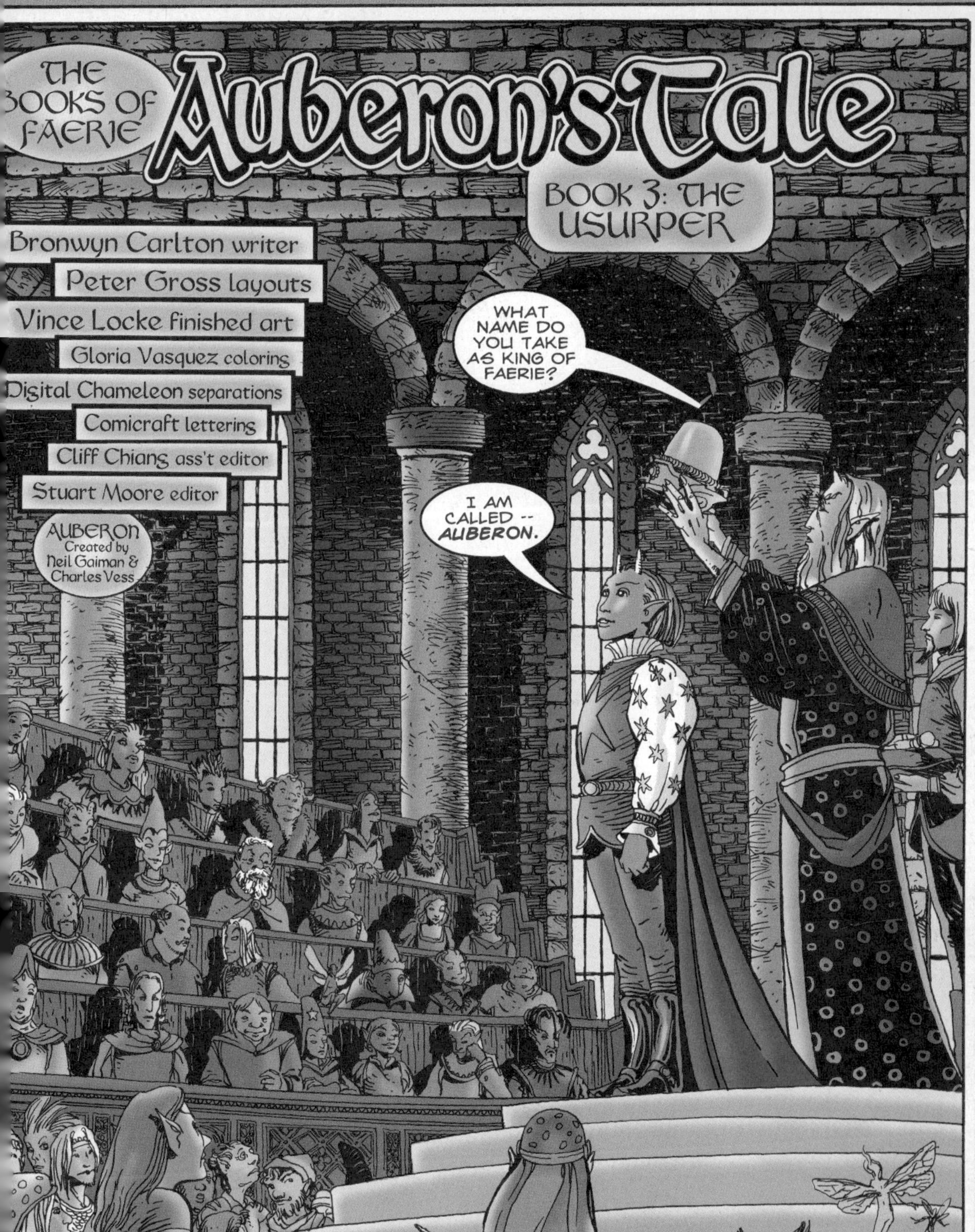
THE BOOKS OF FAERIE
Auberon's Tale
BOOK 3: THE USURPER
Bronwyn Carlton writer
Peter Gross layouts
Vince Locke finished art
Gloria Vasquez coloring
Digital Chameleon separations
Comicraft lettering
Cliff Chiang ass't editor
Stuart Moore editor
AUBERON Created by Neil Gaiman & Charles Vess
WHAT NAME DO YOU TAKE AS KING OF FAERIE?
I AM CALLED -- AUBERON.

[redacted]

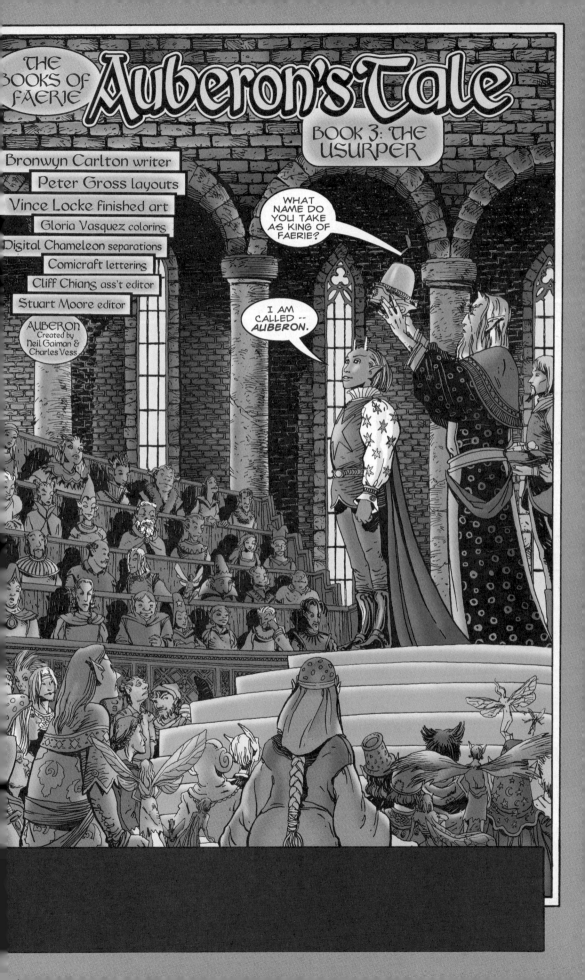

HAIL TO THEE, ALIBERON.

AND WHO SHALL SERVE AS REGENT, GUARDIAN OF YOUR PERSON AND PROTECTOR OF THE REALM, UNTIL SUCH TIME AS YOU SHALL ATTAIN THE FULL POWERS OF MATURITY?

IT IS OUR WISH THAT OUR NEAR KINSMAN, OBREY, LORD WINDAN, SERVE AS REGENT.

SIR, YOUR CHOICE IS IN ACCORD WITH THE JUDGMENT OF THE HIGH COUNCIL OF FAERIE. OBREY, LORD WINDAN --

-- OUR KING IS HEREBY GIVEN INTO YOUR PROTECTION. LONG LIVE KING ALIBERON!

LONG LIVE KING ALIBERON! LONG LIVE THE KING!

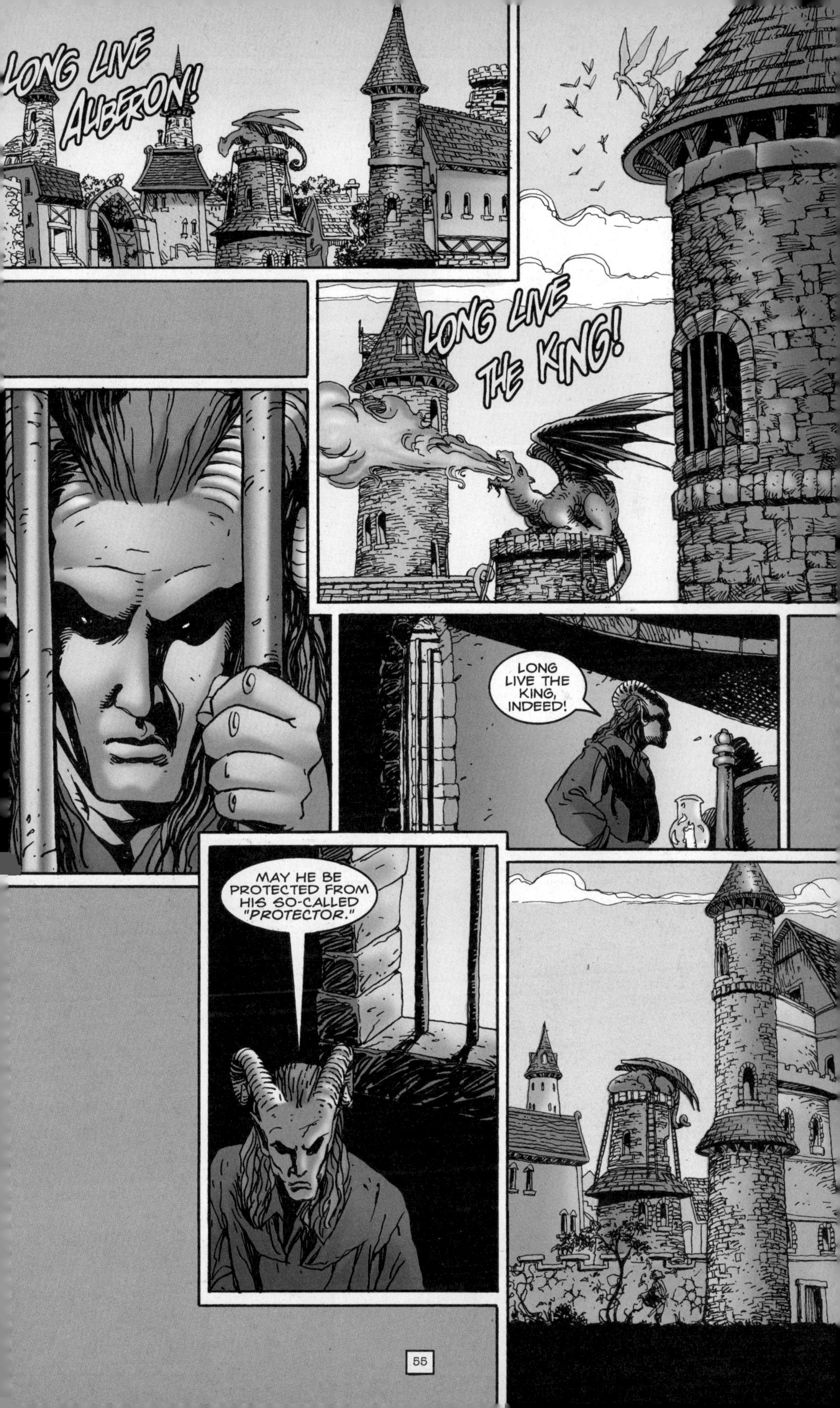
LONG LIVE ALBERON!
LONG LIVE THE KING!
LONG LIVE THE KING, INDEED!
MAY HE BE PROTECTED FROM HIS SO-CALLED "PROTECTOR."

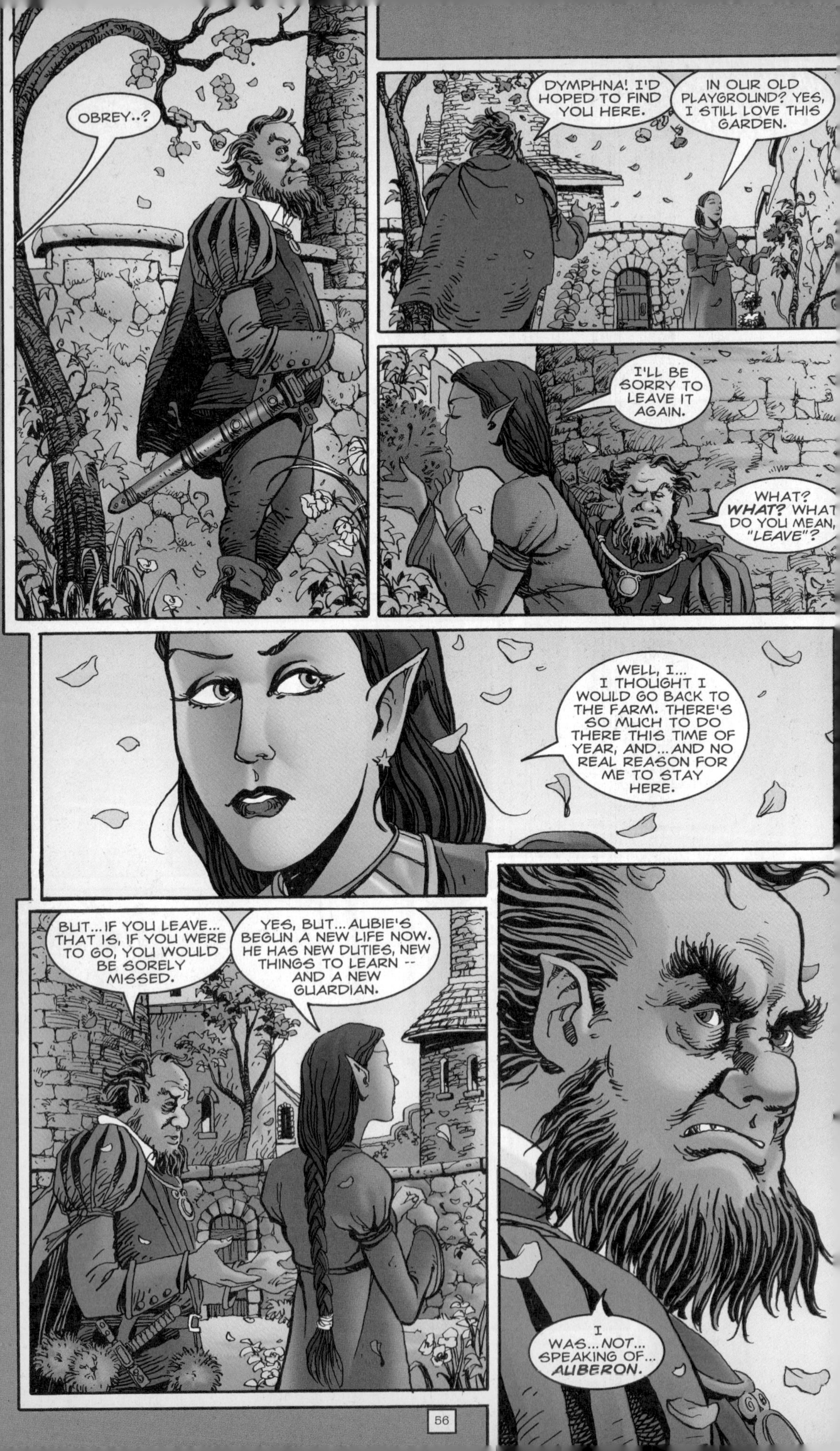
OBREY..?
DYMPHNA! I'D HOPED TO FIND YOU HERE.
IN OUR OLD PLAYGROUND? YES, I STILL LOVE THIS GARDEN.
I'LL BE SORRY TO LEAVE IT AGAIN.
WHAT? **WHAT?** WHAT DO YOU MEAN, *"LEAVE"*?
WELL, I... I THOUGHT I WOULD GO BACK TO THE FARM. THERE'S SO MUCH TO DO THERE THIS TIME OF YEAR, AND... AND NO REAL REASON FOR ME TO STAY HERE.
BUT... IF YOU LEAVE... THAT IS, IF YOU WERE TO GO, YOU WOULD BE SORELY MISSED.
YES, BUT... AUBIE'S BEGUN A NEW LIFE NOW. HE HAS NEW DUTIES, NEW THINGS TO LEARN -- AND A NEW GUARDIAN.
I WAS... NOT... SPEAKING OF... ***AUBERON.***

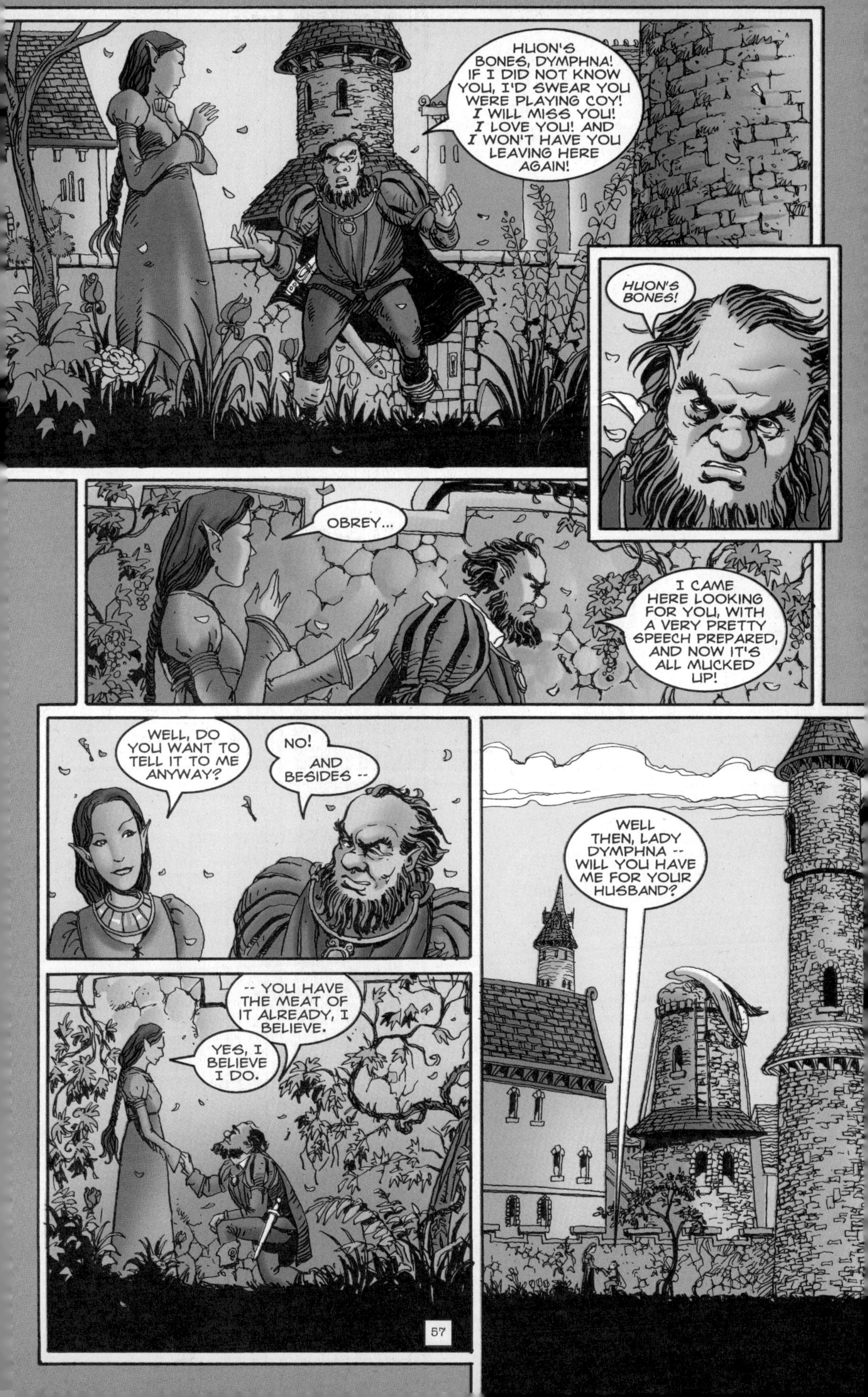
HUON'S BONES, DYMPHNA! IF I DID NOT KNOW YOU, I'D SWEAR YOU WERE PLAYING COY! *I* WILL MISS YOU! *I* LOVE YOU! AND *I* WON'T HAVE YOU LEAVING HERE AGAIN!
HUON'S BONES!
OBREY...
I CAME HERE LOOKING FOR YOU, WITH A VERY PRETTY SPEECH PREPARED, AND NOW IT'S ALL MUCKED UP!
WELL, DO YOU WANT TO TELL IT TO ME ANYWAY?
NO!
AND BESIDES --
-- YOU HAVE THE MEAT OF IT ALREADY, I BELIEVE.
YES, I BELIEVE I DO.
WELL THEN, LADY DYMPHNA -- WILL YOU HAVE ME FOR YOUR HUSBAND?

SEVERAL HOURS LATER...

Oh, BRIDEY! I AM SO HAPPY!

AYE, THAT I CAN SEE, AS COULD ANY BLIND GRUB.

DO YOU REMEMBER WHEN OBREY AND I WERE SMALL, AND WE PLAYED TOGETHER IN THAT GARDEN? AND THEN, WHEN -- WHEN I WENT TO TAKE CARE OF ALIBERON, I THOUGHT I SHOULD NEVER SEE IT, OR OBREY, AGAIN --

-- AND NOW I DON'T EVER, EVER HAVE TO LEAVE!

Hmmm...

COME, OLD BRUNLING, TELL ME WHAT'S THE MATTER. I KNOW THERE'S SOMETHING TROUBLING YOU.

I DON'T KNOW MY OWN MIND NOW, AND THAT'S THE TRUTH. YOU AND YOUNG OBREY ARE A SUITABLE MATCH, AND THERE'S NO DENYING THE FONDNESS THAT'S BETWEEN YOU.

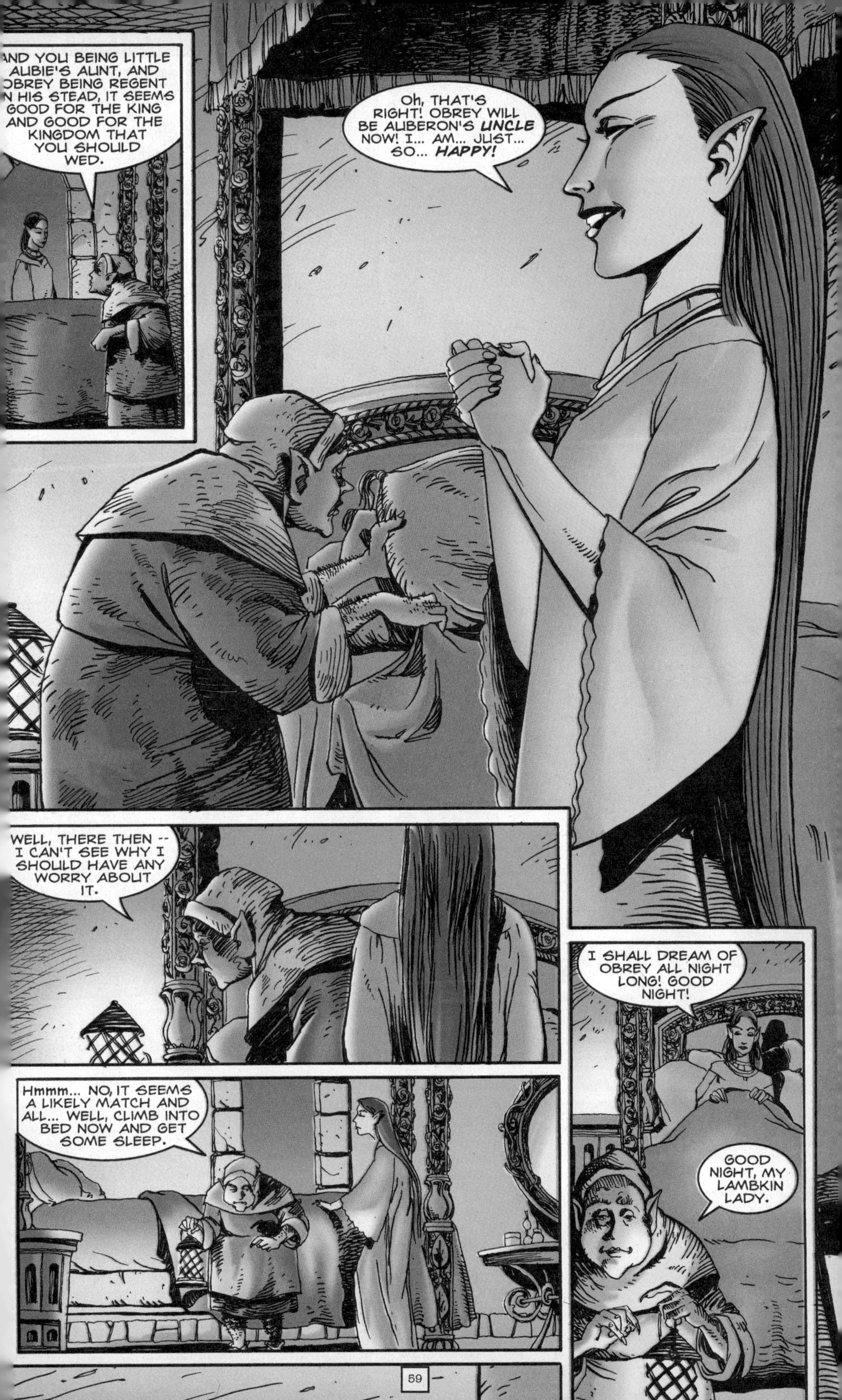
AND YOU BEING LITTLE AUBIE'S AUNT, AND OBREY BEING REGENT IN HIS STEAD, IT SEEMS GOOD FOR THE KING AND GOOD FOR THE KINGDOM THAT YOU SHOULD WED.
Oh, THAT'S RIGHT! OBREY WILL BE AUBERON'S UNCLE NOW! I... AM... JUST... SO... HAPPY!
WELL, THERE THEN -- I CAN'T SEE WHY I SHOULD HAVE ANY WORRY ABOUT IT.
Hmmm... NO, IT SEEMS A LIKELY MATCH AND ALL... WELL, CLIMB INTO BED NOW AND GET SOME SLEEP.
I SHALL DREAM OF OBREY ALL NIGHT LONG! GOOD NIGHT!
GOOD NIGHT, MY LAMBKIN LADY.

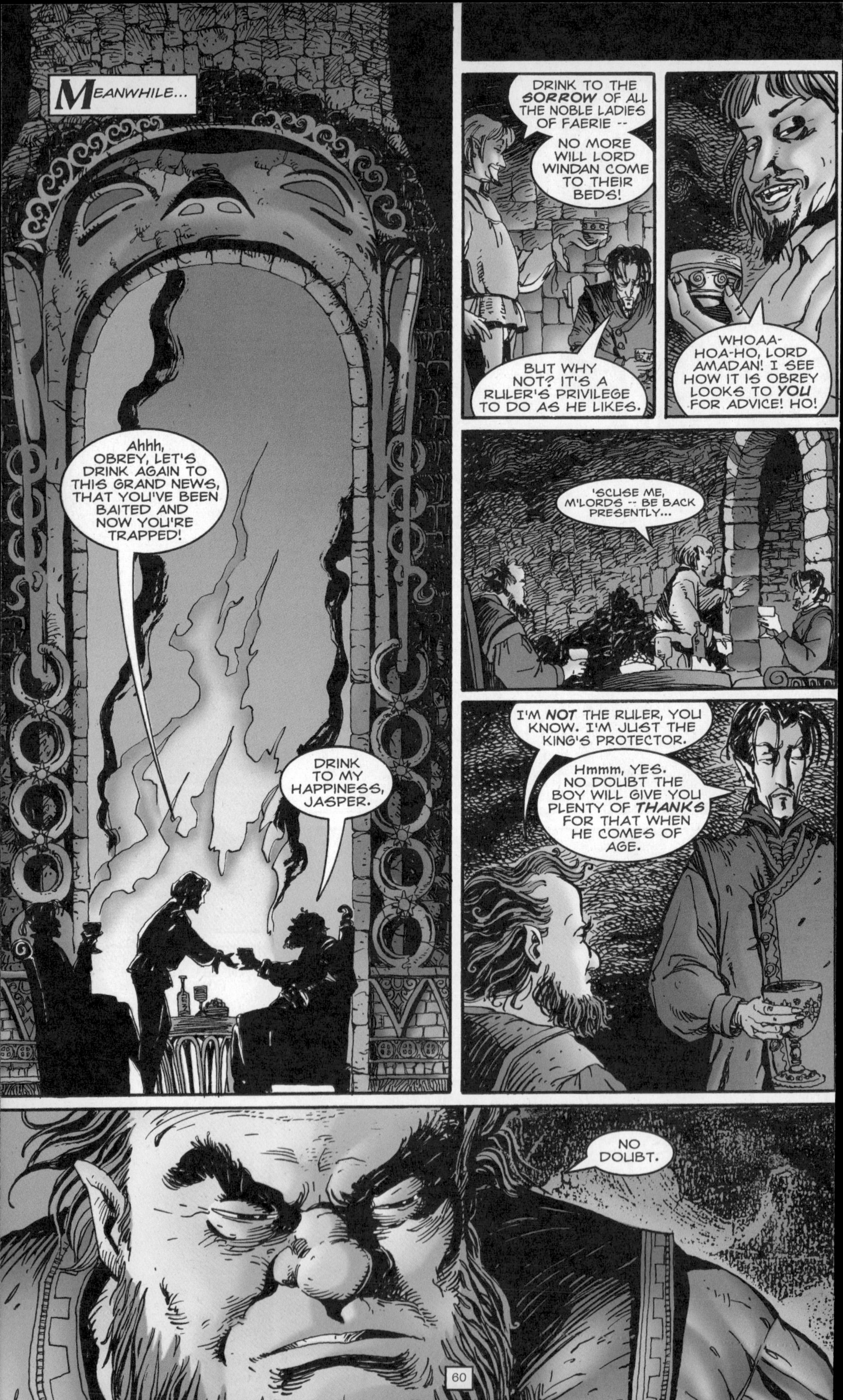
MEANWHILE...
Ahhh, OBREY, LET'S DRINK AGAIN TO THIS GRAND NEWS, THAT YOU'VE BEEN BAITED AND NOW YOU'RE TRAPPED!
DRINK TO MY HAPPINESS, JASPER.
DRINK TO THE SORROW OF ALL THE NOBLE LADIES OF FAERIE --
NO MORE WILL LORD WINDAN COME TO THEIR BEDS!
BUT WHY NOT? IT'S A RULER'S PRIVILEGE TO DO AS HE LIKES.
WHOAA-HOA-HO, LORD AMADAN! I SEE HOW IT IS OBREY LOOKS TO YOU FOR ADVICE! HO!
'SCUSE ME, M'LORDS -- BE BACK PRESENTLY...
I'M NOT THE RULER, YOU KNOW. I'M JUST THE KING'S PROTECTOR.
Hmmm, YES. NO DOUBT THE BOY WILL GIVE YOU PLENTY OF THANKS FOR THAT WHEN HE COMES OF AGE.
NO DOUBT.

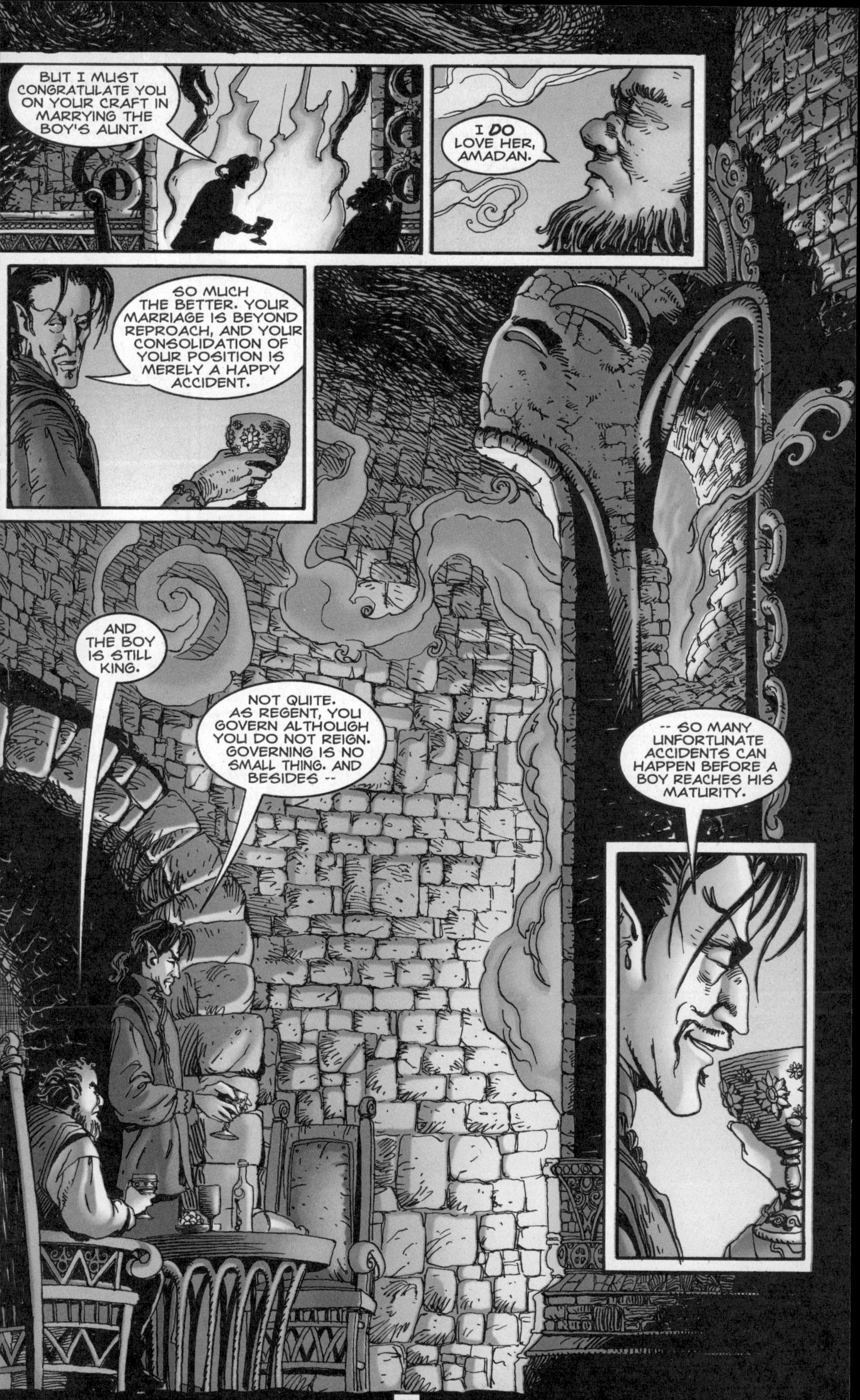
BUT I MUST CONGRATULATE YOU ON YOUR CRAFT IN MARRYING THE BOY'S AUNT.
I DO LOVE HER, AMADAN.
SO MUCH THE BETTER. YOUR MARRIAGE IS BEYOND REPROACH, AND YOUR CONSOLIDATION OF YOUR POSITION IS MERELY A HAPPY ACCIDENT.
AND THE BOY IS STILL KING.
NOT QUITE. AS REGENT, YOU GOVERN ALTHOUGH YOU DO NOT REIGN. GOVERNING IS NO SMALL THING. AND BESIDES --
-- SO MANY UNFORTUNATE ACCIDENTS CAN HAPPEN BEFORE A BOY REACHES HIS MATURITY.

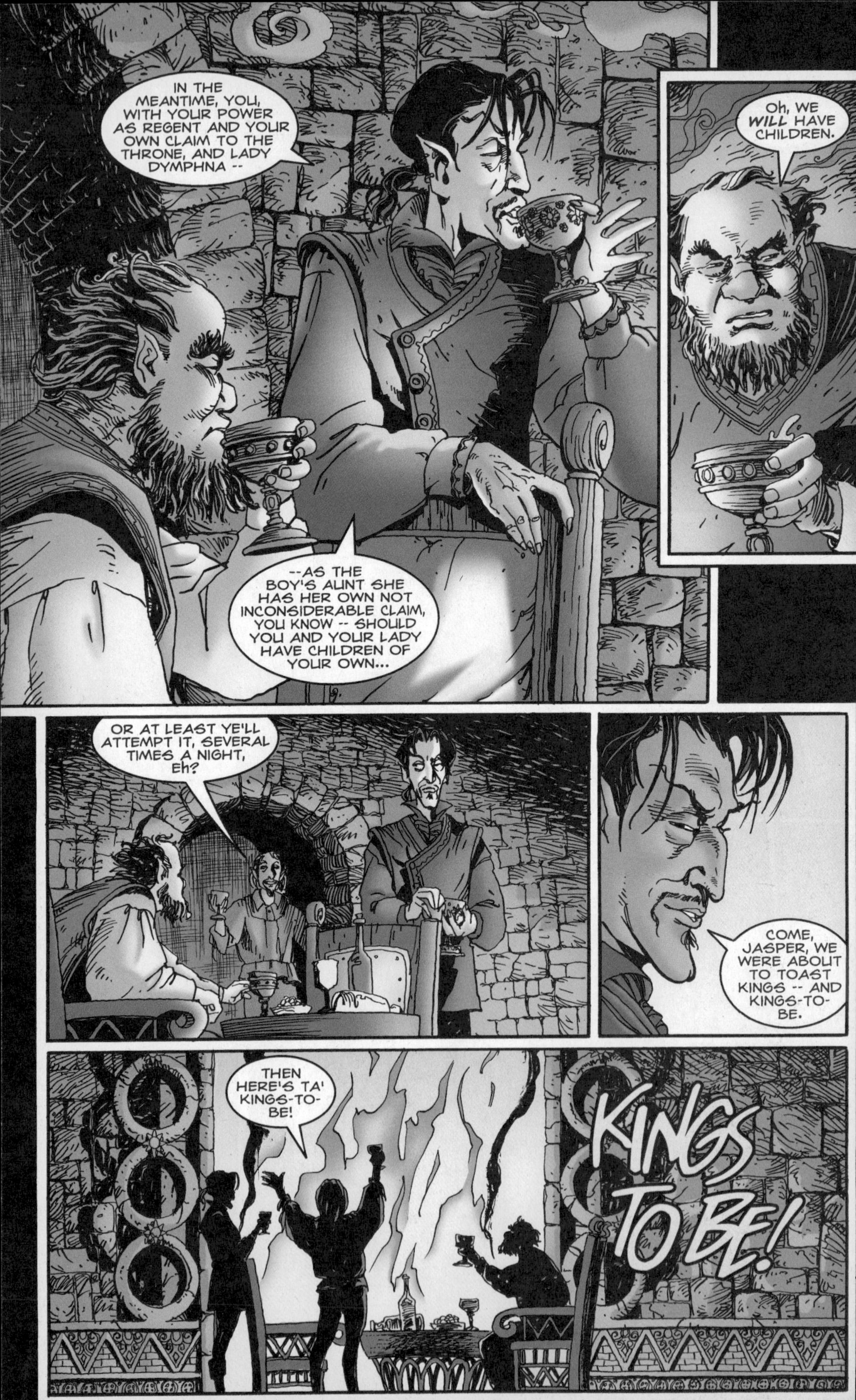
IN THE MEANTIME, YOU, WITH YOUR POWER AS REGENT AND YOUR OWN CLAIM TO THE THRONE, AND LADY DYMPHNA --
--AS THE BOY'S AUNT SHE HAS HER OWN NOT INCONSIDERABLE CLAIM, YOU KNOW -- SHOULD YOU AND YOUR LADY HAVE CHILDREN OF YOUR OWN...
Oh, WE *WILL* HAVE CHILDREN.
OR AT LEAST YE'LL ATTEMPT IT, SEVERAL TIMES A NIGHT, Eh?
COME, JASPER, WE WERE ABOUT TO TOAST KINGS -- AND KINGS-TO-BE.
THEN HERE'S TA' KINGS-TO-BE!
KINGS TO BE!

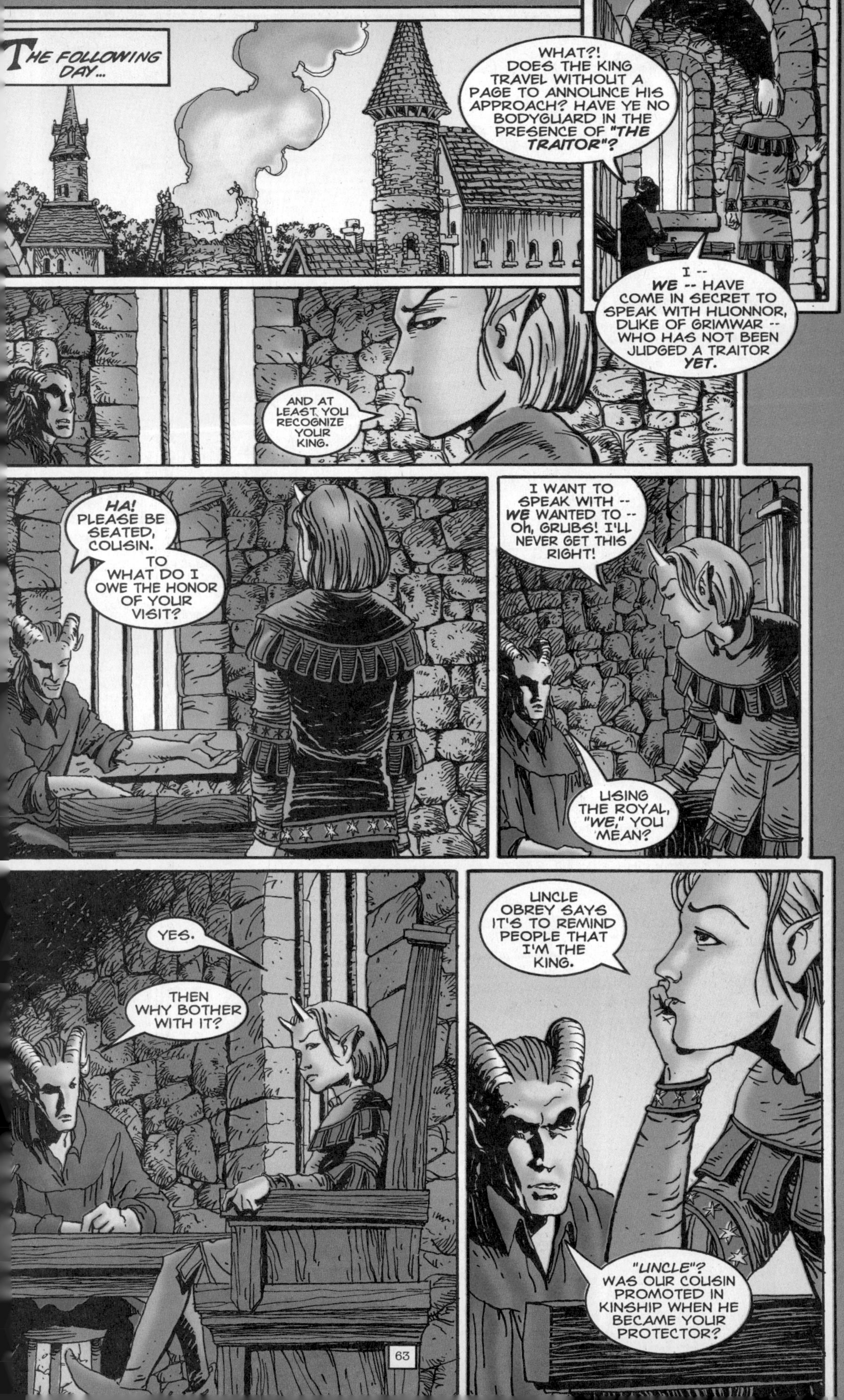
THE FOLLOWING DAY...
WHAT?! DOES THE KING TRAVEL WITHOUT A PAGE TO ANNOUNCE HIS APPROACH? HAVE YE NO BODYGUARD IN THE PRESENCE OF "THE TRAITOR"?
I -- WE -- HAVE COME IN SECRET TO SPEAK WITH HUONNOR, DUKE OF GRIMWAR -- WHO HAS NOT BEEN JUDGED A TRAITOR YET.
AND AT LEAST YOU RECOGNIZE YOUR KING.
HA! PLEASE BE SEATED, COUSIN.
TO WHAT DO I OWE THE HONOR OF YOUR VISIT?
I WANT TO SPEAK WITH -- WE WANTED TO -- Oh, GRUBS! I'LL NEVER GET THIS RIGHT!
USING THE ROYAL, "WE," YOU MEAN?
YES.
THEN WHY BOTHER WITH IT?
UNCLE OBREY SAYS IT'S TO REMIND PEOPLE THAT I'M THE KING.
"UNCLE"? WAS OUR COUSIN PROMOTED IN KINSHIP WHEN HE BECAME YOUR PROTECTOR?

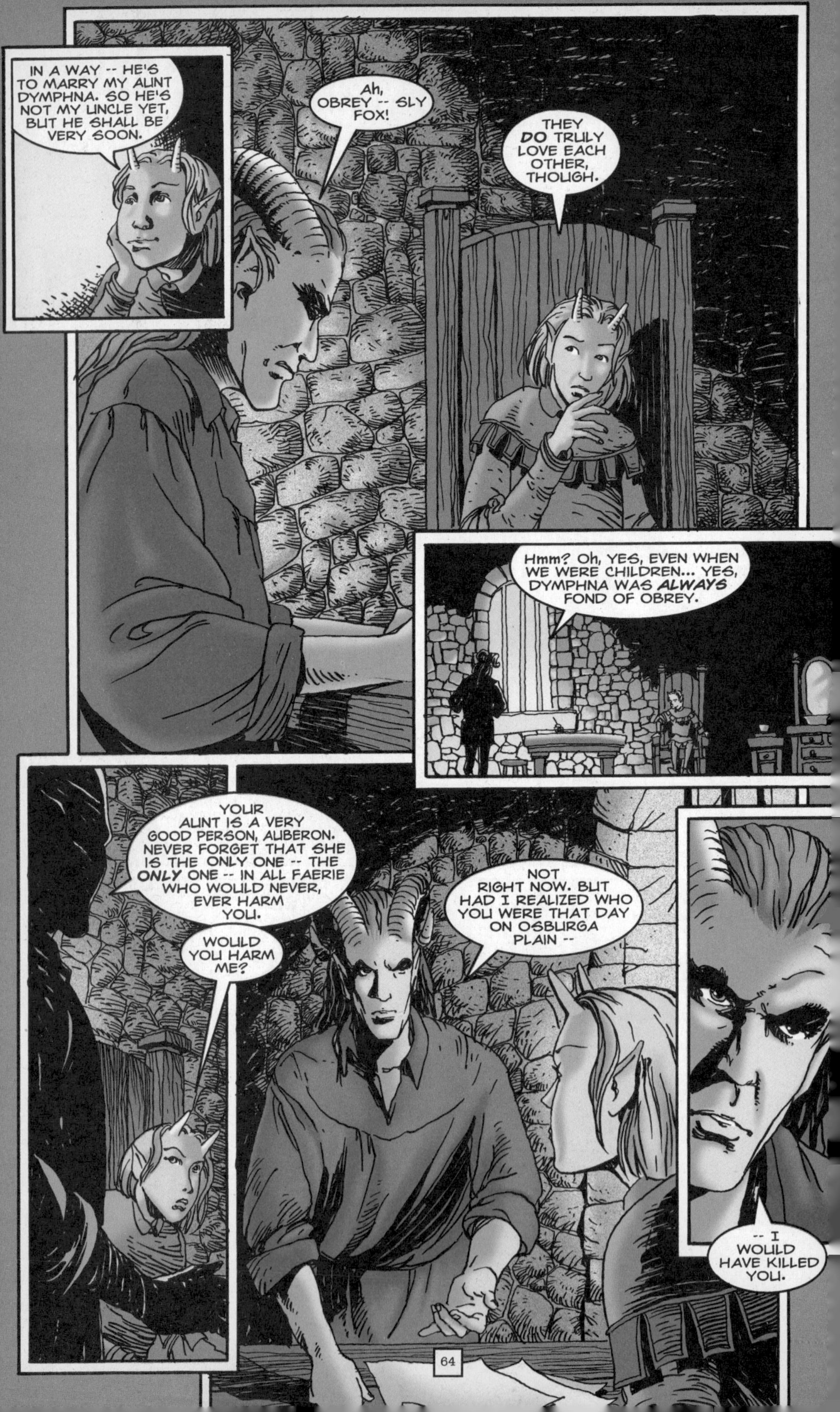
IN A WAY -- HE'S TO MARRY MY AUNT DYMPHNA. SO HE'S NOT MY UNCLE YET, BUT HE SHALL BE VERY SOON.
Ah, OBREY -- SLY FOX!
THEY DO TRULY LOVE EACH OTHER, THOUGH.
Hmm? Oh, YES, EVEN WHEN WE WERE CHILDREN... YES, DYMPHNA WAS ALWAYS FOND OF OBREY.
YOUR AUNT IS A VERY GOOD PERSON, AUBERON. NEVER FORGET THAT SHE IS THE ONLY ONE -- THE ONLY ONE -- IN ALL FAERIE WHO WOULD NEVER, EVER HARM YOU.
WOULD YOU HARM ME?
NOT RIGHT NOW. BUT HAD I REALIZED WHO YOU WERE THAT DAY ON OSBURGA PLAIN --
-- I WOULD HAVE KILLED YOU.

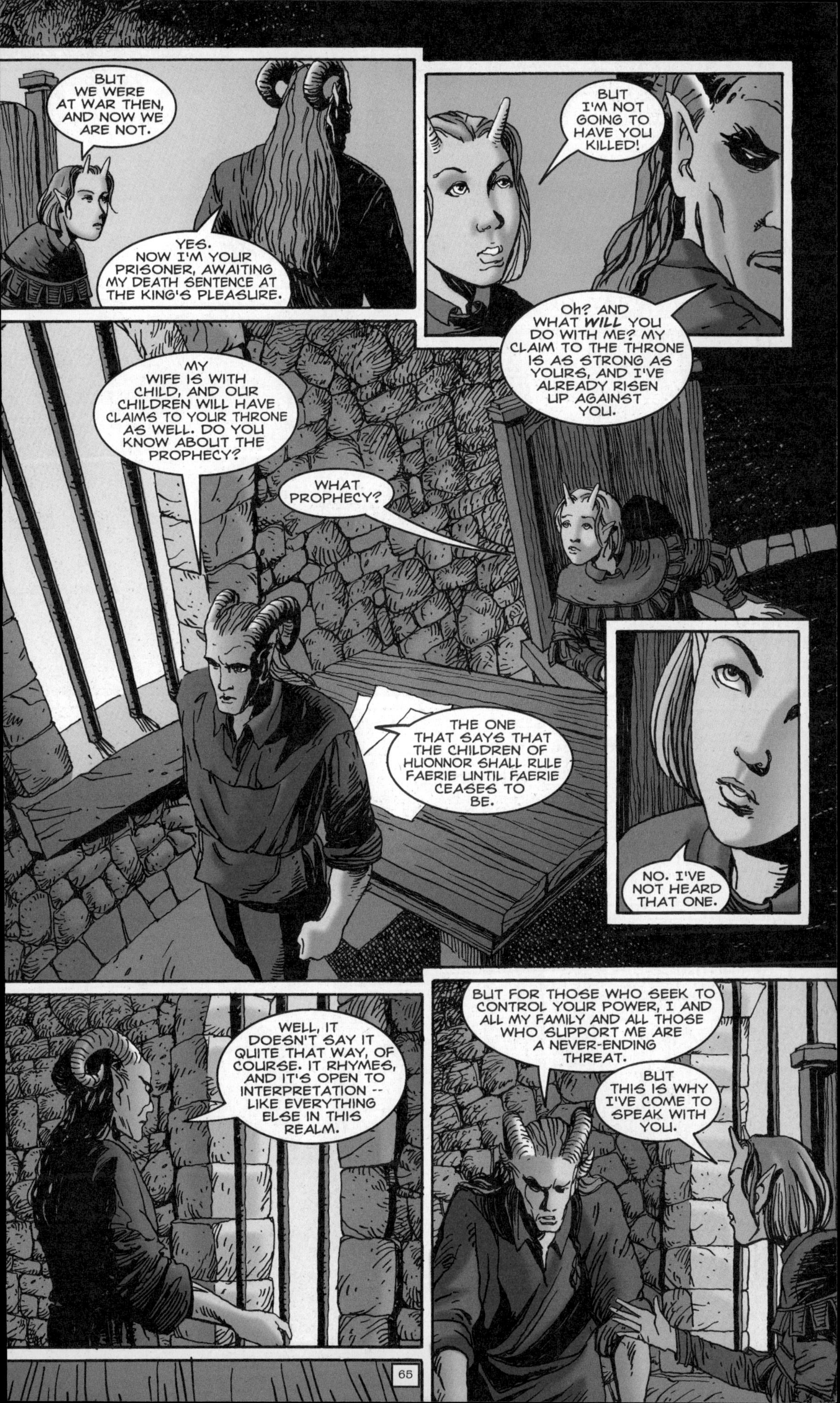
BUT WE WERE AT WAR THEN, AND NOW WE ARE NOT.
YES. NOW I'M YOUR PRISONER, AWAITING MY DEATH SENTENCE AT THE KING'S PLEASURE.
BUT I'M NOT GOING TO HAVE YOU KILLED!
Oh? AND WHAT WILL YOU DO WITH ME? MY CLAIM TO THE THRONE IS AS STRONG AS YOURS, AND I'VE ALREADY RISEN UP AGAINST YOU.
MY WIFE IS WITH CHILD, AND OUR CHILDREN WILL HAVE CLAIMS TO YOUR THRONE AS WELL. DO YOU KNOW ABOUT THE PROPHECY?
WHAT PROPHECY?
THE ONE THAT SAYS THAT THE CHILDREN OF HUONNOR SHALL RULE FAERIE UNTIL FAERIE CEASES TO BE.
NO. I'VE NOT HEARD THAT ONE.
WELL, IT DOESN'T SAY IT QUITE THAT WAY, OF COURSE. IT RHYMES, AND IT'S OPEN TO INTERPRETATION -- LIKE EVERYTHING ELSE IN THIS REALM.
BUT FOR THOSE WHO SEEK TO CONTROL YOUR POWER, I AND ALL MY FAMILY AND ALL THOSE WHO SUPPORT ME ARE A NEVER-ENDING THREAT.
BUT THIS IS WHY I'VE COME TO SPEAK WITH YOU.

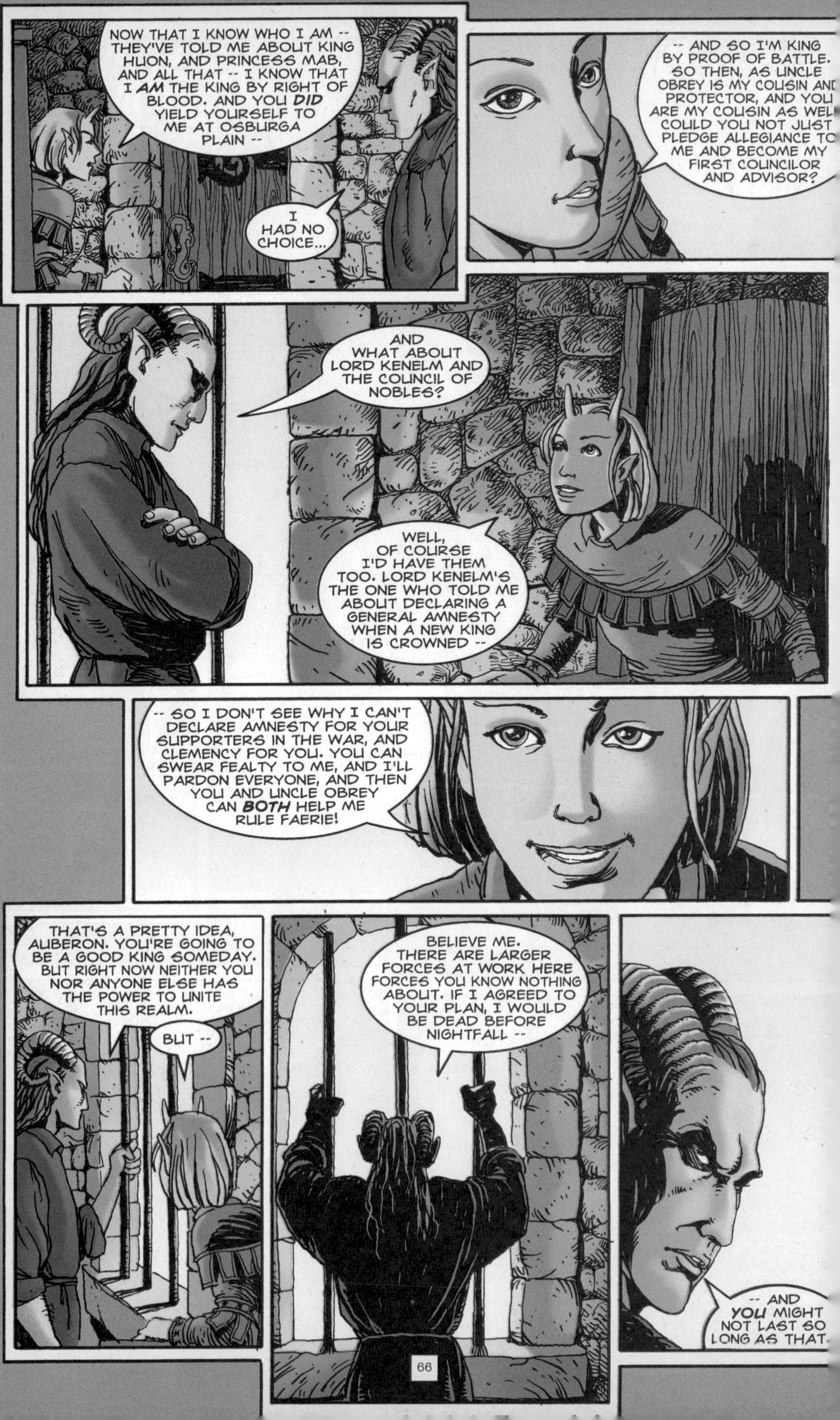
NOW THAT I KNOW WHO I AM -- THEY'VE TOLD ME ABOUT KING HUON, AND PRINCESS MAB, AND ALL THAT -- I KNOW THAT I *AM* THE KING BY RIGHT OF BLOOD. AND YOU *DID* YIELD YOURSELF TO ME AT OSBURGA PLAIN --
I HAD NO CHOICE...
-- AND SO I'M KING BY PROOF OF BATTLE. SO THEN, AS UNCLE OBREY IS MY COUSIN AND PROTECTOR, AND YOU ARE MY COUSIN AS WELL COULD YOU NOT JUST PLEDGE ALLEGIANCE TO ME AND BECOME MY FIRST COUNCILOR AND ADVISOR?
AND WHAT ABOUT LORD KENELM AND THE COUNCIL OF NOBLES?
WELL, OF COURSE I'D HAVE THEM TOO. LORD KENELM'S THE ONE WHO TOLD ME ABOUT DECLARING A GENERAL AMNESTY WHEN A NEW KING IS CROWNED --
-- SO I DON'T SEE WHY I CAN'T DECLARE AMNESTY FOR YOUR SUPPORTERS IN THE WAR, AND CLEMENCY FOR YOU. YOU CAN SWEAR FEALTY TO ME, AND I'LL PARDON EVERYONE, AND THEN YOU AND UNCLE OBREY CAN *BOTH* HELP ME RULE FAERIE!
THAT'S A PRETTY IDEA, AUBERON. YOU'RE GOING TO BE A GOOD KING SOMEDAY. BUT RIGHT NOW NEITHER YOU NOR ANYONE ELSE HAS THE POWER TO UNITE THIS REALM.
BUT --
BELIEVE ME. THERE ARE LARGER FORCES AT WORK HERE FORCES YOU KNOW NOTHING ABOUT. IF I AGREED TO YOUR PLAN, I WOULD BE DEAD BEFORE NIGHTFALL --
-- AND *YOU* MIGHT NOT LAST SO LONG AS THAT.

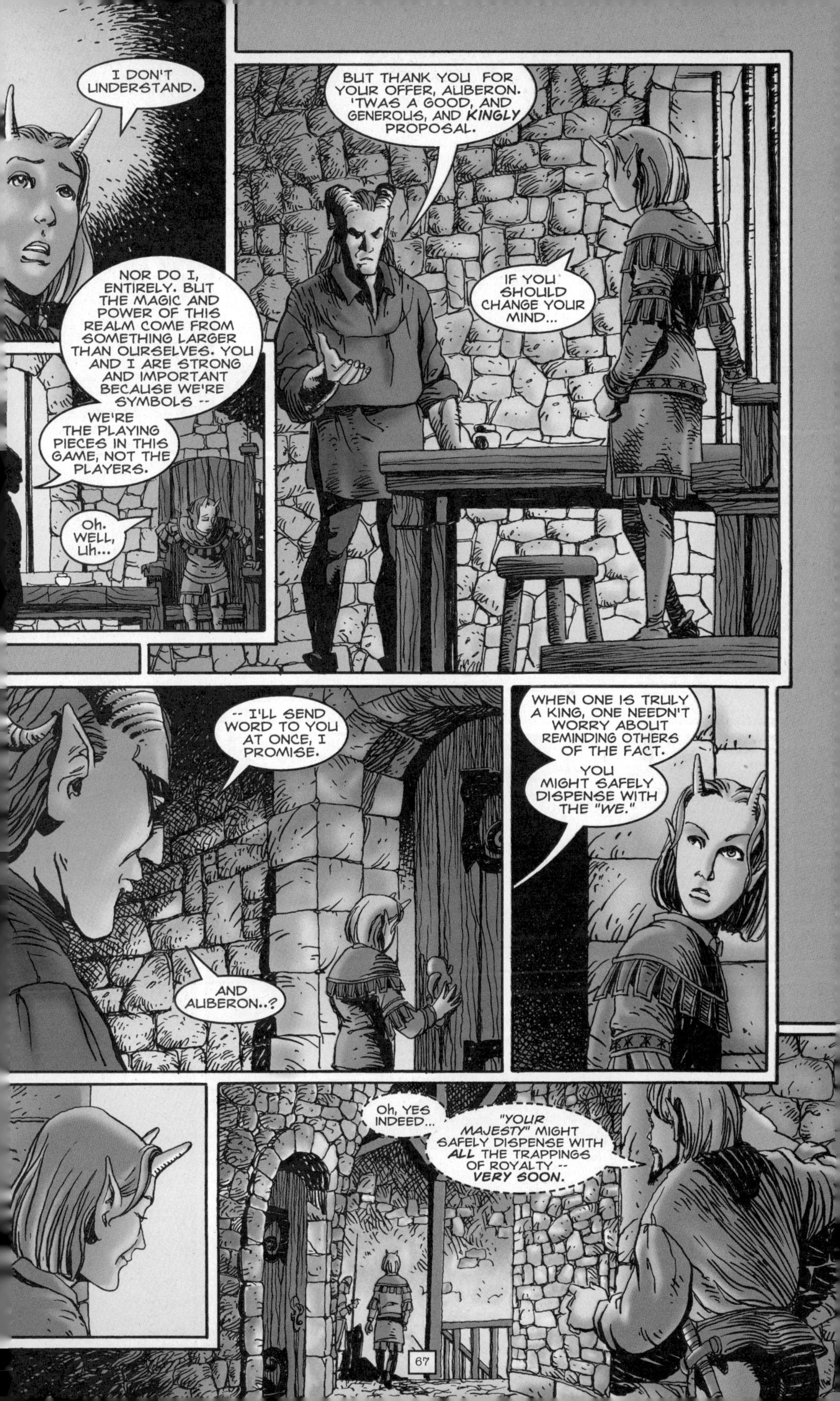
I DON'T UNDERSTAND.
BUT THANK YOU FOR YOUR OFFER, AUBERON. 'TWAS A GOOD, AND GENEROUS, AND KINGLY PROPOSAL.
NOR DO I, ENTIRELY. BUT THE MAGIC AND POWER OF THIS REALM COME FROM SOMETHING LARGER THAN OURSELVES. YOU AND I ARE STRONG AND IMPORTANT BECAUSE WE'RE SYMBOLS --
WE'RE THE PLAYING PIECES IN THIS GAME, NOT THE PLAYERS.
Oh. WELL, Uh...
IF YOU SHOULD CHANGE YOUR MIND...
-- I'LL SEND WORD TO YOU AT ONCE, I PROMISE.
AND AUBERON..?
WHEN ONE IS TRULY A KING, ONE NEEDN'T WORRY ABOUT REMINDING OTHERS OF THE FACT.
YOU MIGHT SAFELY DISPENSE WITH THE "WE."
Oh, YES INDEED...
"YOUR MAJESTY" MIGHT SAFELY DISPENSE WITH ALL THE TRAPPINGS OF ROYALTY -- VERY SOON.

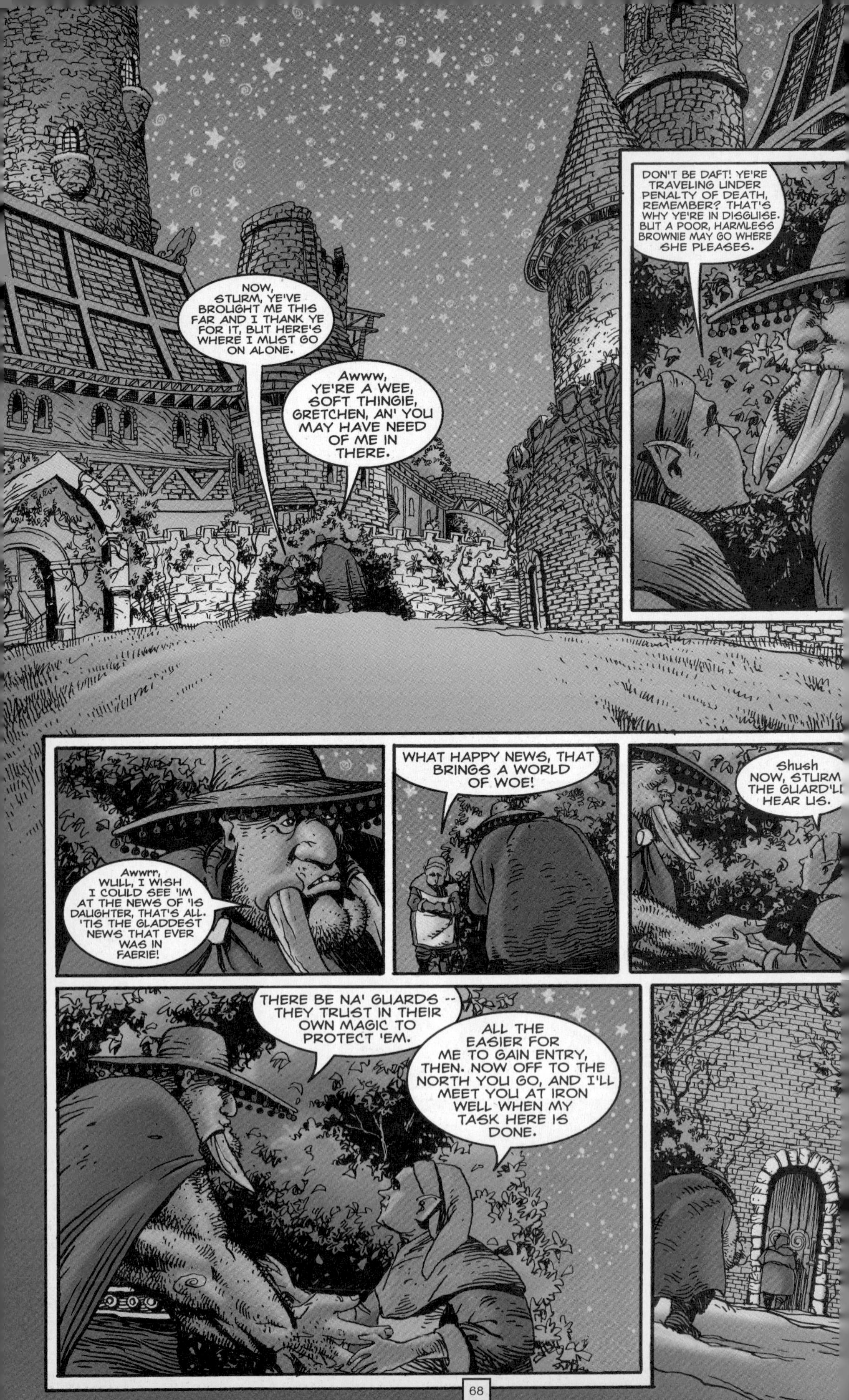
NOW, STURM, YE'VE BROUGHT ME THIS FAR AND I THANK YE FOR IT, BUT HERE'S WHERE I MUST GO ON ALONE.
Awww, YE'RE A WEE, SOFT THINGIE, GRETCHEN, AN' YOU MAY HAVE NEED OF ME IN THERE.
DON'T BE DAFT! YE'RE TRAVELING UNDER PENALTY OF DEATH, REMEMBER? THAT'S WHY YE'RE IN DISGUISE. BUT A POOR, HARMLESS BROWNIE MAY GO WHERE SHE PLEASES.
Awwrr, WULL, I WISH I COULD SEE 'IM AT THE NEWS OF 'IS DAUGHTER, THAT'S ALL. 'TIS THE GLADDEST NEWS THAT EVER WAS IN FAERIE!
WHAT HAPPY NEWS, THAT BRINGS A WORLD OF WOE!
Shush NOW, STURM THE GUARD'LL HEAR US.
THERE BE NA' GUARDS -- THEY TRUST IN THEIR OWN MAGIC TO PROTECT 'EM.
ALL THE EASIER FOR ME TO GAIN ENTRY, THEN. NOW OFF TO THE NORTH YOU GO, AND I'LL MEET YOU AT IRON WELL WHEN MY TASK HERE IS DONE.

WHO'S THERE?

JUST A POOR, WEE BROWNIE SEEKING HOSPITALITY ON THIS DARK NIGHT.

Oh, A *BROWNIE*, ARE YOU? THERE'S A HOVEL FOR BROWNIES DOWN THERE BY THE STABLES -- GO SEEK YOUR HOSPITALITY THERE.

PLEASE, YOUR LORDSHIP, I HAVE NEWS FROM THE NORTH THAT I WOULD TRADE FOR A BIT OF FOOD AND A BED INDOORS.

WHAT NEWS?

IT CONCERNS THE LORD GRIMWAR--THE PRETENDER, AS SOME CALL HIM.

BE OFF WITH YOU, THEN! GRIMWAR HAS NO NEED OF NEWS --

-- NOW THAT HE'S *DEAD.*

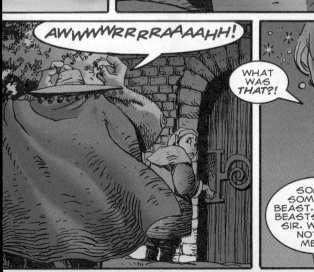

AWWWRRRRAAAAHH!

WHAT WAS *THAT*?!

SOME -- SOME WILD BEAST. THERE'S BEASTS ABOUT, SIR. WILL YOU NOT LET ME IN?

I'VE TOLD YOU WHERE TO GO. BE OFF WITH YOU, BROWNIE, BEFORE YOU COME TO HARM!

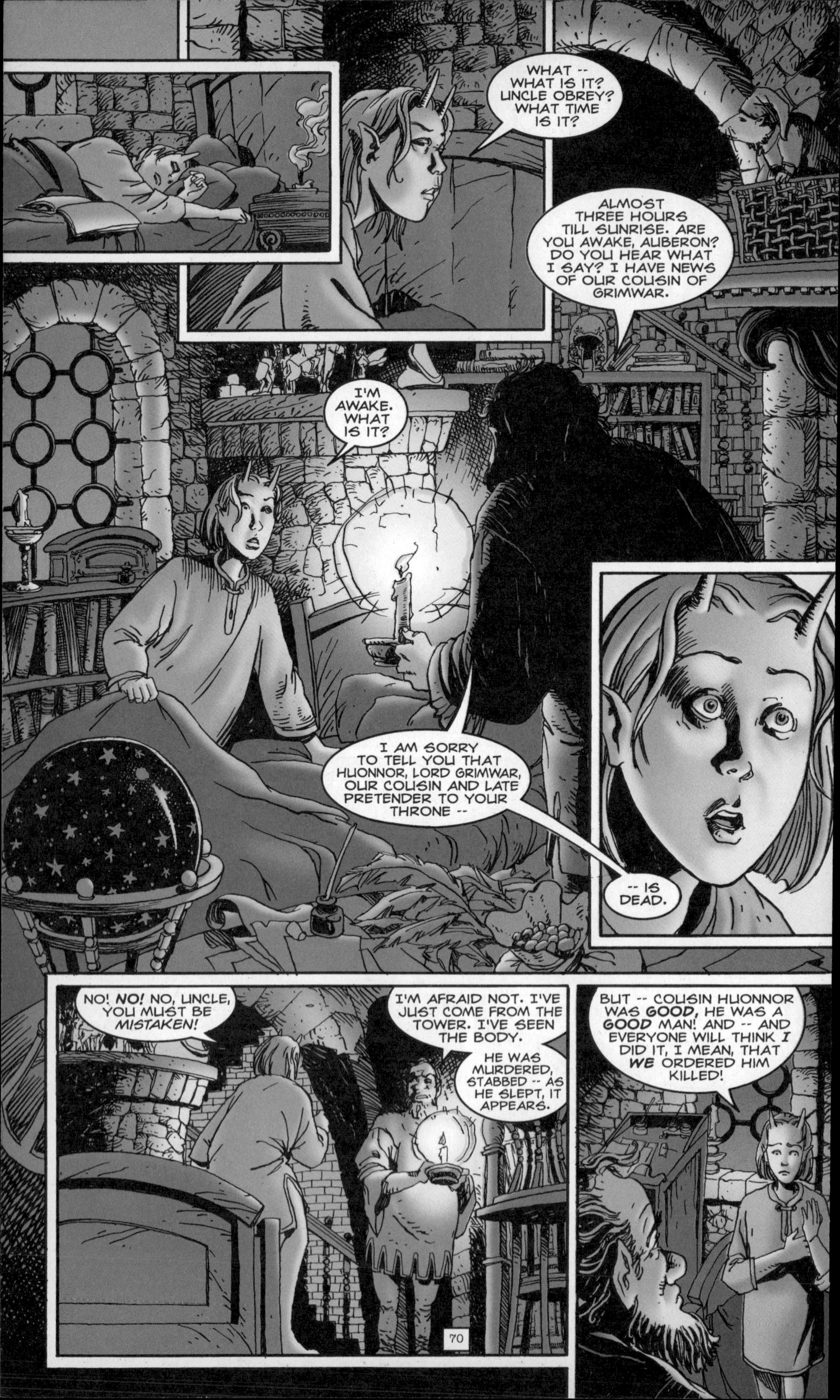
WHAT -- WHAT IS IT? UNCLE OBREY? WHAT TIME IS IT?
ALMOST THREE HOURS TILL SUNRISE. ARE YOU AWAKE, AUBERON? DO YOU HEAR WHAT I SAY? I HAVE NEWS OF OUR COUSIN OF GRIMWAR.
I'M AWAKE. WHAT IS IT?
I AM SORRY TO TELL YOU THAT HUONNOR, LORD GRIMWAR, OUR COUSIN AND LATE PRETENDER TO YOUR THRONE --
-- IS DEAD.
NO! **NO!** NO, UNCLE, YOU MUST BE *MISTAKEN!*
I'M AFRAID NOT. I'VE JUST COME FROM THE TOWER. I'VE SEEN THE BODY.
HE WAS MURDERED, STABBED -- AS HE SLEPT, IT APPEARS.
BUT -- COUSIN HUONNOR WAS **GOOD,** HE WAS A **GOOD** MAN! AND -- AND EVERYONE WILL THINK ***I*** DID IT, I MEAN, THAT ***WE*** ORDERED HIM KILLED!

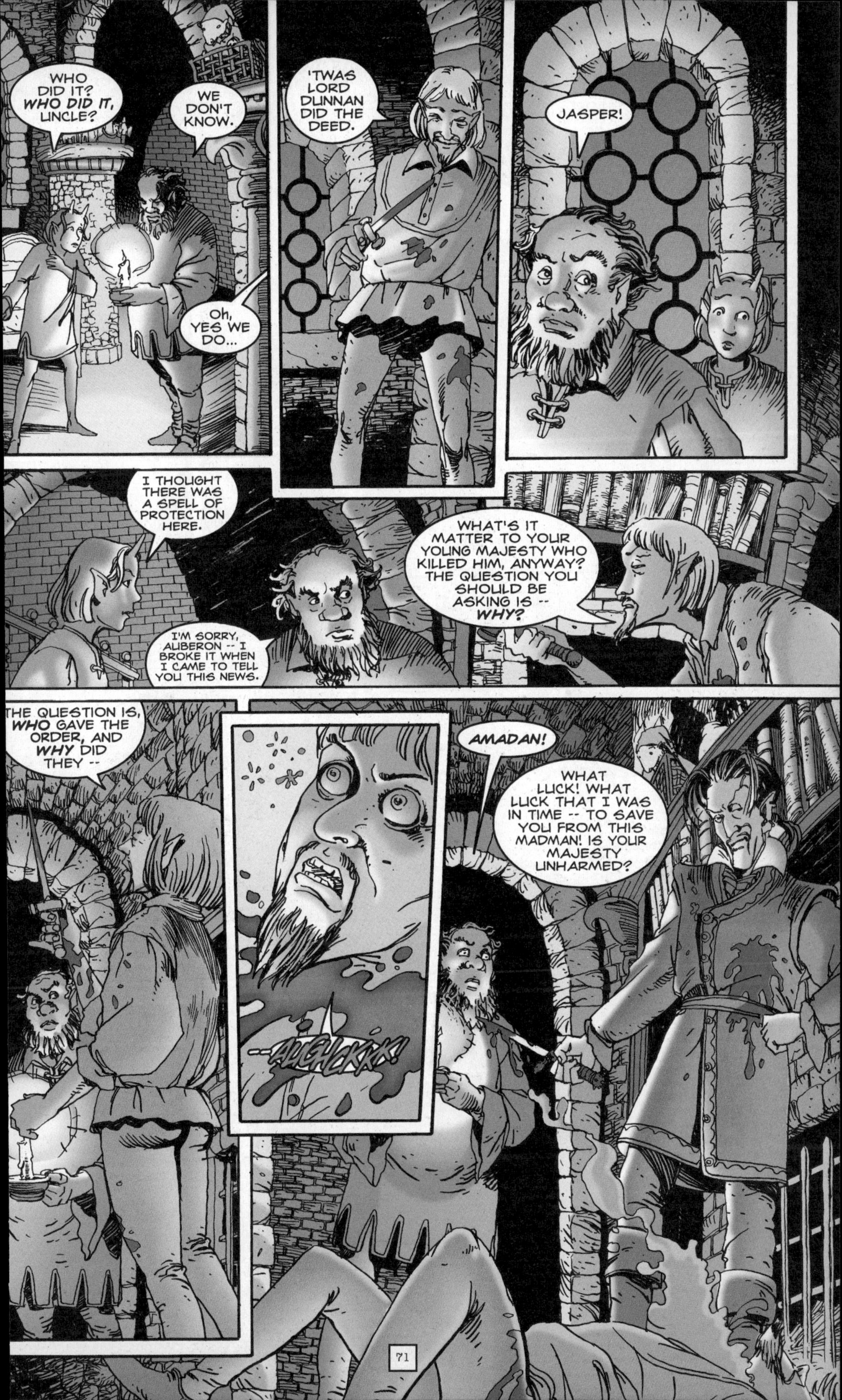
WHO DID IT? *WHO DID IT*, UNCLE?
WE DON'T KNOW.
Oh, YES WE DO...
'TWAS LORD DUNNAN DID THE DEED.
JASPER!
I THOUGHT THERE WAS A SPELL OF PROTECTION HERE.
I'M SORRY, AUBERON -- I BROKE IT WHEN I CAME TO TELL YOU THIS NEWS.
WHAT'S IT MATTER TO YOUR YOUNG MAJESTY WHO KILLED HIM, ANYWAY? THE QUESTION YOU SHOULD BE ASKING IS -- *WHY?*
THE QUESTION IS, *WHO* GAVE THE ORDER, AND *WHY* DID THEY --
--AUGHCKKK!
AMADAN!
WHAT LUCK! WHAT LUCK THAT I WAS IN TIME -- TO SAVE YOU FROM THIS MADMAN! IS YOUR MAJESTY UNHARMED?

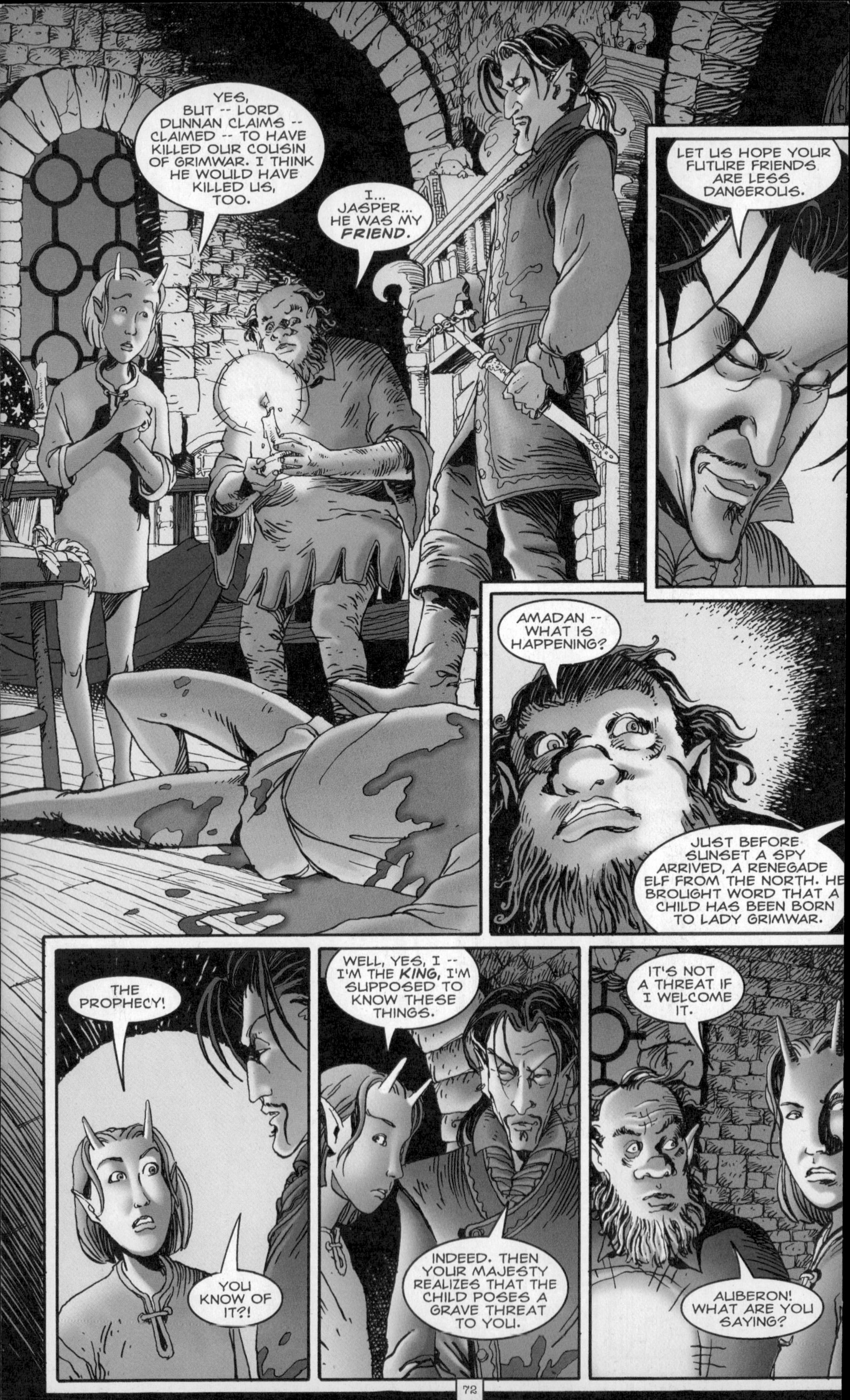
YES, BUT -- LORD DUNNAN CLAIMS -- CLAIMED -- TO HAVE KILLED OUR COUSIN OF GRIMWAR. I THINK HE WOULD HAVE KILLED US, TOO.
I... JASPER... HE WAS MY FRIEND.
LET US HOPE YOUR FUTURE FRIENDS ARE LESS DANGEROUS.
AMADAN -- WHAT IS HAPPENING?
JUST BEFORE SUNSET A SPY ARRIVED, A RENEGADE ELF FROM THE NORTH. HE BROUGHT WORD THAT A CHILD HAS BEEN BORN TO LADY GRIMWAR.
THE PROPHECY!
YOU KNOW OF IT?!
WELL, YES, I -- I'M THE KING, I'M SUPPOSED TO KNOW THESE THINGS.
INDEED. THEN YOUR MAJESTY REALIZES THAT THE CHILD POSES A GRAVE THREAT TO YOU.
IT'S NOT A THREAT IF I WELCOME IT.
AUBERON! WHAT ARE YOU SAYING?

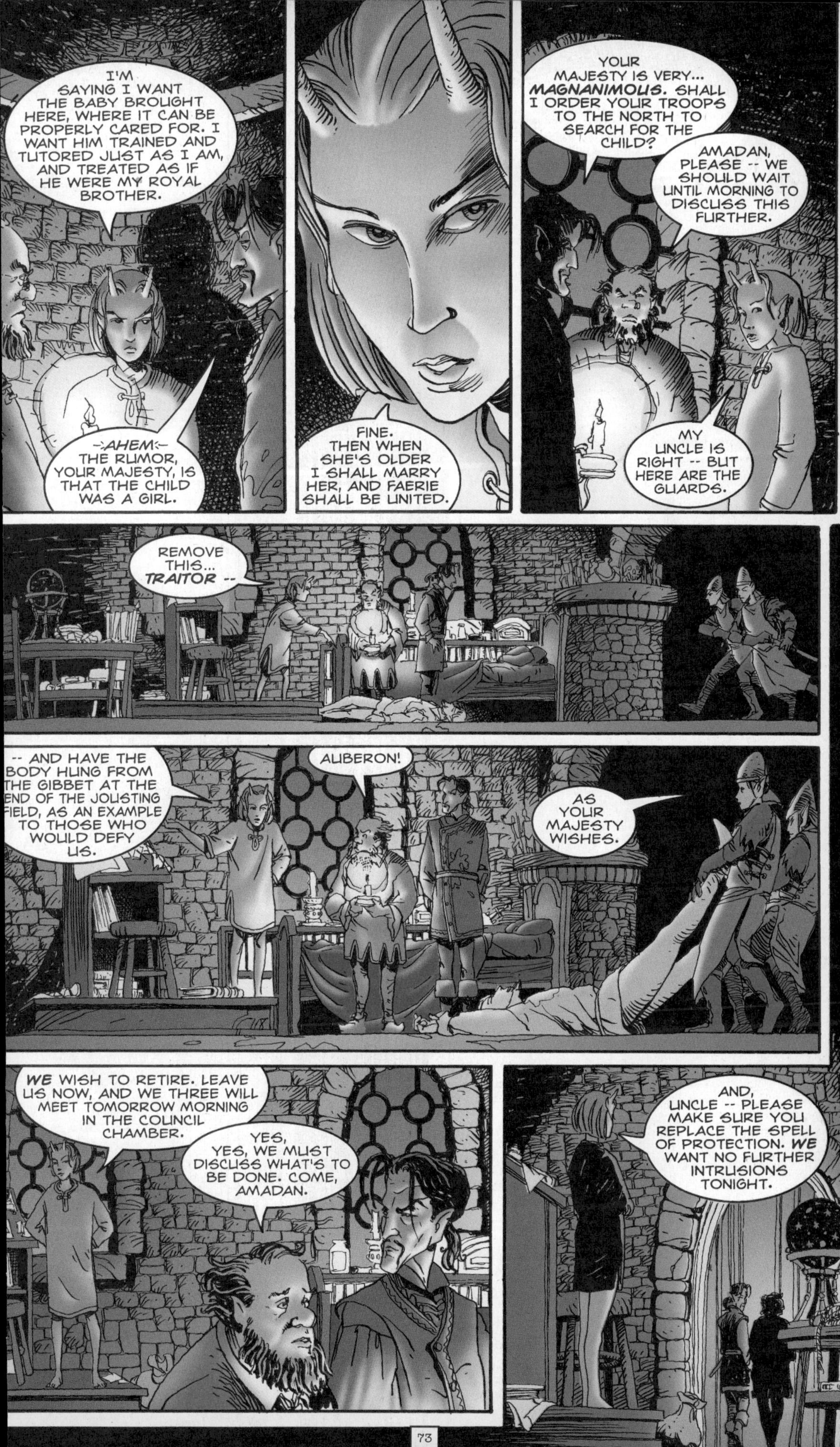
I'M SAYING I WANT THE BABY BROUGHT HERE, WHERE IT CAN BE PROPERLY CARED FOR. I WANT HIM TRAINED AND TUTORED JUST AS I AM, AND TREATED AS IF HE WERE MY ROYAL BROTHER.
-AHEM- THE RUMOR, YOUR MAJESTY, IS THAT THE CHILD WAS A GIRL.
FINE. THEN WHEN SHE'S OLDER I SHALL MARRY HER, AND FAERIE SHALL BE UNITED.
YOUR MAJESTY IS VERY... MAGNANIMOUS. SHALL I ORDER YOUR TROOPS TO THE NORTH TO SEARCH FOR THE CHILD?
AMADAN, PLEASE -- WE SHOULD WAIT UNTIL MORNING TO DISCUSS THIS FURTHER.
MY UNCLE IS RIGHT -- BUT HERE ARE THE GUARDS.
REMOVE THIS... TRAITOR --
-- AND HAVE THE BODY HUNG FROM THE GIBBET AT THE END OF THE JOUSTING FIELD, AS AN EXAMPLE TO THOSE WHO WOULD DEFY US.
AUBERON!
AS YOUR MAJESTY WISHES.
WE WISH TO RETIRE. LEAVE US NOW, AND WE THREE WILL MEET TOMORROW MORNING IN THE COUNCIL CHAMBER.
YES, YES, WE MUST DISCUSS WHAT'S TO BE DONE. COME, AMADAN.
AND, UNCLE -- PLEASE MAKE SURE YOU REPLACE THE SPELL OF PROTECTION. WE WANT NO FURTHER INTRUSIONS TONIGHT.

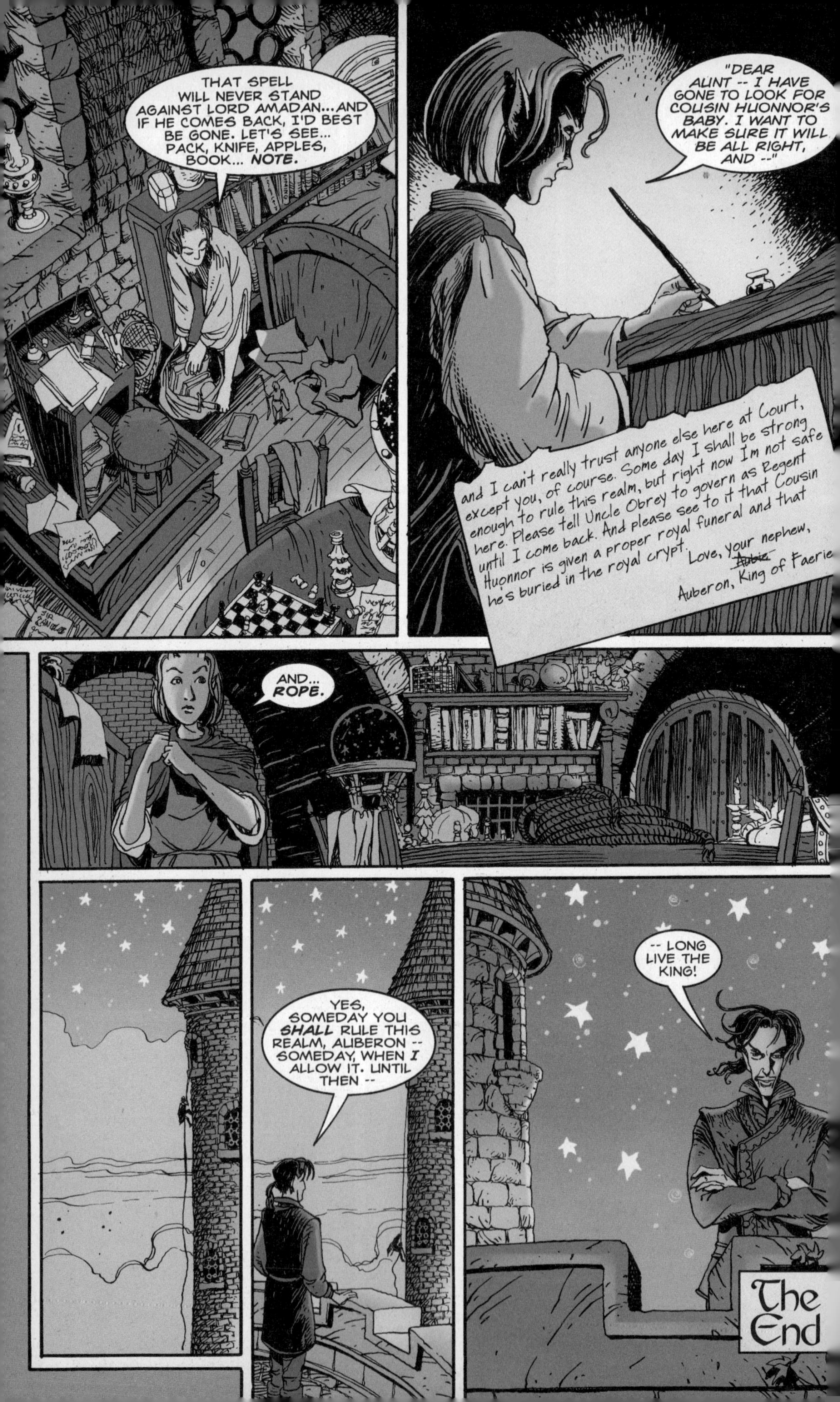
THAT SPELL WILL NEVER STAND AGAINST LORD AMADAN... AND IF HE COMES BACK, I'D BEST BE GONE. LET'S SEE... PACK, KNIFE, APPLES, BOOK... NOTE.
"DEAR AUNT -- I HAVE GONE TO LOOK FOR COUSIN HUONNOR'S BABY. I WANT TO MAKE SURE IT WILL BE ALL RIGHT, AND --"
and I can't really trust anyone else here at Court, except you, of course. Some day I shall be strong enough to rule this realm, but right now I'm not safe here. Please tell Uncle Obrey to govern as Regent until I come back. And please see to it that Cousin Huonnor is given a proper royal funeral and that he's buried in the royal crypt.
Love, your nephew, ~~Aubie~~
Auberon, King of Faerie
AND... ROPE.
YES, SOMEDAY YOU SHALL RULE THIS REALM, AUBERON -- SOMEDAY, WHEN I ALLOW IT. UNTIL THEN --
-- LONG LIVE THE KING!
The End

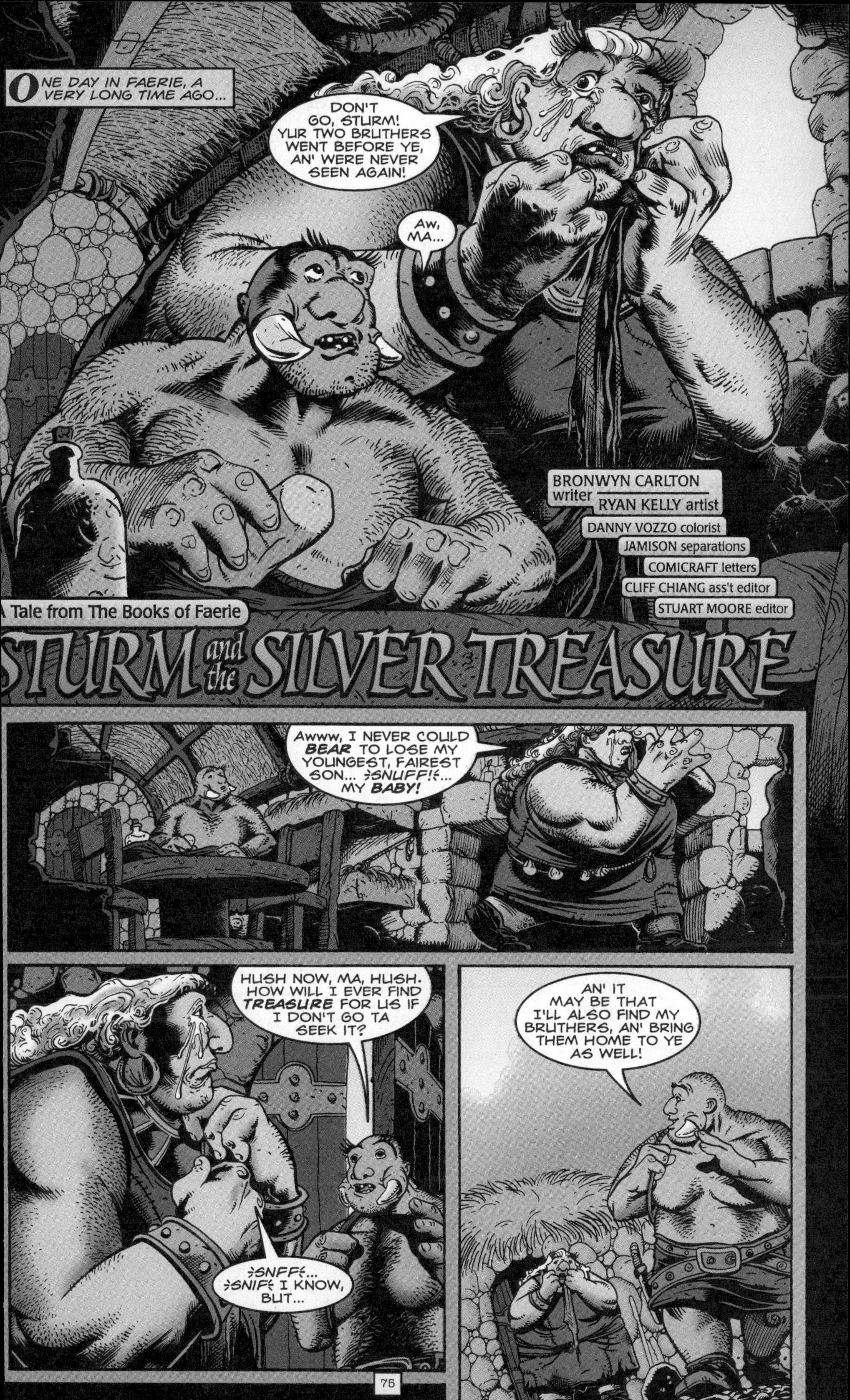

ONE DAY IN FAERIE, A VERY LONG TIME AGO...
DON'T GO, STURM! YUR TWO BRUTHERS WENT BEFORE YE, AN' WERE NEVER SEEN AGAIN!
AW, MA...
BRONWYN CARLTON writer
RYAN KELLY artist
DANNY VOZZO colorist
JAMISON separations
COMICRAFT letters
CLIFF CHIANG ass't editor
STUART MOORE editor
A Tale from The Books of Faerie
STURM and the SILVER TREASURE
AWWW, I NEVER COULD BEAR TO LOSE MY YOUNGEST, FAIREST SON... ≈SNUFF!≈... MY BABY!
HUSH NOW, MA, HUSH. HOW WILL I EVER FIND TREASURE FOR US IF I DON'T GO TA SEEK IT?
≈SNFF≈... ≈SNIF≈ I KNOW, BUT...
AN' IT MAY BE THAT I'LL ALSO FIND MY BRUTHERS, AN' BRING THEM HOME TO YE AS WELL!

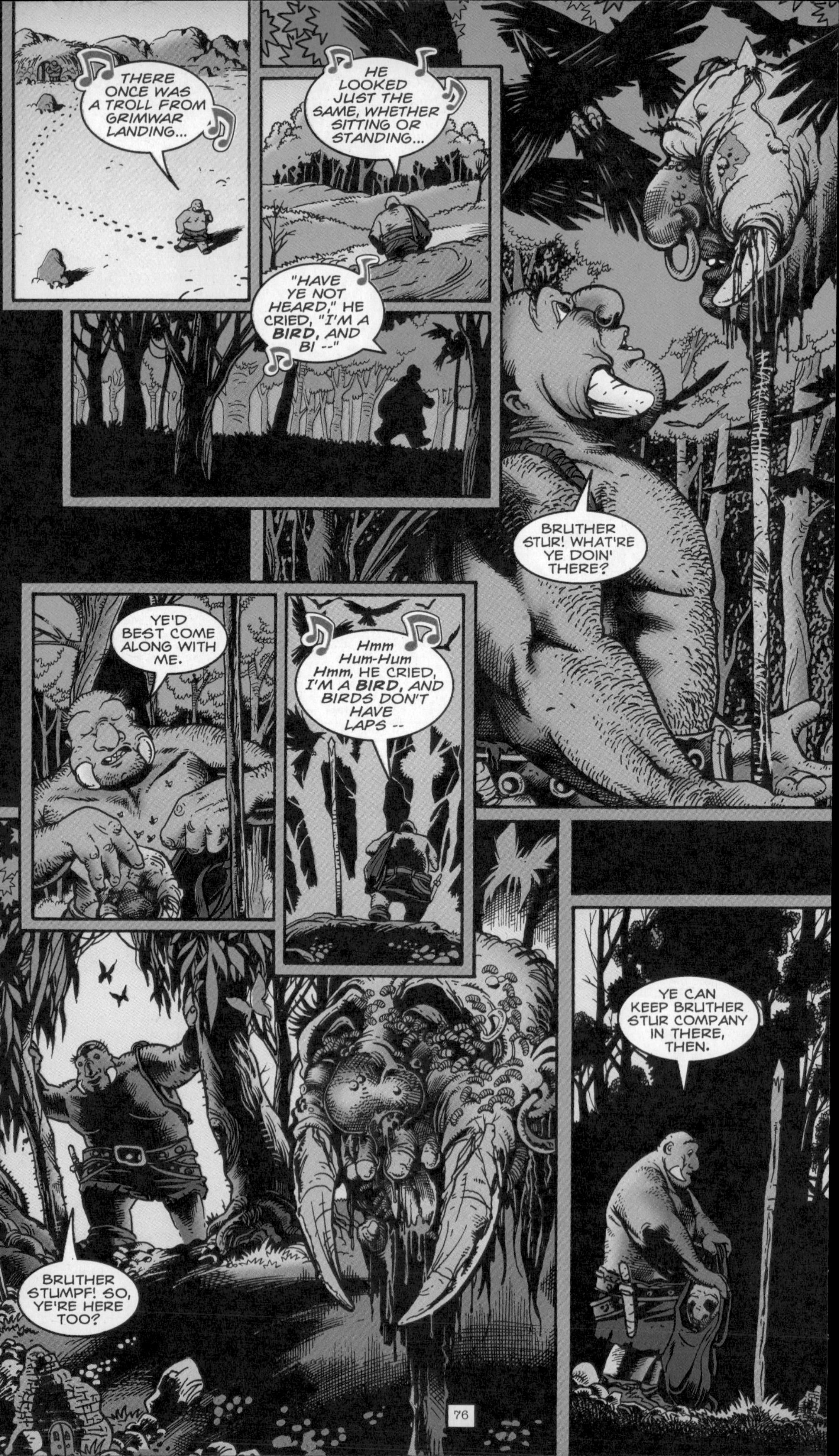

THERE ONCE WAS A TROLL FROM GRIMWAR LANDING...
HE LOOKED JUST THE SAME, WHETHER SITTING OR STANDING...
"HAVE YE NOT HEARD," HE CRIED, "I'M A BIRD, AND BI --"
BRUTHER STUR! WHAT'RE YE DOIN' THERE?
YE'D BEST COME ALONG WITH ME.
Hmm Hum-Hum Hmm, HE CRIED, I'M A BIRD, AND BIRDS DON'T HAVE LAPS --
BRUTHER STUMPF! SO, YE'RE HERE TOO?
YE CAN KEEP BRUTHER STUR COMPANY IN THERE, THEN.

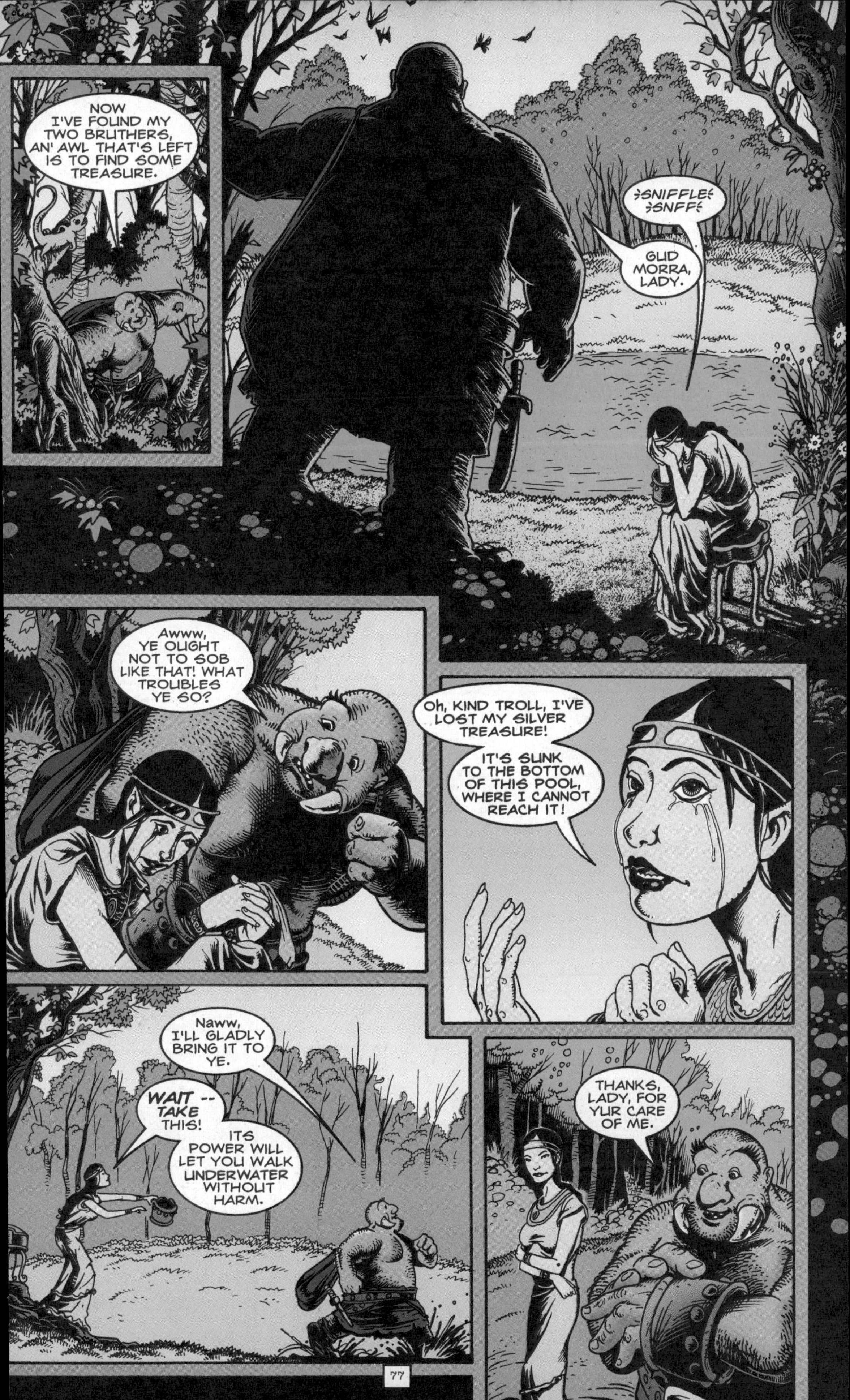
NOW I'VE FOUND MY TWO BRUTHERS, AN' AWL THAT'S LEFT IS TO FIND SOME TREASURE.
SNIFFLE SNFF
GUD MORRA, LADY.
Awww, YE OUGHT NOT TO SOB LIKE THAT! WHAT TROUBLES YE SO?
Oh, KIND TROLL, I'VE LOST MY SILVER TREASURE!
IT'S SUNK TO THE BOTTOM OF THIS POOL, WHERE I CANNOT REACH IT!
Naww, I'LL GLADLY BRING IT TO YE.
WAIT -- TAKE THIS!
ITS POWER WILL LET YOU WALK UNDERWATER WITHOUT HARM.
THANKS, LADY, FOR YUR CARE OF ME.

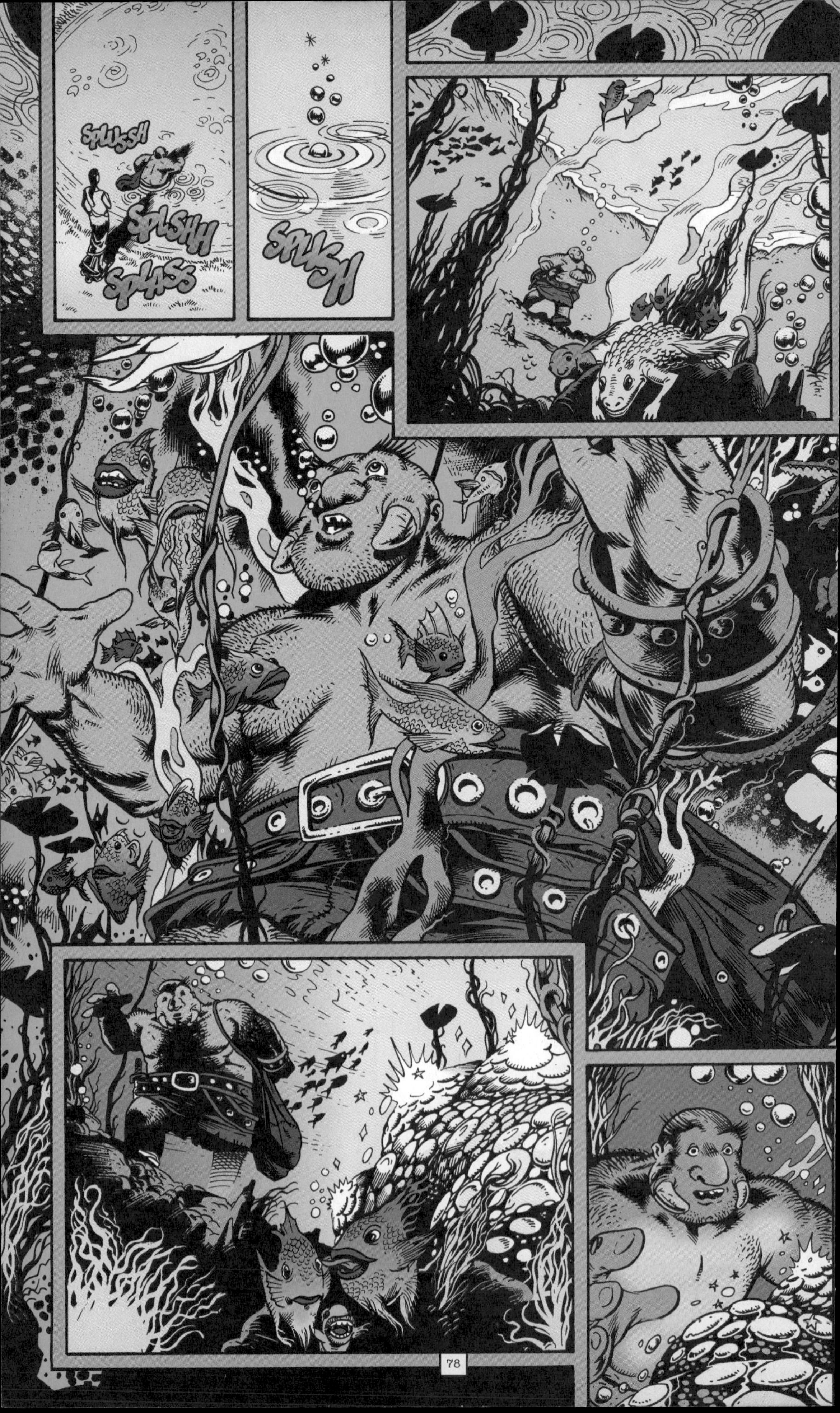
SPLUSSH
SPLSHH
SPLASS
SPLUSH

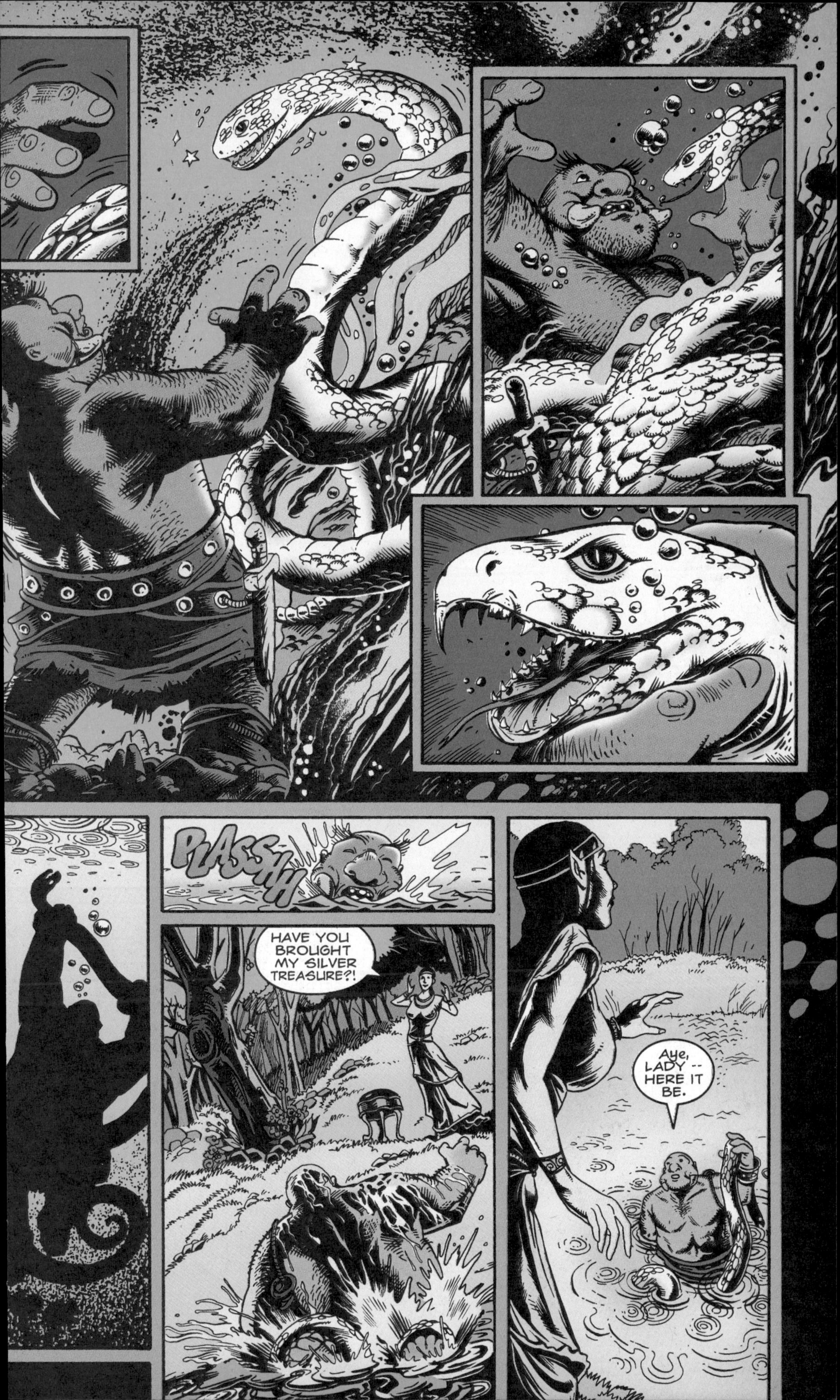
PLASSHH
HAVE YOU BROUGHT MY SILVER TREASURE?!
Aye, LADY -- HERE IT BE.

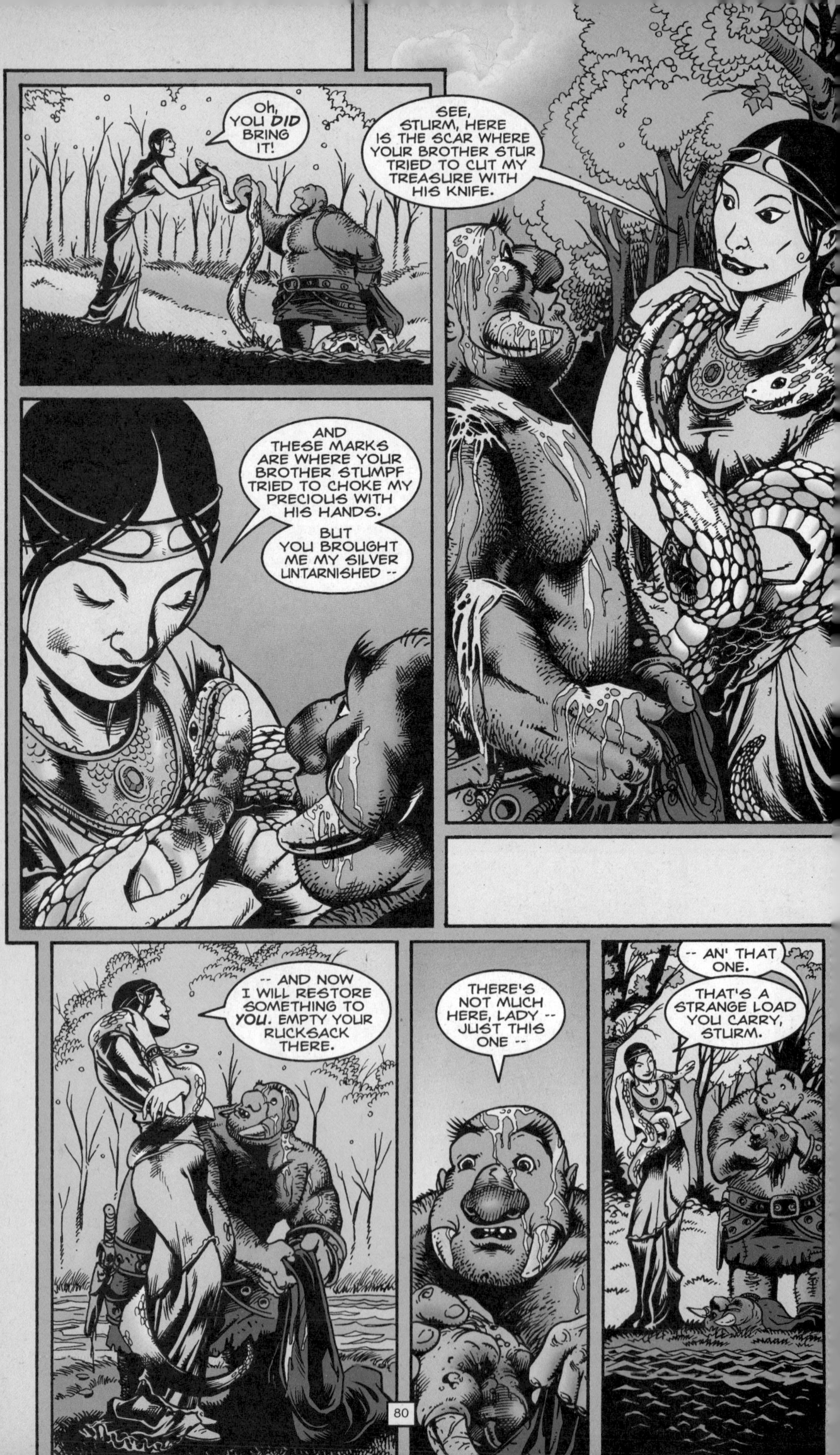
Oh, YOU DID BRING IT!
SEE, STURM, HERE IS THE SCAR WHERE YOUR BROTHER STUR TRIED TO CUT MY TREASURE WITH HIS KNIFE.
AND THESE MARKS ARE WHERE YOUR BROTHER STUMPF TRIED TO CHOKE MY PRECIOUS WITH HIS HANDS.
BUT YOU BROUGHT ME MY SILVER UNTARNISHED --
-- AND NOW I WILL RESTORE SOMETHING TO YOU. EMPTY YOUR RUCKSACK THERE.
THERE'S NOT MUCH HERE, LADY -- JUST THIS ONE --
-- AN' THAT ONE.
THAT'S A STRANGE LOAD YOU CARRY, STURM.

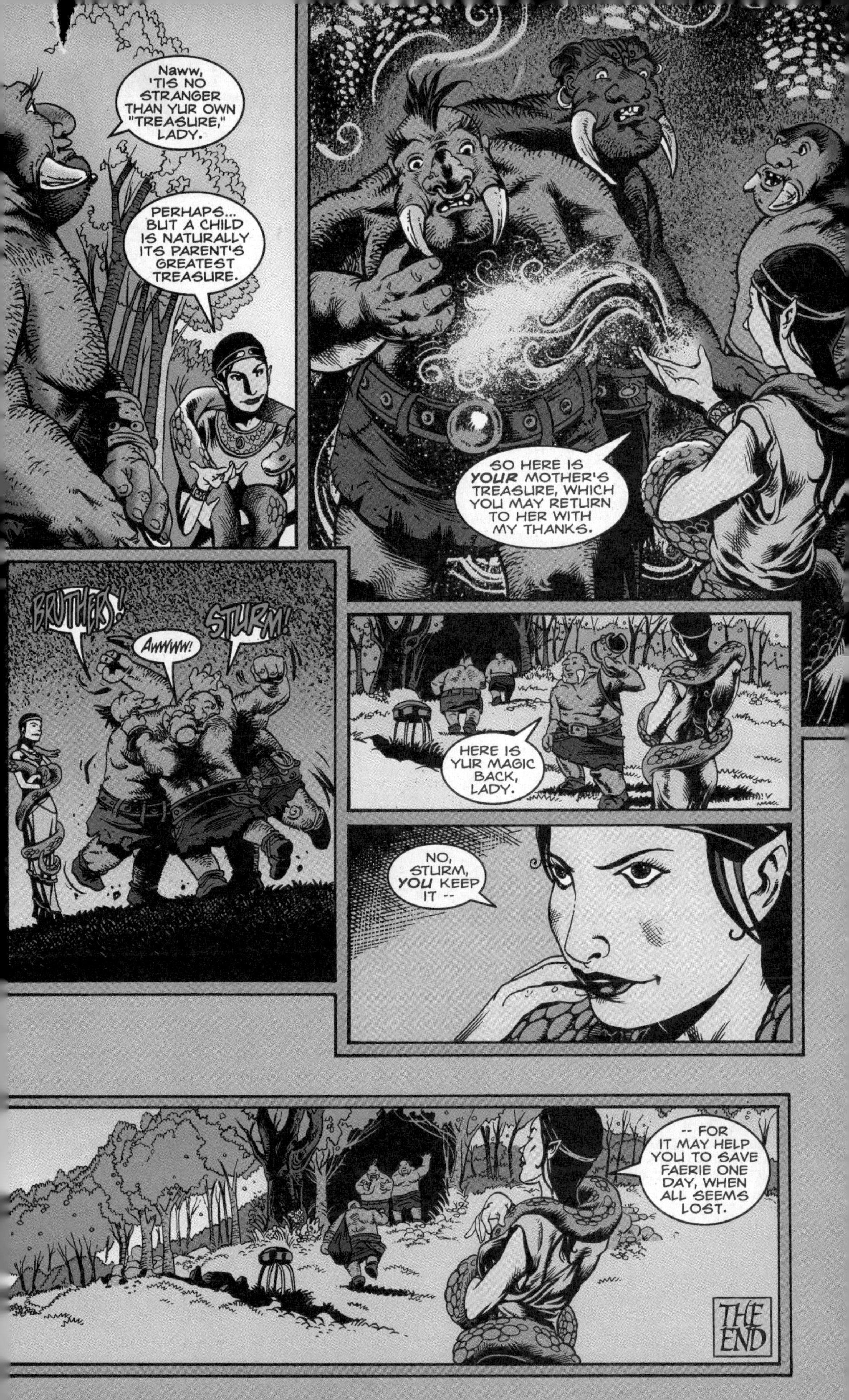
Naww, 'TIS NO STRANGER THAN YUR OWN "TREASURE," LADY.
PERHAPS... BUT A CHILD IS NATURALLY ITS PARENT'S GREATEST TREASURE.
SO HERE IS YOUR MOTHER'S TREASURE, WHICH YOU MAY RETURN TO HER WITH MY THANKS.
BRUTHERS!
AWWWW!
STURM!
HERE IS YUR MAGIC BACK, LADY.
NO, STURM, YOU KEEP IT --
-- FOR IT MAY HELP YOU TO SAVE FAERIE ONE DAY, WHEN ALL SEEMS LOST.
THE END

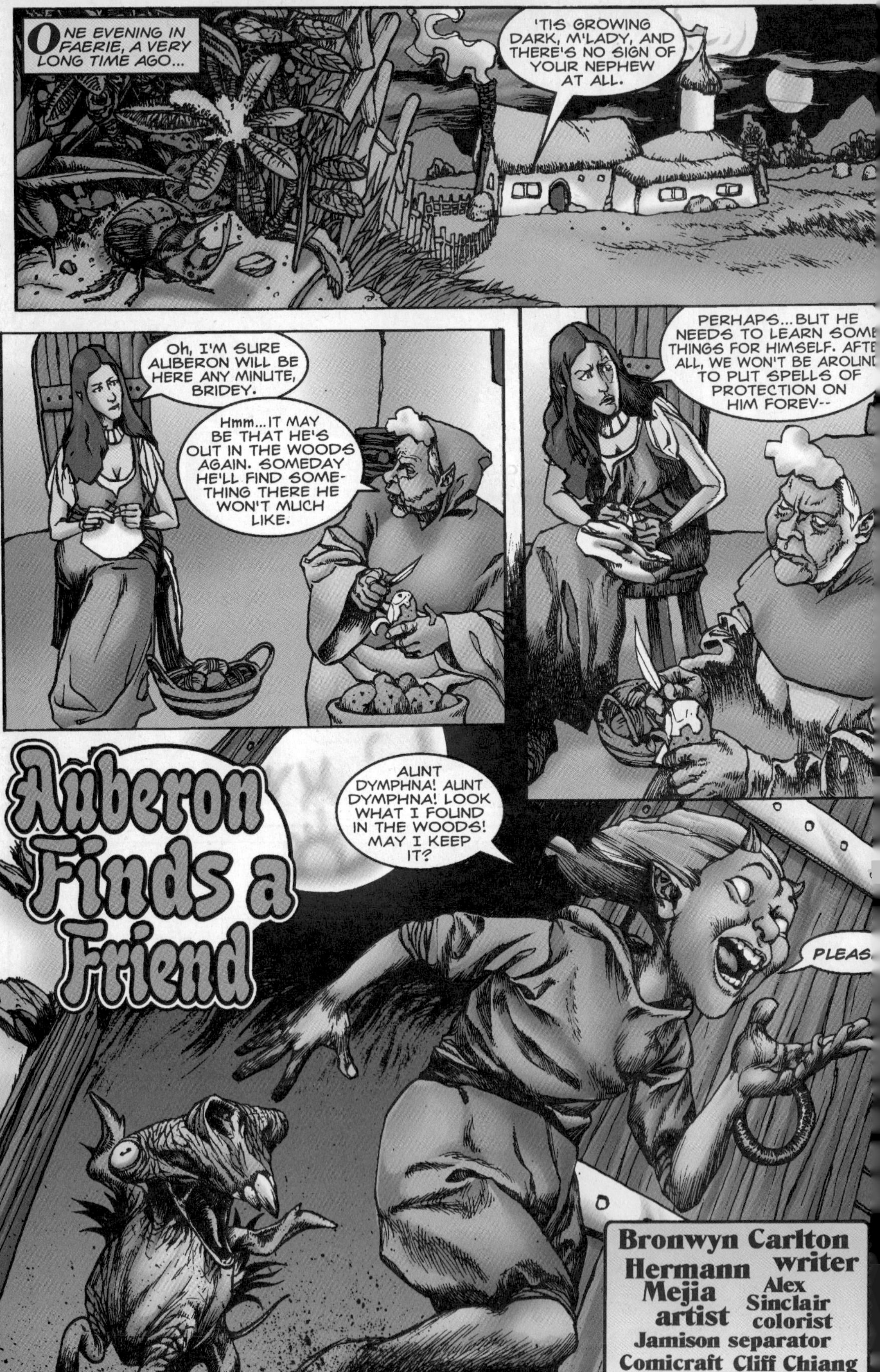
ONE EVENING IN FAERIE, A VERY LONG TIME AGO...
'TIS GROWING DARK, M'LADY, AND THERE'S NO SIGN OF YOUR NEPHEW AT ALL.
Oh, I'M SURE AUBERON WILL BE HERE ANY MINUTE, BRIDEY.
Hmm... IT MAY BE THAT HE'S OUT IN THE WOODS AGAIN. SOMEDAY HE'LL FIND SOMETHING THERE HE WON'T MUCH LIKE.
PERHAPS... BUT HE NEEDS TO LEARN SOME THINGS FOR HIMSELF. AFTE ALL, WE WON'T BE AROUND TO PUT SPELLS OF PROTECTION ON HIM FOREV--
Auberon Finds a Friend
AUNT DYMPHNA! AUNT DYMPHNA! LOOK WHAT I FOUND IN THE WOODS! MAY I KEEP IT?
PLEAS
Bronwyn Carlton writer
Hermann Mejia artist
Alex Sinclair colorist
Jamison separator
Comicraft letters
Cliff Chiang ass't editor
Stuart Moore editor

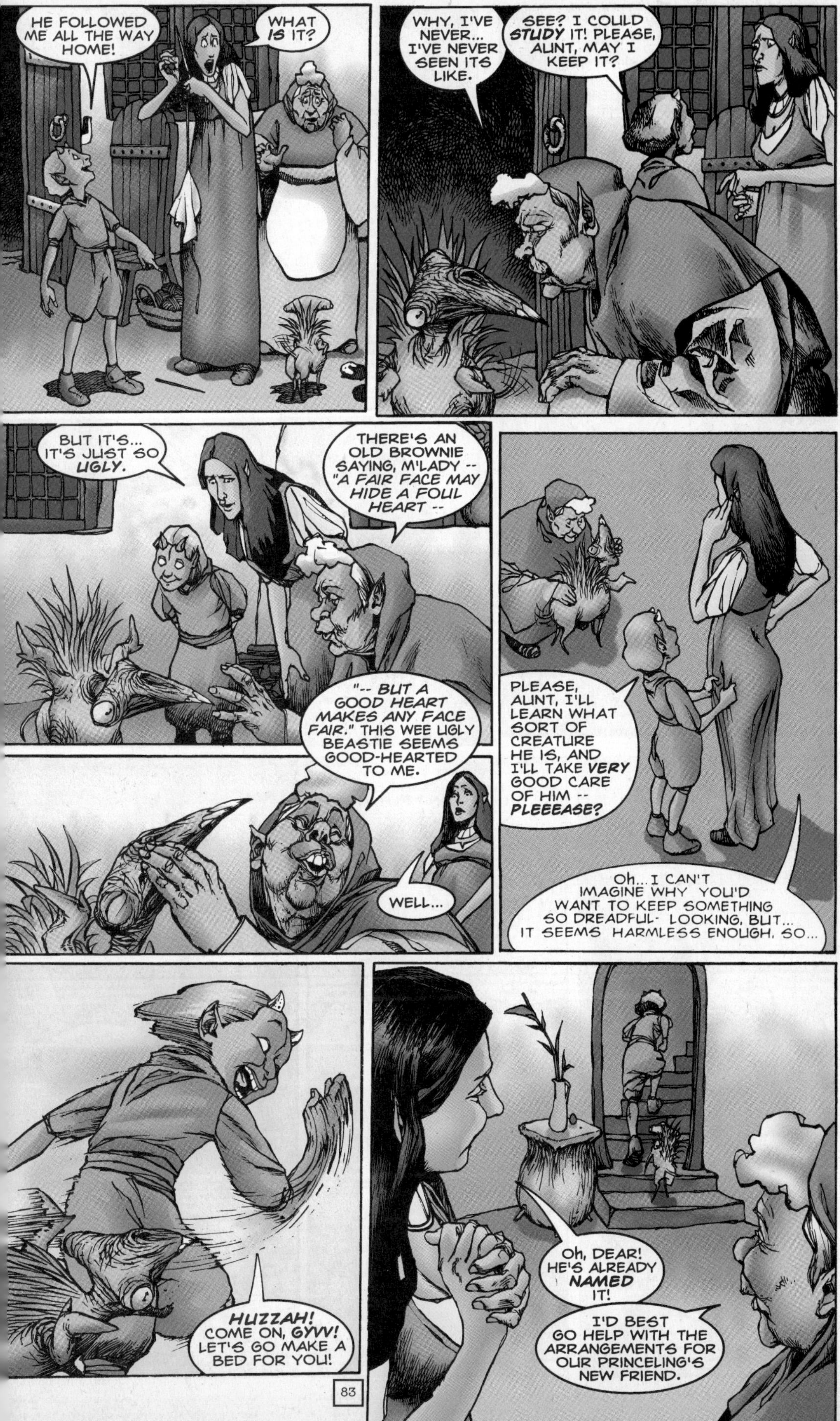

HE FOLLOWED ME ALL THE WAY HOME!
WHAT IS IT?
WHY, I'VE NEVER... I'VE NEVER SEEN ITS LIKE.
SEE? I COULD STUDY IT! PLEASE, AUNT, MAY I KEEP IT?
BUT IT'S... IT'S JUST SO UGLY.
THERE'S AN OLD BROWNIE SAYING, M'LADY -- "A FAIR FACE MAY HIDE A FOUL HEART --
"-- BUT A GOOD HEART MAKES ANY FACE FAIR." THIS WEE UGLY BEASTIE SEEMS GOOD-HEARTED TO ME.
WELL...
PLEASE, AUNT, I'LL LEARN WHAT SORT OF CREATURE HE IS, AND I'LL TAKE VERY GOOD CARE OF HIM -- PLEEEASE?
Oh... I CAN'T IMAGINE WHY YOU'D WANT TO KEEP SOMETHING SO DREADFUL- LOOKING, BUT... IT SEEMS HARMLESS ENOUGH, SO...
HUZZAH! COME ON, GYVV! LET'S GO MAKE A BED FOR YOU!
Oh, DEAR! HE'S ALREADY NAMED IT!
I'D BEST GO HELP WITH THE ARRANGEMENTS FOR OUR PRINCELING'S NEW FRIEND.

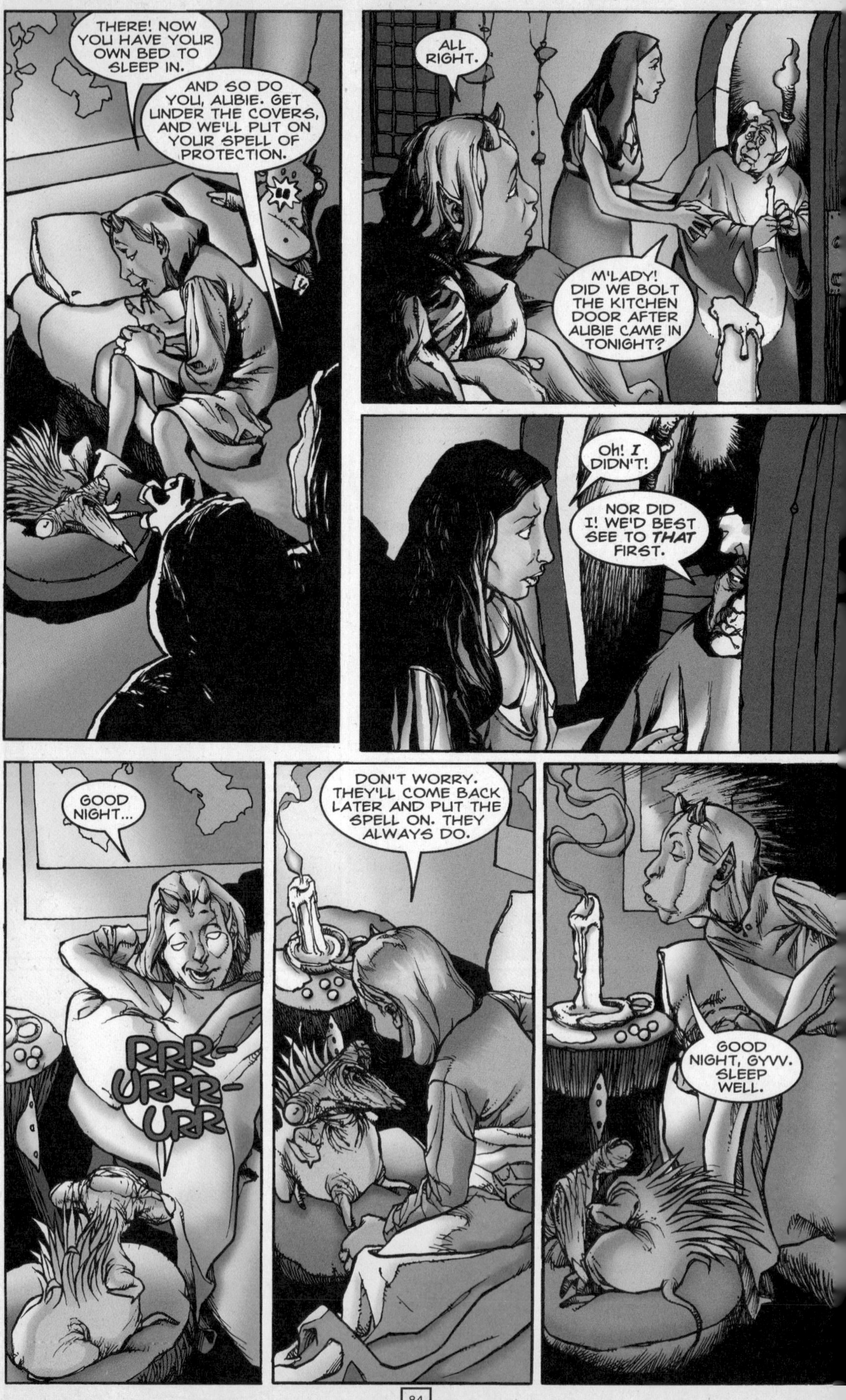
THERE! NOW YOU HAVE YOUR OWN BED TO SLEEP IN.
AND SO DO YOU, ALBIE. GET UNDER THE COVERS, AND WE'LL PUT ON YOUR SPELL OF PROTECTION.
ALL RIGHT.
M'LADY! DID WE BOLT THE KITCHEN DOOR AFTER ALBIE CAME IN TONIGHT?
Oh! I DIDN'T!
NOR DID I! WE'D BEST SEE TO THAT FIRST.
GOOD NIGHT...
RRR-URRR-URR
DON'T WORRY. THEY'LL COME BACK LATER AND PUT THE SPELL ON. THEY ALWAYS DO.
GOOD NIGHT, GYVV. SLEEP WELL.

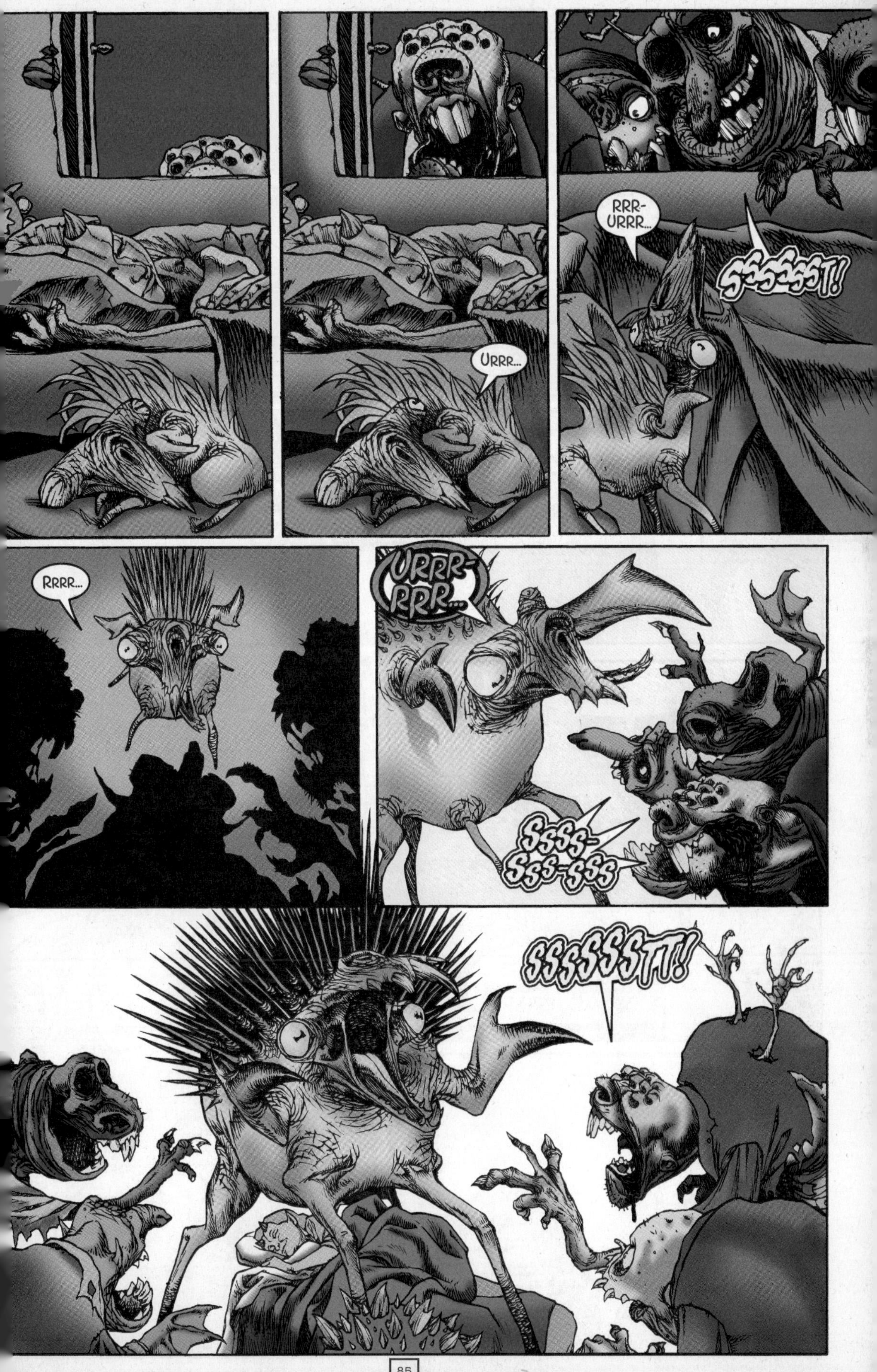
URRR...
RRR-
URRR...
SSSSSST!
RRRR...
URRR-
RRR...
SSSS-
SSS-SSS
SSSSSSTT!

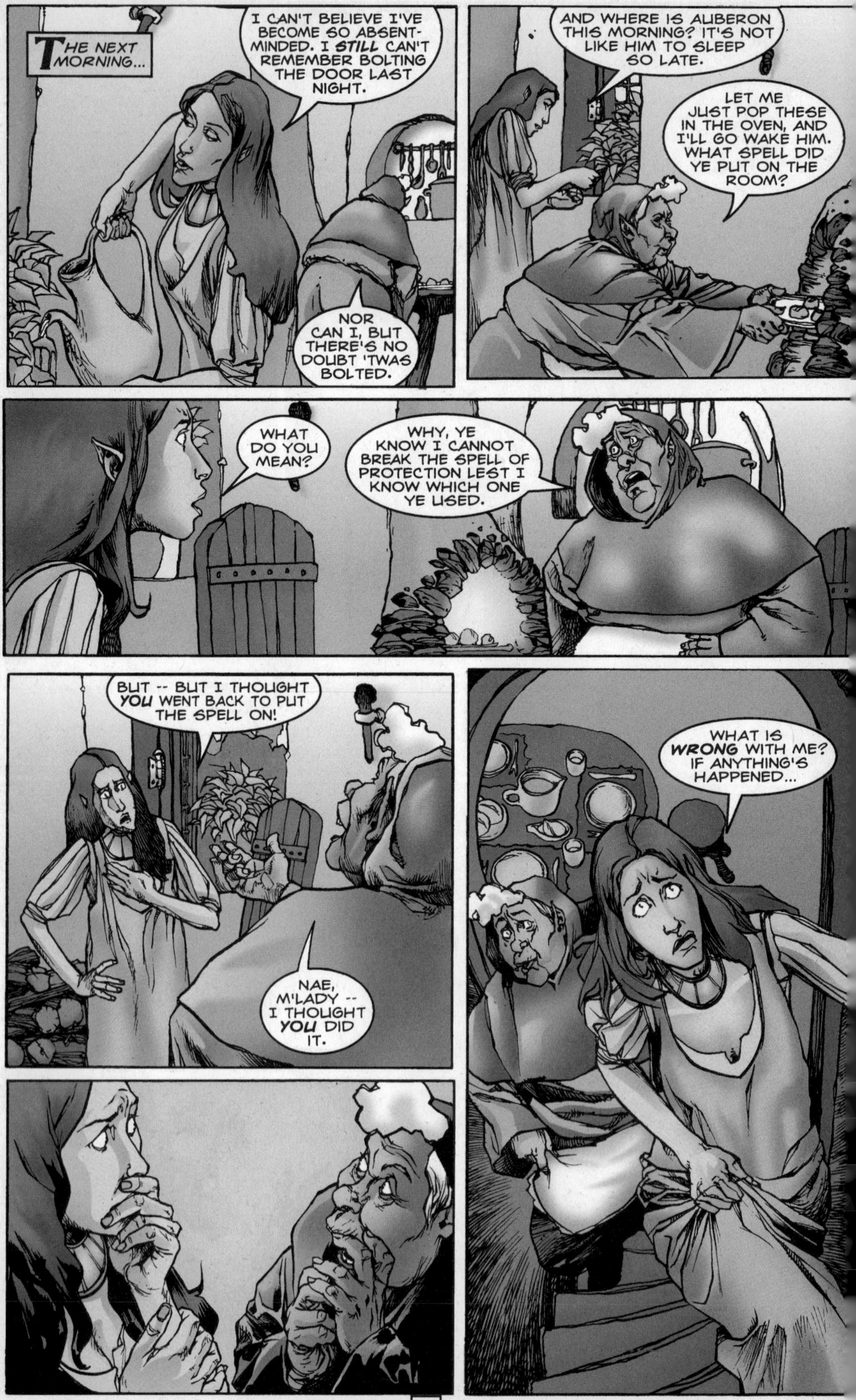
THE NEXT MORNING...
I CAN'T BELIEVE I'VE BECOME SO ABSENT-MINDED. I STILL CAN'T REMEMBER BOLTING THE DOOR LAST NIGHT.
NOR CAN I, BUT THERE'S NO DOUBT 'TWAS BOLTED.
AND WHERE IS AUBERON THIS MORNING? IT'S NOT LIKE HIM TO SLEEP SO LATE.
LET ME JUST POP THESE IN THE OVEN, AND I'LL GO WAKE HIM. WHAT SPELL DID YE PUT ON THE ROOM?
WHAT DO YOU MEAN?
WHY, YE KNOW I CANNOT BREAK THE SPELL OF PROTECTION LEST I KNOW WHICH ONE YE USED.
BUT -- BUT I THOUGHT YOU WENT BACK TO PUT THE SPELL ON!
NAE, M'LADY -- I THOUGHT YOU DID IT.
WHAT IS WRONG WITH ME? IF ANYTHING'S HAPPENED...

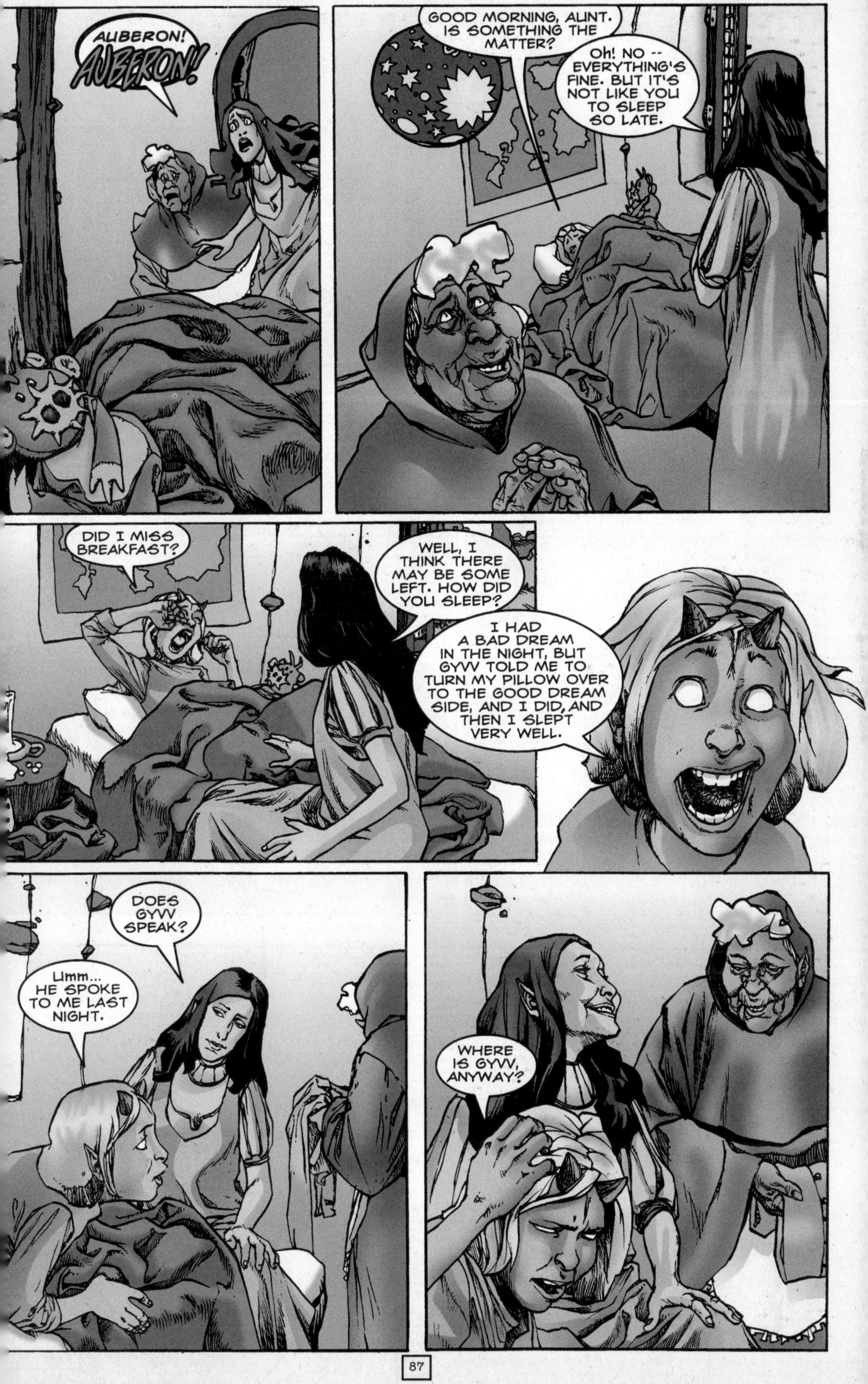
AUBERON!
AUBERON!
GOOD MORNING, AUNT. IS SOMETHING THE MATTER?
Oh! NO -- EVERYTHING'S FINE. BUT IT'S NOT LIKE YOU TO SLEEP SO LATE.
DID I MISS BREAKFAST?
WELL, I THINK THERE MAY BE SOME LEFT. HOW DID YOU SLEEP?
I HAD A BAD DREAM IN THE NIGHT, BUT GYVV TOLD ME TO TURN MY PILLOW OVER TO THE GOOD DREAM SIDE, AND I DID, AND THEN I SLEPT VERY WELL.
DOES GYVV SPEAK?
Umm... HE SPOKE TO ME LAST NIGHT.
WHERE IS GYVV, ANYWAY?

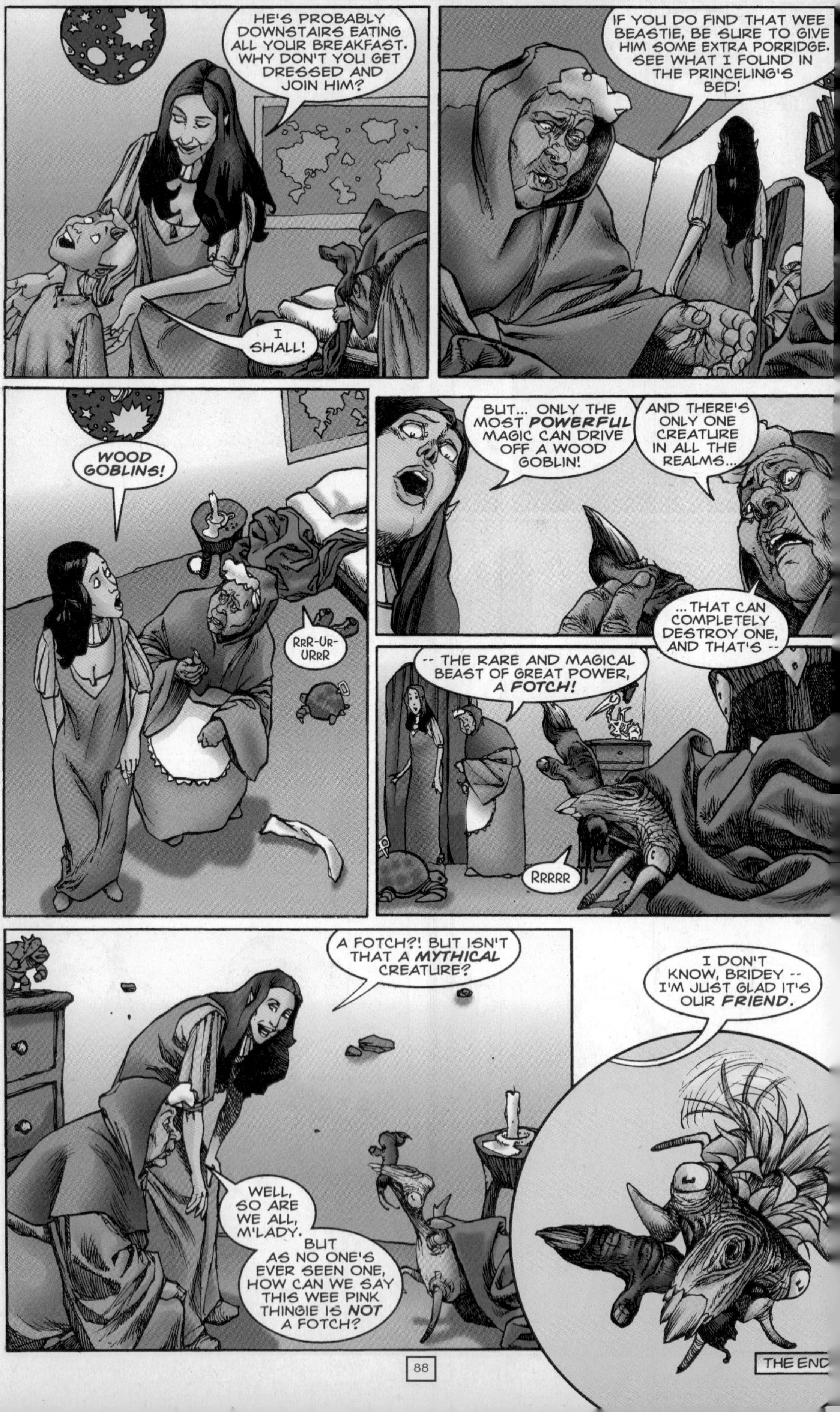

HE'S PROBABLY DOWNSTAIRS EATING ALL YOUR BREAKFAST. WHY DON'T YOU GET DRESSED AND JOIN HIM?
I SHALL!
IF YOU DO FIND THAT WEE BEASTIE, BE SURE TO GIVE HIM SOME EXTRA PORRIDGE. SEE WHAT I FOUND IN THE PRINCELING'S BED!
WOOD GOBLINS!
RRR-UR-URRR
BUT... ONLY THE MOST POWERFUL MAGIC CAN DRIVE OFF A WOOD GOBLIN!
AND THERE'S ONLY ONE CREATURE IN ALL THE REALMS...
...THAT CAN COMPLETELY DESTROY ONE, AND THAT'S --
-- THE RARE AND MAGICAL BEAST OF GREAT POWER, A FOTCH!
RRRRR
A FOTCH?! BUT ISN'T THAT A MYTHICAL CREATURE?
WELL, SO ARE WE ALL, M'LADY.
BUT AS NO ONE'S EVER SEEN ONE, HOW CAN WE SAY THIS WEE PINK THINGIE IS NOT A FOTCH?
I DON'T KNOW, BRIDEY -- I'M JUST GLAD IT'S OUR FRIEND.
THE END

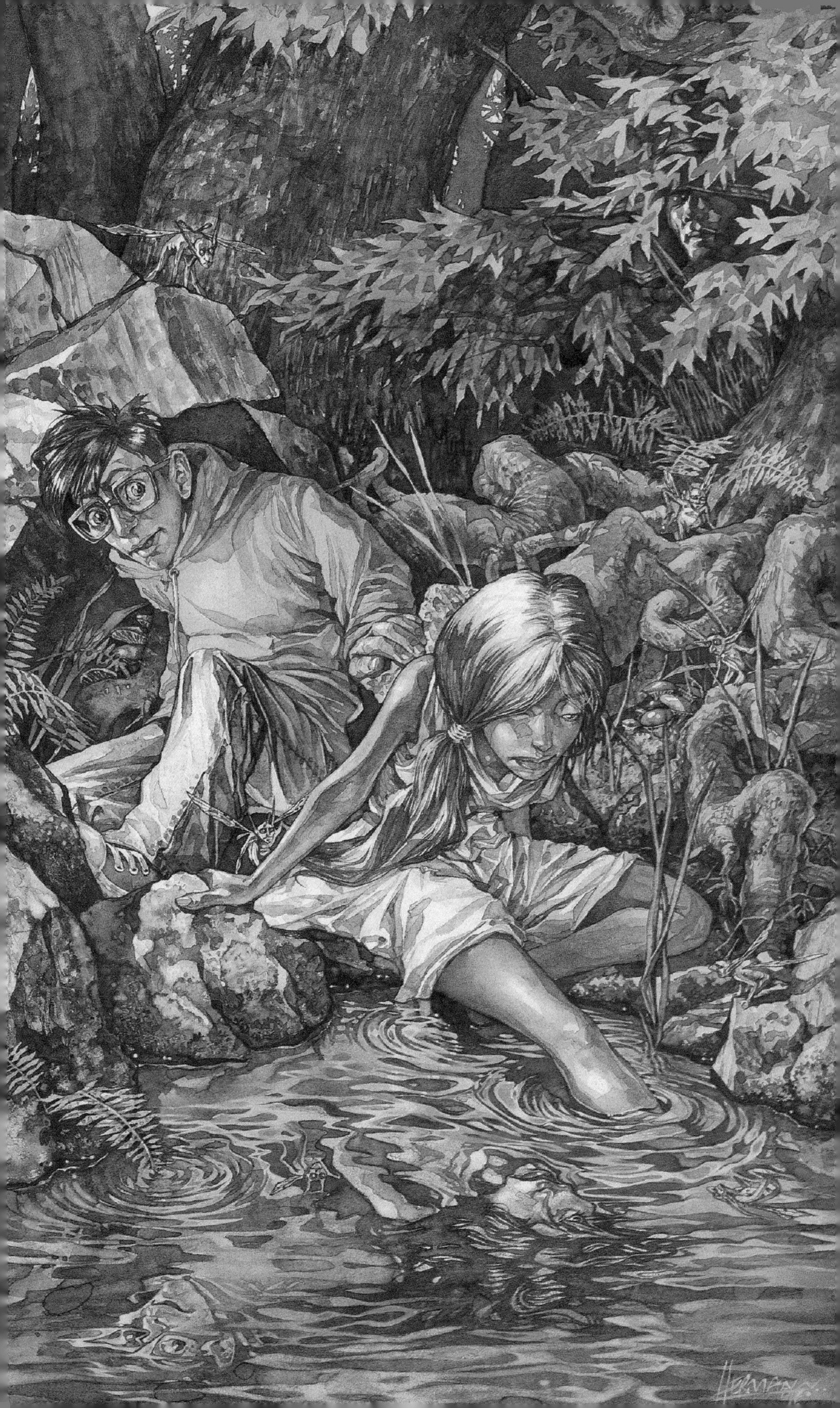

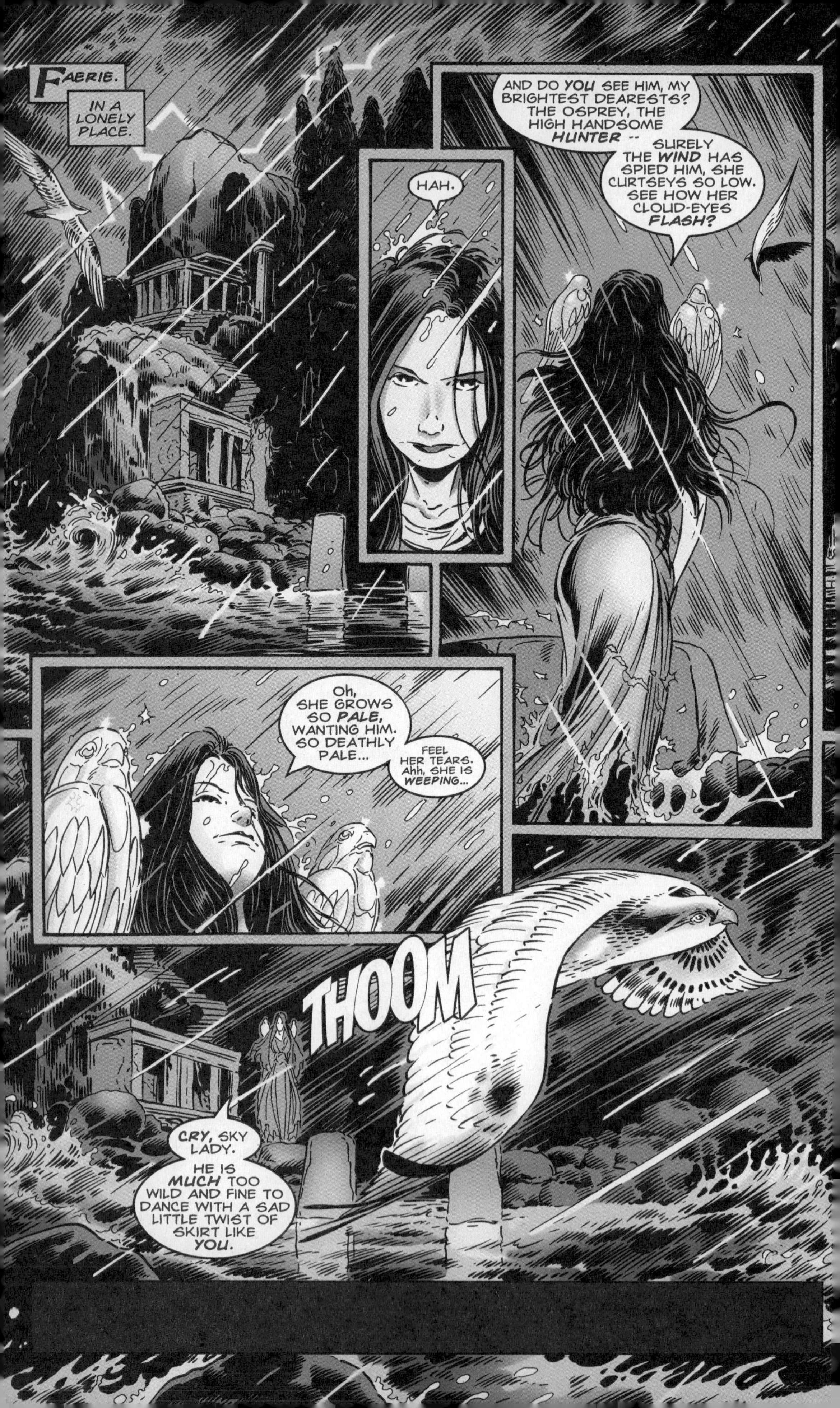
FAERIE.
IN A LONELY PLACE.
HAH.
AND DO YOU SEE HIM, MY BRIGHTEST DEARESTS? THE OSPREY, THE HIGH HANDSOME HUNTER --
SURELY THE WIND HAS SPIED HIM, SHE CURTSEYS SO LOW. SEE HOW HER CLOUD-EYES FLASH?
Oh, SHE GROWS SO PALE, WANTING HIM. SO DEATHLY PALE...
FEEL HER TEARS. Ahh, SHE IS WEEPING...
THOOM
CRY, SKY LADY.
HE IS MUCH TOO WILD AND FINE TO DANCE WITH A SAD LITTLE TWIST OF SKIRT LIKE YOU.

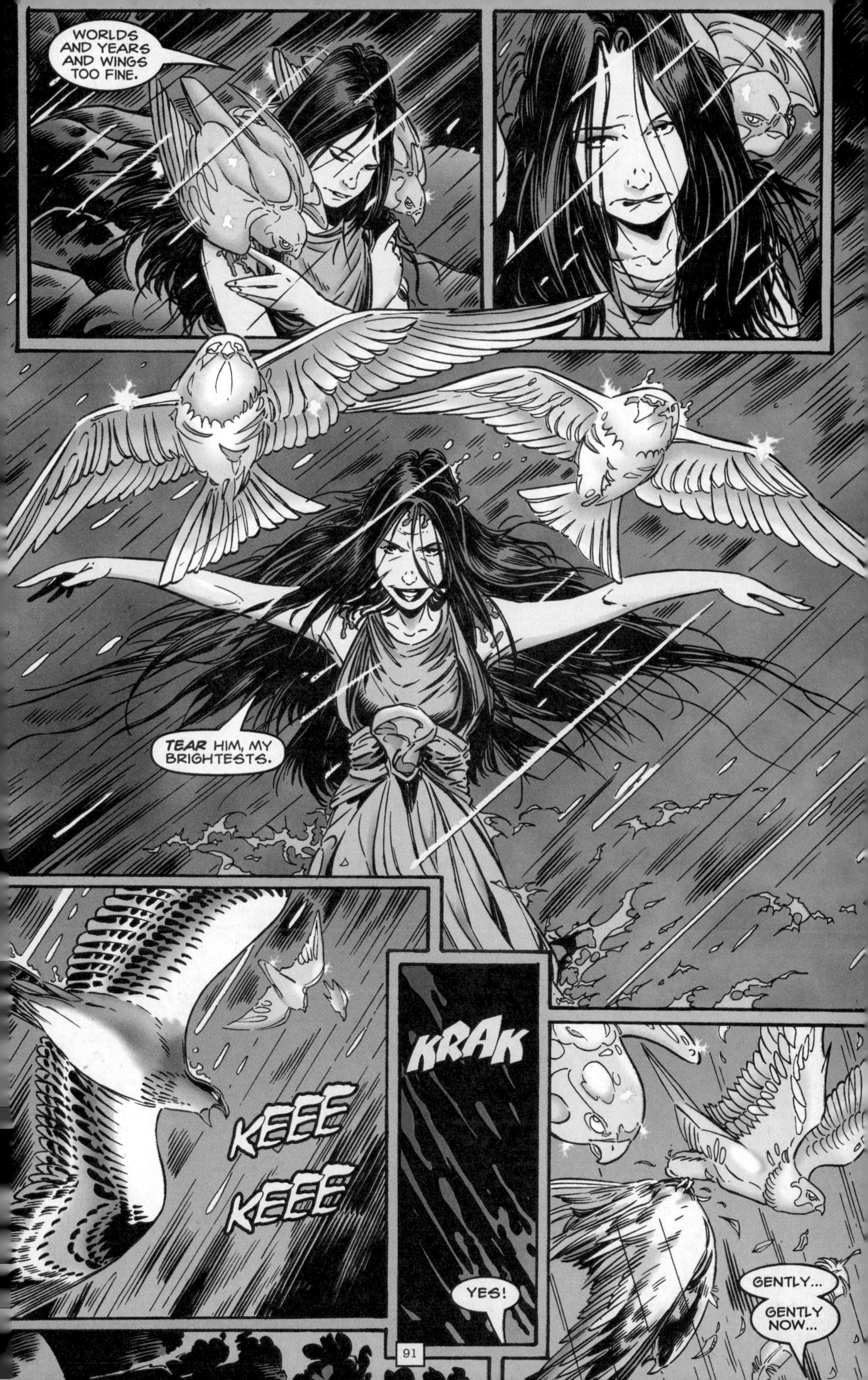
WORLDS AND YEARS AND WINGS TOO FINE.
TEAR HIM, MY BRIGHTESTS.
KEEE
KEEE
KRAK
YES!
GENTLY...
GENTLY NOW...

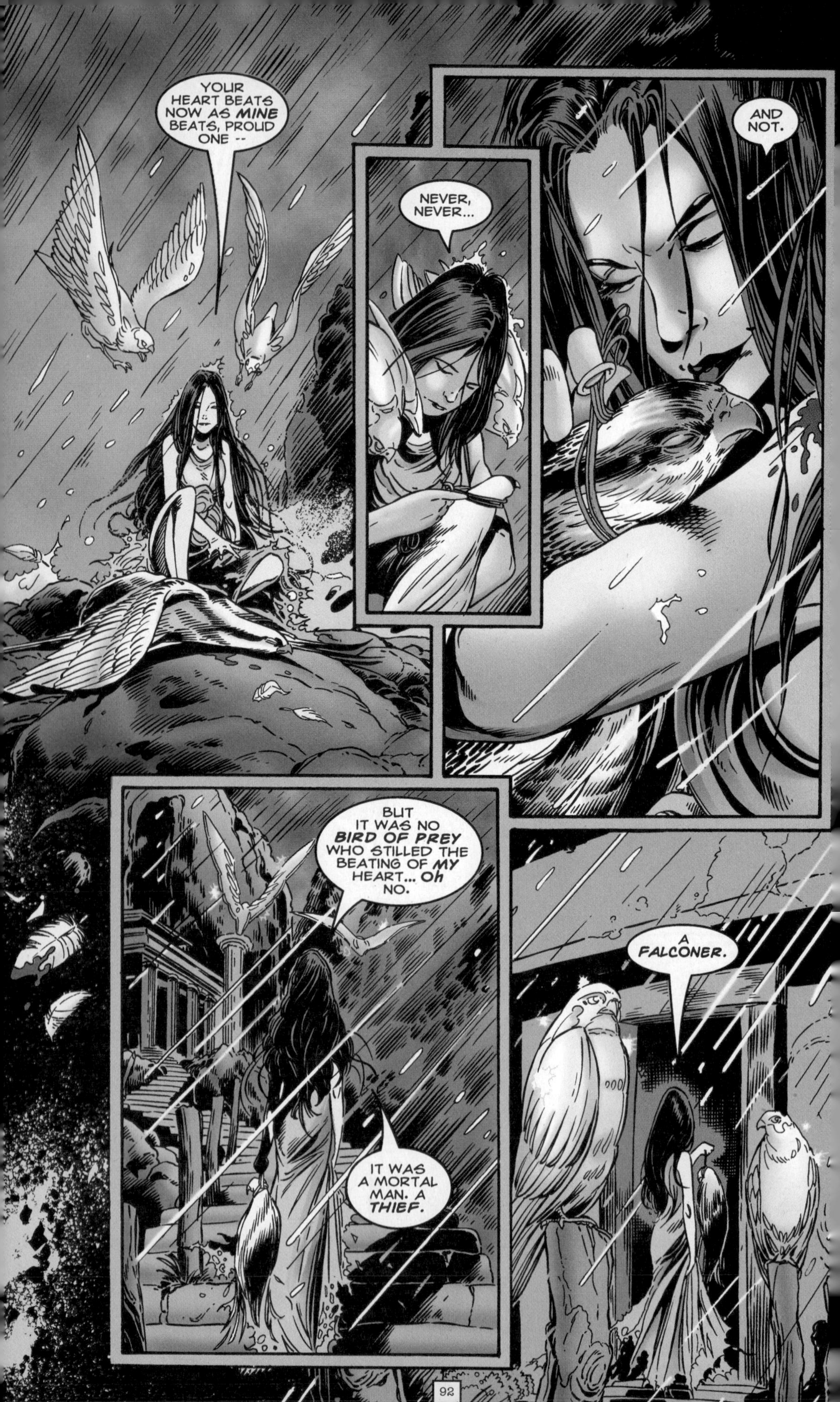
YOUR HEART BEATS NOW AS MINE BEATS, PROUD ONE --
NEVER, NEVER...
AND NOT.
BUT IT WAS NO BIRD OF PREY WHO STILLED THE BEATING OF MY HEART... Oh NO.
IT WAS A MORTAL MAN. A THIEF.
A FALCONER.

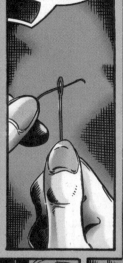

HE IS *DEAD* NOW, MY HIGH HANDSOME SLAYER. COLD IN THE *GRAVE* AND FLOWN BEYOND MY REACH.

I KNOW NOT WHERE HIS SPIRIT NESTS. IN *HELL*, IT MAY BE, OR IN THE *GREY* LANDS.

BUT THIS I *DO* KNOW, MY NEWEST WHITEST WARMEST LOVE.

YOU WILL *FIND* MY DARLING TAMLIN. AND YOU WILL HURRY HIM *BACK* TO ME.

OR YOU SHALL NEVER AGAIN FLY FREE.

DARK AS DAY, MY LADY, BRIGHT AS NIGHT

John Ney Reiber
Writer

Mark Buckingham
Artist

Dick Giordano
Inker
pp 9, 11-13, 19, 20, 23-25, 27-34

James Sinclair
Colorist

Richard Starkings & Comicraft
Letters

Neil Gaiman
Consultant

Julie Rottenberg
Editor

Timothy Hunter & The Books of Magic created by Neil Gaiman & John Bolton

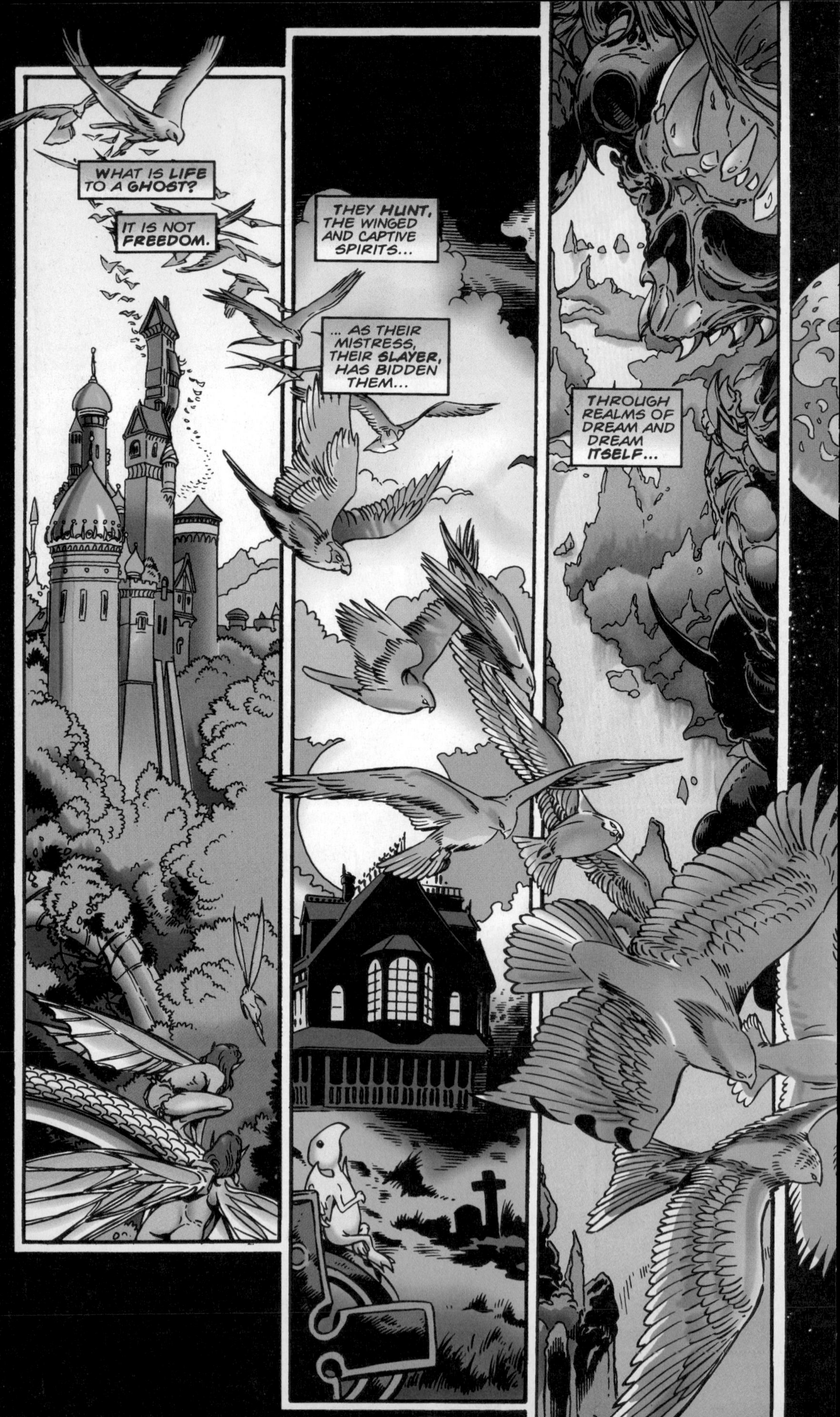
WHAT IS LIFE TO A GHOST?
IT IS NOT FREEDOM.
THEY HUNT, THE WINGED AND CAPTIVE SPIRITS...
... AS THEIR MISTRESS, THEIR SLAYER, HAS BIDDEN THEM...
THROUGH REALMS OF DREAM AND DREAM ITSELF...

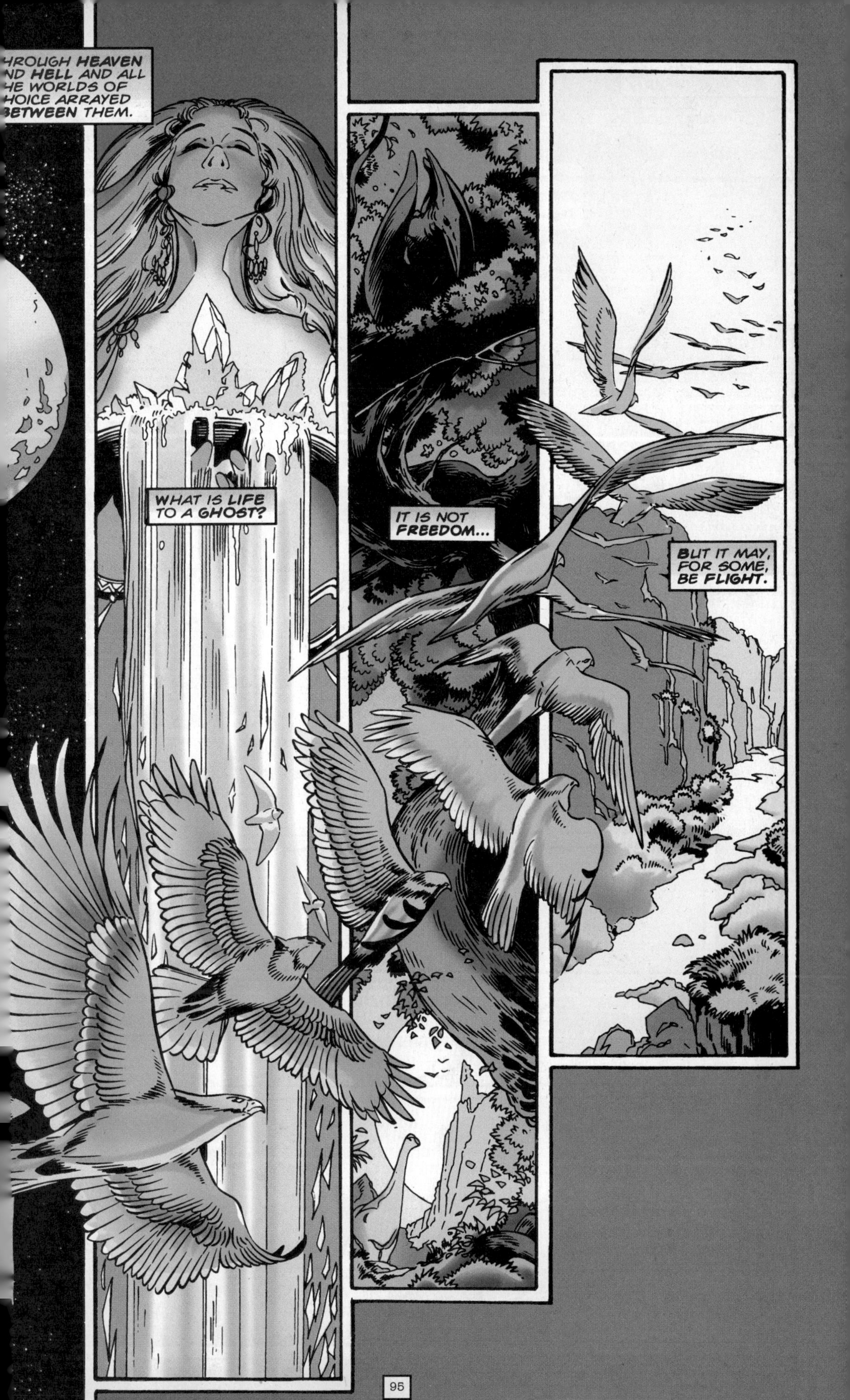
HROUGH HEAVEN ND HELL AND ALL HE WORLDS OF HOICE ARRAYED BETWEEN THEM.
WHAT IS LIFE TO A GHOST?
IT IS NOT FREEDOM...
BUT IT MAY, FOR SOME, BE FLIGHT.

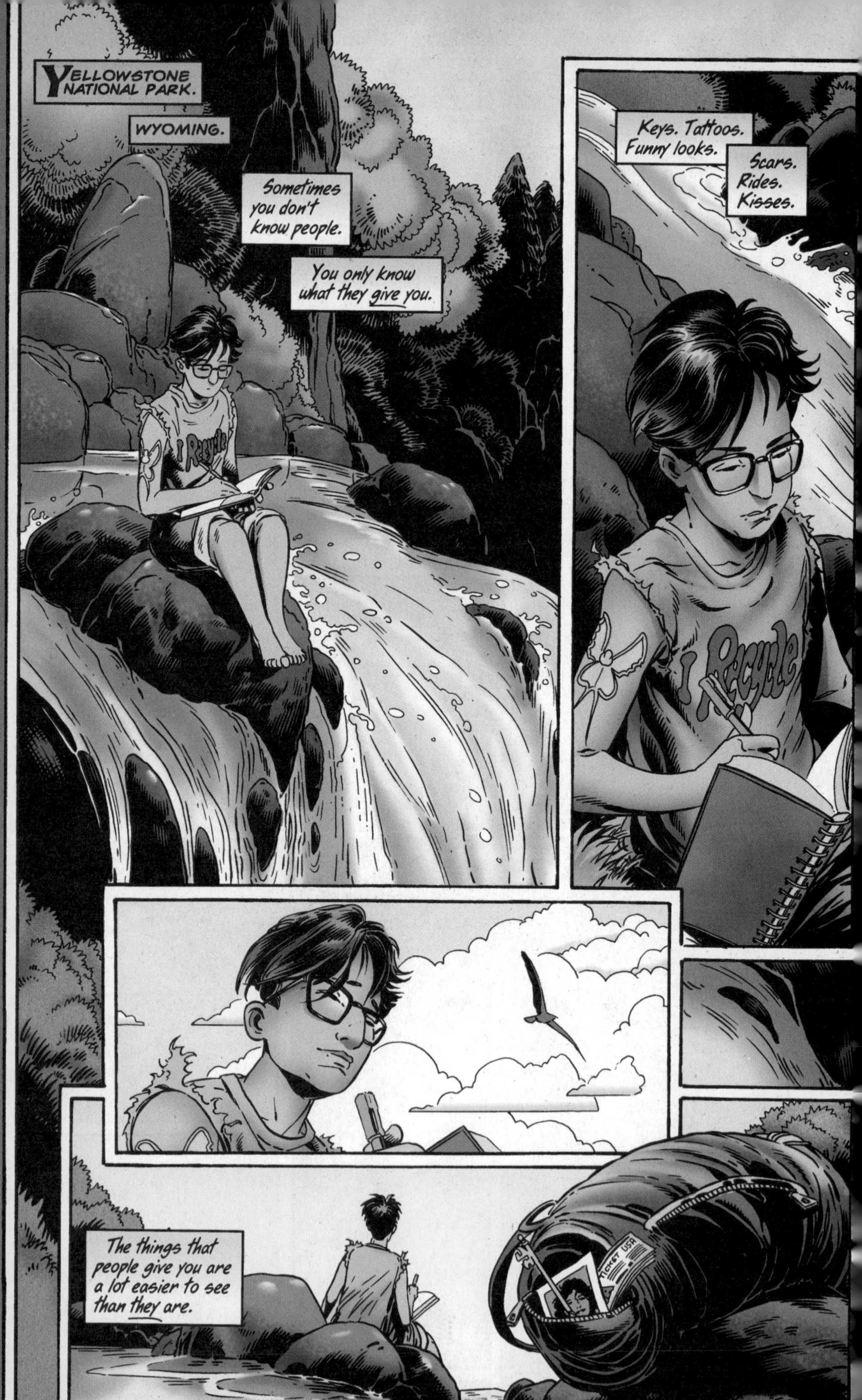
YELLOWSTONE NATIONAL PARK.
WYOMING.
Sometimes you don't know people.
You only know what they give you.
Keys. Tattoos. Funny looks.
Scars. Rides. Kisses.
I Recycle
The things that people give you are a lot easier to see than they are.
TICKET USA

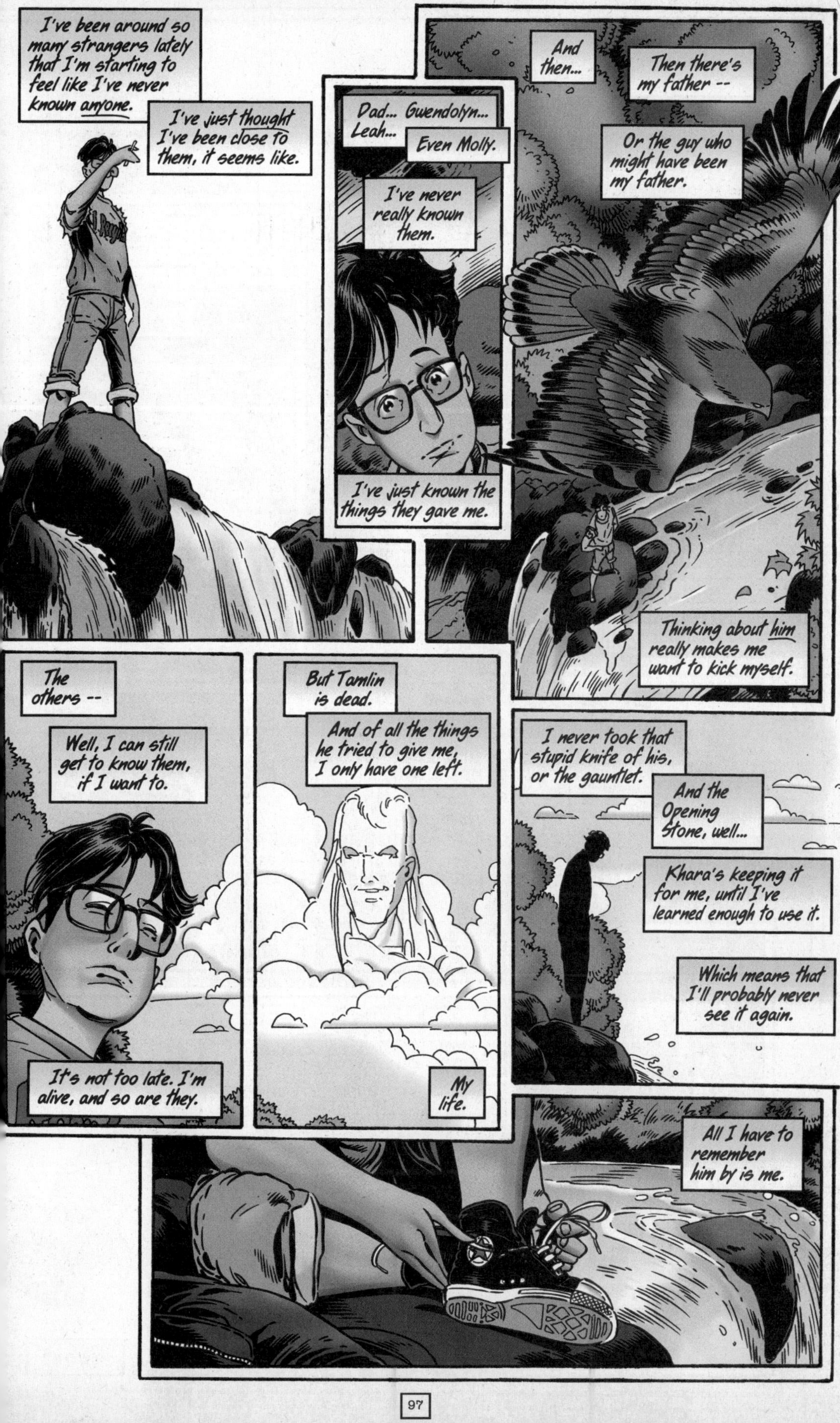

I've been around so many strangers lately that I'm starting to feel like I've never known anyone.
I've just thought I've been close to them, it seems like.
Dad... Gwendolyn... Leah...
Even Molly.
I've never really known them.
I've just known the things they gave me.
And then...
Then there's my father --
Or the guy who might have been my father.
Thinking about him really makes me want to kick myself.
The others --
Well, I can still get to know them, if I want to.
It's not too late. I'm alive, and so are they.
But Tamlin is dead.
And of all the things he tried to give me, I only have one left.
My life.
I never took that stupid knife of his, or the gauntlet.
And the Opening Stone, well...
Khara's keeping it for me, until I've learned enough to use it.
Which means that I'll probably never see it again.
All I have to remember him by is me.

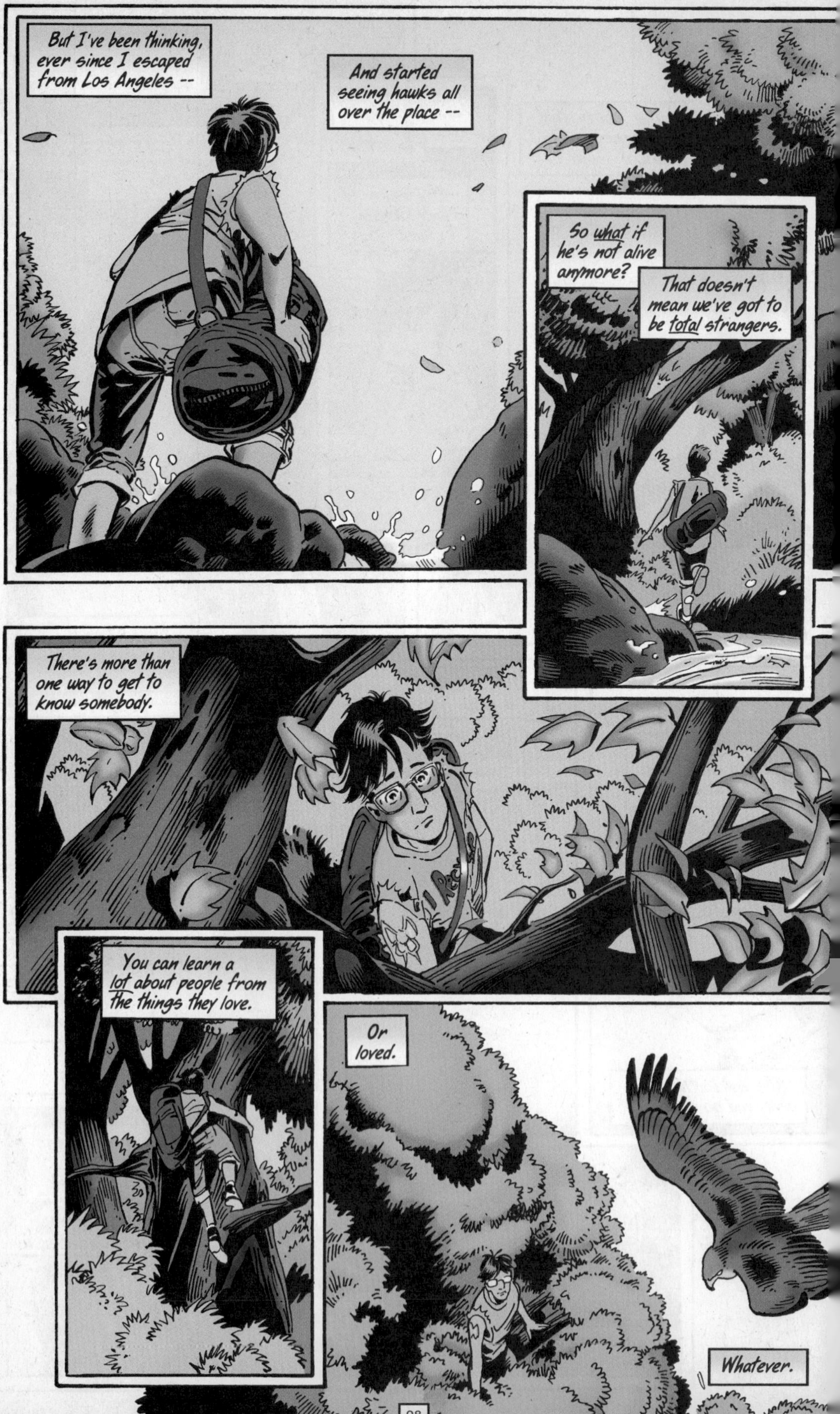
But I've been thinking, ever since I escaped from Los Angeles --
And started seeing hawks all over the place --
So what if he's not alive anymore?
That doesn't mean we've got to be total strangers.
There's more than one way to get to know somebody.
You can learn a lot about people from the things they love.
Or loved.
Whatever.

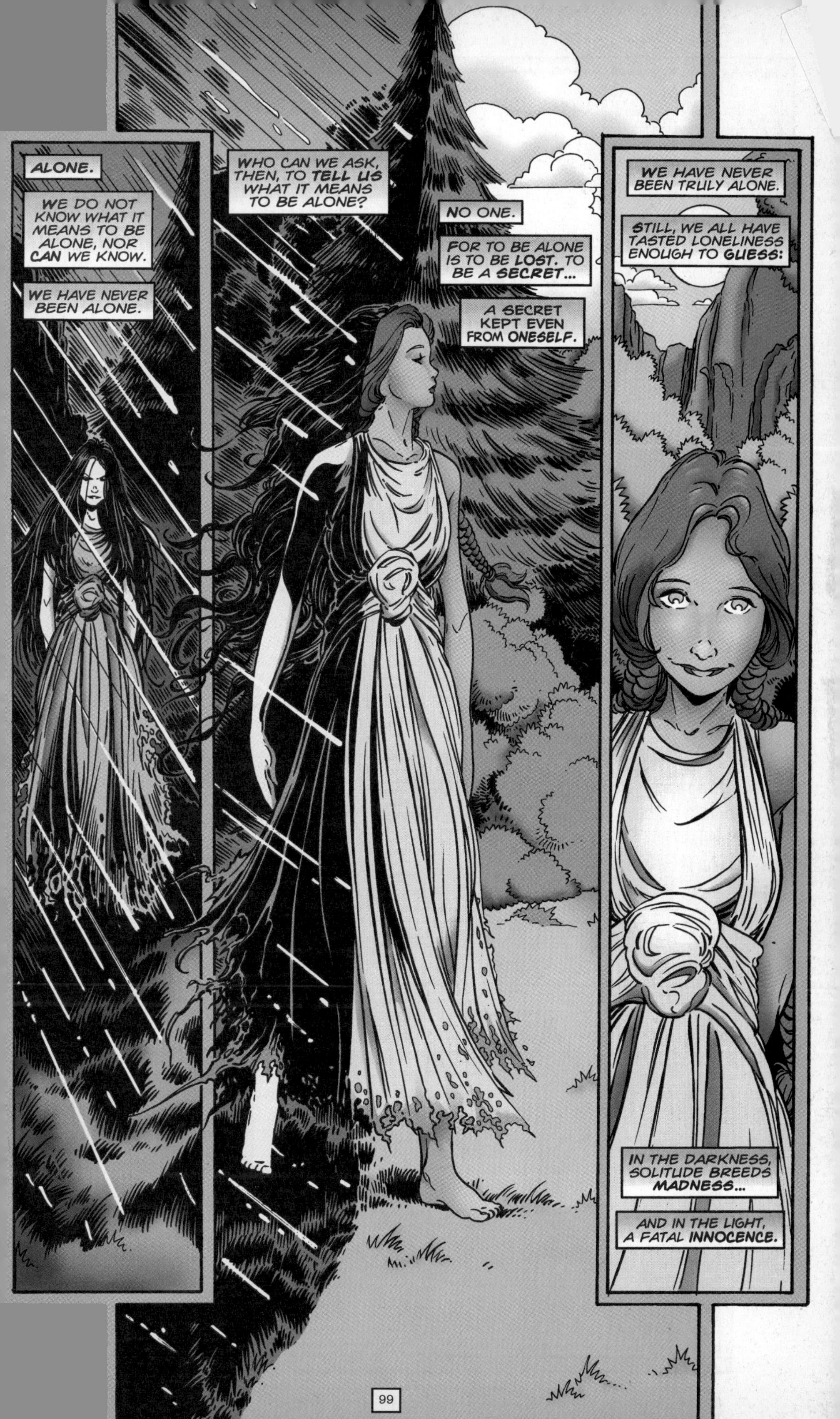

ALONE.
WE DO NOT KNOW WHAT IT MEANS TO BE ALONE, NOR CAN WE KNOW.
WE HAVE NEVER BEEN ALONE.
WHO CAN WE ASK, THEN, TO TELL US WHAT IT MEANS TO BE ALONE?
NO ONE.
FOR TO BE ALONE IS TO BE LOST. TO BE A SECRET...
A SECRET KEPT EVEN FROM ONESELF.
WE HAVE NEVER BEEN TRULY ALONE.
STILL, WE ALL HAVE TASTED LONELINESS ENOUGH TO GUESS:
IN THE DARKNESS, SOLITUDE BREEDS MADNESS...
AND IN THE LIGHT, A FATAL INNOCENCE.

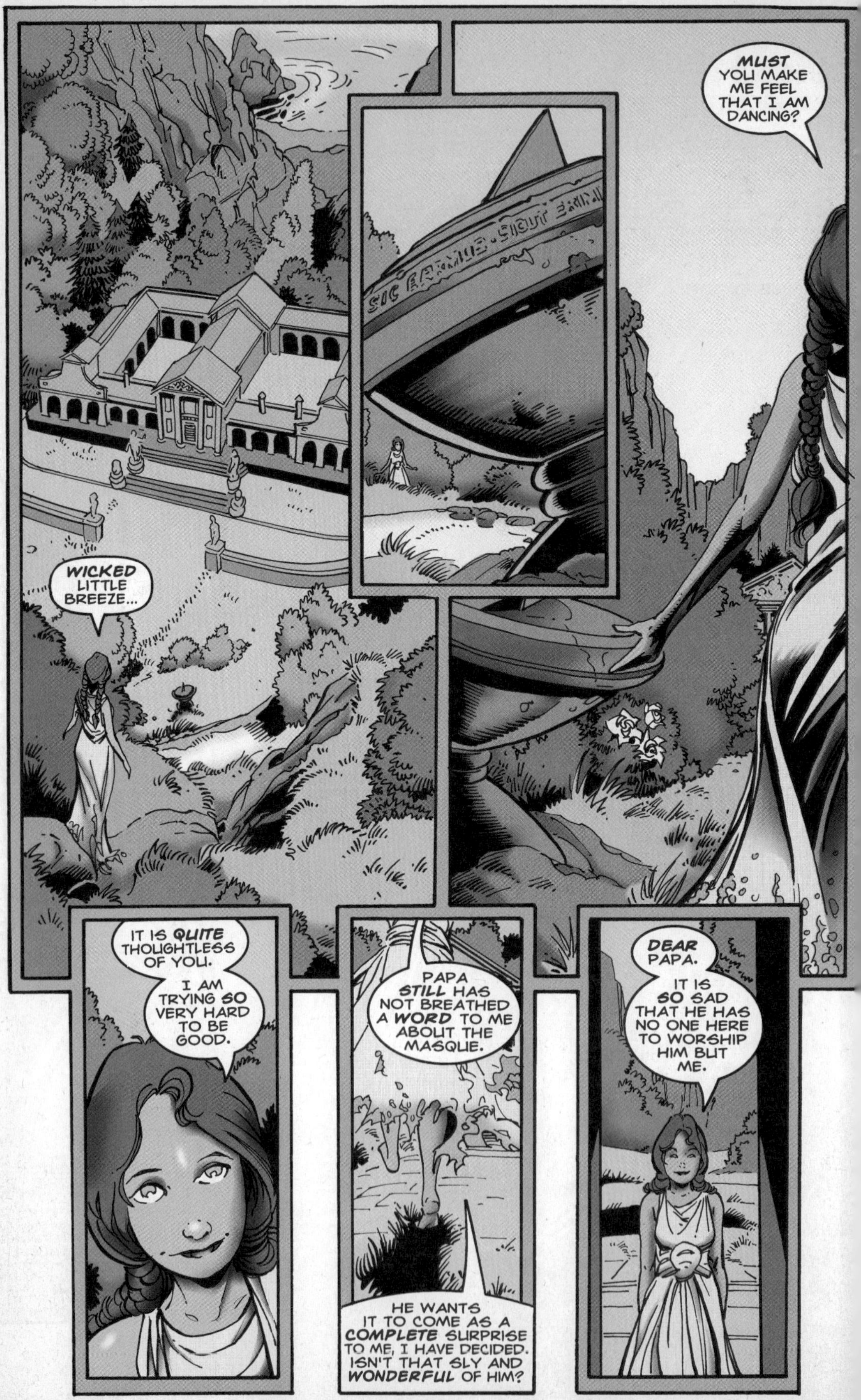
WICKED LITTLE BREEZE...
SIC ERRIMUS - SIC...
MUST YOU MAKE ME FEEL THAT I AM DANCING?
IT IS QUITE THOUGHTLESS OF YOU.
I AM TRYING SO VERY HARD TO BE GOOD.
PAPA STILL HAS NOT BREATHED A WORD TO ME ABOUT THE MASQUE.
HE WANTS IT TO COME AS A COMPLETE SURPRISE TO ME, I HAVE DECIDED. ISN'T THAT SLY AND WONDERFUL OF HIM?
DEAR PAPA.
IT IS SO SAD THAT HE HAS NO ONE HERE TO WORSHIP HIM BUT ME.

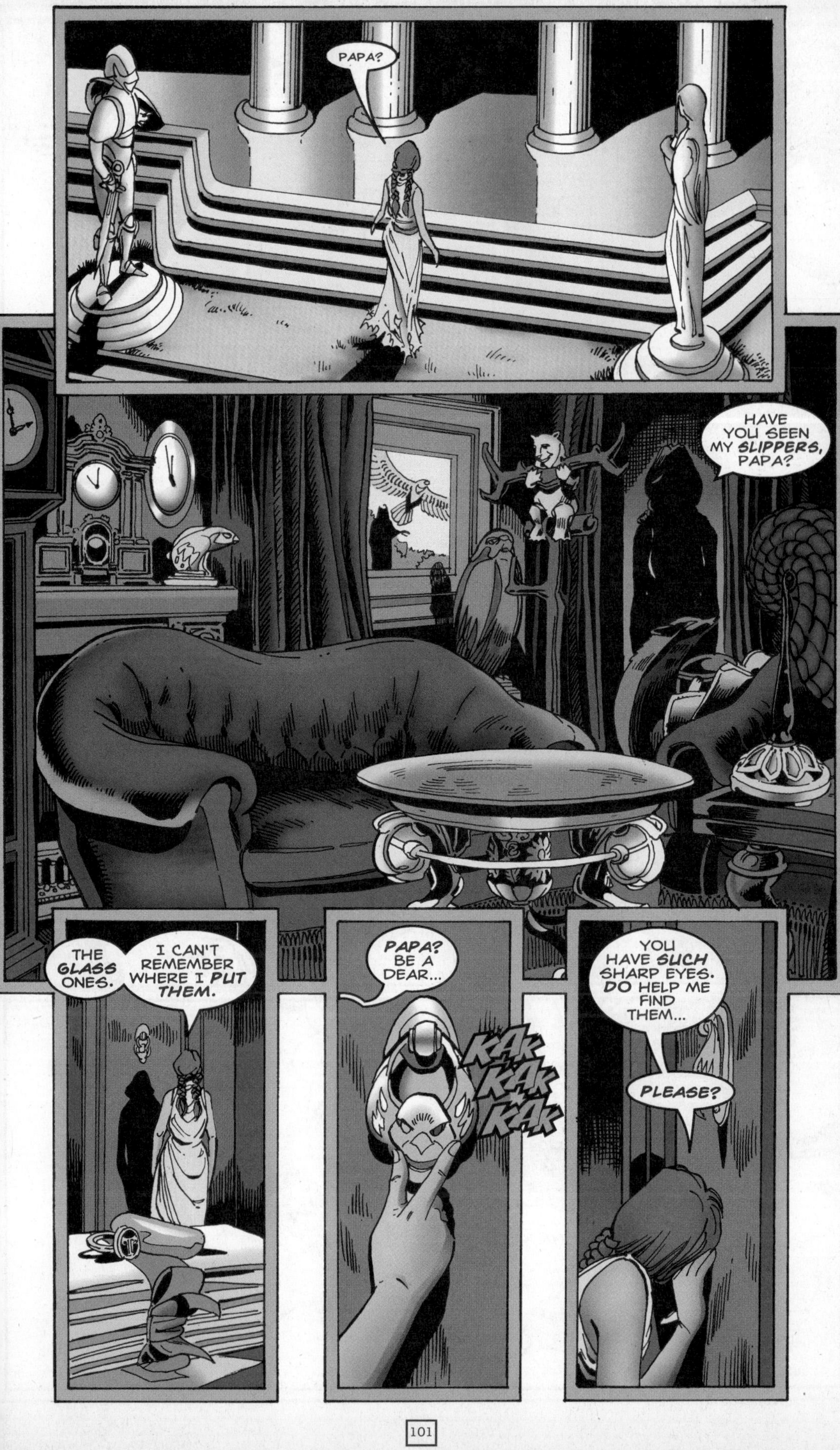
PAPA?
HAVE YOU SEEN MY SLIPPERS, PAPA?
THE GLASS ONES.
I CAN'T REMEMBER WHERE I PUT THEM.
PAPA? BE A DEAR...
KAK KAK KAK
YOU HAVE SUCH SHARP EYES. DO HELP ME FIND THEM...
PLEASE?

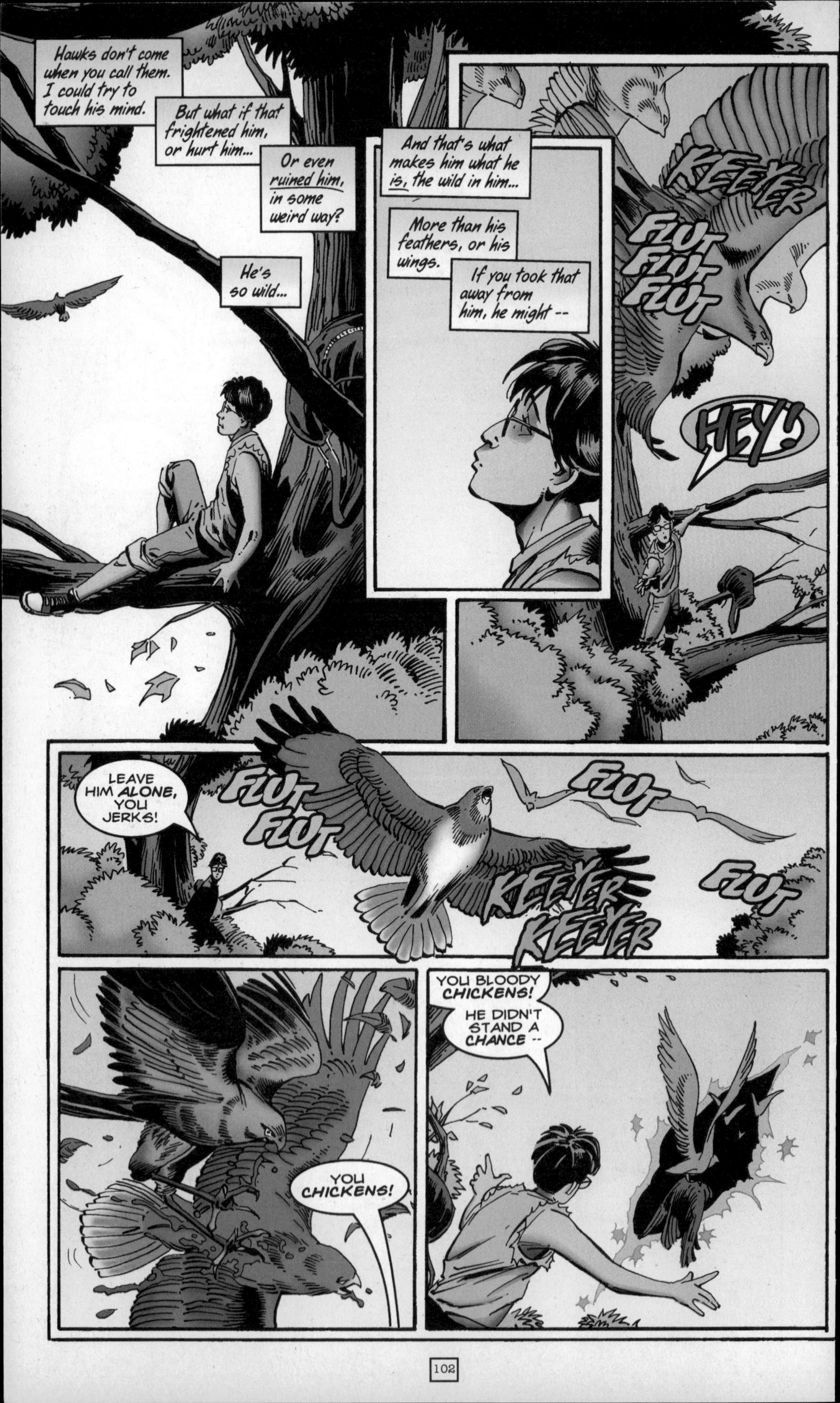

Hawks don't come when you call them. I could try to touch his mind.
But what if that frightened him, or hurt him...
Or even ruined him, in some weird way?
He's so wild...
And that's what makes him what he is, the wild in him...
More than his feathers, or his wings.
If you took that away from him, he might --
KEEYER
FLUT FLUT FLUT
HEY!
LEAVE HIM ALONE, YOU JERKS!
FLUT FLUT
FLUT
KEEYER KEEYER
FLUT
YOU CHICKENS!
YOU BLOODY CHICKENS!
HE DIDN'T STAND A CHANCE --

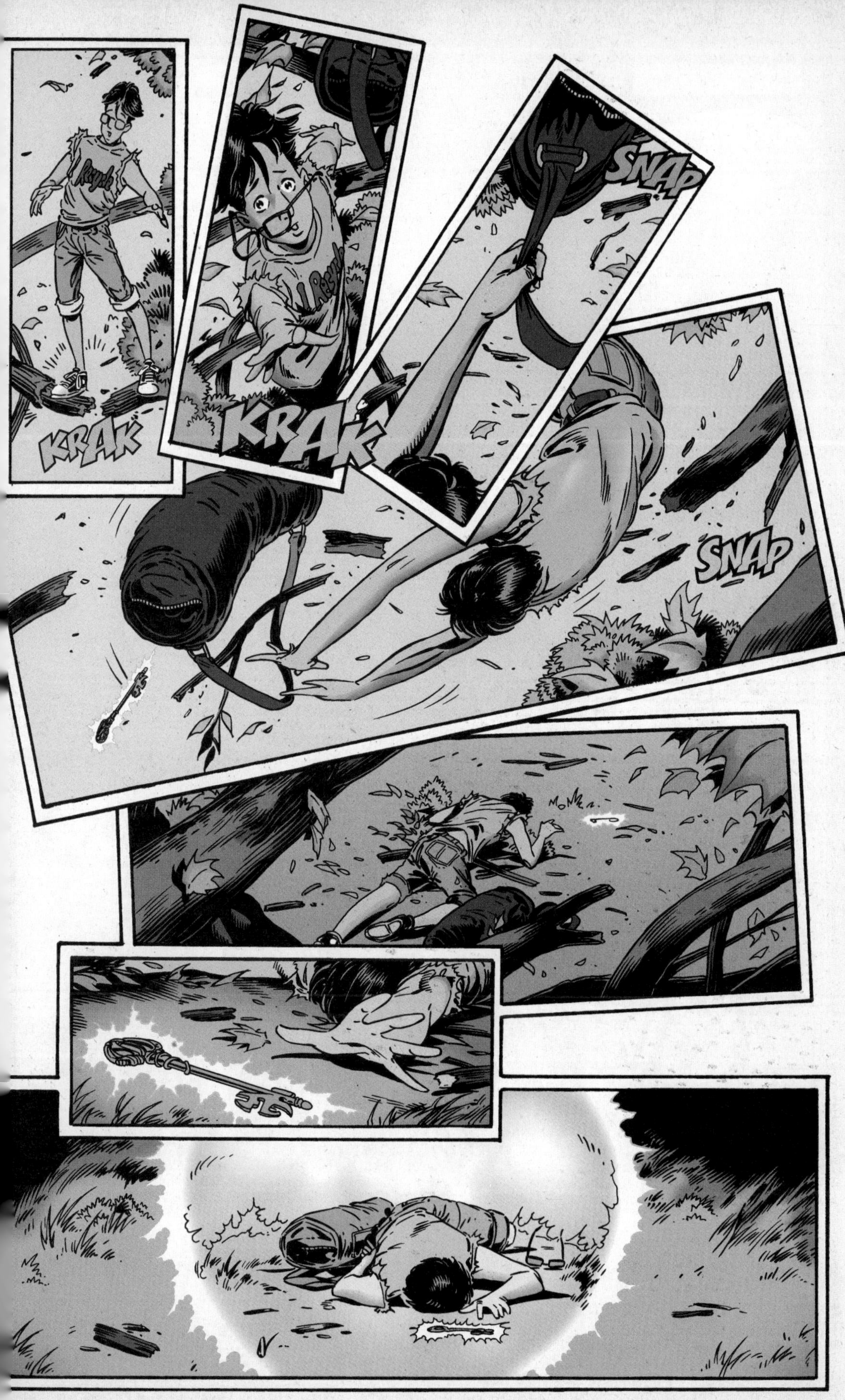
KRAK
KRAK
SNAP
SNAP

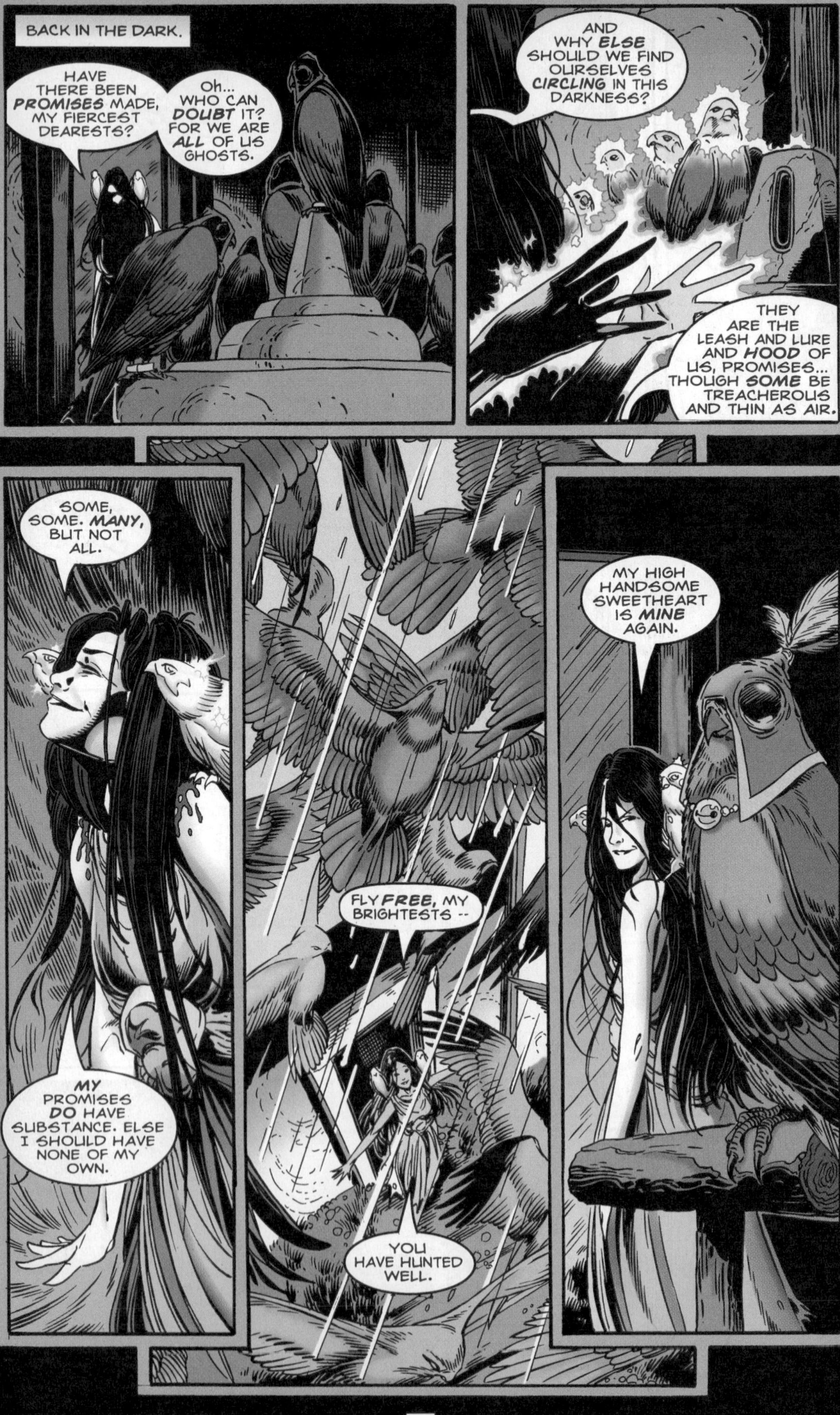
BACK IN THE DARK.
HAVE THERE BEEN PROMISES MADE, MY FIERCEST DEARESTS?
Oh... WHO CAN DOUBT IT? FOR WE ARE ALL OF US GHOSTS.
AND WHY ELSE SHOULD WE FIND OURSELVES CIRCLING IN THIS DARKNESS?
THEY ARE THE LEASH AND LURE AND HOOD OF US, PROMISES... THOUGH SOME BE TREACHEROUS AND THIN AS AIR.
SOME, SOME. MANY, BUT NOT ALL.
MY PROMISES DO HAVE SUBSTANCE. ELSE I SHOULD HAVE NONE OF MY OWN.
FLY FREE, MY BRIGHTESTS --
YOU HAVE HUNTED WELL.
MY HIGH HANDSOME SWEETHEART IS MINE AGAIN.

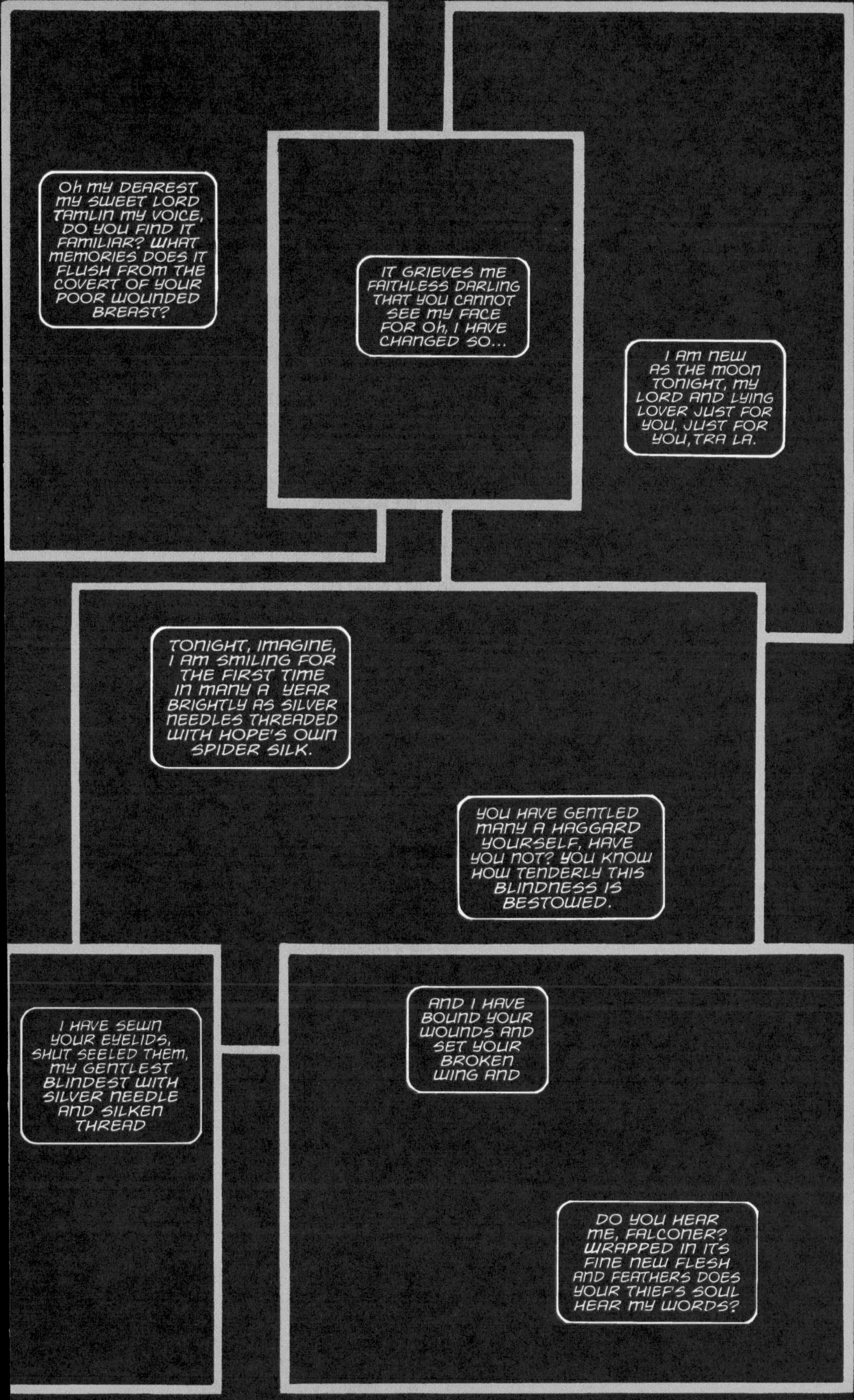
Oh MY DEAREST MY SWEET LORD TAMLIN MY VOICE, DO YOU FIND IT FAMILIAR? WHAT MEMORIES DOES IT FLUSH FROM THE COVERT OF YOUR POOR WOUNDED BREAST?
IT GRIEVES ME FAITHLESS DARLING THAT YOU CANNOT SEE MY FACE FOR Oh, I HAVE CHANGED SO...
I AM NEW AS THE MOON TONIGHT, MY LORD AND LYING LOVER JUST FOR YOU, JUST FOR YOU, TRA LA.
TONIGHT, IMAGINE, I AM SMILING FOR THE FIRST TIME IN MANY A YEAR BRIGHTLY AS SILVER NEEDLES THREADED WITH HOPE'S OWN SPIDER SILK.
YOU HAVE GENTLED MANY A HAGGARD YOURSELF, HAVE YOU NOT? YOU KNOW HOW TENDERLY THIS BLINDNESS IS BESTOWED.
I HAVE SEWN YOUR EYELIDS, SHUT SEELED THEM, MY GENTLEST BLINDEST WITH SILVER NEEDLE AND SILKEN THREAD
AND I HAVE BOUND YOUR WOUNDS AND SET YOUR BROKEN WING AND
DO YOU HEAR ME, FALCONER? WRAPPED IN ITS FINE NEW FLESH AND FEATHERS DOES YOUR THIEF'S SOUL HEAR MY WORDS?

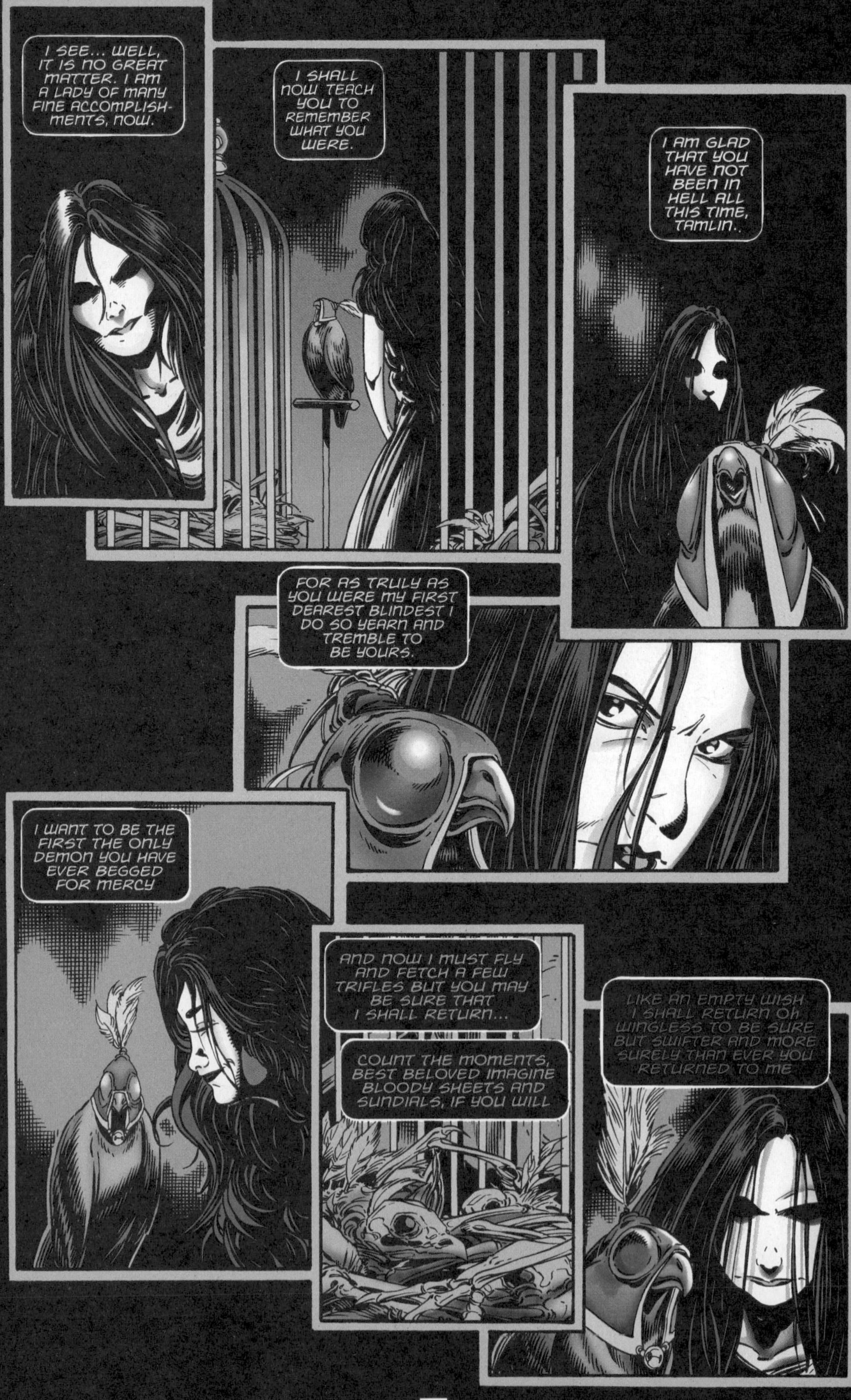
I SEE... WELL, IT IS NO GREAT MATTER. I AM A LADY OF MANY FINE ACCOMPLISHMENTS, NOW.
I SHALL NOW TEACH YOU TO REMEMBER WHAT YOU WERE.
I AM GLAD THAT YOU HAVE NOT BEEN IN HELL ALL THIS TIME, TAMLIN.
FOR AS TRULY AS YOU WERE MY FIRST DEAREST BLINDEST I DO SO YEARN AND TREMBLE TO BE YOURS.
I WANT TO BE THE FIRST THE ONLY DEMON YOU HAVE EVER BEGGED FOR MERCY
AND NOW I MUST FLY AND FETCH A FEW TRIFLES BUT YOU MAY BE SURE THAT I SHALL RETURN...
COUNT THE MOMENTS, BEST BELOVED IMAGINE BLOODY SHEETS AND SUNDIALS, IF YOU WILL
LIKE AN EMPTY WISH I SHALL RETURN OH WINGLESS TO BE SURE BUT SWIFTER AND MORE SURELY THAN EVER YOU RETURNED TO ME

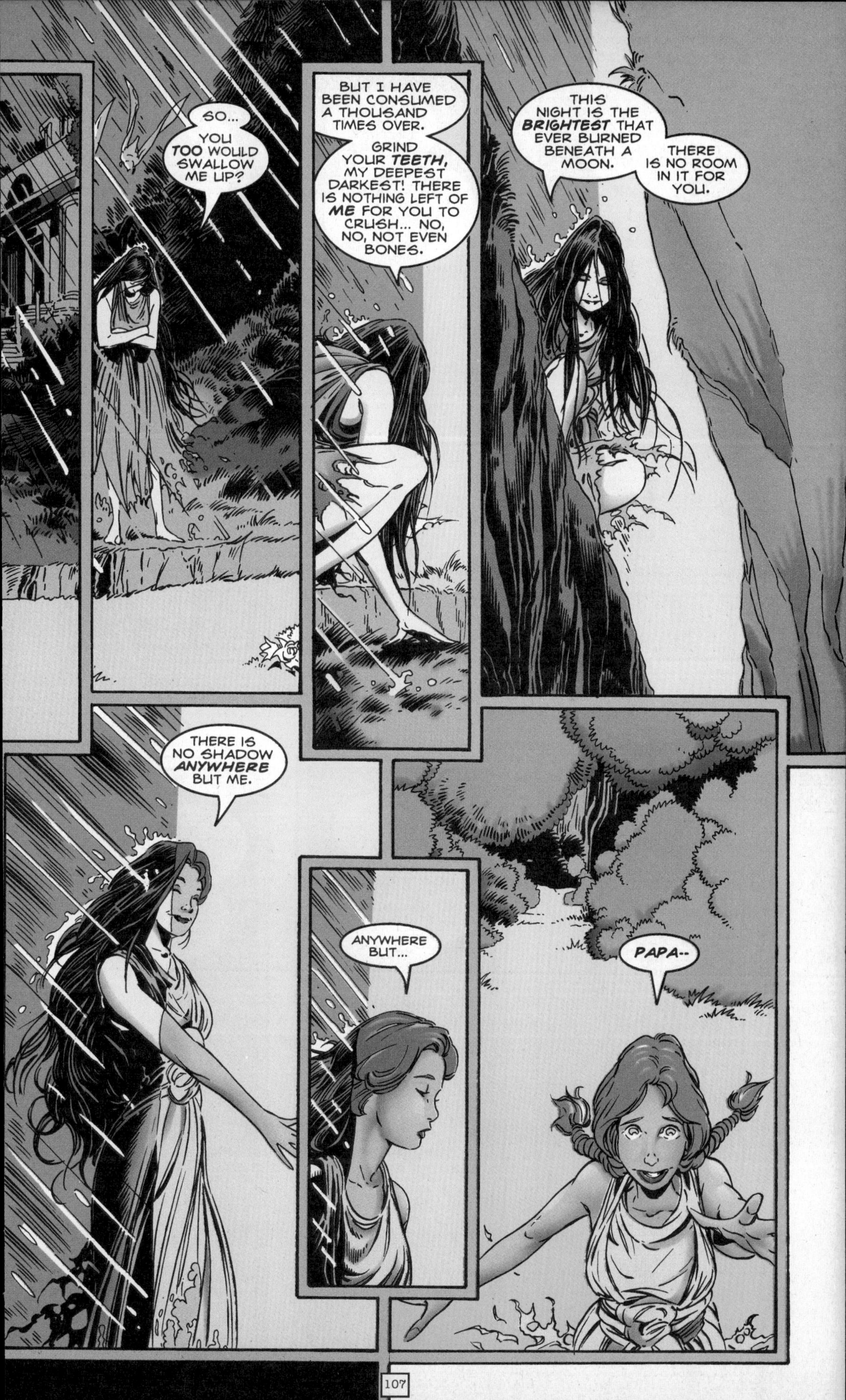
SO...
YOU TOO WOULD SWALLOW ME UP?
BUT I HAVE BEEN CONSUMED A THOUSAND TIMES OVER.
GRIND YOUR TEETH, MY DEEPEST DARKEST! THERE IS NOTHING LEFT OF ME FOR YOU TO CRUSH... NO, NO, NOT EVEN BONES.
THIS NIGHT IS THE BRIGHTEST THAT EVER BURNED BENEATH A MOON.
THERE IS NO ROOM IN IT FOR YOU.
THERE IS NO SHADOW ANYWHERE BUT ME.
ANYWHERE BUT...
PAPA--

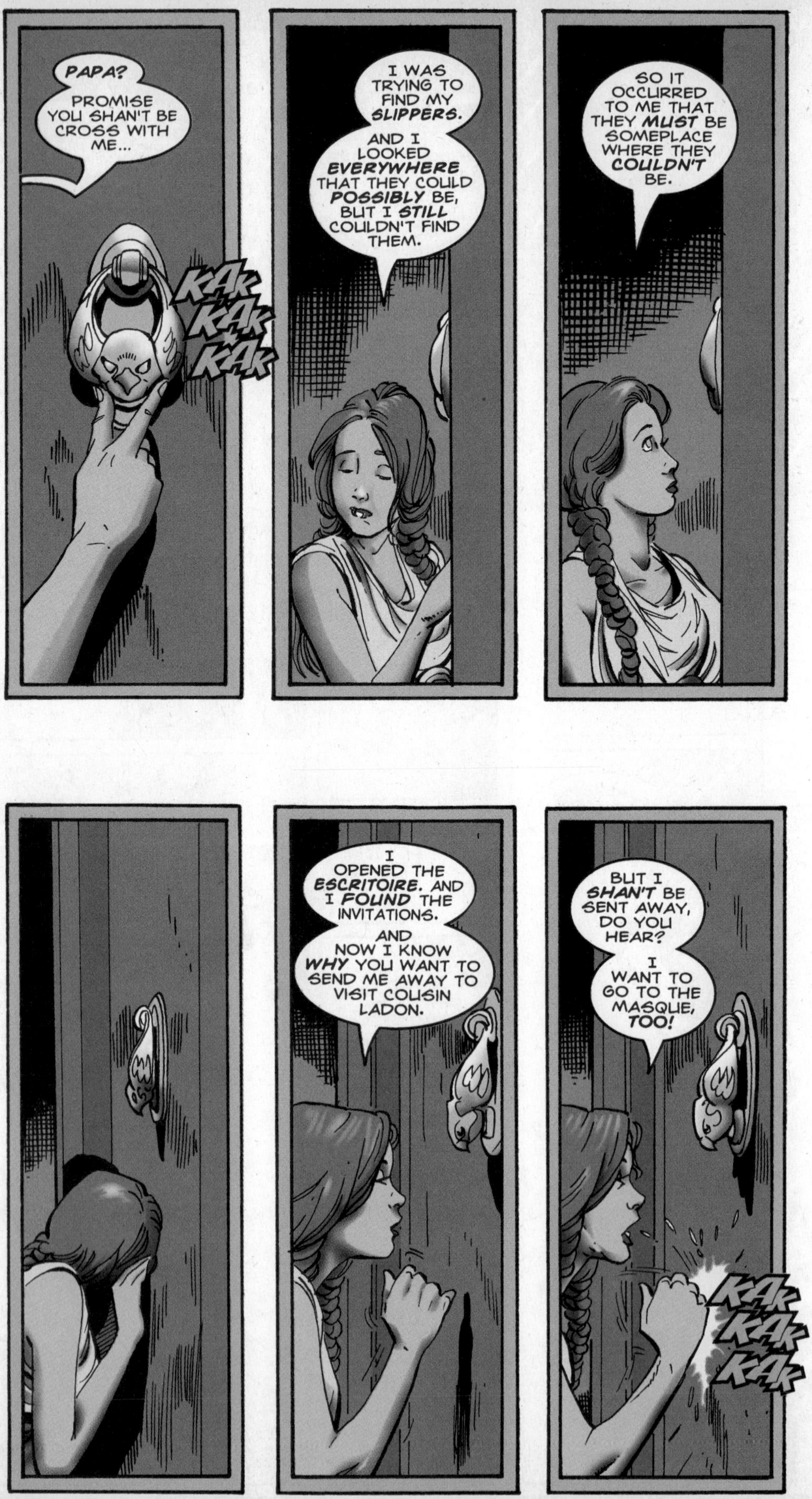
PAPA?
PROMISE YOU SHAN'T BE CROSS WITH ME...
KAK KAK KAK
I WAS TRYING TO FIND MY SLIPPERS.
AND I LOOKED EVERYWHERE THAT THEY COULD POSSIBLY BE, BUT I STILL COULDN'T FIND THEM.
SO IT OCCURRED TO ME THAT THEY MUST BE SOMEPLACE WHERE THEY COULDN'T BE.
I OPENED THE ESCRITOIRE. AND I FOUND THE INVITATIONS.
AND NOW I KNOW WHY YOU WANT TO SEND ME AWAY TO VISIT COUSIN LADON.
BUT I SHAN'T BE SENT AWAY, DO YOU HEAR?
I WANT TO GO TO THE MASQUE, TOO!
KAK KAK KAK

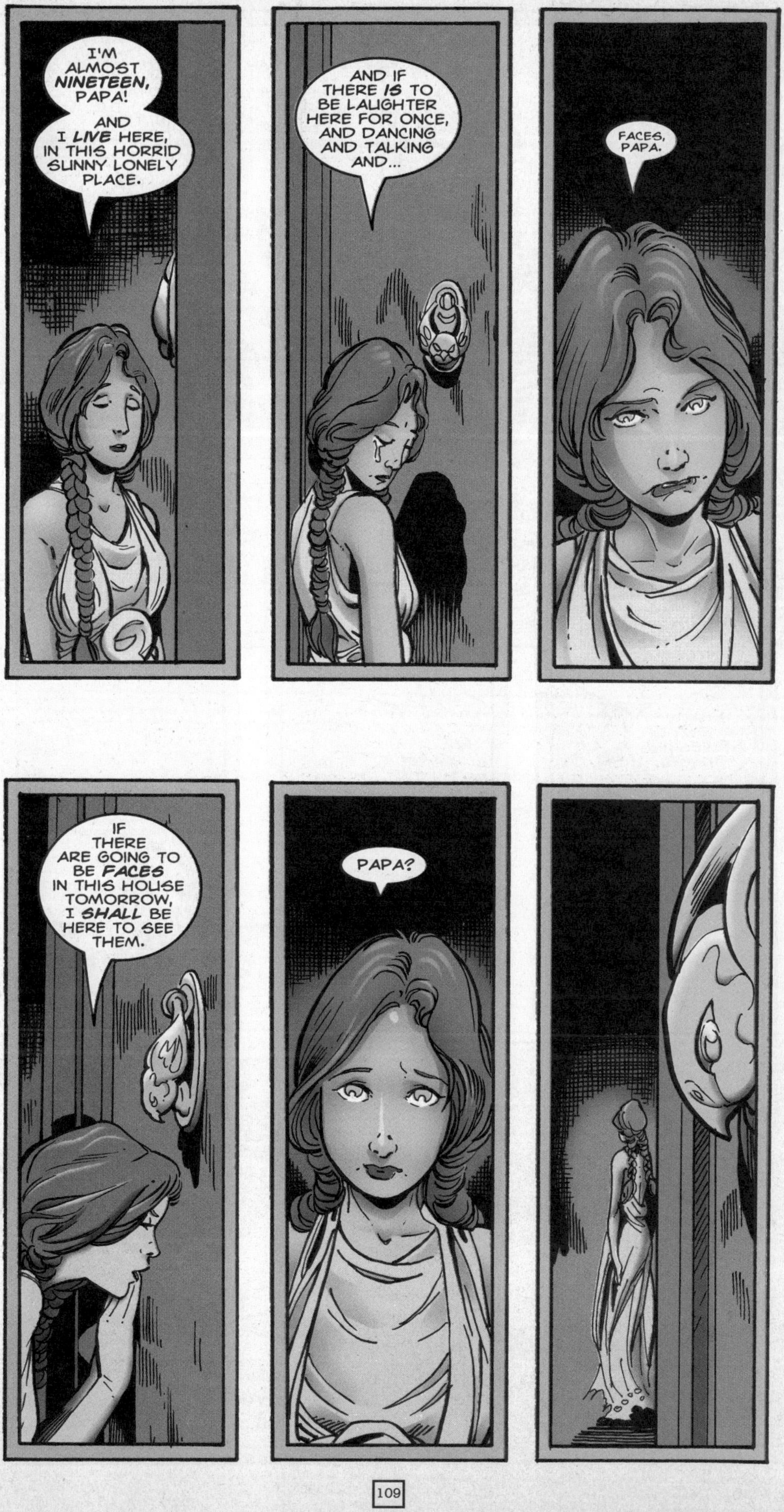
I'M ALMOST *NINETEEN,* PAPA!
AND I *LIVE* HERE, IN THIS HORRID SUNNY LONELY PLACE.
AND IF THERE *IS* TO BE LAUGHTER HERE FOR ONCE, AND DANCING AND TALKING AND...
FACES, PAPA.
IF THERE ARE GOING TO BE *FACES* IN THIS HOUSE TOMORROW, I *SHALL* BE HERE TO SEE THEM.
PAPA?

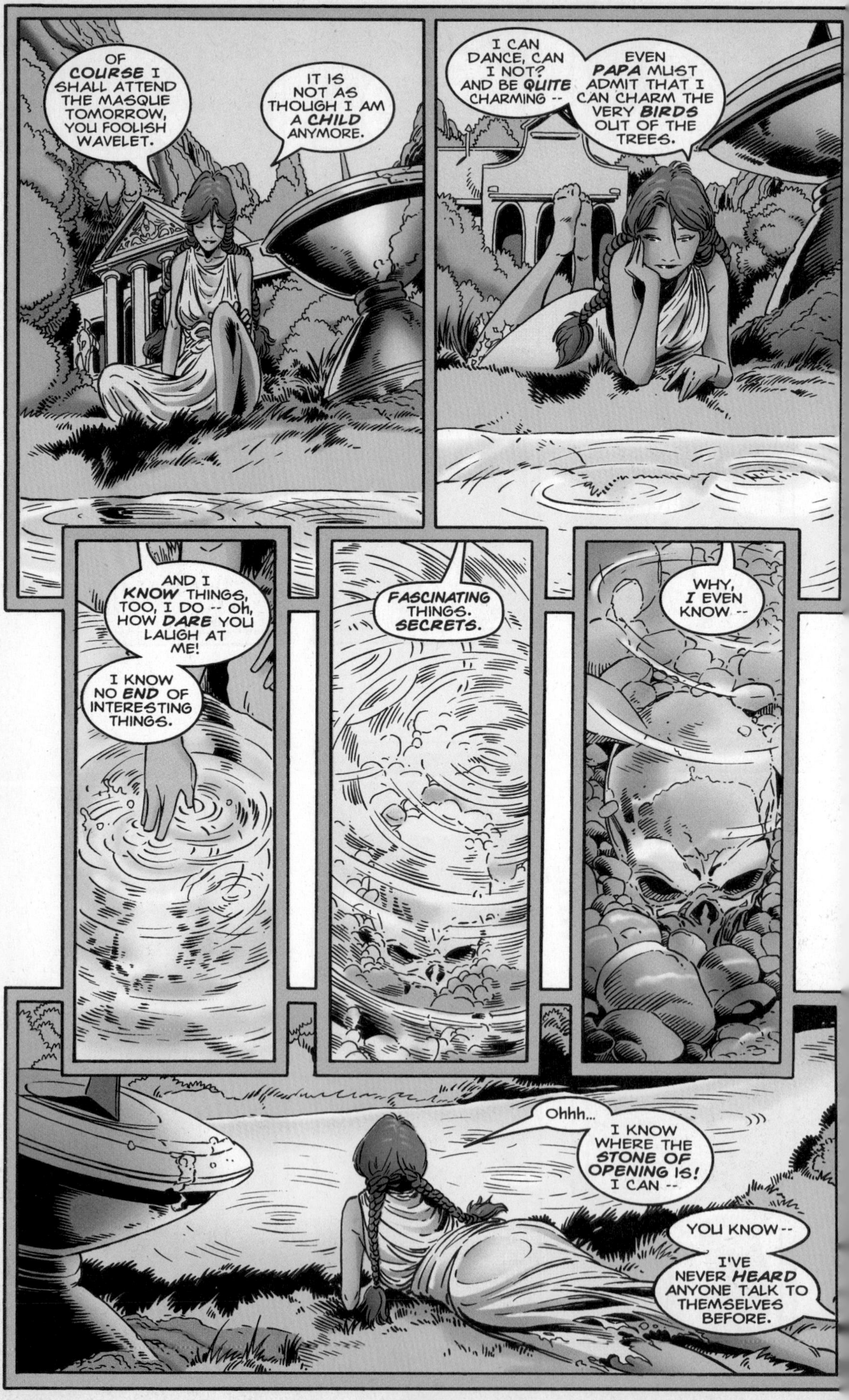
OF COURSE I SHALL ATTEND THE MASQUE TOMORROW, YOU FOOLISH WAVELET.
IT IS NOT AS THOUGH I AM A CHILD ANYMORE.
I CAN DANCE, CAN I NOT? AND BE QUITE CHARMING --
EVEN PAPA MUST ADMIT THAT I CAN CHARM THE VERY BIRDS OUT OF THE TREES.
AND I KNOW THINGS, TOO, I DO -- Oh, HOW DARE YOU LAUGH AT ME!
I KNOW NO END OF INTERESTING THINGS.
FASCINATING THINGS. SECRETS.
WHY, I EVEN KNOW --
Ohhh...
I KNOW WHERE THE STONE OF OPENING IS! I CAN --
YOU KNOW --
I'VE NEVER HEARD ANYONE TALK TO THEMSELVES BEFORE.

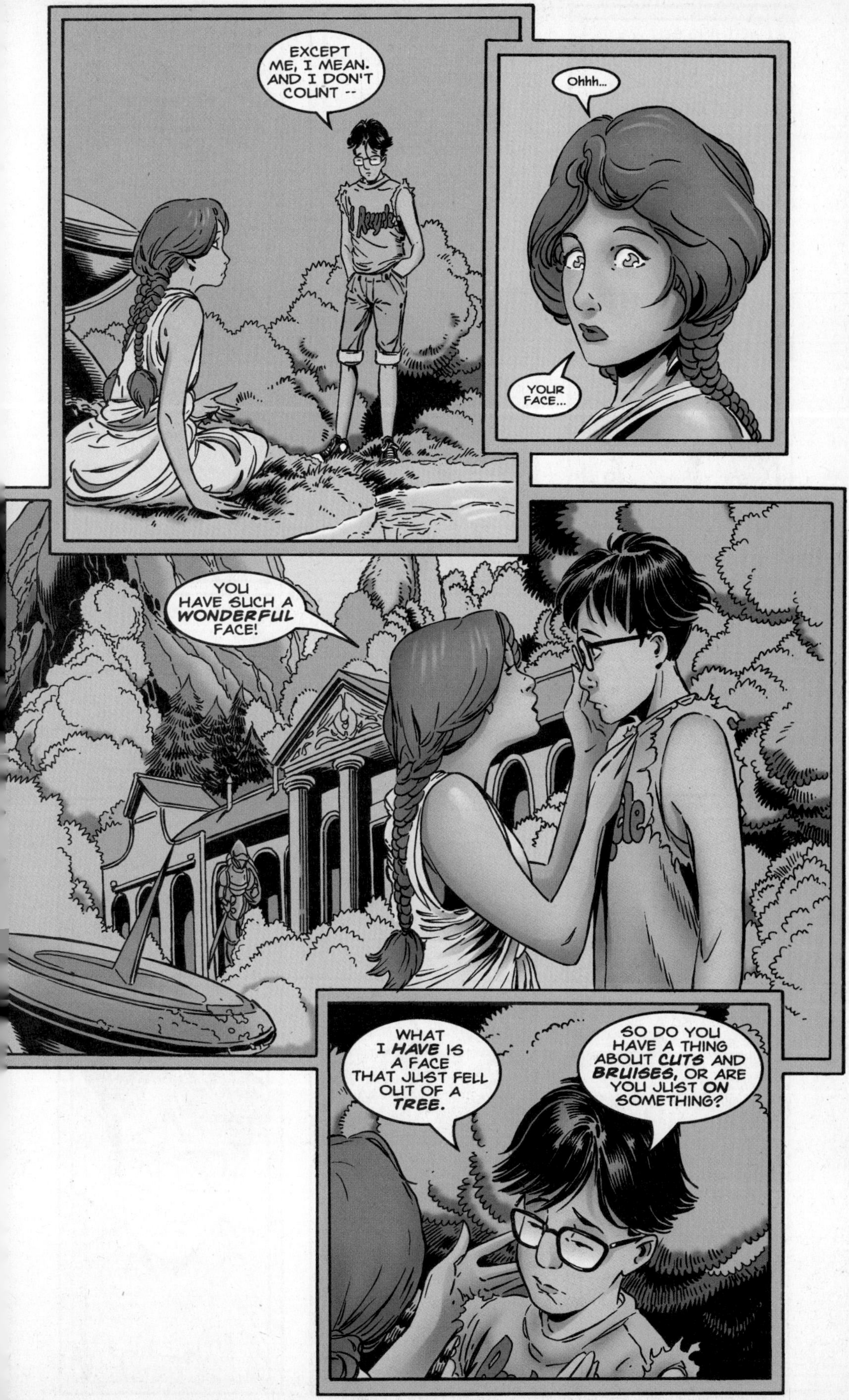
EXCEPT ME, I MEAN. AND I DON'T COUNT --
Ohhh...
YOUR FACE...
YOU HAVE SUCH A **WONDERFUL** FACE!
WHAT I **HAVE** IS A FACE THAT JUST FELL OUT OF A **TREE.**
SO DO YOU HAVE A THING ABOUT **CUTS** AND **BRUISES,** OR ARE YOU JUST **ON** SOMETHING?

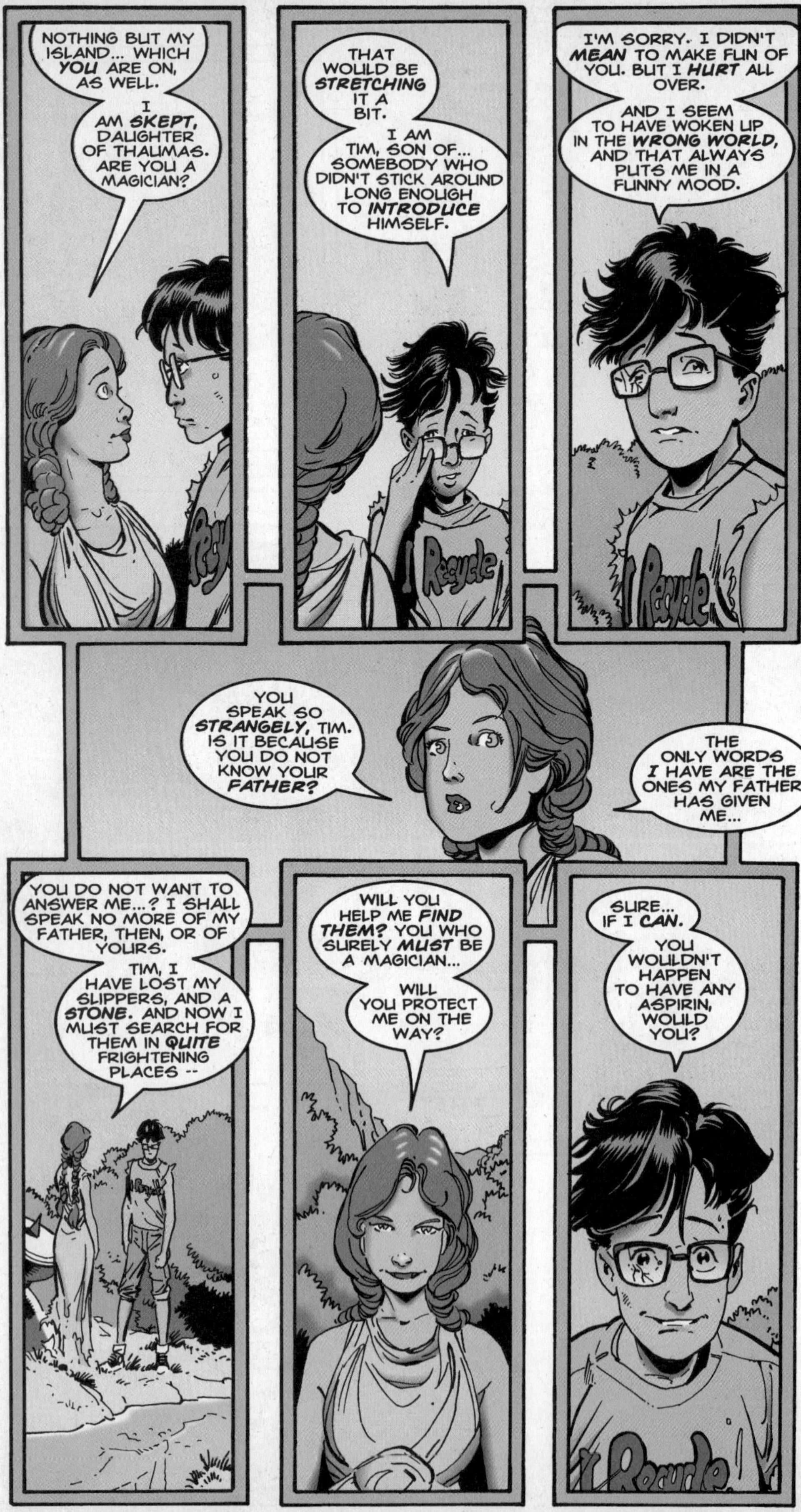
NOTHING BUT MY ISLAND... WHICH YOU ARE ON, AS WELL.
I AM SKEPT, DAUGHTER OF THAUMAS. ARE YOU A MAGICIAN?
THAT WOULD BE STRETCHING IT A BIT.
I AM TIM, SON OF... SOMEBODY WHO DIDN'T STICK AROUND LONG ENOUGH TO INTRODUCE HIMSELF.
I'M SORRY. I DIDN'T MEAN TO MAKE FUN OF YOU. BUT I HURT ALL OVER.
AND I SEEM TO HAVE WOKEN UP IN THE WRONG WORLD, AND THAT ALWAYS PUTS ME IN A FUNNY MOOD.
YOU SPEAK SO STRANGELY, TIM. IS IT BECAUSE YOU DO NOT KNOW YOUR FATHER?
THE ONLY WORDS I HAVE ARE THE ONES MY FATHER HAS GIVEN ME...
YOU DO NOT WANT TO ANSWER ME...? I SHALL SPEAK NO MORE OF MY FATHER, THEN, OR OF YOURS.
TIM, I HAVE LOST MY SLIPPERS, AND A STONE. AND NOW I MUST SEARCH FOR THEM IN QUITE FRIGHTENING PLACES --
WILL YOU HELP ME FIND THEM? YOU WHO SURELY MUST BE A MAGICIAN...
WILL YOU PROTECT ME ON THE WAY?
SURE... IF I CAN.
YOU WOULDN'T HAPPEN TO HAVE ANY ASPIRIN, WOULD YOU?

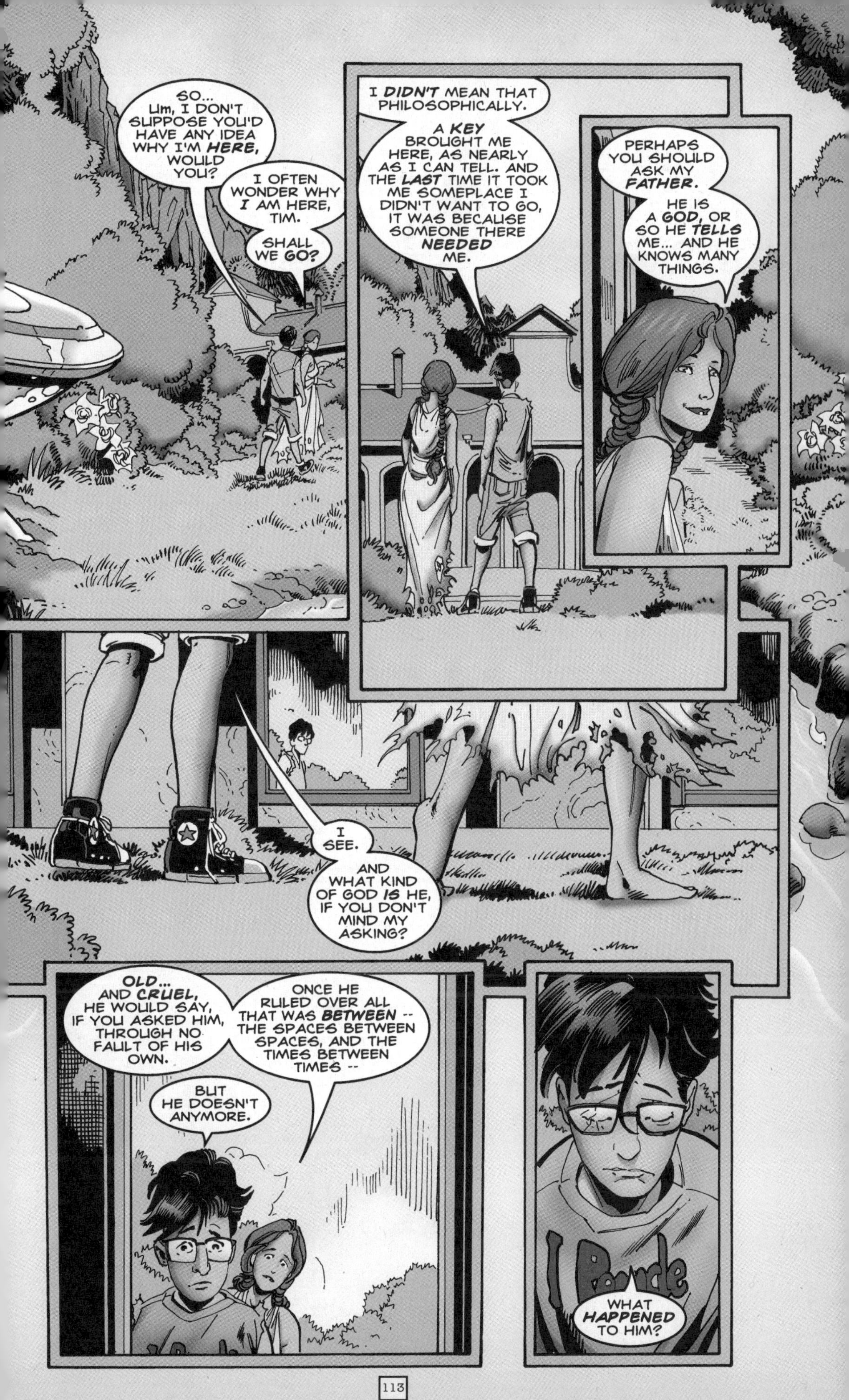

SO... UM, I DON'T SUPPOSE YOU'D HAVE ANY IDEA WHY I'M HERE, WOULD YOU?
I OFTEN WONDER WHY I AM HERE, TIM.
SHALL WE GO?
I DIDN'T MEAN THAT PHILOSOPHICALLY.
A KEY BROUGHT ME HERE, AS NEARLY AS I CAN TELL. AND THE LAST TIME IT TOOK ME SOMEPLACE I DIDN'T WANT TO GO, IT WAS BECAUSE SOMEONE THERE NEEDED ME.
PERHAPS YOU SHOULD ASK MY FATHER.
HE IS A GOD, OR SO HE TELLS ME... AND HE KNOWS MANY THINGS.
I SEE.
AND WHAT KIND OF GOD IS HE, IF YOU DON'T MIND MY ASKING?
OLD... AND CRUEL, HE WOULD SAY, IF YOU ASKED HIM, THROUGH NO FAULT OF HIS OWN.
ONCE HE RULED OVER ALL THAT WAS BETWEEN -- THE SPACES BETWEEN SPACES, AND THE TIMES BETWEEN TIMES --
BUT HE DOESN'T ANYMORE.
WHAT HAPPENED TO HIM?

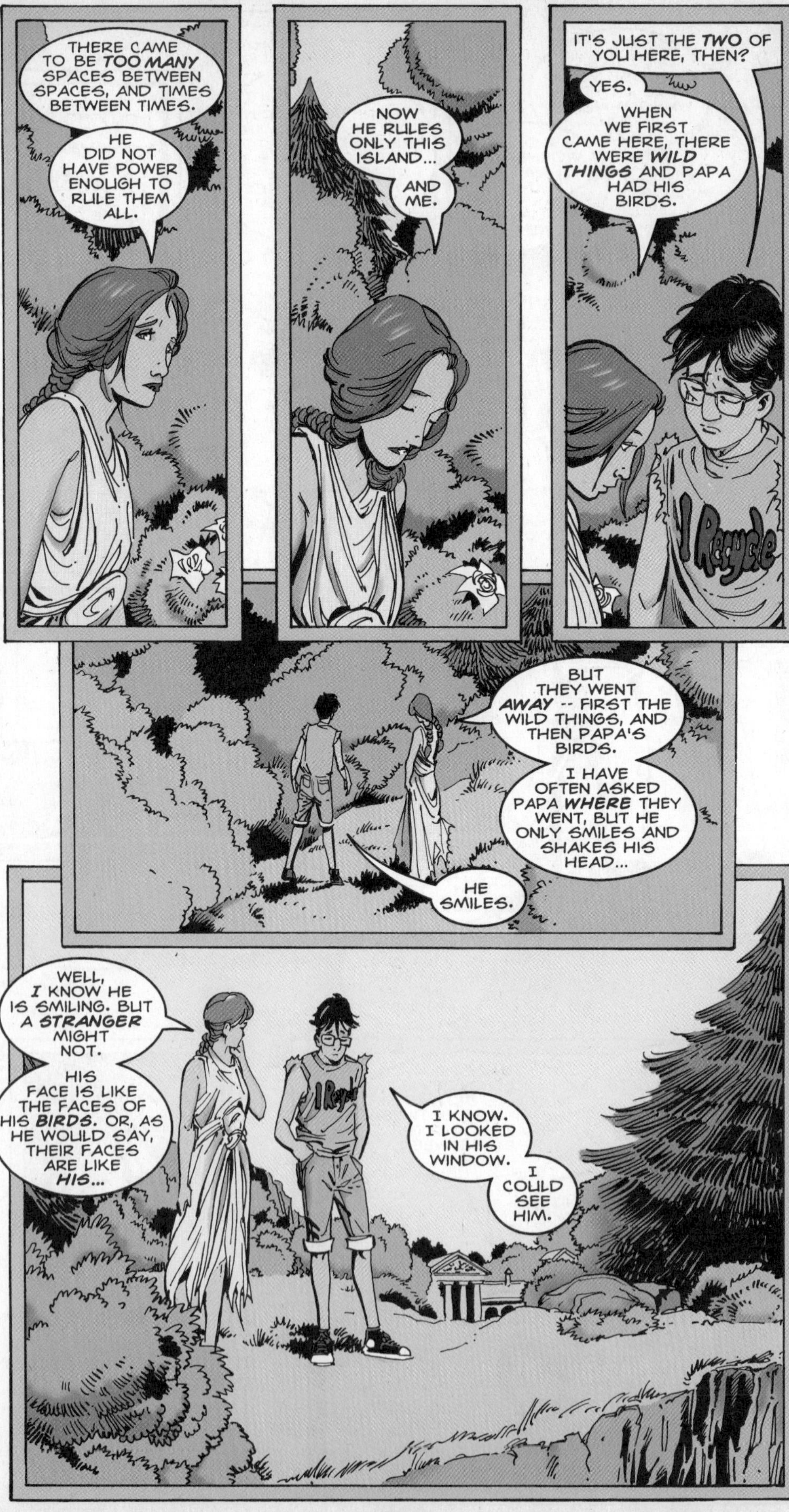
THERE CAME TO BE TOO MANY SPACES BETWEEN SPACES, AND TIMES BETWEEN TIMES.
HE DID NOT HAVE POWER ENOUGH TO RULE THEM ALL.
NOW HE RULES ONLY THIS ISLAND...
AND ME.
IT'S JUST THE TWO OF YOU HERE, THEN?
YES.
WHEN WE FIRST CAME HERE, THERE WERE WILD THINGS AND PAPA HAD HIS BIRDS.
I Recycle
BUT THEY WENT AWAY -- FIRST THE WILD THINGS, AND THEN PAPA'S BIRDS.
I HAVE OFTEN ASKED PAPA WHERE THEY WENT, BUT HE ONLY SMILES AND SHAKES HIS HEAD...
HE SMILES.
WELL, I KNOW HE IS SMILING. BUT A STRANGER MIGHT NOT.
HIS FACE IS LIKE THE FACES OF HIS BIRDS. OR, AS HE WOULD SAY, THEIR FACES ARE LIKE HIS...
I KNOW. I LOOKED IN HIS WINDOW.
I COULD SEE HIM.

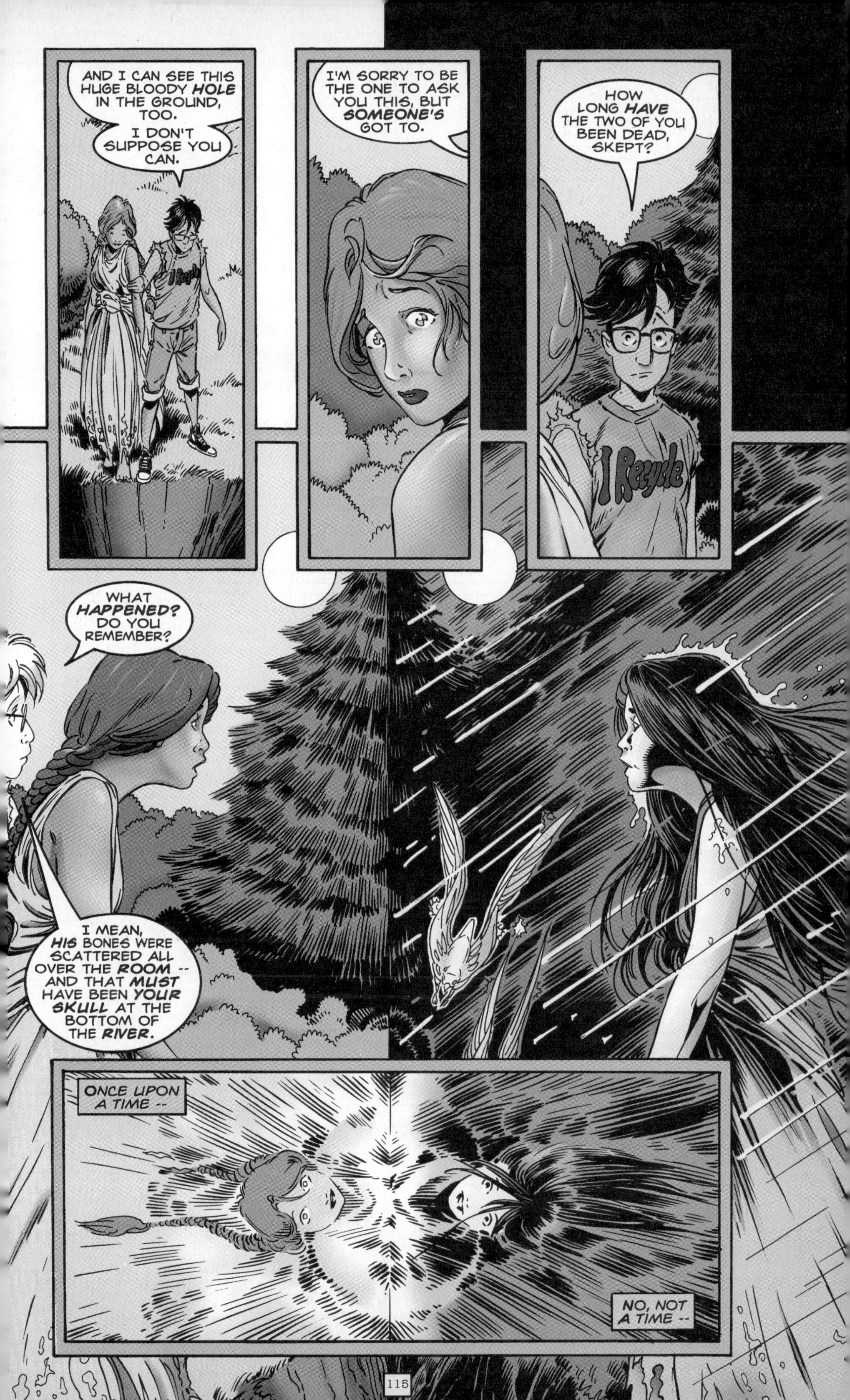
AND I CAN SEE THIS HUGE BLOODY HOLE IN THE GROUND, TOO.
I DON'T SUPPOSE YOU CAN.
I'M SORRY TO BE THE ONE TO ASK YOU THIS, BUT SOMEONE'S GOT TO.
HOW LONG HAVE THE TWO OF YOU BEEN DEAD, SKEPT?
I Recycle
WHAT HAPPENED? DO YOU REMEMBER?
I MEAN, HIS BONES WERE SCATTERED ALL OVER THE ROOM -- AND THAT MUST HAVE BEEN YOUR SKULL AT THE BOTTOM OF THE RIVER.
ONCE UPON A TIME --
NO, NOT A TIME --

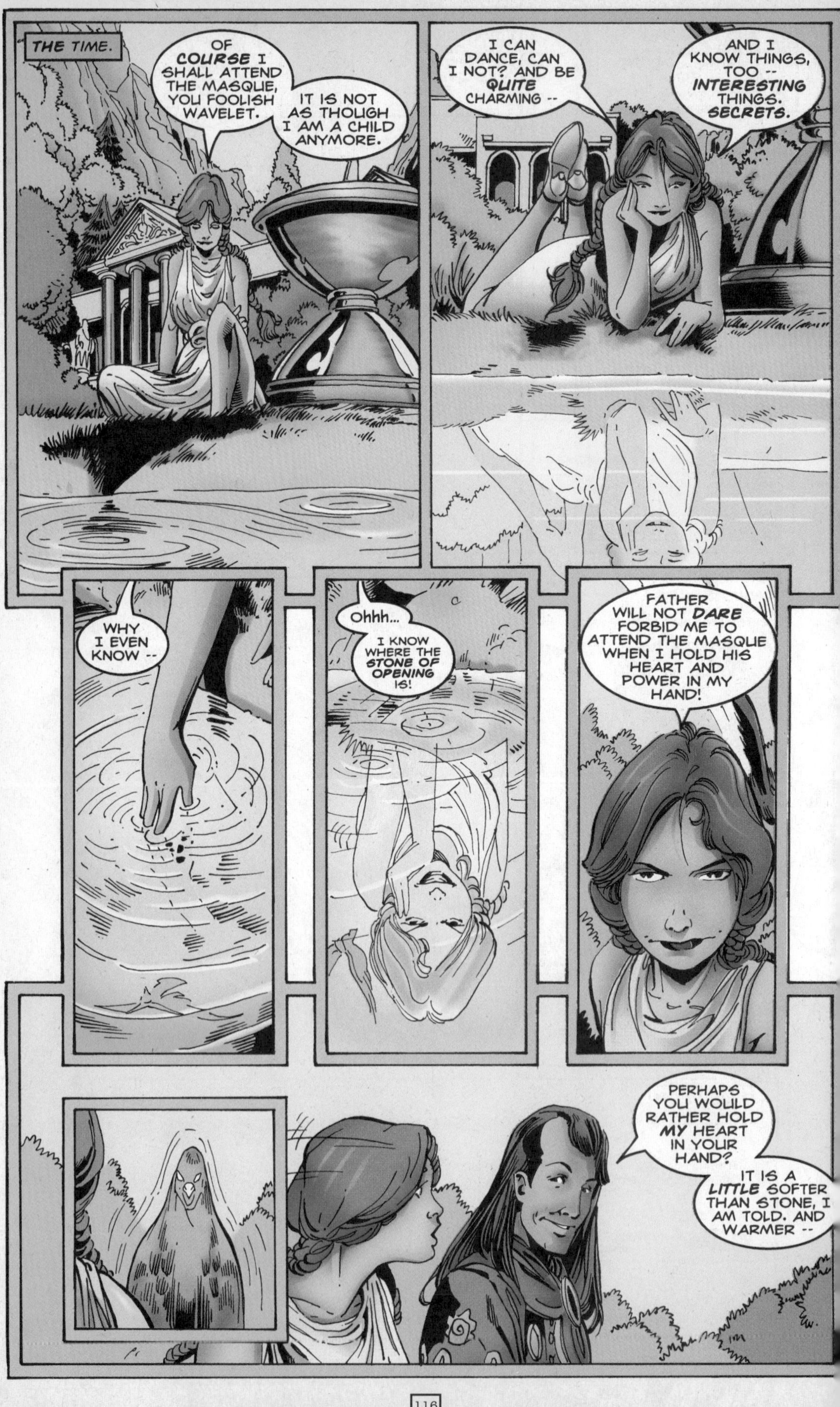
THE TIME.
OF COURSE I SHALL ATTEND THE MASQUE, YOU FOOLISH WAVELET.
IT IS NOT AS THOUGH I AM A CHILD ANYMORE.
I CAN DANCE, CAN I NOT? AND BE QUITE CHARMING --
AND I KNOW THINGS, TOO -- INTERESTING THINGS. SECRETS.
WHY I EVEN KNOW --
Ohhh...
I KNOW WHERE THE STONE OF OPENING IS!
FATHER WILL NOT DARE FORBID ME TO ATTEND THE MASQUE WHEN I HOLD HIS HEART AND POWER IN MY HAND!
PERHAPS YOU WOULD RATHER HOLD MY HEART IN YOUR HAND?
IT IS A LITTLE SOFTER THAN STONE, I AM TOLD. AND WARMER --

Ohhh...

YOUR FACE...

Oh, YOU HAVE SUCH A WONDERFUL FACE!

HAH! IF I DO, YOU ARE CERTAINLY THE FIRST EVER TO SAY SO.

BUT YOU, LADY -- YOU MUST BE QUITE ACCUSTOMED TO BEING TOLD HOW LOVELY YOU ARE.

NO ONE HAS EVER TOLD ME ANY SUCH THING.

I AM SKEPT, DAUGHTER OF THALIMAS. ARE YOU A MAGICIAN?

HARDLY. I COMMAND SOME SMALL MAGICKS... NONE THAT THE DAUGHTER OF A GOD WOULD FIND IMPRESSIVE.

I SERVE THE QUEEN OF FAERIE AS HER FALCONER... AND AS HER COURIER...

WHEN SHE HAS NEED OF ONE WITH WINGS.

I BEAR A MESSAGE FOR THALIMAS; THE QUEEN WILL BE PLEASED TO ACCEPT HIS GRACIOUS INVITATION.

SHE HAS ALSO GRACIOUSLY AGREED TO DISPATCH HER SENESCHAL TO ASSIST THALIMAS IN HIS PREPARATIONS FOR THE MASQUE.

AND YOU, LORD TAMLIN? WILL YOU BE COMING TO THE MASQUE?

117

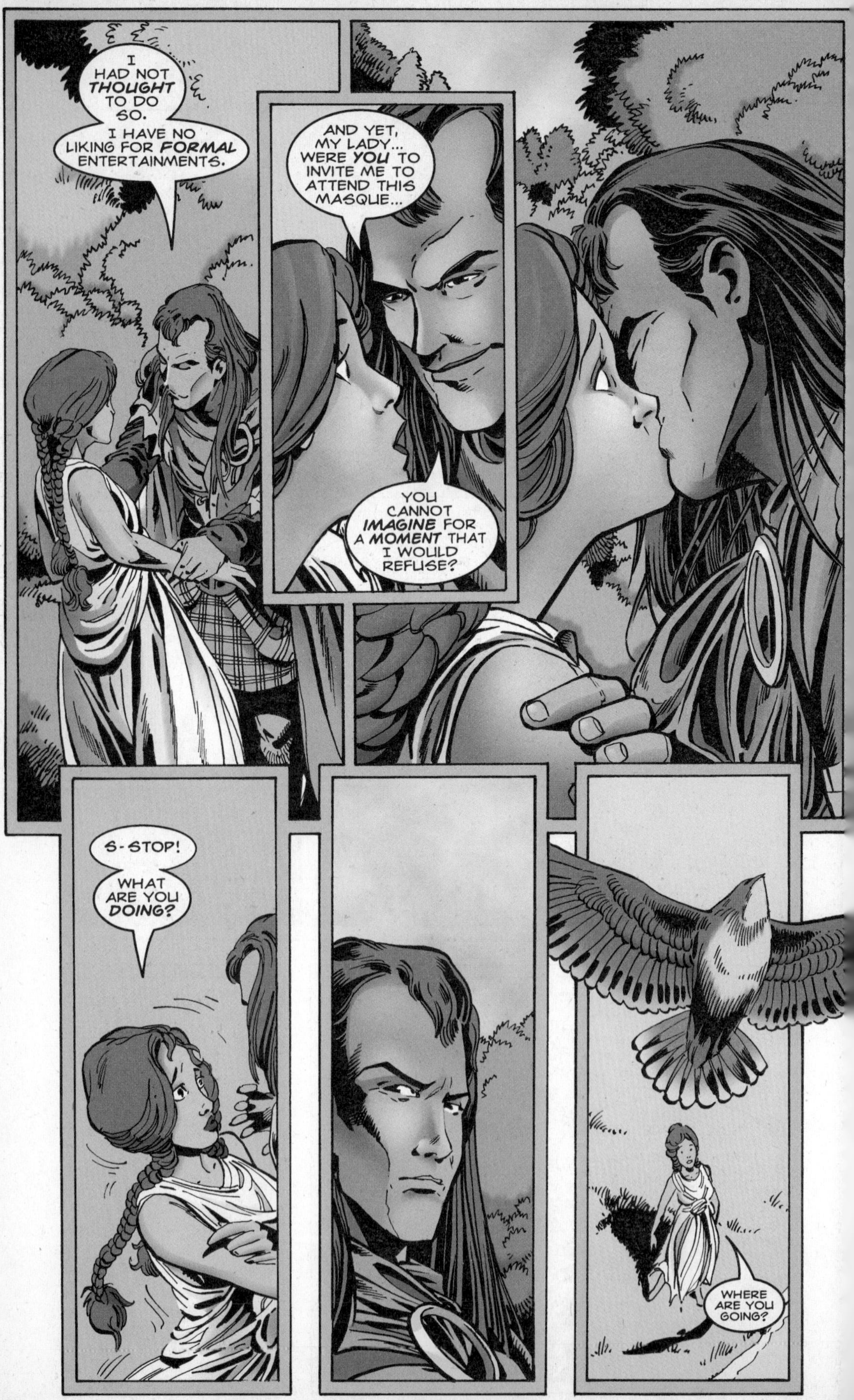
I HAD NOT THOUGHT TO DO SO.
I HAVE NO LIKING FOR FORMAL ENTERTAINMENTS.
AND YET, MY LADY... WERE YOU TO INVITE ME TO ATTEND THIS MASQUE...
YOU CANNOT IMAGINE FOR A MOMENT THAT I WOULD REFUSE?
S-STOP!
WHAT ARE YOU DOING?
WHERE ARE YOU GOING?

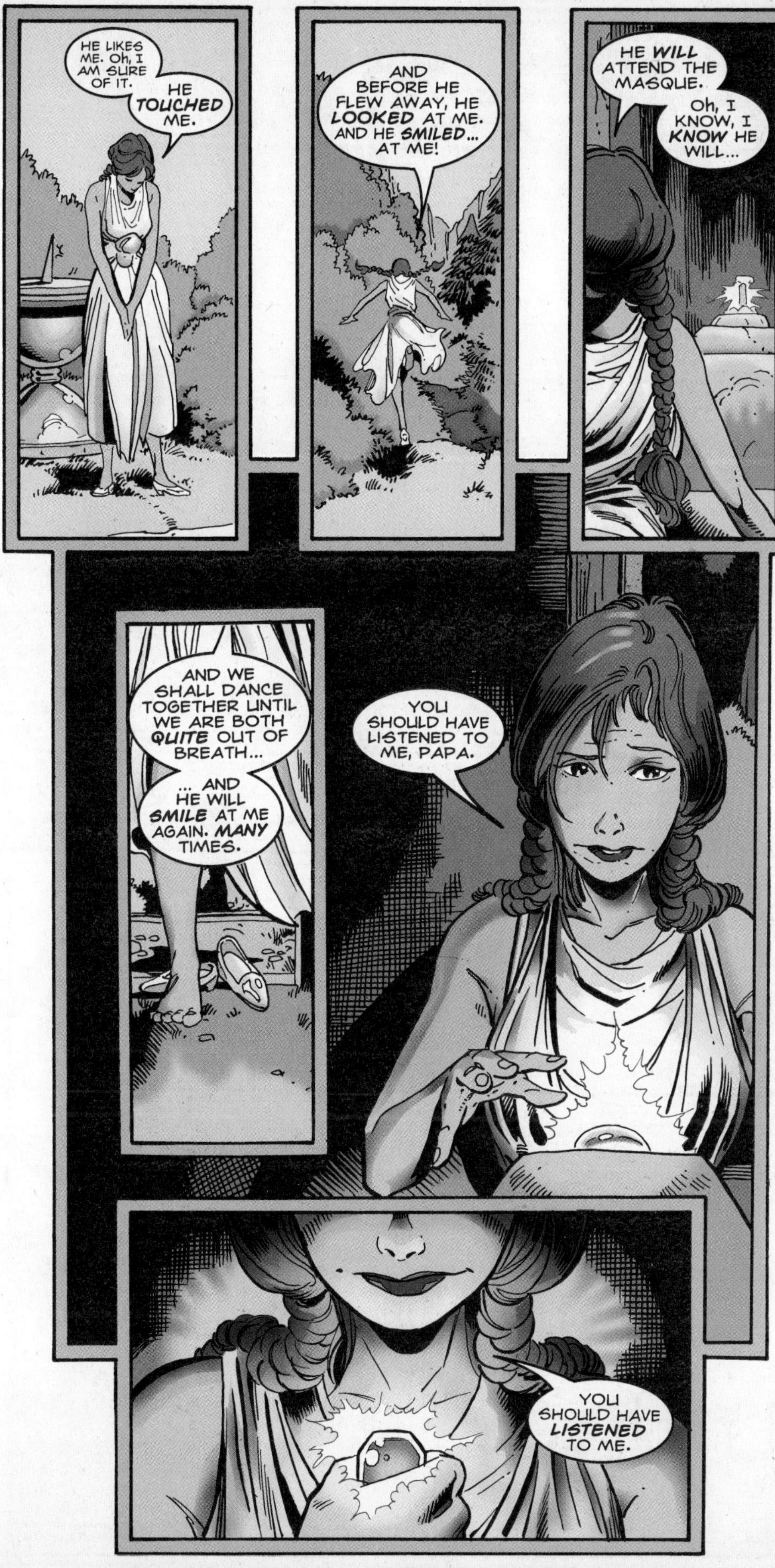
HE LIKES ME. Oh, I AM SURE OF IT.
HE *TOUCHED* ME.
AND BEFORE HE FLEW AWAY, HE *LOOKED* AT ME. AND HE *SMILED*... AT ME!
HE *WILL* ATTEND THE MASQUE.
Oh, I KNOW, I *KNOW* HE WILL...
AND WE SHALL DANCE TOGETHER UNTIL WE ARE BOTH *QUITE* OUT OF BREATH...
... AND HE WILL *SMILE* AT ME AGAIN. *MANY* TIMES.
YOU SHOULD HAVE LISTENED TO ME, PAPA.
YOU SHOULD HAVE *LISTENED* TO ME.

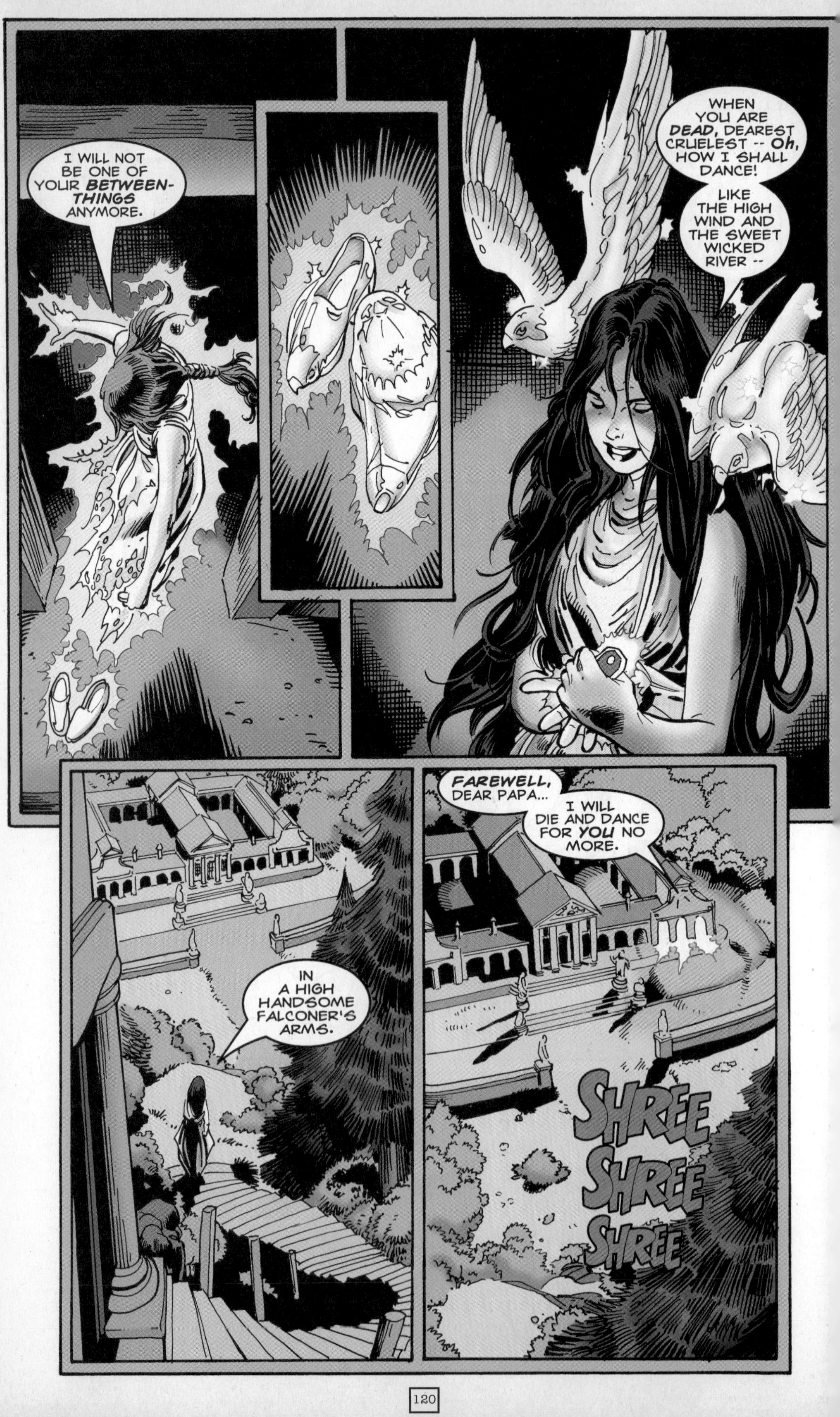
I WILL NOT BE ONE OF YOUR BETWEEN-THINGS ANYMORE.
WHEN YOU ARE DEAD, DEAREST CRUELEST -- Oh, HOW I SHALL DANCE!
LIKE THE HIGH WIND AND THE SWEET WICKED RIVER --
IN A HIGH HANDSOME FALCONER'S ARMS.
FAREWELL, DEAR PAPA...
I WILL DIE AND DANCE FOR YOU NO MORE.
SHREE
SHREE
SHREE

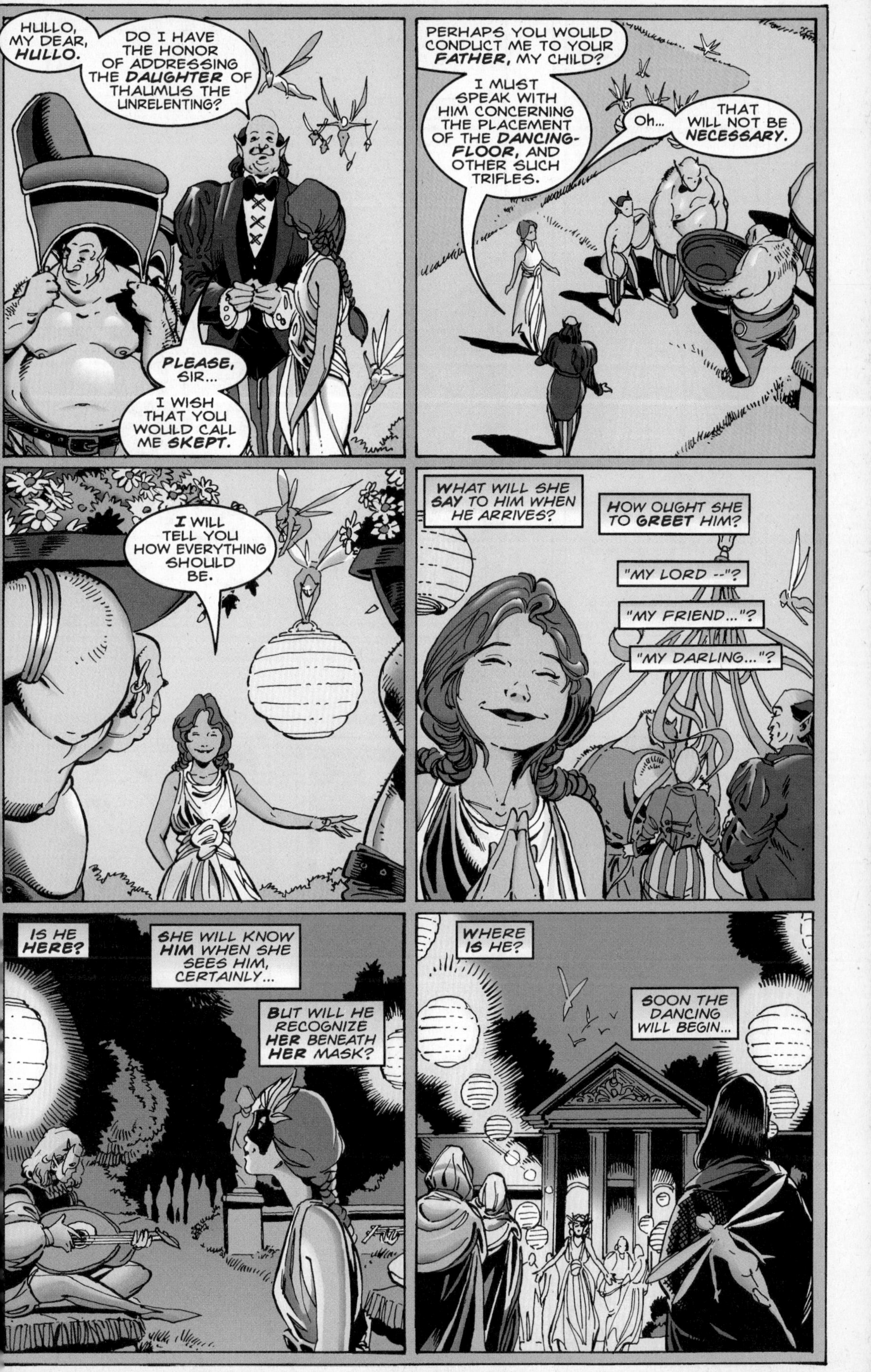
HULLO, MY DEAR, HULLO.
DO I HAVE THE HONOR OF ADDRESSING THE DAUGHTER OF THAUMUS THE UNRELENTING?
PLEASE, SIR...
I WISH THAT YOU WOULD CALL ME SKEPT.
PERHAPS YOU WOULD CONDUCT ME TO YOUR FATHER, MY CHILD?
I MUST SPEAK WITH HIM CONCERNING THE PLACEMENT OF THE DANCING-FLOOR, AND OTHER SUCH TRIFLES.
Oh...
THAT WILL NOT BE NECESSARY.
I WILL TELL YOU HOW EVERYTHING SHOULD BE.
WHAT WILL SHE SAY TO HIM WHEN HE ARRIVES?
HOW OUGHT SHE TO GREET HIM?
"MY LORD --"?
"MY FRIEND..."?
"MY DARLING..."?
IS HE HERE?
SHE WILL KNOW HIM WHEN SHE SEES HIM, CERTAINLY...
BUT WILL HE RECOGNIZE HER BENEATH HER MASK?
WHERE IS HE?
SOON THE DANCING WILL BEGIN...

HE IS NOT COMING.

HE HAS FORGOTTEN HER.

PERHAPS HE DID NOT EVEN REMEMBER HER LONG ENOUGH TO FORGET HER.

THE KISS HE HAD TAKEN FROM HER HAD MEANT NOTHING TO HIM...

WHO IS SHE?

Ohhh, SOME GOD'S DAUGHTER, I SHOULDN'T WONDER. I ASKED HER NAME. AND SHE SPAT ON ME.

SHE HAD MEANT NOTHING TO HIM.

NOTHING AT ALL.

AND TOMORROW SHE WOULD BE ALL ALONE ON THE ISLAND.

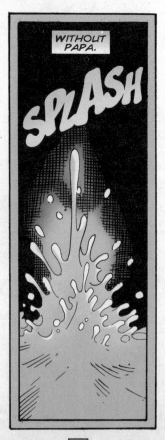

WITHOUT PAPA.

SPLASH

MORE ALL ALONE THAN EVER BEFORE.

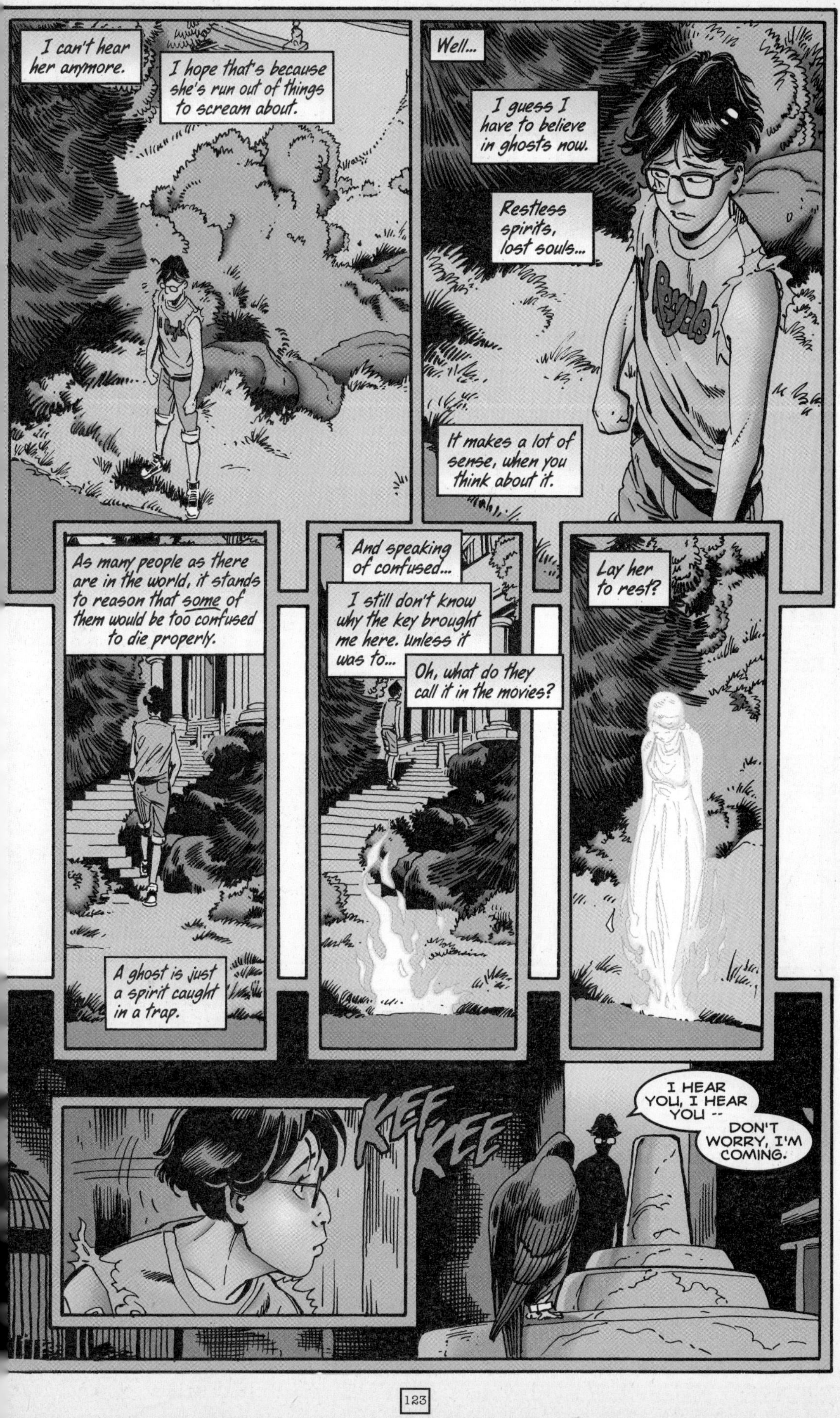

I can't hear her anymore.
I hope that's because she's run out of things to scream about.
Well...
I guess I have to believe in ghosts now.
Restless spirits, lost souls...
It makes a lot of sense, when you think about it.
As many people as there are in the world, it stands to reason that some of them would be too confused to die properly.
A ghost is just a spirit caught in a trap.
And speaking of confused...
I still don't know why the key brought me here. unless it was to...
Oh, what do they call it in the movies?
Lay her to rest?
KEE KEE
I HEAR YOU, I HEAR YOU --
DON'T WORRY, I'M COMING.

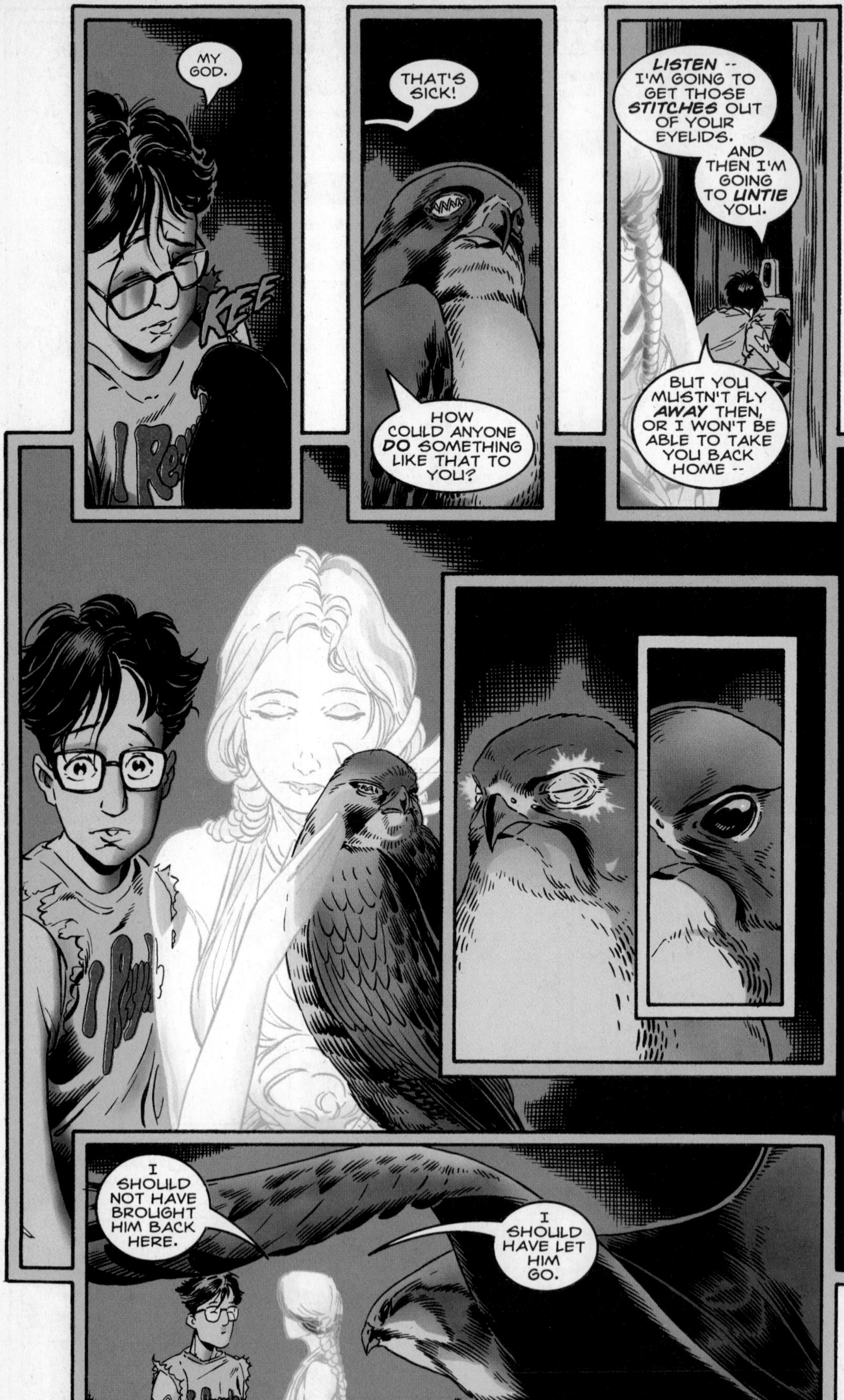
MY GOD.
KEE
THAT'S SICK!
HOW COULD ANYONE DO SOMETHING LIKE THAT TO YOU?
LISTEN -- I'M GOING TO GET THOSE STITCHES OUT OF YOUR EYELIDS.
AND THEN I'M GOING TO UNTIE YOU.
BUT YOU MUSTN'T FLY AWAY THEN, OR I WON'T BE ABLE TO TAKE YOU BACK HOME --
I SHOULD NOT HAVE BROUGHT HIM BACK HERE.
I SHOULD HAVE LET HIM GO.

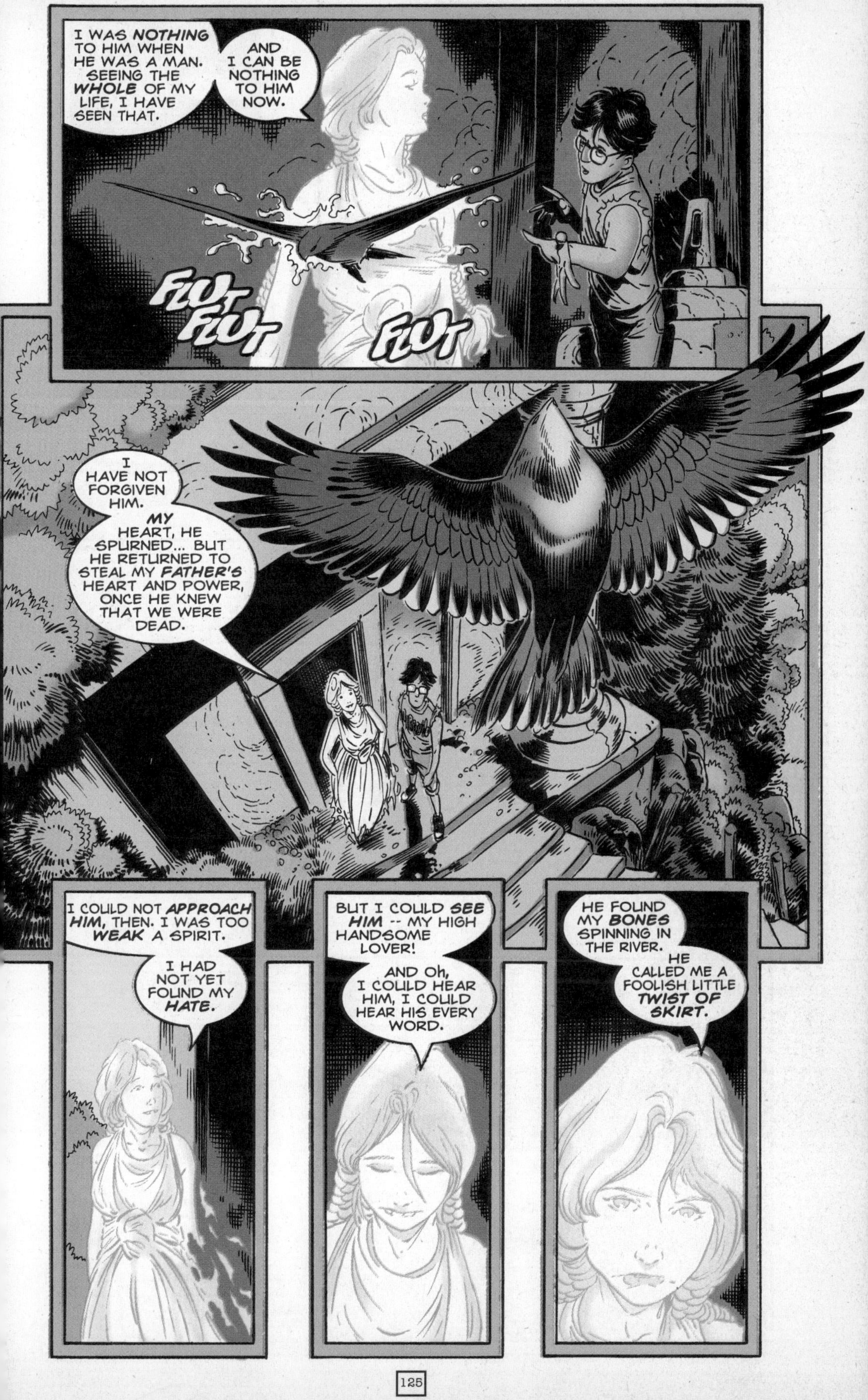

I WAS NOTHING TO HIM WHEN HE WAS A MAN. SEEING THE WHOLE OF MY LIFE, I HAVE SEEN THAT.
AND I CAN BE NOTHING TO HIM NOW.
FLUT FLUT
FLUT
I HAVE NOT FORGIVEN HIM.
MY HEART, HE SPURNED... BUT HE RETURNED TO STEAL MY FATHER'S HEART AND POWER, ONCE HE KNEW THAT WE WERE DEAD.
I COULD NOT APPROACH HIM, THEN. I WAS TOO WEAK A SPIRIT.
I HAD NOT YET FOUND MY HATE.
BUT I COULD SEE HIM -- MY HIGH HANDSOME LOVER!
AND Oh, I COULD HEAR HIM, I COULD HEAR HIS EVERY WORD.
HE FOUND MY BONES SPINNING IN THE RIVER.
HE CALLED ME A FOOLISH LITTLE TWIST OF SKIRT.

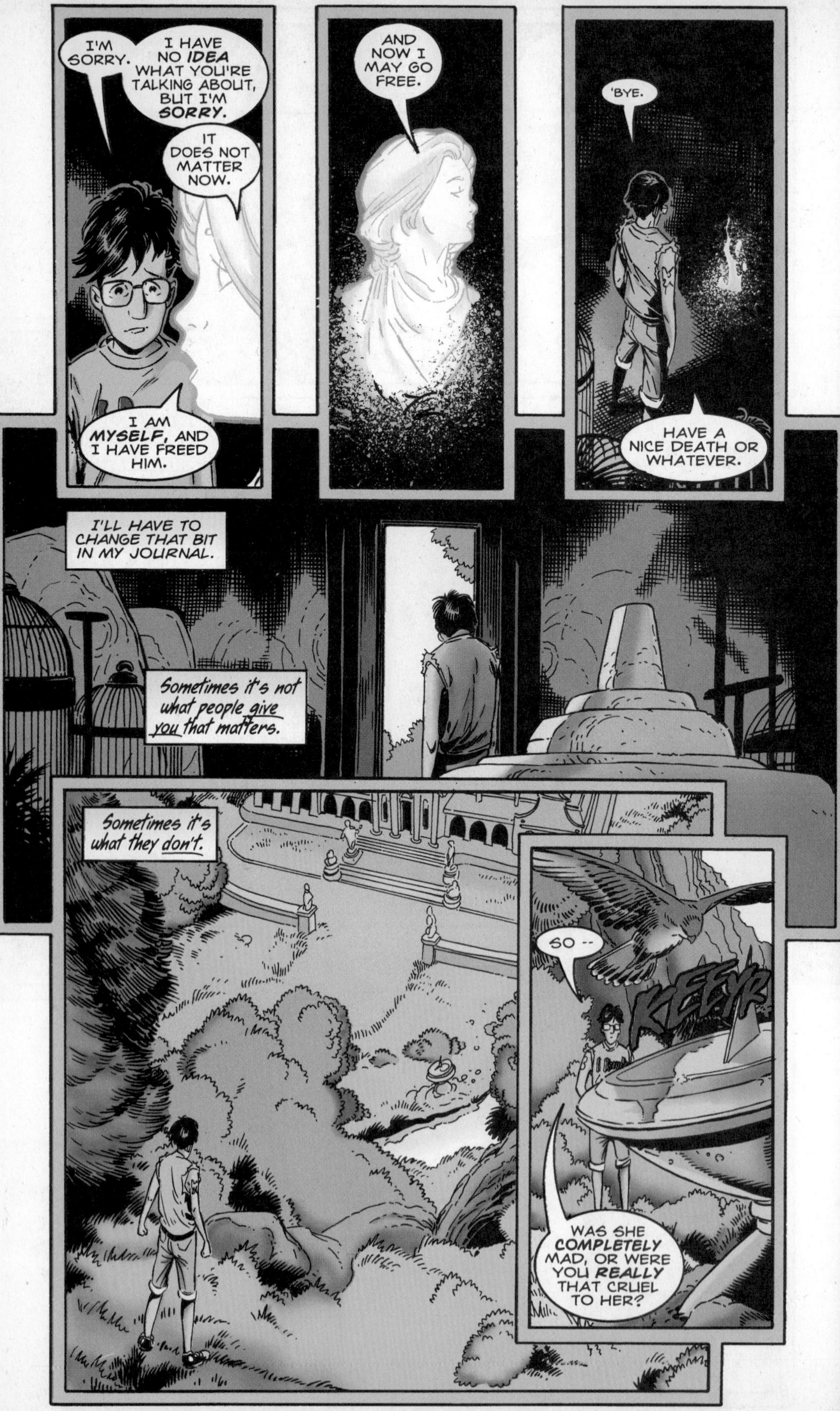
I'M SORRY.
I HAVE NO IDEA WHAT YOU'RE TALKING ABOUT, BUT I'M SORRY.
IT DOES NOT MATTER NOW.
I AM MYSELF, AND I HAVE FREED HIM.
AND NOW I MAY GO FREE.
'BYE.
HAVE A NICE DEATH OR WHATEVER.
I'LL HAVE TO CHANGE THAT BIT IN MY JOURNAL.
Sometimes it's not what people give you that matters.
Sometimes it's what they don't.
SO --
KEEYR
WAS SHE COMPLETELY MAD, OR WERE YOU REALLY THAT CRUEL TO HER?

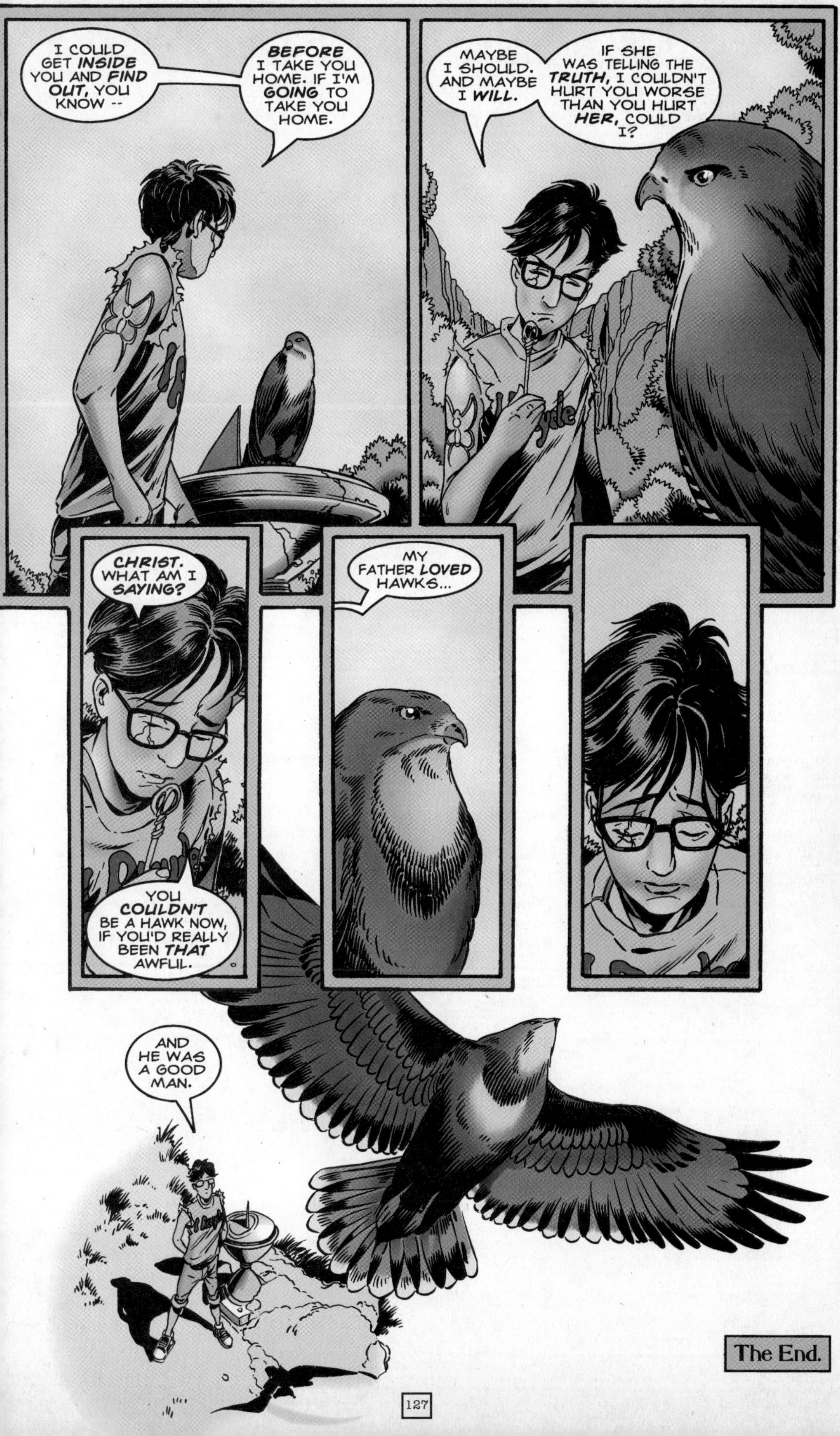
I COULD GET INSIDE YOU AND FIND OUT, YOU KNOW --
BEFORE I TAKE YOU HOME. IF I'M GOING TO TAKE YOU HOME.
MAYBE I SHOULD. AND MAYBE I WILL.
IF SHE WAS TELLING THE TRUTH, I COULDN'T HURT YOU WORSE THAN YOU HURT HER, COULD I?
CHRIST. WHAT AM I SAYING?
YOU COULDN'T BE A HAWK NOW, IF YOU'D REALLY BEEN THAT AWFUL.
MY FATHER LOVED HAWKS...
AND HE WAS A GOOD MAN.
The End.

LOOK FOR THESE OTHER VERTIGO BOOKS:

All VERTIGO backlist books are suggested for mature readers

GRAPHIC NOVELS

KILL YOUR BOYFRIEND
Grant Morrison/Philip Bond/D'Israeli

MR. PUNCH
Neil Gaiman/Dave McKean

WHY I HATE SATURN
Kyle Baker

YOU ARE HERE
Kyle Baker

COLLECTIONS

BLACK ORCHID
Neil Gaiman/Dave McKean

THE BOOKS OF FAERIE
*Bronwyn Carlton/John Ney Rieber/
Peter Gross*

THE BOOKS OF MAGIC
*Neil Gaiman/John Bolton/
Scott Hampton/Charles Vess/
Paul Johnson*

**THE BOOKS OF MAGIC:
BINDINGS**
*John Ney Rieber/Gary Amaro/
Peter Gross*

**THE BOOKS OF MAGIC:
SUMMONINGS**
*Rieber/Gross/Snejbjerg/
Amaro/Giordano*

**THE BOOKS OF MAGIC:
RECKONINGS**
*John Ney Rieber/Peter Snejbjerg/
Peter Gross/John Ridgway*

**THE BOOKS OF MAGIC:
TRANSFORMATIONS**
John Ney Rieber/Peter Gross

BREATHTAKER
Mark Wheatley/Marc Hempel

THE COMPLEAT MOONSHADOW
J.M. DeMatteis/Jon J Muth

**DEATH:
THE HIGH COST OF LIVING**
*Neil Gaiman/Chris Bachalo/
Mark Buckingham*

**DEATH:
THE TIME OF YOUR LIFE**
*Neil Gaiman/Chris Bachalo/
Mark Buckingham/Mark Pennington*

**DOOM PATROL:
CRAWLING FROM THE WRECKAGE**
Grant Morrison/Richard Case/ various

**THE DREAMING:
BEYOND THE SHORES OF NIGHT**
Various writers and artists

ENIGMA
Peter Milligan/Duncan Fegredo

HELLBLAZER: ORIGINAL SINS
Jamie Delano/John Ridgway/various

**HELLBLAZER:
DANGEROUS HABITS**
Garth Ennis/William Simpson/various

**HELLBLAZER:
FEAR AND LOATHING**
Garth Ennis/Steve Dillon

HELLBLAZER: TAINTED LOVE
Garth Ennis/Steve Dillon

**HOUSE OF SECRETS:
FOUNDATION**
Steven T. Seagle/Teddy Kristiansen

**THE INVISIBLES:
SAY YOU WANT A REVOLUTION**
*Grant Morrison/Steve Yeowell/
Jill Thompson/Dennis Cramer*

**THE INVISIBLES:
BLOODY HELL IN AMERICA**
*Grant Morrison/Phil Jimenez/
John Stokes*

**NEIL GAIMAN & CHARLES VESS'
STARDUST**
Neil Gaiman/Charles Vess

PREACHER: GONE TO TEXAS
Garth Ennis/Steve Dillon

**PREACHER:
UNTIL THE END OF THE WORLD**
Garth Ennis/Steve Dillon

PREACHER: PROUD AMERICANS
Garth Ennis/Steve Dillon

PREACHER: ANCIENT HISTORY
*Garth Ennis/Steve Pugh/
Carlos Ezquerra/ Richard Case*

PREACHER: DIXIE FRIED
Garth Ennis/Steve Dillon

THE SYSTEM
Peter Kuper

TERMINAL CITY
Dean Motter/Michael Lark

**TRANSMETROPOLITAN:
BACK ON THE STREET**
Warren Ellis/Darick Robertson/various

TRUE FAITH
Garth Ennis/Warren Pleece

UNKNOWN SOLDIER
Garth Ennis/Kilian Plunkett

V FOR VENDETTA
Alan Moore/David Lloyd

VAMPS
Elaine Lee/William Simpson

THE SANDMAN LIBRARY

**THE SANDMAN:
PRELUDES & NOCTURNES**
*Neil Gaiman/Sam Kieth/
Mike Dringenberg/Malcolm Jones III*

**THE SANDMAN:
THE DOLL'S HOUSE**
*Neil Gaiman/Mike Dringenberg/
Malcolm Jones III/Chris Bachalo/
Michael Zulli/Steve Parkhouse*

**THE SANDMAN:
DREAM COUNTRY**
*Neil Gaiman/Kelley Jones/Charles Vess/
Colleen Doran/ Malcolm Jones III*

**THE SANDMAN:
SEASON OF MISTS**
*Neil Gaiman/Kelley Jones/
Mike Dringenberg/Malcolm Jones III/
various*

**THE SANDMAN:
A GAME OF YOU**
Neil Gaiman/Shawn McManus/various

**THE SANDMAN:
FABLES AND REFLECTIONS**
Neil Gaiman/various artists

**THE SANDMAN:
BRIEF LIVES**
Neil Gaiman/Jill Thompson/Vince Locke

**THE SANDMAN:
WORLDS' END**
Neil Gaiman/various artists

**THE SANDMAN:
THE KINDLY ONES**
*Neil Gaiman/Marc Hempel/
Richard Case/ various*

**THE SANDMAN:
THE WAKE**
*Neil Gaiman/Michael Zulli/
Jon J Muth/Charles Vess*

**DUST COVERS-THE COLLECTED
SANDMAN COVERS 1989-1997**
Dave McKean/Neil Gaiman

For the nearest comics shop carrying collected editions and monthly titles
from DC Comics, call 1-888-COMIC BOOK.

VER9811